SUMMER'S CHILD

by

Sherry Wille

THE CREEK
Whiskey Creek Press
www.creekpress.com

Published by
THE CREEK

Whiskey Creek Press

P.O. Box 726
Lusk, Wyoming 82225
307-334-3165
www.thecreek.com

ISBN 1-59374-012-3

Printed in the United States of America

Dedication

To Mom:
You rejoiced at my minor accomplishments, and cried with
me over rejections. I know your heavenly tears are ones of joy
for my success. This one is for you.

To Linda

Hope you enjoy
: the gang.
Solving

Best Wishes

Perry Dorn-Wilu

Solveig

Prologue

Norway 1939

The nightmare came again!

Hundreds of soldiers marched across the fields and into his village in Norway. Wherever the soldiers went the land ran red with blood and cries of anguish filled the night. Above the gore and the din, a strong, calm voice began speaking. For the first time, Erik could hear the words.

Take your family and leave Norway. A great war will come and no place in Europe will be safe. Leave now!

Erik sat up in bed, terrified and drenched in sweat. The dream had been so real, the voice so strong and calm. He could hear it still in his mind. The cries of anguish filled the night and consumed his soul. The streets running with blood sickened him. For the rest of the night, sleep would be a stranger.

Did God speak the words in his dream? Could he dare to believe God appeared to him, Erik Jorgenson, a poor Lutheran pastor from a small Norwegian village?

Beside him, his wife, Solveig, slept peacefully. In the soft light of Norway's midnight sun, her long blonde hair formed a halo around her face. No one had ever considered her to be a small woman, nor would people call her attractive, but to him, she was the most beautiful woman in the world. She was his beloved wife, the mother of his children. His life would be over if he ever lost her.

Quietly, he slipped out of bed and put on his robe. Before he left the room, he pulled the covers around Solveig's shoulders

Down the hall he looked in on the children. Eight-year-old Karl and six-year-old Johann slept peacefully. Across the room, three-year-old Kristin was curled into a ball, sucking her thumb. Sometimes Kristin kicked off her covers. Once Eric readjusted the lightweight dena, he left the room. As he started down the stairs, the grandfather clock began to strike. He stopped momentarily and counted the chimes; one-two-three-four. Far too early to be up, but he knew sleep would be a stranger if he stayed in bed.

Moses' face glowed when he came down from Mount Sinai with the Ten Commandments and his hair turned white. In the Bible these were the things that happened when the prophets dared to speak with God. What made him think he, Erik Jorgenson, a poor Lutheran pastor, would have heard God speak to him?

Chapter One

"Jorgenson residence," Solveig Jorgenson answered the ringing telephone. It still annoyed her that the church council thought it necessary to install this machine in her home to interrupt her routine with its incessant ringing.

"I have a long-distance call for you, overseas," the operator said. "Can you hold?"

"Of course I can," she replied.

"Hello, Solveig," the voice on the other end of the line said.

"Yes, this is Solveig." She did not recognize the voice, and yet she knew to whom it belonged.

"This is Sven, is my brother Erik there?"

"Sven? From America?" she questioned foolishly.

"Yes, is Erik there?" He seemed only slightly annoyed with her being so hesitant about putting her husband on the line.

"Just a minute, Sven." Trembling she called Erik to the phone. "Erik, it is your brother, Sven, from America."

"Sven?" Erik questioned, glancing at the clock as he spoke into the receiver. It would be early, only eight in the morning in Minnesota.

"Yes, I called as I need to ask a favor of you."

"A favor, what favor could I possibly do for you from so far away?"

"I have just returned from the hospital. I am dying, Erik."

Sven said the words so calmly Erik could hardly comprehend them. "You are what?" he questioned.

"I am dying. I have cancer. The doctors have given me three months to live. My condition will weaken steadily. I met with the church council last evening. They would like you to come and take my place."

"Are you serious?" Erik asked.

"I know it means uprooting your whole family and coming to America. It is too much to ask, but it would mean so much to me to have you here for the last few months, to know you would be caring for these people."

"I've prayed for another sign, but I never expected a sign like this."

"What are you saying, Erik?"

"I've been having a dream. In the dream, God told me to take my family and leave Norway. I was going to post a letter to you, asking if there were any openings in America."

"God does answer prayers," Sven said, sounding relieved. "Then you will come, you and your family?"

"Of course I will come, but what of your family?" Erik asked, realizing his acceptance would leave Sven and Ruth without a home.

"Ruth has her teaching certificate. She's been teaching now for several years. We've been putting aside some money for the children's educations as well as for our retirement. This community needed someone to teach who understood the language and loved the children. It has been a good arrangement all around. By being frugal and not trusting in the banks, we have not suffered as badly as most of the people in this country. "

"What about your own children?"

Sven seemed to relax and even managed to laugh. "Matthew is in college, he will graduate next year. Mark is working in Minneapolis and plans to be married at Christmas, and Martha is already married. She and her husband will make us grandparents soon. They are no longer children. You forget there are many years separating us. Ruth and I have been married for almost twenty-five years."

Erik smiled. He momentarily forgot people aged. To him, Sven would always be the young man of twenty-five whom he watched sail away from Norway almost twenty-seven years ago. More than just age separated the brothers. He realized when he arrived in America he would be meeting a stranger.

Sven continued to talk, eager to tell his brother as much as he could in this unconventional way of talking across the ocean. "The money we have saved will make the down payment on a small home. With the Depression coming to an end, Ruth's salary will enable her to live comfortably, when ..." he left the rest of the sentence unsaid. "I'm so pleased you are coming," he continued, composing himself.

"So am I," Erik said, swallowing the lump in his throat.

"The church council will look into voyages from Bergen. They will send passage for you and your family. There are still only three children, aren't there?"

"Yes, Sven, there are only three."

"Then it is settled. They would like you to sail the end of July or the first of August. Can you be ready so soon?"

"I think so. Solveig's father can take over until a new pastor is found."

"Good, then I'll speak with the church council today. They will send you a cable shortly. I can hardly believe it. In two short months we will be together again. It seems like an impossible dream. Until we meet in America."

"Until we meet in America, Sven," Erik said, before Sven broke the connection.

Solveig went outside, not wanting to hear even one side of Erik's conversation with his brother.

What could the call from America mean? She'd fallen deep into thoughts of the future when she felt Erik's hands on her shoulders.

"Do you need more of a sign, Solveig?" he asked.

She turned to face him, knowing something must be terribly wrong. She gasped at the sight of his face wet with tears, tears she never saw him shed before. Her questioning look prompted him to repeat the entire conversation.

After he told her of Sven's illness, she began to cry. "I--I can't believe Sven is sick. I never meant for such a thing to happen. I never wanted such a sign."

"It is God's will, Solveig. You did not will anything to happen. It happened long before I ever knew the meaning of the dream. God has prepared a place for us. He will take care of us."

"Yes, He will take care of us. I have many plans to make, Erik, many things I must do."

Erik returned to the house, leaving Solveig with her thoughts. Over the past days she had been in such turmoil. Erik has been so certain God spoke to him in a dream and yet she could not comprehend it.

Solveig allowed her mind to wander back to the morning when her whole world seemed to become turned upside down.

She had awakened, as though she had set an alarm. She automatically got up at six. As usual, she turned to rouse Erik, but to her amazement she found his side of the bed empty. Where could he be so early in the morning? Perhaps he had become ill. That would be the only reason she could think of for him to be out of bed.

Not stopping to dress, she put on her robe and slippers. Before going downstairs, she opened the drapes. Seeing Erik crossing the short distance between the church and the house surprised her. A strange smile graced his face and a faraway look glistened in his eyes. Worried, she hurried down the stairs and met him as he entered the kitchen. "Are you all right?" she questioned.

"Yes, Solveig," he said calmly, his manner somehow seeming out of character. Usually he would not have been up before she got out of bed. If he were she knew she would not have found him sitting at the table drinking coffee.

"You're up so early," she stammered, unable to conceal her concern.

"I've been up for hours," he said.

"What is wrong?"

"There is nothing wrong, Solveig. I told you before. Sit down. Let me get you a cup of coffee. Let me tell you about my dream."

Solveig rolled her eyes. *The dream.* He had pondered over this dream for months. At least it seemed like months. It was a dream with no meaning, a dream that kept returning. "What about the dream Erik?" she asked as she accepted the cup of coffee.

"Remember how I told you the soldiers were all faceless, and they were marching, ever marching. Remember the blood, the voice?"

"Yes, Erik, I remember, you have told me before," she sighed, taking a sip of the coffee.

"This time I could hear the voice, the voice of God."

"The voice of what?" she exclaimed, almost choking on her coffee.

"Not what. Who. The voice of God. God spoke to me as He spoke to Joseph and Paul, as He spoke to Abraham, Moses, and David."

"Do you consider yourself in a class with them?" Solveig scoffed. "You are nothing but a poor Lutheran minister."

"What were they before God spoke to them? Abraham lived as a nomad, Moses a hired man, David a simple shepherd boy,

Joseph a carpenter, and Paul, who was known as Saul, a persecutor of the early Christians. They were ordinary people, just like us. I tell you, He spoke to me, Solveig! He spoke to me in the words Joseph heard. He told me to take my family and leave Norway. He said a great war is coming and no place in Europe will be safe."

"Did He tell you where you were going or what you would do?" she asked.

"I'm a minister, I will preach the Gospel. He didn't tell me where I'd go, but He will show me. When I sat praying on it, it came to me. My brother, Sven, is in America. I will write to him, and he will find me a position there."

"Oh, Erik, I remember Sven's letters as well as you. There has been a great Depression in America. How could Sven find you a job?"

"They are coming out of the Depression, Solveig," he reminded her.

"You think there are no ministers in America?"

"God will make room for one more. All my life, I've known God has been preparing me for something, but I knew not what. My father was a master of languages, a professor, who taught in all the major capitals of Europe. He taught me to speak those languages. He made certain I spoke perfectly no matter what the tongue I chose to speak. On my own, I've learned Greek and Hebrew in order to study the ancient scriptures. All of this knowledge has been God's will. He has a purpose for me somewhere and I think that place is America."

"Oh, Erik, I wish I could be as trusting as you, but you just had a dream. I dream all the time. Dreams are meaningless."

"Meaningless, unless God speaks to you in one," Erik argued. "Don't you see? Everything has meaning in my life. Even Sven going to America when I was so young has meaning. God prepared a place for Sven and now God is preparing a place for me."

"It is just too much to comprehend. You don't even know if Sven will be able to find a placement for you, and yet you are asking me to leave my home, my family, to pick up my roots and move to a country where I don't even speak the language," Solveig said, knowing her words betrayed her despair.

"You will learn the language, Darling. You will see. God will help us." Erik took her in his arms in an attempt to reassure her. "Once the children are out playing, we will go and talk to your parents. They will be as excited as I am about this."

"I am happy for you, I am just not excited the way you are. What happens if we get to America and there is no position for you?"

"Oh, Solveig, consider the lilies of the field and the birds of the air. They ..."

"Don't quote the scriptures to me Erik. I grew up in this house. My father served as pastor here before you. I know the scriptures and I have faith. It is just in this day and age God does not speak to poor Norwegian Lutheran ministers. God does not come to them in dreams and tell them to leave their homes. I'll need more of a sign than your dream."

"Oh, ye of little faith," Erik sighed. "You will have more of a sign, God will show you. Perhaps God will even speak to you."

"God is not going to speak to me Erik. I'm little more than a poor housewife and this poor housewife has a lot of work to do today."

Tears brimmed in her eyes as she went back upstairs. Once she washed and dressed for the day, she began to braid her long blonde hair. She watched the automatic process in the mirror and allowed her mind to wander. Could she survive anywhere but in Kinsarvik? Could she live anywhere but on the fjord? Could her life ever be complete without the mountains? The mountains, the fjords, the people, the lakes, she could live nowhere else. Nowhere else on earth could she ever live and be happy.

It turned into a strange day. Secretly, she was relieved when Erik said nothing to the children.

At last, they were alone and at Erik's insistence they went next door to see her parents. Erik told them the story of the dream. He related the many times he experienced it and how last night's dream revealed its meaning. Tears formed in Solveig's father's eyes as he looked at his son-in-law in awe. Her mother was also crying when she hugged them both tightly.

"Solveig, you are truly blessed among women," her mother said, as she held her at arms length and stared into her eyes. "You husband has spoken with God."

"I speak with God daily, Mama. I pray to him all the time, so do you and Papa. We all speak with God."

"But God has verbally answered Erik. You are blessed."

Solveig shook her head. "Mama, those are the words Elizabeth spoke to Mary when she learned she was pregnant. *You are blessed among women*. I am certainly not Mary. I have not had an immaculate conception, nor am I going to give birth to the new Christ. Don't you understand? Erik wants to take me and the children to America."

"Perhaps it is God's will, my dear child," her father said

"Now you sound like Erik."

Her father seemed unable to understand her apprehensions. He took her in his arms, as though she were a child, and said, "Trust a little more, my child. Just trust a little more. God knows what He is doing."

Solveig lingered, secure in her father's embrace. "I know He knows what He's doing, but I don't know what I'm doing. America is so far away, Papa. I don't speak the language. I don't know the customs. Where will I find the mountains and the fjords? How can I live so far from you and Mama, from Thomas and Gerta and their families? I may never see you again."

"If not in this life, my Darling, then we will surely meet in the next. Be like Ruth, *'wither thou goest, I shall go, wither thou lodgest, I shall lodge, your people shall be my people, your land shall be my land.'"*

"But, Papa," she protested, "Erik's people are here, Erik's land is here."

Erik took her hand in his. "Not really, the people who raised me when my parents died, are here in Norway, living in Stavanger, but they are not my people. My only family is in America. My parents have been dead for more years than I care to remember. We must trust in the Lord and do His bidding."

They stayed for almost an hour, and at last Solveig tired of trying to explain her dread. They did not understand her, just as Erik did not understand her. Were they right? Could she be the only one who did not understand? Was Erik truly blessed having been spoken to by God? Had God chosen to bless her by arranging for her to move, to leave behind everything she held precious?

They returned home, but said nothing to the children. Erik glowed, while Solveig thought tears would spring to her eyes at any moment. Although they said nothing, the children seemed to sense something amiss and became edgy.

Automatically, she went about her daily tasks of cooking, cleaning, and gardening. With each completed task, she wondered how many times she would do it again in this house, in this country?

"We need to talk about what has happened," Erik said, bringing her back to the reality of the phone call. "We need to talk about going to America."

The lump in Solveig's throat would not allow any words to pass. Instead she nodded her head in agreement.

Chapter Two

During the next few days, the parsonage became a hub of activity. The children, as well as the parishioners, were told about *the dream* and their forthcoming move. Solveig found herself forced into silent acceptance.

Erik's friends were pleased for him. Solveig's friends told her how much they would miss her, and how thrilled they were over her move to America.

Somehow, she could not muster the same enthusiasm as everyone else. How could she become excited over something so unknown and so terrifying?

Her life seemed to turn upside down. With each passing day, her organized routine ceased to exist. Each morning when she should have been baking bread and cleaning the house, Erik insisted they set aside time for lessons. She, along with the children, spent two hours every day learning to speak a few words in English.

The children excelled. Her English seemed very poor in comparison.

"Children always learn faster than adults," Erik assured her. "You'll learn English soon."

Solveig was not so certain. Not only did he expect her to learn to speak English but she had to learn to read and write

English as well. Frustration became her constant companion. Her only recourse was to continue to try in order to please Eric.

By mid-morning, her friends would arrive with coffee and pastry to share, while they helped with the sorting and packing. There were times when she wanted to scream, *just leave me alone. I can pack my own things,* but she couldn't turn down the help of her friends. These were friends she had known all her life, friends she was unlikely to ever see again.

Evenings were always spent poring over Sven's letters, searching for clues to life in America. Erik had even gone to Oslo on an overnight trip and returned with several books on the subject.

"Where did you find them?" Solveig asked, as she paged through the books that were written in Norwegian.

"I asked your brother-in-law, Gustaf. He has access to the University library. He said we could borrow as many books as we wanted and he would return them after we leave."

The books were filled with information. America was so vast, they said, that Norway could fit into one small section of coastline. It seemed so huge, so imposing, so frightening.

Putting her fears aside, Solveig continued to read, greedy for the knowledge. She learned of small farming communities and large cities. From what Sven had told them, New Oslo fell into the category of the former. She liked the idea of living in a place not so unlike Kinsarvik.

She read about the government and thought how strange it would be not having a king and queen, but a President instead, a President elected by the people! What did common people know about leadership? How did they know if a man was good or bad? Why couldn't they just have a king who was appointed for life, rather than a man who stood for reelection every four years?

America's struggle to become a country, its fight against England for independence, confused her. Weren't they now allies? Hadn't they fought side by side in the big war? She could not comprehend how enemies could so easily become friends.

The days and weeks passed all too quickly and soon it was time to leave her homeland. Would she be able to trade her old life for a new life?

"I've had no time for myself, Erik," she announced one last evening in their old home as they prepared for bed. "Tomorrow will be just for me."

"To do what, Solveig?"

"To be alone. You can surely care for the children for one day."

"But, what will you do?"

"I will say good-bye to Norway."

"I do not understand you at all," Erik said, shaking his head. "Why do you feel this need to be alone when there is so much to do?"

"I do not expect you to understand, only to allow me this one concession. Tomorrow will be my day. I realize how much there is to do, but I must have this time. Whatever needs to be done, will be done, just not tomorrow."

"Then I cannot stop you?"

"No. The packing and sorting are done. There is enough food for you to eat. You will not miss me for a few hours."

"What about our lessons?"

"One day without lessons will not hurt me. There will be time for lessons on the ship. I will learn English. I may not be good at it, but I promise you I will try."

Early the next morning, she was up and eager to begin. She packed herself a lunch of cheese, bread and a flask of tea. With her food safely packed in her oldest son's knapsack, she silently left the house.

The path she, Gerta and Thomas had used as children was now overgrown. She didn't mind the bushes tugging at her skirt and scratching her legs. Her objective lay ahead. No amount of discomfort could override her excitement.

In her mind she could see the three of them as the children who so often walked this path to their secret hideaway.

She could see Thomas, nine, and Gerta, seven, being forced to take five year old Solveig with them on their outings. As she did, a long forgotten conversation flooded her mind.

"Mama," she had cried. "Thomas and Gerta always go away. They never play with me!"

"You are not old enough, Solveig," her mother admonished.

"But I want to go."

Unable to say no to her youngest child, she called to her older children. "Thomas, Gerta, take your sister with you."

"But Mama," Thomas pleaded. "She's a baby."

"I said to take your sister with you. Do as I say."

Reluctantly, they had taken the overjoyed Solveig with them.

"Where we are going," Thomas warned, "is a secret. You may tell no one of its existence."

"Not even Mama?"

"Not even Mama," Gerta repeated. "Mama does not know where we go when we leave the house to play." Slowly, they made their way up the path to the waterfall. The climb seemed to take forever. Once they neared their destination, Solveig became frightened. The sound of the pounding water, coupled with the fine mist that sprayed her face made her tremble. "I don't want to go by the waterfall, Thomas. I'm scared."

"You wanted to come with us," Thomas scolded, "and now you are here. You must come inside because we are not taking you home."

Taking her by the hand, he led her behind the waterfall into a small cavern. Inside, a rock served as a table and a makeshift holder held the stub of a candle. Thomas struck a match and immediately the cave became illuminated. Highlights sparkled on the walls and stalactites and stalagmites grew in the back.

"This is our hideaway, but you must never tell anyone," Gerta reminded her.

Solveig kept her promise. She never told anyone of the existence of the cave, not Erik and especially not Mama. She always promised herself when her children were old enough, she would bring them here.

Thomas and Gerta had grown up and abandoned the hideaway. For Solveig, it became a refuge, a place where she could escape whenever she was troubled. The last time she came was to say good-bye to her childhood. She remembered climbing the pathway on the day before she married Erik.

Today, she would say good-bye to so much more. Today, she would bid farewell to the home she had known all her life. She would say good-bye to Norway.

She slipped behind the curtain of water and from her pocket produced the stub of a candle. When she lit the wick, the cave sprang to life. Lights sparkled on the walls and the water of the stream running through the cavern behind her made the gurgling sound she found so comforting.

"I love you, old cave," she said, aloud. "Have other children found you? Has Thomas brought Gunnar here?"

Solveig sat, dreaming of bygone days, of childhood memories all too soon past, all too soon forgotten.

She didn't think she had been there long, when to her surprise, she felt the first pangs of hunger. As she reached into her knapsack for the bread and cheese, she thought she heard someone call her name. It must be the wind, she surmised, no one knows where I am.

Again the wind whispered her name. She shook her head. It couldn't be. The third time, the voice was loud and clear. It was the voice of a man. Had Erik followed her, invaded her private moment? She decided if it had been Erik, he would have overtaken her long before this.

A man stepped into the cavern, silhouetted by the sunlight against the waterfall. She smiled as she recognized Thomas.

"I thought I would find you here, Little Sister."

"I am not hard to find, if you know where I prefer to be. How did you know I had come?"

"I saw Erik. He's very worried about you. I told him I was certain I knew where you would be. What are you doing here?"

"I am saying good-bye to Norway," she replied, wiping away a tear. "In my own way, I am saying good-bye. Why does it all have to end?"

Thomas pulled her to her feet, and held her while she cried. "I see no ending, Solveig, only a new beginning."

"Everything ends. God has ended my childhood, the lives of friends, even my life in Norway. Why is He doing this to me? Nothing will ever be normal again."

"Of course it will, only just in a little different way. You are embarking on an adventure, one everyone in the village envies you for having."

"Everyone but me," she sobbed. "What if I don't fit in? What if I never speak English?"

"Oh, Solveig, you will learn English and you will fit in. Speaking of such things, how is your English coming?"

"You sound like Erik," she sniffed, her sobs subsiding. "So far all I can do is ask the grocer if the vegetables are fresh and how expensive the meat is. I can say good morning and good evening, hello and good-bye, and little more."

"My dear sister, it will come easier once you are around people who speak it daily. Once you are in America, I guarantee you will begin to even think in English."

Solveig sighed. "Erik keeps telling me the same thing. Are you hungry, Thomas?"

"You are changing the subject."

"Yes, I am. Now, are you hungry?"

"You know me, I am always hungry." Thomas' laughter at her question, as well as his answer, filled the cavern.

"Then sit down. I have bread and cheese and tea. It will be like when we were small children. Have you ever come back here?"

Thomas accepted the bread and cheese and chewed thoughtfully. After washing it down with the tea, he said, "I brought Gunnar here when he was seven. I don't think he was impressed. He had more important things to do, with his friends, not his papa. How about you?"

"I vowed I would bring the children when they were old enough. It's strange they never seemed to be old enough. I never had the time and now it's too late. Perhaps it is for the best. This was our place, not theirs. I would hate to have them intruding on what we had."

They talked long into the afternoon, before starting the long trek back to Kinsarvik.

"It was all so long ago," Solveig commented, when at last they reached the parsonage. "It is hard to believe any of it ever happened."

Thomas gave her a brotherly hug. "Our lives change, you know that, nothing ever stays the same. You wouldn't want to live without change."

Solveig knew Thomas was right, she just didn't want to accept the changes that seemed to be coming so fast.

Erik's last Sunday at the church proved to be a bittersweet day, a day for memories. It was a day for anticipation. Inwardly, Solveig cried, but outwardly, she smiled. She could not allow her friends to remember her tears, nor would she let them know how uncertain she felt about her future.

After church, large tables were set up on the lawn between the church and the parsonage, and they groaned with an abundance of food. It was the last time they would see their friends and they were making the most of every precious minute.

The next morning, they boarded the train for Bergen. Trunks were being loaded as Solveig and Erik prepared to leave. Thomas and Sonja, along with their family and Solveig's parents also accompanied them. In Bergen they would meet Greta and Gustaf for a holiday in the seaport city prior to sailing.

The hotel, just a block from the wharf, was a stately old building. The rooms were luxurious.

While the children played on the docks, the women explored the shops. One evening, they all rode the Finicular to the top of Mt. Floren, where they enjoyed dancing until the wee hours of the morning. In the pale hours of twilight that separated night from day, they made their way down the mountain in the small cars of the Finicular and walked back to their hotel.

Mornings were spent in the marketplace. There, Solveig relished all the sights and sounds. Fresh fish, as well as flowers and vegetables, were in abundance and sellers hawked their wares.

All too soon, it was August first and time for the Jorgenson family to sail for America. The ship was to sail at noon, but they had to be at the dock by eight in the morning. Trunks and baggage were loaded and staterooms assigned.

Solveig's family stayed aboard and visited until the last call for visitors to go ashore was made.

Solveig stood at the railing as slowly her family and Norway disappeared from view. Only then did she give in to the exhaustion that had plagued her for the last few weeks.

"I am very tired, Erik. I think I will go down to the cabin and rest a bit. You and the children will be all right, won't you?"

"You know we will," he replied, concern showing in his voice.

Once in the cabin, she eased herself wearily onto the lower bunk. She would let Erik be the one to maneuver the upper. It pleased her that the children would be in the adjoining cabin. The accommodations were cramped for two, let alone five. She fell asleep almost instantly. Only vaguely did she remember Erik trying to wake her for dinner. "Let me sleep," she mumbled. "Just let me sleep."

It was morning when she awoke and for some strange reason her stomach churned. *The boat,* she thought, *it must be the movement of the boat.* Once she was sick, her stomach settled down and she was able to enjoy her first full day at sea.

Grudgingly, she admitted to becoming excited. Leaving Norway was extremely hard, but as Thomas promised, the future lay ahead.

To her dismay, the next morning her sickness returned and then disappeared as quickly as it had the day before. Mentally she began to calculate and realized she was pregnant.

"Erik," she said, "I think we are going to be parents."

"What are you talking about, Solveig? We are already parents."

"I mean, I think we are going to be parents again. If my calculations are correct, the child will be born in about seven months, around the first of March. Our baby will be born in America."

Erik was thrilled. She watched as he hurried from the cabin to bring the ship's doctor to confirm Solveig's suspicions.

Once the doctor left, Erik took Solveig's hand. "A child," he began, "a baby, born in America. Not a Norwegian child, but an American child of Norwegian parentage! Perhaps this was why God is leading us from Norway to the promised land of America. Perhaps He has planned for this child to be an American citizen in order for him to do great things."

"What if the child is another girl?" she asked.

"It will not be. I can tell it will be a boy, a boy we will name Sven for my bother. You will see, Solveig, our son will become a great man. Not only will he be born of Norwegian parents but he will be an American. There, he will have many more opportunities than he could have ever hoped to have in Norway. All of our children will, but I know this one will be special."

Chapter Three

When at last the ship docked in New York, the passengers were taken to a large room with signs reading Customs And Immigration.

Solveig envied those with American passports, those who needed only to go through customs.

There were a few, like themselves, who were immigrating. There weren't the throngs she read about at Ellis Island, only four families on the entire ship. The remainder of the passengers had traveled for pleasure. Many were returning from visiting families in the old country. Others were returning from what they called the Grand Tour of the capitals of Europe and their splendor.

"It wouldn't have been complete," she heard one woman say, "without going to Norway. Everything there seemed so beautiful."

Solveig's heart ached for the beauty of Norway, the beauty she had left behind.

As they waited with the other immigrants, Erik answered questions over and over again. Always the questions were the same. How many are there in your family? Where do you come from? Do you have a sponsor in America? Where will you be living? Do you have a position?

Erik answered each question patiently, until Solveig wanted to scream. The room was large and yet it began to close in on her. The children fidgeted so she made them sit next to her on the floor, while she sat on the trunk.

"There are other children here," Karl pleaded. "Why can't we play with them?"

"Because I told you, you must be good. I want you to stay here by me. Papa will be done soon, then we can go out to meet Mr. Einerson and he will take us to Minnesota."

"How far is it to Minnesota, Mama?" Johann asked.

"It will take several days by train. It will be a long and exciting journey."

Johann's eyes mirrored the excitement she spoke of, while Karl pouted. She knew he wanted to play and was in no way interested in how long or exciting their journey would be. He had been so good all during the sailing and she knew he needed to run and play, to get rid of his energy.

At last Erik joined them. "We are finished here," he said. "We can go now."

The boys carried the trunk, while Erik struggled with the other baggage. At Erik's insistence, Solveig carried only a small traveling bag. Once outside the room, they found themselves in another waiting area. Across the room, a man of about fifty years of age stood holding a sign that read, *Pastor Jorgenson and Family*.

"Mr. Einerson?" Erik inquired, as he approached the man.

"Pastor Jorgenson, it is good to have you here," the man said in English.

"It is good to finally be through customs," Erik said, shaking the man's hand. "This is my wife, Solveig, and our children, Karl, Johann and Kristin."

"How was your trip, Mrs. Jorgenson?" the man asked, drawing her into the conversation.

It surprised Solveig, to realize she actually understood what the man said to her. "It was long, very long."

"Let me get a porter," Mr. Einerson continued, as he motioned to a black man. "We will be taking the luggage, but I'd like to ship the trunk on this evening's train to New Oslo."

The man spoke so fast Solveig did not comprehend what he had said. To her horror, two black men came and began to pick up the trunk. She started to protest about strangers taking away her belongings, but Erik silenced her. He quickly explained in Norwegian what she had not understood in English.

"We will spend two nights in New York," Mr. Einerson explained, this time speaking in Norwegian. "It will give you time to rest and see the city. You should have more time to see New York, but we must make do with what we have."

Solveig didn't want to see anything. She only wanted to be in her own home, to be able to sleep in a soft bed and to relax.

Outside, Mr. Einerson hailed a cab and showed them the sights of New York as they sped through the city.

"What hotel will we be staying in?" Solveig asked.

"Hotel?" Mr. Einerson sounded horrified at her question. "We won't be staying at a hotel. Thor, a young man from our congregation, has just been ordained and is serving a church in New Jersey. We will be staying with him and his wife, Rebecca."

Solveig was disappointed. She didn't like the idea of imposing on another pastor. She wanted to be alone.

Pastor Torsevite and his wife were a nice young couple. Their home was nothing like she expected.

"I'm English and Dutch," Rebecca said when she and Solveig shared a cup of tea in the kitchen. "I met Thor while he was in school. We fell in love and are so happy."

Although Solveig understood only a few of the words the girl had spoken, her meaning was clear. The glow on her face said it all.

Solveig could not help but compare the shabby furnishings of the parsonage with the beautiful handcrafted furniture she left behind. All that was here were hand-me-downs, various things other people donated. This table from that parishioner, that chair from this one, so that nothing matched. She wondered if this was what she could expect in her home in New Oslo.

"We have a small community here," Thor said, that evening at supper. "It reminds me of home. Even though these people aren't farmers, they are good people. I'd be pleased if you would join me in the pulpit tomorrow, Pastor Jorgenson."

Thor's proposal shocked Solveig. Could it be Sunday, already? She had lost track of time on the ship. True, Erik gave the Sunday sermon, but how could it have already been a week ago?

The next morning, they went to church with the Torsvites. Solveig's excitement quickly faded when she realized the entire service would be conducted in English.

She caught certain phrases and was pleased when Thor introduced Erik as the visiting pastor. Her heart swelled with pride as he greeted the congregation in his perfect English.

On Monday, they were again traveling, moving closer and closer to New Oslo and home.

"We will spend the night in Chicago with Pastor Bondehagen, then go on to New Oslo," Mr. Einerson announced on the morning of their second day on the train.

Solveig didn't protest. It would do her no good. She simply nodded her head and agreed. She didn't want to stay in Chicago. She didn't want to impose on Pastor and Mrs. Bondehagen. She merely wanted to be in her own home.

Chicago, like New York, was a dirty city. The stockyards, the smoke that seemed to come from everywhere, even the lake of which Pastor Bondehagen seemed so proud was dirty. Solveig expected the crystal clear water of the lakes at home, not this murky water filled with human contamination.

"It is not Norway, is it my dear?" Mrs. Bondehagen asked, in Norwegian, as they worked together to prepare supper.

"I'm afraid it is not. All of this is overwhelming. How do you survive in a city like this? The only mountains I can see are the buildings. There is no natural beauty."

"I know what you mean. I felt the same way when Harold first brought me here. Although Illinois does not have mountains, it does have beautiful lakes. I have learned to look beyond the city to the people in our congregation. It will not be easy, but you will learn to do the same."

The next morning they boarded the train and Solveig vowed to heed Mrs. Bondehagen's advice.

As they wound their way through the fertile farmland of Southern Wisconsin, Erik became more and more excited. "It reminds me of Denmark," he exclaimed.

Solveig smiled. Erik would certainly know of such things. He had traveled extensively as a child. He could describe any of the European capitals in vivid detail.

"Ja," Mr. Einerson said, "and you will find Northern Wisconsin and Minnesota will remind you of Sweden. Perhaps it is the reason so many people from Scandinavia have settled here."

"What reminds you of Norway?" Solveig asked, wistfully.

"There is nothing like Norway," Mr. Einerson replied. "Norway is a dream."

"An impossible dream," Solveig commented.

If Erik caught the irony of her words, he didn't acknowledge them. He remained lost in his own thoughts, his own dreams. With each mile he came closer to his brother, to his congregation and the fulfillment of God's prophesy.

Throughout the day, they rode through the changing countryside. While Solveig found the trip to be long and tedious, Eric and the children talked excitedly about the new things they were seeing.

At last they arrived in New Oslo. At the station two women met them.

"Pastor Jorgenson, Mrs. Jorgenson, this is my wife, Helga, and your sister-in-law, Ruth," Mr. Einerson said, making the necessary introductions.

Solveig assessed the two women. Mrs. Einerson was short and heavyset, her long gray hair coiled tightly around her head in braids. In any country, she would be a typical housewife. Solveig liked her immediately.

Ruth stood in direct contrast. She was tall and slender. Her hair was cut in a stylish bob and the strain of the past months showed on her face. Sven's illness had indeed been hard on Ruth.

"I am so pleased your family is here," Ruth said, embracing both Eric and Solveig.

"I thought Sven would be here to meet us," Erik's voice betrayed his disappointment.

"I am sorry," Ruth apologized. "Sven isn't having a good day. He decided to wait for you at the parsonage."

Together, they walked to the parking lot and Solveig was surprised to see two black automobiles parked side by side. "Do you drive an automobile?" she asked, in amazement.

Ruth laughed. "You will find driving in America is almost mandatory. Country towns here are just that, country towns. They are not the self-contained villages of Norway. It is a vast distance from here to there and you will find many things that require the use of an automobile. Although New Oslo is small, it is not compact. Many of the parishioners are farmers in far outlying areas. A car makes visits easier and less time consuming.

You'll get used to it. Perhaps you will even learn to drive yourself."

Solveig was horrified. Riding in a car was one thing, but driving one was quite another.

"Think about it, Solveig," Ruth said, breaking into Solveig's thoughts. "Driving has been my salvation since Sven became ill. It enables me to take him for rides when the weather is nice, as well as take him to the doctor's office. It lifts his spirits."

"Is he that ill?" Erik asked, concern sounding in his voice.

"I am afraid he is. It is only a matter of time. I am certain he has willed himself to live to see you take his place. Once that has successfully happened, he will be able to let go and find the rest he needs."

"There is nothing that can be done?"

"There are no miracle cures."

"Why doesn't God do something?" Solveig asked, knowing as soon as the words were said how terribly naive they sounded.

"He did do something," Ruth said, holding her hand as she smiled. "He brought you here. You will never know how the knowledge of your arrival has raised Sven's spirits. As for the cancer, there is nothing that can be done. Years ago, before doctors knew about such things, people died. At least we have an idea why Sven is going to die. We can prepare for it."

Solveig agreed. She pitied her sister-in-law for the burden she was carrying.

Once the luggage had been collected, Eric and the boys joined the Einersons, while Solveig and Kristin went back to the parsonage with Ruth.

"An ending and a beginning," Solveig commented, as they pulled away from the station.

"What a curious thing to say," Ruth said. "What do you mean by it, Solveig?"

"Sven's life is ending and I am carrying a new life. It is almost as though it is all part of God's master plan."

Ruth glanced at her and smiled. "You are pregnant? You are going to have a child?"

"Yes. We confirmed it while we were on the ship. With all the excitement, it took us by surprise."

"When will the child be born?"

"March, although I already feel as big as a house."

"Erik will want you to see the doctor right away. Dr. Olsen is excellent."

"A doctor? Why? I have always had a midwife."

"There are not many midwives here. Dr. Olsen will take very good care of you. I am certain you will like him."

Solveig was not as sure as Ruth seemed to be, but she said nothing. It had been a long and draining trip. The discussion of doctor versus midwife could wait for another time.

When at last they arrived at the parsonage, several parishioners as well as Ruth and Sven's children greeted them. Luncheon had been prepared for them, and for a short while being pleasant took precedence over emotional reunions and much needed rest.

After they ate and everyone left, it was time to get to know their family. For the first time, Solveig assessed her surroundings. The house was large, perfect for their growing family and the furnishings reminded her of home. Each piece suited the house, and had been made especially for the place where it stood.

Sven was an older, thinner, sicker version of Erik. Even their mannerisms were the same. Solveig ached seeing the shell of a man who was so alien and yet so familiar.

By late afternoon, Sven's strength seemed to drain and he was content to allow Ruth to take him home. Although Solveig needed to rest herself, she knew Erik was disappointed that his brother needed to go home. She knew her own misgivings and her own adjustment were just that, her own. Erik needed this time to get to know his brother to glean whatever knowledge Sven had to offer.

The weeks flew past quickly and soon it was October. Bright, crisp October, with brilliant blue skies and cold clear nights seemed a relief from the overly warm weather of August and September.

Sven had rallied after their arrival in August and seemed much stronger in September. For these reasons, his sudden death in October shocked and saddened the community.

The day of the funeral was a perfect October day. As Solveig stood in the small cemetery behind the church, she drank in every detail. The sky, she noted, was as blue as the glacier Papa had taken her to see as a child. The sky was clean, as though God had washed it and scented it especially for them to remember Sven. It seemed like a blessing that the entire community turned out to honor this man who had given them so much of himself, asking nothing in return.

Erik performed the funeral service with tears in his eyes. Solveig, too, felt a great loss, not for herself, for she hardly knew Sven, but for Erik and Ruth. Dear sweet Ruth, who had lost more than her husband, her lifelong companion. She had lost her home, her standing in the community, her identity. Although her small bungalow was cozy and neat, and she professed a great fulfillment from her job, Solveig still worried. Nothing she could imagine could ever take the place of home and husband. Even though she still had her husband, she knew she would never recover from the loss of her home.

December brought on the onset of winter and Solveig felt the depression of pregnancy closing in on her. Unlike her previous pregnancies, she felt no bonding with the child growing within her. Although she was only in her sixth month, she felt and looked much further along. Her body was swollen out of proportion and her breasts ached.

Unlike December in Norway, the sun did not completely disappear. The days were shorter, but the sun did peek through the clouds that dropped snow at least once or twice a week. The few hours of sunlight during the day did work to lift her spirits.

Erik was too busy to notice her depression and the children were too young to care. Although she occasionally spoke to Ruth, she hesitated to open herself too much to her American sister-in-law. Solveig missed her mama. She could have told Mama anything and she would make everything better. Now, when Solveig needed Mama the most, she was too far away. Letters took so long to arrive that the small worries her mother addressed were long forgotten by the time they were answered.

By February, even the every-day tasks of dressing the children and preparing the meals exhausted Solveig. "I can't go on like this, Erik," she said, one night after the children were in bed. "I am too tired to perform the simplest of tasks."

To her surprise, Erik looked at her in disbelief. "How can this be any different from the other times?"

"I don't know why it is different, Erik, it just is." The discomfort she had learned to live with suddenly became unbearable. Awkwardly she got to her feet when the first pains of labor began.

"Oh, Erik," she said, clinging to a chair for support. "It's the baby, but it can't be, it's too early."

Erik was immediately on his feet and at her side to help her to sit back down in the chair. "I will call Ruth and Dr. Olsen."

The pain was so sudden, so intense, that Erik's words were lost on her. Ruth arrived and helped her into a nightdress and into bed. She heard bits and pieces of the conversations around her, but understood little.

31

Eric paced the length of the parlor while the doctor attended to Solveig. He could not understand what was taking so long.

"It has been hours, Pastor," Dr. Olsen finally said. "The child is not going to be born naturally. We will have to take her to the hospital and take the child surgically. Help me get her to the car."

Unable to protest, drained from the ordeal, Solveig allowed them to take her away from her home and her children.

Hours later, Solveig awakened in a sterile white room in a strange bed. Beside her, Erik dozed in a chair. Even asleep, he looked drained.

"Erik," she said softly.

His eyes opened and he broke into a smile, which encompassed his entire face. "I was afraid I had lost you, too," he said, taking her hand in his.

"Lost me, too?" she questioned. "Did I lose the baby?" Her hand went, instinctively, to her now flatter belly.

"One baby died. You had twins," Eric said, softly.

"Twins?"

"Yes, darling, a boy and a girl. I christened him Sven, just before he died," Eric said, choking back tears.

"And the girl?" Solveig asked, crying at the loss of their son. She felt as though asking about the surviving child was necessary. They had only expected one, only planned for one, and now only had one. For some reason their daughter had survived, while their son perished.

"I named her Anne." Erik's voice sounded strangely strained.

"Do you resent her?" Solveig couldn't help but ask the hurtful question. "Is it so terrible that she is the one who survived and not your son?" Her voice was flat, drained of emotion, for she knew these were her feelings, her misgivings.

"God brought us to America for a great reason," Erik began, tears rolling down his cheeks. "When I found you were carrying our child, I was certain that child was the great reason. Our child, our son, would be destined for greatness in this country. Now, that hope is gone. Little Sven will never know the thrill of knowledge, will never play games, never grow up, never love a beautiful woman."

"Is it so hard to believe that a daughter could be destined for greatness?"

"You know the answer as well as I. She'll marry and have children. What mark will she make on this country?"

"Perhaps her children are the ones God meant, or maybe the dream was for Karl and Johann," she pleaded.

"I have no answers, Solveig. I only know this child is not destined for greatness."

She closed her eyes, knowing she should inquire about the baby. "How small is she?"

"Just under five pounds."

"I want to see her, to hold her," Solveig said.

Erik left the room and she steeled herself to meet her daughter, to hold the child who had stolen life from her brother.

When Erik returned, he brought with him a nurse and the baby. Although Anne's tiny mouth searched for the nipple and sucked at her breasts, Solveig knew there was nothing there. Her breasts were hard and yielded no milk. Again and again she tried, until at last it was decided Anne should be bottle-fed.

The nurse took Anne back to the nursery and Erik held Solveig while she cried. She ached for the small mouth suckling at her breast, taking nourishment from her body.

"I have nothing, nothing to give to her, Erik," she managed to say through her sobs.

"It was a difficult birth. It has drained you. The doctor says that is why you have no milk."

33

Solveig cried even harder at the words, for she was too exhausted, too sore from surgery to protest in any other manner.

Within two weeks she was up and walking around and able to go down to the nursery to see Anne. The nurses brought her in to be fed, but it wasn't the same. She ached for the feel of the baby pulling at her nipple, for the warm feeling as the tiny hands kneaded the flesh of her full breasts. This was how it had always been in the past. Now her breasts were empty and Anne did not need them for her nourishment.

Although the baby was beautiful, her complexion fair, her hair a tuft of blonde down, Solveig felt nothing for her. Had it been the difficulty of the pregnancy and birth, the loss of her twin brother, or Erik's disappointment about her gender?

When at last they went home, Solveig was pleased to find the women of the church willing to come and care for her and the children. They held Anne and cooed over her the way Solveig knew she should be doing. Although she fed and diapered the baby, she could not hold her tightly or kiss her lovingly.

It was as though Erik had no child. He spent his time with the older children, but seemed to ignore the cradle in the corner of their bedroom.

The children were thrilled with their baby sister and they were constantly at the cradle, talking to her in English and Norwegian and touching her head. Anne thrived on the attention and began early to build a bond with her siblings, if not with her parents.

Chapter Four

April 9, 1940, just two months after Anne's birth, seemed to mark the beginning of years or terror for the community of New Oslo. While they were safe in America, Hitler's armies had crossed the North Sea and invaded Norway.

For months the papers had been filled with stories of Hitler and Mussolini. One by one the major countries of Europe were falling under the control of the two dictators. The war of Erik's dream became a harsh reality.

With the fall of Norway, all correspondence ceased and phone calls were impossible to make. The members of Erik's congregation could only pray for friends and relatives thousands of miles away.

When, occasionally, a letter did slip through, the news was not good. Friends, family, acquaintances, none were missed by the brutality of the Germans.

Solveig received a letter almost a year after the beginning of the occupation, not from Thomas or Gerta, but from her nephew, Gunnar.

> Dear Aunt Solveig and Uncle Eric,
> I write to you from the top of the world. I am with the Laps, skiing with the resistance against the Germans. Aunt Gerta

returned to Kinsarvik for a visit just before the beginning of the occupation and has been a prisoner there ever since.

From what I have heard, Uncle Alfred was arrested and taken to a prison camp, along with several other professors.

Grandpa and Grandma were killed when they protested the intrusion of their home. I do not like to be the one who breaks this news to you, but I know there will be no letters from home.

The information I have received comes from new recruits, from various villages and cities. There is little time to write and receiving word is almost impossible as we move daily.

Pray for me, and the others who are with me who are working to free our country.

Gunnar

Solveig cried at the words. Alfred was in a prison camp and her parents were dead. It was all too much to comprehend. It brought her loss of Norway and family to the forefront. She had sacrificed so much, how could God ask her to give up even more?

The atrocities in Europe the bombing of Pearl Harbor pulled the United States into the dreaded war. Young men from every state in the Union enlisted. Men from small towns, large cities, farms and plantations were thrown together in a melting pot and trained to fight the enemy.

Young men from New Oslo said good-bye to family and friends. Among those to go were Mark and Matthew Jorgenson.

Although Erik comforted Ruth at their leaving, he secretly rejoiced that his own sons were too young to enlist.

Throughout the war years, Solveig became engrossed with her family. The older children spoke English with only a slight trace of an accent. As Anne grew, she spoke her first words in English. Solveig grieved that her youngest child would never speak Norwegian, would never see the beauty that was Norway, would never know the excitement of summer's twenty-four hours of sunlight after a winter with twenty-four hours of darkness.

At last the war was over. Hitler was dead, Mussolini hanged and Japan bombed. One by one the men came home, among them Mark Jorgenson, Matthew having lost his life in France.

The ending of the war brought to light the atrocities of the Nazis. Jewish death camps, murders carried out in the name of the Third Reich, and Russian stalags for the Allied prisoners of war were all exposed.

One by one, families in the sleepy farming town of New Oslo heard from loved ones in Europe. For some, the news was good. Entire families had survived by going to summer farms high in the mountains, areas where the Nazis were reluctant to follow. For others, the news was sad. Deaths were recorded in long awaited letters. Periods of mourning were sometimes delayed by as much as five years.

Erik and Solveig knew they were fortunate having had a preview of what other families were learning in their one letter from Gunnar. Still, they worried.

At last they also received a letter from home. The letter confirmed everything Gunnar told them and added more.

Alfred had perished in the prison camp, leaving Gerta a widow. She would not be returning to Oslo. She had decided to remain in Kinsarvik, teaching in the village, living in the home where her parents had died at the hands of their captors.

Gunnar was missing. There had been no word from him for many months prior to the end of the war. Thomas was certain his son, like his parents, was dead, lost to him forever.

Thomas' letter ended with the words Solveig remembered him saying to her when he found her saying 'good-bye' to Norway in the cave where they had played as children.

My dear Solveig, you were so right when you said it was so long ago. It is hard to believe any of it ever happened. Was there ever a time when we were carefree children? The future we dreamed of has disappeared. I do thank God for saving you from the Occupation. Had you stayed, you would have been dead now, as is the pastor who took your place.

Solveig could read no further. Bitter tears stung her eyes and sadness tore at her heart. Everyone she loved, all that she held dear had been torn asunder.

It was Erik who finished reading the letter, Erik who explained to the children, as best he could, the consequences of the events described by their uncle.

The boys, now twelve and fourteen, were keenly interested in the happenings in Norway. They remembered their native land and the relatives they left behind. Even though Gunnar was missing and presumed dead, he became their hero.

Kristen's memories of Norway were dimmer, but they had been kept alive, nurtured by her parents. At the age of nine, she was becoming a young lady and the knowledge of what happened to her home and her family pained her deeply.

For Anne, there were no memories to be reinforced. Norway, like the people Mama and Papa talked about, was alien. No amount of description could bring alive the nonexistent scenes of a home she'd never seen.

On a Saturday morning in December of 1946, the family was returning from Christmas program practice at the church.

Solveig walked beside them. She knew Karl was pleased that he was old enough to be exempt from the pageant and able to sing in the junior choir. Since his voice had changed, his once clear soprano had deepened to a delightful baritone and he'd been asked to sing a solo.

Johann had been chosen as narrator, while Kristen and Anne were angels and sang with the children's choir.

"Why do we have to practice every Saturday?" Anne whined. "Nobody says anything but Johann, and we know all the songs by heart. I've been singing *Away in a Manger* ever since I was a baby. My friend, Marcia, says they say recitations in their church. They don't have a dumb old pageant and they practice in Sunday school, not on Saturday."

"Unfortunately, Little One, you go to our church and in our church the Christmas pageant is a tradition," Erik said.

Solveig could hear the exasperation in his voice. More and more she noticed it whenever he talked to Anne, especially since she had started school in the fall. Since that time, she had talked incessantly of Marcia. The child's father moved to New Oslo, just after the war. The story Solveig had heard was that he had returned from the war to find his wife gone, his child with his parents. He now ran the family business, a textile plant in Minneapolis. After taking his child back to his own home he was forced to leave Marcia in the care of constantly changing housekeepers. Erik was not impressed with Anne's choice of friends, but no matter how much they protested, they were unable to pressure her into finding friends within their own church.

Solveig noticed that Karl had begun to fidget and told him to run ahead and get the mail. When they finally entered the kitchen, he was excitedly waving a letter in an onionskin envelope.

"Mama, Papa, it's a letter from Gunnar and it's postmarked Germany!"

Everyone except Anne went into the living room, so they could listen to the contents of the letter. Solveig ignored the younger of her two daughters' attitude. She was used to Anne's lack of interest in the family. She was too excited about the letter to worry about Anne's attitude. It had been over a year since they first learned of Gunnar's disappearance and now it seemed he was returning from the dead. To her dismay, the letter was written in English. Although she now spoke and read the language, she felt more comfortable having Erik read the letter, knowing his flawless English would not miss any of the words.

Dear Aunt Solveig and Uncle Erik,

An American nurse is writing this letter for me, as I am still far too weak to write for myself. It has taken almost a year for me to be able to talk about the war and find someone in the hospital who could understand Norwegian.

Of my comrades who were taken prisoner, I am the only one to survive.

I fought with the resistance and was captured in 1943 after being wounded. The stalag where I was kept had no medical treatment and many of the prisoners were tortured for the slightest infraction of the rules. I was among those who were beaten and starved. I know not why God spared my life, such as it is.

Once we were liberated and taken to the American hospital, I stayed in a twilight state, unable to even tell them my name for many months. Now, thanks to their care, I am progressing well.

I made many friends among the Laps and plan to visit them as soon as I am able. The doctors say I can return to Norway at Easter. I know your love and prayers have brought me through this ordeal. Being in Germany, I miss the long months of darkness, as I know you must miss them in America.

I am not sorry I chose to fight. I like to believe I had some small hand in helping to bring freedom to Europe.

I look forward to whatever role I will play in the rebuilding of my beloved Norway.

With prayers and thanksgiving,
Gunnar

Solveig dabbed at her eyes with her handkerchief as Erik comforted her. The children cheered their cousin, their cheers mixed with excited tears.

Out of the corner of her eye, Solveig saw Anne standing in the doorway. As usual, she was on the outside, looking in. She could almost read Anne's mind. She had no idea who Gunnar was, or why her family was so excited about listening to a narrative of the war.

Anne

Chapter Five

Solveig wondered where the years had gone. It was already 1958. They had been in America for nineteen years. Their lives, like those of their family in Norway continued to prosper.

In Norway, Thomas had become a member of Kinsarvik's city council. Gerta had remarried and still lived in her parents' small home. Gunnar had finished college and taken his grandfather's and uncle's place in the pulpit of the village church.

In America, Solveig's children had grown and were beginning their own lives. Karl was just finishing his medical training and would soon be starting his practice in Saint Peter a small rural community, much like New Oslo, and only sixty miles away. It meant less than an hour and a half trip by car, a short drive that she could even make alone. Being able to so easily visit her oldest son and his family, made her glad she'd learned to drive.

Johann, too, would soon be embarking on a new life. In another year, he would finish seminary and begin looking for a pastorate. She prayed it would be close to home, but she knew God would send him wherever he was needed.

Kristen was already married with two children and a third on the way. She and her husband, Lars Olsen, owned a small farm outside of New Oslo and were members of Erik's church.

The grandchildren, Nels and Gretta were the light of her life. Sadly, she realized these children, like her own Anne, would never know the beauty of Norway.

Anne, too, was almost grown. She would be graduating from high school in a few weeks and Solveig wondered what Anne's future would bring. By the time Kristen was preparing for graduation, a wedding was being planned, but there was no wedding in Anne's future, not even a special young man in her life. Even though they encouraged Anne to date, she declined. Her grades were excellent. Her study habits bordered on perfectionism, but what did this matter? She was just a girl. What did a girl's intelligence have to offer to the world? Solveig kept her own council concerning Anne, since Erik refused to comment on the subject.

They had just finished grace and were beginning to eat Sunday supper, when Anne brought up the subject. "Papa, I would like to go to college."

Solveig nearly choked on her soup, but it was Erik who loudly voiced his opposition. "College? Whatever for?"

"For Art, Papa. I want to be a fashion designer. I can't learn what I need to know without going to college." The tone of Anne's voice sounded determined, her arguments well rehearsed.

"But such a waste," Erik protested. "Are you sure this is something important or do you just want to find a husband? Perhaps you just want to go because your friend, Marcia, is going."

"No, Papa. I want to be a fashion designer, more than anything else in the world."

Solveig couldn't help but intervene on behalf of her daughter. "She does have a talent, Erik. Her stitches are even finer than mine. All of her handwork is perfect. It is as though she was born knowing how to do it."

"It's a gift, Papa. It's my gift from God. I don't think He meant me to be a farmer's wife, like Kristen. I know I wasn't meant to be a doctor or a minister, either. I'm certain He wants me to be a fashion designer, to use my talent to make clothes for people to enjoy."

"You shouldn't twist God's desires to fit yourself," Erik scolded.

"I'm not twisting anything, Papa. I honestly believe this is God's gift. I can sketch clothes on paper and then turn them into beautiful garments."

"I have seen your skill with a needle, but I am still skeptical. College for a girl is so expensive."

"I know it is, Papa. I've received a scholarship."

"Behind our backs?"

"My art teacher sent my sketches with my grades to a college in Minneapolis and they were so impressed, they sent a full four-year scholarship."

Anne's announcement impressed Solveig. "What else will you be studying at this school?"

"Fashion design, art, English, mathematics, history, and business management, they have a full program."

Solveig could hear the excitement in Anne's voice and see it in her eyes. She could tell Erik was equally impressed, but he was still skeptical.

"Where in Minnesota will you work?"

"I wouldn't be in Minnesota, Papa. I will go wherever there is a position. It could be California or New York, I don't know."

"Those places are so far away from home," Solveig lamented.

"America was far away from Norway, but God sent you here. I will go where God sends me. He has given me this talent, how can I deny it?"

"We will think about it and talk more tomorrow," Erik said, patting her hand. "Now, finish your supper and prepare for devotions."

Erik spent a restless night. He had never seen Anne so excited about anything. He disapproved of college for a girl, but she was so unlike her mother and sister, so unlike any woman he had ever known, any woman except Solveig's sister, Gerta. He wondered if his father-in-law had felt like this when she wanted to become a teacher. He wished he could talk to Solveig's father. Perhaps then he would be able to make sense of Anne's desire for a higher education.

The next day while Anne was at school, it was Marcia's father, Mr. Bower, who called. "Pastor Jorgenson," he began, "I know you don't approve of me, but I'd like to intercede for Anne. She has told me she would like to go to college ..."

"It seems as though everyone knew about Anne's decision but us. She only just told her mama and me last night." Erik felt defeated. It was as though Mr. Bower was Anne's father, not him.

"Just give me a minute, Pastor. The school she has been accepted to is close to where my factory and outlet store are located. I've checked it out and it is an excellent institution. I would be very happy to take her with me every day. In that way she would not need a car and she could continue to live at home. I will be taking Marcia with me to go to the teacher's college, so it would be no imposition."

"Will Marcia be at the same school as Anne?" Erik asked.

"No. She will be at a school several blocks away."

"And you think this will be good for Anne?"

"I think it will be very good for her. She is extremely talented. As a matter of fact, if I were in the business of making dresses, rather than fabric, I would definitely hire her. She has taught Marcia so very much. Let me give a little back. You and your family have been very good for my daughter. It has been hard with the hours I have to work and only housekeepers and nannies for Marcia. With my wife gone ..."

Mr. Bowe, paused and Erik wondered if the man ever heard from the wife who had deserted Marcia when she had been so small.

"It has been hard raising a daughter alone," Mr. Bower continued, "but your family has eased the burden. Let me give this gift back to you."

"I will think about it," Erik promised.

After talking to Mr. Bower, Erik contacted Anne's art teacher and she too praised Anne's qualifications. Outnumbered, he agreed to Anne's education.

Anne was overjoyed and hugged her father tightly when he gave her the news. "I'll make you and Mama so proud of me. I'll work hard and you'll see this is what I was meant to do."

Erik remained skeptical, but Anne had learned to live with his skepticism, had learned not to expect outward displays of affection from her parents.

"It's because I'm different," she confided to Marcia the next day when they were talking about Anne's parents agreeing to her education. "I wasn't born in Norway and things are so different here."

Marcia shook her head. "Do you actually think that is the reason, or do you think it's because your twin bother died when you were born?"

Anne nodded her head sadly. She'd always known her papa resented the fact she hadn't been a boy. "You're right. Papa did want a son, someone he could be proud of, someone who could aspire to greatness. Of course, he's proud of the boys, but they weren't born in America. You'll see, though, it will all work out. Once I get my diploma and am working for a big design house I just know they'll be proud of me."

The four years at college were long, the work hard. In order to take the courses she needed, Anne endured the academic courses as well. It meant long hours of study, but it was worth it. Her grades were high and she made the dean's list consistently.

She soon learned that if she wanted to be on top, she needed to spend every free minute in her room, studying. College was so different from high school. The professors didn't constantly remind her of deadlines. The decision to study had to be hers and hers alone. She begrudged even the hour a day that Papa demanded she dedicate to God.

"Isn't there some young man you'd like to be seeing?" Solveig asked, one Sunday after church. "I worry about you spending all your time studying."

"If I want to make good grades, Mama, I have to study. There will be plenty of time for young men once I graduate and get established."

"But isn't there someone special?" her mother pressed.

"No, Mama, there is no one special. There is no young man from church that I want to date."

Solveig was not content to let the argument rest. "Mrs. Einerson was telling me about her grandson ..."

Anne smiled and hugged her mother tightly, not allowing her to finish her sentence. "Oh, Mama, Edward Einerson is not my idea of a perfect date, nor am I his. He and Marta Carlson are planning to be married soon and are very happy together. You don't have to play matchmaker for me. I will find someone. I won't always be an old maid, contrary to what you might think."

Karl Jorgenson pulled his car into the familiar driveway of the parsonage. His fiancée, Janet Page, sat next to him. In just one week he would make her his wife. She had been his office nurse ever since he started his practice four years ago.

Today, his sister, Anne, would do the final fittings for the wedding dress. Although he hadn't seen the dress, he knew it would be elegant. Everything Anne did was special.

Anne settled herself on a blanket in the yard to put the finishing touches on the altar clothes with her special hardanger cutwork. The clothes, displaying the Norwegian designs cut from the fabric and bound with tight stitching were for Karl's wedding. Even though they were to be for the wedding, the clothes were meant to be a gift to the people of her father's congregation in New Oslo.

The following weekend was to be a busy one. Karl and Janet would be getting married on Saturday and Anne would be graduating from college on Sunday. It had been planned so the two events would coincide and Anne could attend the wedding.

With her top grades and beautiful designs, everyone was certain she would be leaving for a choice position right after graduation. Now, with the big event just a week away, she was having doubts. Perhaps Papa had been right and she had wasted the past four years. Her classmates, even those whose portfolios were not as prestigious as her own, had received offers from New York, Los Angeles and Chicago. She wondered why she had been passed over. Was God punishing her for her grandiose aspirations?

"Why so glum?" Karl asked as he came over to the blanket. "You look like you lost your best friend, Little One."

"I was just thinking," she said as she got to her feet and hugged her brother. "What if I don't ever get a job? What if Papa is right?"

Karl held her at arm's length and then began to laugh. "Is this my baby sister talking? It can't be."

"I'm afraid it is. Not a single design house has accepted me. What else can I think?"

"I think God has something special in mind for you. You'll see, you just have to be patient."

Anne smiled at how Karl sounded like her when she was arguing with Papa.

"Are you ready for your final fitting?" she asked Janet, changing the subject.

"I'm as ready as I'll ever be. Did my sister Linda come over for her fitting?"

"Oh, yes, she was here Wednesday evening. The deep pink suits her perfectly. I'm glad you decided to make her dress a different color from ours. Kristin and I would look terrible in the deep color and Linda wouldn't look good in the pale pink you chose for us."

Anne reached down to pick up her sewing as Karl folded the blanket. They were just heading for the house when Solveig came to the door.

"Anne," she called. "There is a phone call for you."

Anne saw no reason to hurry. Marcia could wait. Putting her sewing on the hall table her mother prompted her to hurry. "Don't dawdle Anne. I think it is long distance."

Once in her father's study, she picked up the phone. "Hello. Is this Anne Jorgenson?" the woman on the other end of the line asked. "I know that you don't know me. My name is JoAnna Bergendahl.and I own a chain of dress shops in Colorado called Jo's. I hope I'm not too late, but I had several arrangements to make before I could offer you a position."

"A position?" Anne interrupted, knowing she sounded more like an excited schoolgirl than a professional designer.

"Yes. I've decided to feature my own line of clothing in my shops. There are only three shops at the moment, but I'm opening three more out of state in the next two years. Would you be interested in coming to work for me?"

Interested, Anne wanted to shout *of course I'd be interested!* Instead, she took a deep breath and replied, "Yes, I'd be very interested! Do you already have a senior designer?"

JoAnna laughed. "You'd be the only designer. I've been toying with a name, in the event you weren't already obligated. I've come up with Fashions By AJ. It could stand for Anne Jorgenson or Anne and Jo, whichever way you want to think about it. Of course if it doesn't work out, that could all be changed."

"Fashions By AJ," Anne repeated, letting the words roll across her mind. "I can't believe it."

"Then your answer is yes? You aren't previously committed? If not, we could meet and work out the details. I'll be in Minneapolis for a trade show this week. Could we meet at the Hilton Wednesday at four in the afternoon?"

"Yes. The time would work out well. Especially considering my last class is over at three. I'll see you on Wednesday." After hanging up, she wrote down the name of the hotel as well as the scheduled time of the meeting before relaying her news to her family.

"I just had a job offer," she announced as she entered the kitchen.

"That's wonderful," Karl said, swinging her high in the air. "Sit down and tell us all about it."

As Anne repeated the conversation, even she had trouble believing it. Had she imagined the whole thing? Was JoAnna Bergendahl real?

Janet and Karl were enthusiastic at the news, but her parents seemed more reserved, almost disbelieving of what she was telling them. She was relaying the most important news of her life and her own parents were staring at her in disbelief. Just once, couldn't they be happy for her?

* * *

JoAnna Bergendahl hung up the phone and remained seated at her desk. Had she made a wise move? She didn't know. She certainly hoped so. She wished Paul were here. He would put her fears to rest.

"What would you have done?" she asked the smiling photograph on her desk. There was no reply, but she needed none. Hiring a designer had been Paul's idea five years ago, before he died. Be it grief, or whatever, she had not acted on his idea until now.

She remembered when they had first married, just before he shipped out for the South Pacific to fight the Japanese. They had been so young and had such great plans for the future. There should have been kids, lots of kids. When the war ended, they returned to Paul's grandfather's ranch, the Lazy B. His Grandfather had raised Paul and the ranch was his legacy. During the war, the foreman had run the operation and everything was waiting for Paul's return.

At first she had loved the ranch, but with each month when no child was conceived, she became more and more depressed. In 1950, out of desperation, they had consulted a doctor. It had been a blow when he told them that JoAnna would never have children.

"I have a wonderful idea," Paul had said that afternoon as they drove home. "We're going to involve you in the ranch. We'll remodel the house and turn it into a dude ranch. We'll still keep the cattle, keep this a working ranch, but we'll cater to tourists as well."

The idea grew and soon construction was underway. The sprawling ranch house was enlarged and guest cottages were constructed. Even the bunkhouse was upgraded to house the college students who comprised the summer staff. The working ranch was relocated to the south end of the property, where Paul built a new house in a secluded valley. The Lazy B had been kept intact but the dude ranch was renamed *The Lady Jo*.

They had opened in 1952. By 1954, the Lady Jo had exceeded their first expectations. Paul suggested opening it in the winter to cater to the growing skiing industry. It started as an outlet for riding clothes in the summer and ski togs in the winter, but slowly more fashionable clothing was added to the racks. The dress shop had been a natural progression.

Just before Paul's death, he suggested finding a designer. To Jo it seemed like too big a step. "Hiring a designer is a big commitment. Especially since I can order from the large design houses."

"You could, but that would never make the shop special. If you hire a designer you could feature an exclusive line of clothing. It would make *Jo's* unique."

The idea intrigued Jo to the point that she allowed Paul to add a studio to their home, which had now stood vacant since his death.

She had toyed with the idea of presenting her own line every year since Paul's death. Each year she had ordered portfolios from several schools across the country; each year she looked for something exciting, something unique; and each year, she ended up disappointed.

This year she was out of town when the portfolios from the various art schools arrived. As she leafed through them, she felt the same disappointment she had always experienced in the past. At first, she thought she may have been too late with this year's samples, but as the mundane pieces of artwork were spread before her, she wondered if she was just being too picky.

The last portfolio in the stack was marked Anne Jorgenson. Slowly she opened it, even though she knew what she would find. Her hand's shook as she dreaded the usual disappointment. However, to her delight, the designs were exactly what she was looking for. They were new, fresh, exciting and carried a hint of old country allure. There were dresses trimmed in hardanger cutwork and ski sweaters and mittens that could have been imported from Scandinavia.

She immediately began consulting with her business manager and lawyer. Things were moving quickly. In less than a week she had begun to assemble a staff. Seamstresses, pattern makers, even her friend, Colette had offered her assistance. She knew she was doing it all too prematurely, but she couldn't resist the urge to get things started. If Anne didn't work out, the people she had contacted would understand. They were her friends and neighbors. They had been hearing of her dream for years and were willing to become a part of it, even if it were only in theory at this point.

Joe had been almost afraid to place the call to Minnesota. She worried that someone else had already discovered the talent that jumped out at her from the pages that she had received in the mail. Putting aside her doubts, she had placed the call and listened to Anne's excited acceptance of the suggestion that they meet. Shaking her head, she smiled, secure in the knowledge Anne had said yes and had agreed to meet with her next week in Minneapolis. Perhaps it had all been prearranged by some higher power. The tradeshow she was to attend corresponded perfectly with the graduation ceremonies at the college Anne attended. Talking to Anne, it seemed as though Anne had been waiting for the call, the offer to become the brains behind Fashions By AJ.

* * *

Anne worked on Janet's fitting. She wished she could go over to Marcia's house and share her wonderful news with someone who would be supportive.

When the fitting was at last completed, they all sat down to supper. As usual, the table was laden with a bounty of food. Although Anne was not hungry, manners compelled her to stay at the table. To leave before eating would be an insult not only to her mother but in her father's eyes, to God.

"Dear Father in Heaven," Erik began to pray. "Thank you for the blessings You have bestowed on Anne and on the rest of this family. The talent she has developed is truly a gift from You. With Your guidance, she has nurtured that gift and allowed it to grow. Help her to use it wisely and to praise You for Your generous guidance."

Erik's prayer continued. Although Anne kept her head bowed and her hands clasped, her mind wandered to the phone call from JoAnna Bergendahl. Fashions By AJ seemed to be too much to comprehend.

At her father's Amen, Anne raised her head, relieved the long prayer was over. After eating enough to satisfy her parents, she left home to spend the remainder of the evening with Marcia.

The Bower house was only a few blocks away and over the years had become Anne's refuge. As she anticipated, her friend was excited about her wonderful news.

"This calls for a celebration," Marcia said, as she opened two cold beers. "Daddy just stocked the fridge and he'll never miss a couple of them." Anne poured the cold, amber liquid into her frosted mug. The beer bit at her tongue and warmed her throat and stomach. Taking a drag from her cigarette, she settled back into the overstuffed chair.

"Now, tell all," Marcia demanded.

Elvis sang sweetly from the stereo as Anne related every detail of the phone call from Colorado. In actuality, she realized she knew absolutely nothing about JoAnna Bergendahl and Fashions By AJ. How could she be so certain she hadn't been duped, that JoAnna Bergendahl actually existed?

The next afternoon, Anne was surprised when Kristen and Lars, Johann, and Karl and Janet all gathered at the parsonage.

"We decided to give you your graduation present early," Kristen said. "We figured it was something you could use on Wednesday."

Anne was bewildered. Her brothers and sister were acting like children who were sharing a playful secret from their baby sister.

"Are you ready?" Karl asked, tying a blindfold over her eyes.

"Ready for what?" she questioned.

"Your surprise," Johann teased, as he took her hand and led her out of the house.

"Surprise? What kind of surprise?" she asked, trusting them not to walk her into a wall. When they stopped her and removed the blindfold, Anne was astonished to see a bright yellow Volkswagen standing in the driveway.

"Congratulations, Anne," they said in unison.

"A car? For me?"

"Of course for you, silly," Kristen said, as she handed her the keys. "We found it two weeks ago. It's been almost impossible to keep it a secret."

Johann put his arm around her shoulders. "We were planning to wait until next Sunday, but with your interview on Wednesday, we thought you could use it now."

"You know I can, but it's so expensive. You shouldn't ..."

"Nonsense," Karl said. "You've worked very hard for this. With all of us chipping in, it didn't cost too much. I'd say this is the perfect gift, since it looks like you'll be needing transportation to Colorado."

She hugged them all in turn and then drove the car around the block. As impossible as it had seemed just twenty-four hours earlier, her life was coming together. She had a future.

Wednesday seemed to drag. Final exams and preparations for Sunday's graduation seemed unimportant compared to her upcoming meeting with JoAnna Bergendahl.

Over the past three days, her parents had become more and more skeptical, voicing their concern loudly and often. Listening to their fears, she too was beginning to doubt the existence of JoAnna Bergendahl, Jo's dress shops, and even Fashions By AJ.

Anne arrived at the hotel shortly before four and asked to be directed to Mrs. Bergendahl's room.

The desk clerk excused himself while he placed a call to confirm he should send her up. "Mrs. Bergendahl is in Suite 1432," he said, once he hung up the phone. "Just take the elevator to the fourteenth floor. You'll find it at the end of the hall to your right.

Once she was in the elevator, Anne's nerves kicked in. By the time the doors opened, she would be only moments away from her future. When she stepped from the elevator, she turned to her right and headed toward the end of the hall. Her timid knock was answered immediately.

The woman who answered the door was very attractive. Anne judged her to be in her early forties. Her dark hair was streaked with gray and her brown eyes sparkled with excitement.

After they exchanged greetings, Jo outlined her current operations and what she had planned for Fashions By AJ. Like a child describing Christmas toys, she drew a verbal picture of the home she and Paul had built with its well-lighted studio. When she spoke of the pattern makers and seamstresses who would bring Anne's designs to life, her eyes sparkled even more than before.

"The ranch attracts some very rich and famous people, both winter and summer. When those people go home with their purchases, your designs will be seen in New York, Los Angeles, Dallas, Chicago, in all corners of the country. I just know that with the proper designs the company will grow quickly."

"Why don't you want a more experienced designer?" Anne asked, almost afraid of the answer.

"I didn't see the need. This company is as new to me as your chosen profession is to you. I think the two of us will be like a child and a puppy growing up together."

"This is like a fairytale," Anne replied. "It's all too good to be true. You're offering me a future as well as a home. I only hope I prove worthy of the trust you're putting in me."

Jo laughed. "From what I saw in your portfolio, I don't think I'll be disappointed. I do want to meet your family before I return to Colorado, though."

Anne bit at her lip. How would Mama and Papa react to a woman as self assured, as successful, as JoAnna Bergendahl?

"I don't know," she said, hesitantly. "It's a busy week. My brother is being married on Saturday. Why don't you come to graduation on Sunday and then join us for supper?"

"I'd like that," Jo said. "I think you'd better check with your mother first. Why don't you call her from here?"

* * *

Solveig glanced at the clock. It was after four. Surely Anne was meeting with Mrs. Begrendahl?

Solveig wanted to be excited for Anne. She knew her daughter's desire to be a fashion designer, but in the end would Eric be correct? Would she give up her dream when a man came along and swept her off her feet?

She was proud of Anne, but her promise never to cross Eric again loomed ever present in her mind. When they left Norway, her doubts had been proven wrong when Eric learned of his brother's impending death. Since then she had deferred to her husband's opinion, as was her duty as his wife. To put Anne between herself and her husband at this point was easier said than done.

Solveig was putting the finishing touches on supper when the phone rang.

"Mama," Anne's voice came over the wire. "I'm calling you from Mrs. Bergendahl's suite."

"You shouldn't be calling long distance, Anne. It's so expensive," Solveig cautioned.

"You don't understand, Mama. Jo wanted me to call you. She ..."

"Don't be disrespectful, Anne. You should call her Mrs. Bergendah. You've been taught better than that."

"She asked me to call her Jo, Mama. She wants to meet you and Papa. I asked her to join us after graduation for supper."

For a moment, Solveig was speechless. Was her home good enough for someone who was as wealthy as JoAnna Bergendahl appeared to be? "You know there's always room for one more at our table." The reply surprised even Solveig. In her voice she could hear her own mama making the same comment many years earlier when her papa had insisted she invite Erik to come to supper so he could meet Solveig. At the time he was the worldly young minister who was coming to Kinsarvik to take her papa's place. Solveig knew her father wanted her to meet the young man in the hopes he would want her as his wife. Mama had been as anxious for Eric and Solveig to meet as Papa. She had always been an incurable matchmaker.

Sunday's graduation was the highlight of Anne's week. Around her the friends she'd made in school congratulated her on not only her job offer, but also on the award for top scholarship she would be receiving. When comparing notes with her classmates, she found that although they would be making more money for the first couple of years, they would be only associates. Their designs would be meaningless, since they worked for someone else, expanding only on the work of others. It would take them several years to reach the point where their work would be taken seriously.

Jo joined the Jorgenson family, along with Marcia and her father, at the parsonage for supper.

"I'm so excited about this new venture," Jo said, when at last they finished eating. "Your daughter is extremely talented, Pastor Jorgenson. You must be very proud of her."

Erik said little, causing Jo to wonder about him. She would have thought he would be singing his daughter's praises instead of sitting sternly at the head of the table. Her mother, too, seemed to be reserved. Anne's grades and her designs were all reasons for pride. Did they consider pride sinful? Was it sinful to be proud of the academic excellence of God-given talent?

Anne's brothers and sister seemed aloof as well. It was a strained relationship, a tense household. Everyone was happy for Anne, but they didn't seem overly passionate about their happiness.

To her surprise, it was Mr. Bower and Marcia who highly praised Anne's accomplishments.

"When will you be expecting Anne to be in Colorado?" Kristen asked.

"She'll need time pack to and get ready to leave. The fifteenth of June should be soon enough. By that time the seamstresses will be ready to begin and the knitting machines will be manufactured and in place."

"Knitting machines?" Solveig questioned, taking an interest in the conversation for the first time.

"I have a friend, Colette Rollins. She was injured in a skiing accident. It left her paralyzed, with very limited use of her hands. She was an avid knitter, so her husband designed a machine to help her continue with her hobby. When I saw Anne's beautiful sweaters I called them. Her husband, Bill, assured me he could adapt the machine to reproduce those patterns. He's making two more machines for me and will teach the women how to use them. Colette will head that department."

"A skiing accident," Marcia said. "How terrible!"

"Yes, it was tragic. She was in the Olympics just two years before the accident. It was such a freak accident. It shocked us all. A sudden storm caught her in a secluded valley. We'll never know exactly what happened, as she doesn't remember much and her skiing partner died."

Jo could hear the sadness in her own voice. Each time she related the details of Colette's accident, it tore anew at her heart.

"Tell us more about Crystal Creek," Anne said, changing the subject to a more positive one.

Jo was relieved for the change of subject. "It's a beautiful area. The Lady Jo is about ten miles out of town. Along with the dude ranch, I have a working ranch, the Lazy B. I keep the two businesses separate. The Lazy B has been in my husband's family over a hundred years. When we decided to establish the Lady Jo, I insisted the Lazy B remain intact."

"What is a working ranch?" Johann asked.

Jo smiled, glad to be talking about her passion. "We run cattle and horses. Luckily it's a large enough operation that we can make a living from it. It was my husband's idea to open a dude ranch, just like it was his idea to start the ski lodge and the dress shops. It was even his idea to hire a designer. It just took me several years to realize he was right."

"Does your husband also live in Crystal Creek?" Erik asked.

"Paul was killed in a hunting accident five years ago." Even now it was hard to say the words. As soon as they passed her lips, she could feel the tears that started to pool in her eyes. Before continuing, she dabbed at her eyes with her napkin. "Hiring a designer was actually his idea, but taking the first steps seemed to be the most difficult thing to do. I'm fortunate to have found Anne before anyone else did."

Around the table, the Jorgenson's expressed their sympathy over Jo's loss of her husband and for the first time, Jo realized the pain was easing. Paul had finally become a pleasant memory rather than an empty spot in her heart. She prayed Anne would open a new chapter in her life.

Chapter Six

Anne had waved until the plane carrying Marcia became a speck in the Colorado sky.

For the first time in her life, she was completely on her own. Behind her lay New Oslo, as well as her friends and family. Before her, the Lady Jo Ranch, which held her future.

Marcia had accompanied Anne as far as Denver, sharing the last remnant of their childhood friendship. In what Anne considered a twist of fate, Marcia and her father seemed more like family than the people who shared her name.

Papa's disappointment that she lived and her twin brother died had driven the initial wedge between them. The emotional cavern had widened when Anne chose her friends, not from the members of the Lutheran Church where her father served as pastor, but from outside the church community. Her desire for a college education rather than an early marriage, her independence, even her ignorance of the Norwegian language, acted as a barrier between herself and those she loved and wanted to love her.

Her thoughts returned to Colorado and her new home. To the left a white board fence ran parallel to the road. Beyond the fence lay the Lady Jo, as well as the working ranch, the Lazy B. Within a mile, she found a break in the fence jealously guarded by large metal gates that stood invitingly open. The words Lady Jo graced the wrought iron grillwork. She turned her car onto the country lane leading away from the road and up to the lodge. Ahead of her the Lady Jo promised an exciting future, one that promised acceptance.

If I'm going to start a new life, it will be as AJ. Today I will leave Anne behind. AJ will become so much more than Anne could ever be.

As she drove up the paved driveway, she passed guest cottages resembling Swiss Chalets and corrals filled with beautiful horses. She had a feeling she would like it here. The countryside enchanted her and she'd become caught up in the adventure of beginning a new life.

She parked the car outside the lodge. Although it looked like an old ranch house, she remembered Jo telling her how she and her husband had built it only a few years earlier. Its charm and beauty so perfectly depicted a bygone era.

Sitting in the car for just a moment, she took in everything around her. The mountains seemed to call to her, to whisper their secrets. Were these like the mountains in Norway that Mama so often described? The mountains in Norway were laced with fjords and were the homes of the Neese and the beautiful Hulda of Norwegian folk legends. *No, these are the Rocky Mountains. They aren't like Norway. They aren't like anything else on earth. Their snow-capped elegance surpassed all else.*

Stepping out of the car into the bright Colorado sunshine, a young man who looked to be only a few years older than her with dark hair and equally dark eyes approached her. He wore blue jeans and a plaid shirt, making him look like the cowboy he was meant to depict. The way he assessed her made Anne feel as though she was a mouse and he a cat, ready to devour her for his dinner. Once she stepped from the car, the way he looked at her long tanned legs accented by her white shorts caused her to be very self-conscience.

"Can I help you find someone?" he asked.

"I'm looking for Jo," she replied.

"You must be *the* one," he commented, again looking her over from head to toe.

"*The* one?"

"Fashions By AJ. Everyone on the ranch knows about you. Jo said you should be arriving soon. My name is Logan-Logan Prescott,"

"I'm AJ," she replied, smiling brightly. "I'm pleased to meet you, Logan Prescott." Just the touch of his hand made her tingle with excitement

"The pleasure is mine, AJ. I'm certain we'll be seeing a lot more of each other." He held her hand just a bit longer than necessary. His gaze brought alien feelings to her mind as well as her body. Never before had a perfect stranger been able to so completely unnerve her.

Trying to regain her composure, she kept her handshake firm and her smile sincere but not too inviting. She remembered how Karl told her that people equated a firm handshake and a sincere smile with a confident person.

"You'll find Jo in the lodge, probably in the dress shop."

AJ thanked him and entered the lodge. Without him staring at her she breathed a sigh of relief. She'd been unable to think straight when he was with her. Now she hoped she hadn't appeared to be too nervous.

The main building bustled with activity. Young people wearing the same kind of blue jeans and plaid shirts as Logan manned the reservations desk. It was evident that their attire was the accepted uniform for all of the employees. Meanwhile, thee guests, were more causally dressed.

Off to the side, she saw the dress shop and hurried inside. It didn't take long for her to see Jo standing at the counter.

"It's so good to see you," Jo said, taking her hands. "Did you have a good trip?"

"Yes, I had a wonderful time. Since I've never been more than sixty miles away from New Oslo, I didn't realize such beauty could exist just a few days from home."

"Did Marcia's plane leave on time?"

"Yes, and I've come to a decision. I like your name 'AJ'. It's what want to be called from now on."

Jo smiled. "A new life deserves a new name. I've already registered the name of the company. Carolyn can take care of things here for a time. I'll take you up to the house."

To her surprise, Jo drove a sleek, pink Cadillac, making AJ's well-used Volkswagen look shabby in comparison. The drive to the house took only about five minutes, but it was as though they entered another world. Grassy foothills and majestic peaks surrounded the valley where the house stood. AJ took a deep breath trying to absorb everything, excited to be part of this beautiful world.

The interior of Jo's house was magnificent. The living room, dominated by handcrafted furniture and windows, easily blended the indoor beauty with the outdoor serenity. A soot blackened stone fireplace filled the wall opposite the door. AJ relaxed immediately. She had always longed for this kind of a home. Here, she knew Jo led a very private life and perhaps she could as well.

"Your belongings arrived the first of the week," Jo said, interrupting her thoughts. "I had them put in your room."

She led AJ to a spare bedroom with a spectacular view. Every room had a spectacular view. In it sat several boxes. It seemed strange to see the labels in her own hand writing which read JoAnna Bergendahl, c/o The Lady Jo Ranch, Crystal Creek, Colorado.

"I'll leave you to your unpacking," Jo said. "I have to get back to the lodge, but I'll show you where the studio is first."

* * *

Awestruck AJ looked around the studio. A tilted sketching table sat in front of the window that faced the mountains, the rich green of the valley stretched before her. A desk stood by the door and overstuffed chairs were clustered to form an informal sitting area with its own view of the rolling foothills.

AJ saw Jo smile as AJ explored the room that was to be her domain. "Lunch for the staff is served at 1:30 sharp. I'll send someone to get you later. It will be better to have someone bring you down than for both of us to have our vehicles at the lodge." Without adding more, Jo left, leaving AJ to her unpacking.

The clock struck 11:00 as Jo pulled out of the driveway. The amount of work AJ completed before she heard it strike 1:00 pleased her. Knowing someone would be coming to get her soon, she quickly changed into her favorite jeans and new boots.

She had just finished securing her blonde hair into a ponytail when she heard a knock at the door.

"Jo said you'd be expecting me," Logan said, when she greeted him. "Are you ready to go down for lunch?"

"I'm ready," she replied, checking her reflection in the mirror beside the door before stepping outside.

"Are you really going to wear those boots?" As he had earlier, Logan took inventory of every inch of her body, making her feel as though a slight jolt of electricity had traveled throughout her system.

"I have them on, don't I?"

"Is this the first time you've worn them?" he pressed.

"Maybe it is, maybe it isn't. Why is it any of your business?"

"It isn't any of my business, but I know you'll be sorry later on."

"Sorry? Why? What are you talking about?"

Logan laughed. "I wouldn't wear them. I'd wear tennis shoes or something comfortable until I broke them in."

"Nonsense, I've never worn ordinary shoes this comfortable in my whole life. These boots feel like they were made especially for me."

"Talk to me tonight and tell me then how comfortable they feel. You do ride, don't you?" he asked, changing the subject.

"Ride? As in ride a horse? No, I don't ride. You didn't really bring a horse did you?" AJ tried to peek around his bulk to see if there were horses tied to the railing of the front porch.

"No, I brought the surrey. I wanted to bring a horse for you, but Jo didn't know if you rode."

AJ relaxed. "I'm from Minnesota, not Colorado, you know. I lived in town. My sister is the farmer and I doubt if she has ever ridden a horse."

"I suppose you don't ski either, then," he teased.

"I cross country," she defended herself.

"That's not really considered skiing. I mean downhill ski."

"I can learn can't I?"

" Of course you can learn. Not only am I the ski instructor in the winter, I'm riding instructor during the summer. I just happen to have some free time this afternoon, so Jo wants you to start learning to ride a horse today. As for the skiing, that will have to wait for snow."

She could almost see him picking her up in his strong arms when she fell. "Both riding and skiing sound wonderful, but I'm afraid I'll have so much work to do, I won't have much time for either activity."

"You'll get the work done, but on Jo's schedule, not yours. She wants you to get to know the staff, to enjoy yourself. By enjoying yourself, she means riding and skiing. The first step is for you to get to know everyone. That will happen at lunch."

"You sound like you know everyone very well."

As he helped her into the surrey he said, "Well, I should, I've been at the Lady Jo for three years now. I spent two summers here while I went to college. When I graduated last year, I signed on full time. Jo knew I was from Stowe, Vermont. When I told her how much I liked to ski, she asked if I wanted to become the ski instructor."

"Do you plan to make skiing a career?" AJ asked.

"I'll spend a couple of more years here while I finish my book, but that will be all. It's fun playing cowboy and teaching people to ski, but it's not the career I see for myself."

"Your book? I'm impressed. What's your book called?"

"*Lost Innocence*."

"I like the title. Are you an authority on the subject matter?" She couldn't help the smile that crossed her lips at the thought of the title.

"It's possible," Logan said giving her a sly wink. "We don't have time to find out, though. The cook doesn't like the staff to be late for meals."

As Logan urged the horses ahead, AJ looked around. "Jo mentioned this is a working cattle ranch."

"You're on the ranch now. She has a good business here. The Lady Jo is just for fun. The Lazy B is for profit."

AJ smiled at his comment, "Which one makes the most profit?"

"I'm not the accountant here, but I'll wager it's the Lady Jo."

"You said everyone knew I was coming. Is that good or bad?"

"Jo told everyone about the new designer. She's very excited about you. The girls are anxious to meet you, to find out what you're like."

"The girls? And what about the boys?"

Logan turned and peered at her from beneath the brim of his hat. "They're curious too."

"So you've appointed yourself the means to satisfy their curiosity. Do you think you're up to the task?"

"Oh, I think so," Logan commented with a wink, as the Lady Jo came into view.

The employee dining room was very informal, really little more than a large hall. Jo had furnished the room with picnic tables that were covered with red-and-white, checkered, vinyl covers.

Young people stood in line at a bountiful buffet table. AJ felt insignificant, as everyone seemed to be good friends and the room buzzed with conversation. No one seemed to take particular notice of her as she joined the line just ahead of Logan. To her surprise, he placed his hand protectively on her arm, as if signaling to the entire staff that she belonged to him.

Choosing a small amount of salad, fresh fruit, and a roast beef sandwich, she picked up a glass of milk and turned to see Jo motioning her to a table in the middle of the room.

"I see Logan got you here in one piece. I want you to meet more of the staff," Jo said.

AJ looked around to see Logan joining a group of young people at another table.

"Don't worry about remembering everyone's name, there won't be a test," Jo continued. "In time they'll all fit the faces. This is Julie, Brenda, LiAnn, and Miriam. They will be some of your models for the fall showing."

"Models?" AJ asked, not so much in disbelief, but because she never considered doing a showing with models so soon. "I didn't even think about a show."

Jo laughed. "You're young, AJ. It won't take long for you to learn the ways of big business, though. Fashions By AJ will not just be clothing that flatters pencil thin models. These will be clothes for real, robust girls, girls like these. I want you to get to know them soon, as you'll be designing an outfit especially for each of them for the fall line."

AJ looked for a moment at each of the girls. Each presented a definite figure problem. The challenge would be exciting. Brenda was tall and thin, so thin she would need something to make her figure look fuller. Julie was pleasingly plump, so her outfit should be slimming. LiAnn was Asian and petite. The design for her would need to make her look taller and something to accent her coloring. Miriam was tall and big boned.

"This is going to be a fantastic challenge. I almost feel guilty taking money for having fun.

Jo smiled, apparently pleased with AJ's comment. "There are fifteen models in total. They are all on staff. You will be designing for each of them. We'll keep you busy."

"Do I get to design something for you?" AJ asked Jo.

"Good heavens, no," Jo said, on the verge of laughter. "I'm far too old to be one of your models."

"We'll see," AJ teased. In her mind, she could hear Jo saying that the designs were for real girls. Since they would be sold at the ranch, it would be foolish not to include fashions for more mature women. Most of the patrons of the ranch were older. There was a need to cater to them as well.

The girls at the table seemed to enjoy the idea of Jo being in the show along with them and did their best to try to persuade her to join them. Before returning to work, they each made an appointment to meet with AJ for measurements and sketches.

"Did you call your parents?" Jo asked, just before Logan joined them.

"No," she confessed.

Jo turned to greet Logan. "What time did we schedule AJ's riding lesson?"

"Not until three o'clock," he replied.

"Good." She turned back to AJ. "I'll take you up to my office so you can call home."

Finally alone in Jo's office, AJ called her parents, for the first time not reversing the charges. "Hello Mama," she said when, her mother answered the phone.

"Anne, where are you?" Solveig asked.

What a silly question.. "I'm at the Lady Jo. I got here this morning. Jo thought I should call and let you know that I arrived safely."

They talked for a few more minutes, but the strain was not lost on AJ. The fact that the call was long distance seemed to make her mother uncomfortable. As she chatted about the trip, the people she met, the beauty of Colorado, her mother seemed eager to end the conversation.

Hanging up the phone, she sat rethinking her life. *Why aren't my parents proud of me? Why am I the only one excited about my accomplishments and brilliant future? There are just too many unanswered questions.*

* * *

"It's three," Logan said, entering the office without knocking.

"Already?" AJ asked, a note of sadness in her voice.

"What's this? A long face?"

"I just called home," she said, wiping her eyes with the back of her hand.

"I know," Logan replied. "Everyone gets homesick at first."

AJ agreed. *Let him think I'm just homesick. I certainly don't want him to know how much my family disapproves of my new life.*

Logan took her hand and led her outside. "The horses are in the small corral."

"Horses?" she asked. "As in more than one horse?"

"You and I are going for a ride together."

"Around the corral," she said.

71

"No. A ride. A real ride." Logan guided her toward the fenced area where two saddled horses stood patiently waiting for them.

"I don't know about this," she protested.

"Believe me, you'll learn. Everyone here learns to ride. It's not hard."

"Oh, it's not huh? And what if I land on my bottom?"

"Trust me, you won't."

"Trust you? I've only known you a few hours and I'm supposed to trust you?"

"Of course you are. I've picked out a good little mare for you."

"Is that what you do, pick out good little mares for the guests?"

"Only for those who can't ride. I'll make an expert rider of you in no time."

Before they left the corral, he instructed her on the correct way to mount a horse and how to properly neck rein the mare.

By 4:30, she thought she'd become glued to the saddle. He took her back up around Jo's house and further into the valley where he reined his horse to a halt and instructed AJ to do the same.

"This is the most beautiful ride on the ranch. It's a shame no one gets to see it. It's off- limits to the guests and most of the staff."

"But not to you?"

"I rode up here alone one day and Jo caught me. She gave me a good tongue lashing until I told her I got lost."

"Which you didn't. You lied to her," AJ accused.

"My, aren't you Miss Prim and Proper. Of course, I lied. I wanted to save my ass. Today, she told me to bring you here. She thought you would enjoy the scenery."

AJ agreed and thought about what Logan said. *Am I prim and proper? Not if you listened to Papa.*

"You'd better get down and stretch your legs a bit," Logan said, holding out his hand to her.

He helped her dismount and when her feet hit the ground she knew what Logan meant about the boots. Her feet hurt and her legs felt like Jello. She stumbled and found herself protectively encircled in his arms.

"Oh!"

Logan righted her and began to laugh. "Which is I? Have you lost your land legs or are your boots doing you in?"

"Both," she admitted sheepishly. "I've never worn a pair of shoes that hurt my feet so much."

"What do you mean you've never worn shoes which hurt so much? What about your first pair of high heels? I've heard girls say those are killers," he teased.

AJ sank to the ground. "I've never worn high heels," she confessed.

Logan lowered himself beside her. "That seems hard to believe. You're a fashion designer and you've never worn high heels?"

"Well, it's true," she said defensively. "Papa said they were sinful."

"Sinful? Where did he ever get that idea?"

AJ thought how silly she must have sounded. "Papa is a pastor, so he thinks just about everything is sinful. He did let me wear Queen Anne heels, though."

"Are they those shoes that look like some fat woman wore them and squashed them? Sounds right generous of him. Whatever made him approve of them?"

"He saw the Queen wear them once," she replied.

"What Queen?"

"The Queen of Norway. My family came to Minnesota from Norway before I was born. If the Queen can wear them, they must be all right."

Logan got to his feet and extended his hand to her. "You're an interesting lady," he said, helping her up. "Jo's been telling everyone how talented you are, and in reality you're just a little girl who is scared of her Papa."

"I guess I do sound like that, but I plan to make a lot of changes."

"Let's start with you changing those boots. You might as well be comfortable for tonight's barbeque. It's mandatory for the entire staff."

"I'll have to change more than my boots," AJ said, thinking of the fancy dresses she and Marcia wore in Denver.

"You look perfect. No one dresses up for the barbeque."

They returned to the lodge just in time to eat. "I thought you two got lost," Jo said.

"Not really, we just lost track of time and then I needed to change my boots. I think I have blisters on my blisters," AJ confessed.

"I told her not to wear those boots on her first day," Logan teased.

Jo assessed the two of them. From the look on AJ's face, she wondered if something happened between them. Perhaps she'd made a mistake by pushing worldly Logan at sheltered AJ. Somehow though, she knew they would have eventually gotten together. She made it happen sooner rather than later.

"You'll learn the "do's and don'ts" in time. Once you get those boots broken in, you'll never be out of them. Now hurry along, we'll be late for the barbeque."

"Logan told me about it. I'm excited. I've never been to a real western barbeque before."

"This will be an experience for you then. I want you to meet the guests."

AJ looked surprised. "I don't know if I'm ready for guests. It's just my first day here."

"The guests are an important part of our lives. They're especially important to you. These are the people who will be buying your designs and it's going to be the best part of this endeavor. They'll be able to meet you here, get to know you. People like to be able to say they know someone famous. Once we're up and running, these people will be anxious to get personal designs."

"I don't know if I'm up to all of this so soon!"

"I know this is all overwhelming, but starting next week, it will all fall into place. I've already contacted the pattern makers. They've started on some of the designs from your portfolio."

Jo put her arm around AJ's shoulders and guided her toward the yard where long tables were set up.

Guests were already filling their plates with meat sliced from the steer that had been roasting in the pit for two days. As Jo approached them, many greeted her, calling her by name.

"Ladies and gentlemen," Jo began, as she held up her hands for silence. "Tonight, I would like you to welcome a young woman that joined our staff today, Miss AJ. We are going into a new venture called Fashions By AJ. We hope to see all you lovely ladies back here next year to enjoy her exciting new designs, because Jo's dress shops will be the only place you will be able to purchase them."

Jo helped AJ to her feet as the guests applauded her. "I'm very happy to be here. I'm looking forward to meeting you and creating some personal designs for you in the future. By this time next year, we will be ready to cater to your every need."

AJ found a seat at one of the tables next to a perky little brunette and her husband.

"Where are you from AJ?" the woman asked.

"Minnesota,"

"We're from Iowa. My husband likes to play summer cowboy. We've been coming to the Lady Jo for the past three years. I'm looking forward to next summer."

AJ smiled. "I'll be looking forward to seeing you next year. It will be a pleasure to design something special just for you."

The woman laughed. "I'd never be able to afford one of your personal designs, but I'll buy something off the rack. You can bet your boots on it."

AJ looked down at her tennis shoes. "I think I already did."

"Overdid is more like it," the woman's husband said. "I think everyone does that when they first come here. I know I did the first time. It took me about two weeks to be able to even look at those boots again, but I did break them in right. You will too, and then you won't be comfortable in anything else."

The evening passed quickly, and at last AJ was able to collapse for her first night's sleep in her new home. Dreams of her brilliant future dominated her sleep time. She dreamed of her designs, of her success, and of the young man named Logan, who, she was certain, would soon be turning her world upside down.

Chapter Seven

Monday morning finally arrived. The sketching table that pulled AJ like a magnet all weekend was at last hers to command.

She sat with Jo lingering over their breakfast coffee, as they went over the schedule for the day.

"Now remember," Jo said, "lunch is served promptly at one thirty. I don't want you overworking. Do you have your appointments for this morning set up?"

"Yes, the first is at eight, then nine, then ten. I can sketch in the afternoon."

"I'll be spending the morning at the Crystal Creek shop," Jo said, as she dug into her purse for the keys to her car. "I do plan to be back in time to join you for lunch, though."

"I'll see you then," AJ replied, as Jo left the house.

AJ cleared the table and washed up the few dishes before heading for the bright studio. The sun streamed in the windows and sunbeams played across the floor and over the sketching table.

She had just set her cup of coffee on the table when she heard a knock at the door. Checking her watch, she saw it was exactly eight o'clock. The promptness of her first appointment pleased her.

As she sketched and took measurements, she recorded the questions and answers of her interview on a small tape recorder.

It had been a gift from Mark Bower when she graduated from high school. It had become invaluable at college for taping lectures. She knew it would be equally useful for interviews. The more she knew about the girls, the easier it would be to design the perfect outfit for each model.

Each interview took about forty-five minutes and by eleven, she had enough information on each girl to know her likes and dislikes, as well as her lifestyle.

When at last she sat alone in the studio, she began to work in earnest. It surprised her to be interrupted by the ringing of the phone. "Hello," she said, tentatively.

"Where are you?" Jo's tone sounded stern.

"Why?" AJ asked, puzzled by the question. "It certainly can't be lunch time yet."

"AJ, it's three o'clock! You missed lunch."

"Don't worry about me, I'm thoroughly and utterly engrossed in my project," AJ said, trying to put an end to Jo's worry about her overworking herself.

"Well, enjoy yourself," Jo said. With the words, she could imagine Jo shaking her head, trying to understand her newest arrival.

The next few days followed much the same pattern. Interviews were conducted and by the time AJ looked at the clock she knew she missed lunch again. Although she knew her missing lunch upset Jo, she rationalized her actions with the argument that she had rarely eaten lunch in college. She found the time she had set aside for eating to be better used for studying.

At noon on Friday, she was annoyed by a knock on the door that interrupted her concentration. She was surprised to find Logan standing outside the studio.

"Jo sent me up here to drag you to lunch," he said.

"Oh, Logan, Jo's not happy with me, is she?" AJ asked.

"Just worried. She says you don't eat enough to keep a bird alive. You're to bring a swim suit and clothes for dinner."

"I don't understand, a swim suit and dinner clothes, why?"

"Because Jo has decided you need the afternoon off to loll around the pool."

"All right, if it will make Jo happy, I'll relax this afternoon. Will we be riding horses down to the lodge? If we are, I'd better change my clothes."

Logan laughed at her comment. "No, I brought the jeep. Now hurry up, we don't want to be late."

"So how is it going?" Logan asked, as they drove to the lodge.

"I've finished the interviews and most of the preliminary sketches. Once I've decided what to make for each girl, I can finally get down to work."

"It sounds like you've made progress," Logan said, shaking his head. "You know what they say about all work and no play making AJ a dull girl. Everyone at the lodge misses you."

"How can they miss me? They don't even know me."

"You know what I mean. It was nice seeing you at last night's barbeque. I miss you at lunch, miss seeing you around."

"I'm like you, I have work to do. Speaking of work, don't you have more to do on a Friday afternoon than come after tardy fashion designers and drag them off to lunch?"

"By this time, the guests don't need a riding instructor, and on Fridays a lot of them are so tired out they prefer to vegetate around the pool."

"Is that what I'm supposed to do, vegetate around the pool?"

"It's a beautiful day for it," Logan replied. "I suppose now you're going to tell me you don't swim."

"I grew up in Minnesota, remember, the land of ten thousand lakes. My friend, Marcia, and her dad used to take me to their lake cottage in the summers. Her father taught me how to swim."

"You talk about your friend, Marcia, and her father, but I rarely hear you talk about your own parents. The one time you did, you told me that your father thinks everything is sinful. I don't understand what you mean by that."

"It's the way I view my parents. My father is a very stern man."

"If he's so stern and so set in his ways, whatever made him come to America in the first place?"

"You wouldn't believe me if I told you," AJ said, punctuating the statement with a nervous laugh.

"Try me."

AJ took a deep breath, knowing he would probably not budge until she gave him the answer he wanted. "Before Hitler became a household word, to be feared, my father kept having a dream, a vision. He experienced it for several months. It was always the same, men marching through rivers of blood, and a voice he couldn't understand. In the early summer of 1939, the voice became clear. He called it the voice of God telling him about the coming war and advising him to take his family and leave Norway. My father believed, wanted to believe, needed to believe, I don't know what. No matter what it was, he insisted God spoke to him in order to save our family. Because of the dream, he came to America bringing with him my mother, my two older brothers, and my sister."

"He came here with nothing?" Logan asked.

"Not really, he had his ministerial skills and his brother, Sven, served as the pastor of the church where Papa ministers now. My mother was skeptical about coming, but she accompanied him, just happy to be by his side. She brought him great pleasure when she agreed to come. She begged God for another sign. When my uncle called from America and told them he was dying of cancer and he wanted Papa to take his place, she became filled with guilt."

"Why did they feel they needed to bring a minister from so far away? Weren't there ministers in Minnesota?"

" My Papa speaks many languages. In our community there are Norwegians, Swedes, Danes, Fins, even Laps. My Papa speaks all those languages. He was viewed as a great asset to the church. He is a very learned man."

"It sounds like it. Does he ever have time for fun?"

"His fun, as well as his life, is the church and the scriptures." She paused for a moment before continuing. "I never became the child he wanted."

"What could he have wanted he didn't get?" Logan asked, bewildered.

"He wanted a son and if not a son, a carbon copy of my sister, Kristin. She chose her friends from within our own church and married a farmer right after graduation from high school to start her family. He certainly didn't want a worldly fashion designer."

Logan laughed at her comment. "Do you consider yourself worldly?"

For the first time AJ smiled. "No, but Papa does."

"And Papa is the one who counts?"

"I always wanted Papa and Mama to love me. Perhaps Mama wanted to love me as well, but I didn't come along at an opportune moment. She was trying to rebuild her life in a country where she knew neither the language nor the customs and giving birth to a child didn't make things easy for her. It didn't help when I came early and my twin brother died at birth. None of it helped. I'm different from my brothers and sister and nothing will ever change."

Logan sat quietly for a moment. As he started the Jeep he said, "Well, maybe we can't change the past, but there's nothing to say we can't change the future, starting with your work habits."

Once at the lodge, he helped her out of the jeep and stood back looking at her for a long minute.

AJ enjoyed his company but his overly long gaze unnerved her. "What are you staring at?"

"Your skirt, I've never seen anything like it before."

AJ looked down at her split denim skirt. "Oh, it's just a little something I whipped up before I left home. I saw it in an old cowboy movie once."

"And Papa approves of old cowboy movies?"

"Only the ones where the hero just kisses his horse. I certainly didn't go to cowboy movies with Papa."

"Ah ha, some lucky boy, no doubt."

"No lucky boys. I went with Marcia."

"You and Marcia must be very close."

"We are, but her life is in Duluth and mine is here. We grew up and got on with our lives."

On that rather sad, note AJ ended the conversation and went into the dining hall. Everyone seemed genuinely happy to see her, and even more pleased she would be spending both the afternoon and evening at the lodge.

To her surprise, Jo was nowhere to be found. "So where is the lovely lady who insisted I join her for lunch?" AJ asked.

"She got a call from Crystal Creek. There was an emergency at the shop," Julie said, indicating she should join her at a table on the far side of the room. "Did you bring your swim suit?"

"What is this? A conspiracy to get me out of the studio?"

Julie nodded. "Jo is very concerned, and the rest of the girls also think you are working way too hard. You need a break."

"Well, it worked. I'm prepared for an afternoon of total leisure."

After she finished lunch, AJ changed into her swimsuit in the girl's dorm. At the pool she found a beehive of activity. Families were enjoying the beautiful Colorado afternoon, sunning themselves and playing in the pool.

Standing at the edge of the pool she realized it wasn't the crystal clear lake she played in back home, but it did look cool and inviting. Swimming vigorously across the pool and back again, she eased herself out of the water and went to the towel she left on the grass. She picked up the book Julie had loaned her and began to read as the sun warmed her body.

"Good afternoon," a man's deep voice said, interrupting her concentration. "Are you a new guest?"

Raising up on one elbow and taking off her sunglasses she smiled. "No, I work here."

"I haven't seen you before. You're not one of the waitresses."

"No, you wouldn't have seen me at the lodge. I work at the other end of the ranch, for a company called Fashions By AJ."

"You mean there is more than just the Lady Jo?" The man inquired as he seated himself beside her on the grass.

"There's the dress shop, Jo's, the working ranch, The Lazy B, and Fashions By AJ," she replied.

"Just where do you fit in?"

"I'm AJ."

"You're too young to have a company named after you."

"Just ask anyone," AJ said. She was comfortable having a conversation with the young man. She liked his easy manner.

"I guess I just have to take your word for it. Are you free for dinner this evening, AJ?" he asked.

She thought for a long moment before answering. Would Jo approve? Jo encouraged her to mingle with the guests. AJ remembered seeing the young man at last evening's cookout.

Logan had taken up her time then and she had not been able to pay attention to anyone else.

"I don't even know your name."

The young man smiled, "My name is Breck, Marshall Breck."

"Well, Marshall Breck, I'll have to think about it."

"Better think quickly, I see the boss lady coming," Marshall replied.

AJ laughed. "I guess the answer is yes. I'll meet you in the dining room at six."

Marshall winked at her slyly and dove into the pool as AJ turned to greet Jo.

"Sorry I missed you at lunch AJ," Jo said. "I certainly am glad to see you relaxing. Who was the young man you were talking to?"

" Jo, you surprise me. I thought you knew all your guests by name. He's Marshall Breck. I can't believe I did it, but I agreed to have dinner with him this evening. Wouldn't Papa think me sinful?"

"I don't think you're sinful at all. It's high time you met some young men, and experienced a few summer romances."

AJ laughed heartily. "I'd hardly call meeting a guest for dinner a summer romance, but it will be fun. I'm glad I brought along something special to wear tonight."

"You'll have a good time, I'm certain of it," Jo said.

AJ thought Jo sounded just a bit tired. "Is everything all right?" she asked.

"Just a minor crisis at the Crystal Creek shop, nothing for you to worry about. One of the girls got a call from her babysitter. Her baby was sick. I covered for her until we could get someone to come in. I don't mind working the shops, but I am worried about her little one."

"And you talk about me overworking," AJ scolded. "What about you?"

"I guess you're right. I'll get my suit and join you for a swim."

AJ entered the dining room just before six. She wondered if Marshall Breck would be waiting for her or if she would be dining alone.

"AJ?" Logan said, posing her name as a question, as if her presence here came as a surprise. "Do you have any plans for this evening?"

Before she could answer, Marshall joined them. "Are you ready for dinner, AJ?" he asked.

She nodded, thinking perhaps she should introduce the two young men, but Marshall took her by the arm and swept her into the dining room. Glancing back, she saw Logan leave the dining room and experienced a moment of indecision.

After dinner, Marshall led her out by the pool. "I wish we'd met earlier in the week," he said, touching her face with his hand. "I have to go home in two days."

"And I have work to do," she replied.

"I would have liked to have been able to get know you better."

"Isn't that the way it is with vacations? They come to an end and all too soon, we have to return to reality."

"You're wise beyond your years," Marshall said, holding her hand just a little tighter.

She shook her head, unable to believe the words he had just said. "I wouldn't say so," she replied.

His lips brushed against hers and before she could comprehend what happened, he whispered, "good bye" and walked away.

She stood alone, her eyes closed, as though she needed the time to engrave the poignant memory on her soul.

"Who was that dude?" Logan asked as he came out of the darkness, startling her.

"Just a guest."

"Why did you let him kiss you?"

"I didn't "let" him kiss me, it just happened."

"You didn't stop him!"

"My goodness, Logan, are you jealous?" she asked.

Logan lit a cigarette. "Why should I be jealous? I hardly know you."

"That's right, you hardly know me," she retorted, wondering if she wanted him to be jealous.

"How are you getting back up to the house?"

"If Jo's not ready, I just might walk. It's such a beautiful night."

Logan moved closer to her and put his hands on her shoulders. "I'll take you home."

"AJ, are you out there?" Jo called.

"Right here Jo," she answered, wondering if she should be relieved or sorry to hear Jo's voice.

"Are you ready to go back to the house?" Jo asked, moving close enough to see Logan for the first time. "Oh, Logan, I didn't know you were with AJ."

"I wasn't," Logan said, not giving AJ a chance to answer for herself. "It's been a long day. I think AJ needs some rest."

AJ opened her mouth to reply, but Logan simply turned and disappeared into the night.

"Mr. Breck looked like a nice young man," Jo said, as they walked toward the parking lot. "Did you have a good time?"

"Yes. He thinks he's smitten with me, but you know how it is with summer romances."

Jo laughed as her words from earlier in the afternoon came back to haunt her. "Was Logan upset?"

"I think so. He didn't think it was right for me to be out with Marshall. He seemed especially upset because he saw Marshall kiss me. I think he's jealous, although I don't know why. I'm not his personal property."

"That is where the problem lies," Jo teased. "No one has informed Mr. Prescott of that fact. He thinks he's the apple of your eye. He is very taken with you. Don't let it bother you. This too will pass, it always does."

After that, life fell into a routine. At Jo's insistence, AJ found an old alarm clock and set it to remind her when it was time for lunch. The Friday afternoons around the pool soon became a necessary source of relief. On Thursday evenings, she attended the barbeque and Friday nights were spent with the guests at dinner.

As for Logan, AJ hardly saw him. No matter when she visited the lodge, he seemed to be occupied elsewhere.

"I guess I can just chalk Mr. Logan Prescott up to experience," she told Julie one day over lunch. "I don't really have the time for a relationship right now anyway, but it was flattering when I thought he actually cared."

Inwardly, she was hurt. Logan was the first man who ever paid any attention to her, even if it hadn't been that much attention.

The summer passed quickly and AJ took pride, not only in her designs but also in the quality of work produced by the seamstresses and the knitting-machine operators.

As the date of the fall showing drew nearer, excitement ran high. With the show only a week away, AJ spent her evenings teaching the girls the skills of modeling. To her delight, two of the girls had modeled before and were able to help with the training. They worked diligently amid cries of "I'll never get this right!"

"Now listen to me," AJ said. "If something goes wrong, just go on. No one but you knows what we planned and what we didn't. If you mess up, continue on and smile, and no one will ever know what happened."

At last the day of the show arrived. Since Jo would be the commentator, she read and reread the cards describing the ensembles, committing as much information as possible to memory.

When the girls were assembling back stage, AJ brought out a beautiful blue hostess gown. "We all want you to be a part of the show. I designed this especially for you. I hope I judged your measurements more or less correctly. It was a bit of a challenge, considering you didn't want to be a model."

"It's beautiful," Jo exclaimed, as she took the dress, fingering the silky material. "I never expected anything like this. Thank you!"

While Jo went to change into the gown, the other girls chatted excitedly. Their big moment was at hand and they were all nervous.

The staff had completely transformed the dining room for the event. Guests, as well as the fashion editors of the local papers, formed the audience.

AJ watched as Jo took the stage, quickly assessing her creation. Everyone else looked perfect too, right down to the line of young men in blue jeans, plaid shirts, and bandanas who waited to escort the models across the stage.

"Ladies and gentlemen, it is my pleasure to introduce the creations of Jo's exclusive designer, AJ. You will begin by seeing her collection and then you will meet the brilliant mind behind them. The first of her designs is the creation that I am wearing. This hostess gown is perfect for every occasion. Who knows, you may even see me wearing it around the ranch. In all seriousness, it is perfect for attending the many parties the

Denver social season demands. You will light up the room with glitz and glamour when you swirl in wearing this creation." For emphasis, Jo walked across the stage with all the poise and grace of a professional model, executing perfect turns at just the right places.

As the models and their escorts floated across the stage and into the audience, Jo described each ensemble.

From her backstage vantage point, AJ could tell the people were enjoying the show. The models came in all shapes and sizes, in various ethnic backgrounds. There were black, white, Indian, Asian, and Hispanic, as well as being tall, short, pudgy, slim, big bones and petite. Each girl was very definitely her own person, and each creation perfectly suited the model wearing it.

At the end of the show, Jo again turned toward the audience. "Now ladies and gentlemen, it is my great pleasure to introduce to you, AJ."

A round of applause sounded and flash bulbs popped as AJ took the stage. From the wings, Logan appeared with a dozen long stemmed red roses. It stunned AJ to see the audience on its feet and feel Logan's kiss on her cheek.

She stepped to the microphone. "Thank you for coming. Today was my trial by fire. I hope I impressed everyone. I want to begin by thanking Jo for taking a chance on an unknown. I look forward to a long and prosperous relationship. I also would like to thank my models. Without them, none of this would have been possible. These girls are like you and me, with busts, waistlines, and hips. They are girls who buy clothes to wear every day, not for a one time party or event. This is my clientele." She extended her hands toward the girls who stood on either side of the stage and again the room exploded with applause.

As the audience quieted, various reporters rushed to ask questions.

"Where are you from, AJ?"

"Minnesota."

"How did you meet JoAnna?"

"She sent for a copy of my portfolio from the school I attended. She called and offered to give me a chance. I couldn't have been happier than when we met and I accepted her offer."

The questions went on and on. When at last the session ended, she found Logan waiting for her.

"I didn't expect to see you here today. I thought you had disappeared," she said.

"I've been busy," Logan replied.

"Busy?"

"All right, I was jealous. It seemed like you were so busy with the show and the guests, I didn't think you would find time for me."

"I could have found a way to fit you in," she said, surprised by her forward statement.

Logan smiled. "We have time now. We'll go over to the dining hall and get something to eat."

To AJ's surprise, the dining hall was decorated much as the guest dining room. Rather than reporters, Jo and the majority of the staff greeted her. Congratulations sounded from every quarter when she entered the room.

"If you're all here, who's taking care of the guests?" she asked.

"The winter staff," Jo assured her. "These kids are done today and they always stay on as guests for another week. After next week's show in Denver, they'll all be going back to school."

The following Wednesday they held the show in Denver. AJ met fashion reporters from as far away as New York, Chicago, and Los Angeles.

"How did they know to be here?" AJ asked, when they were on their way back to the lodge in the vans Jo had rented for the trip.

Jo laughed. "We must get you away from the ranch more often. The wire service picked up on last weekend's story."

Wire services, reporters, successful shows, it was almost incomprehensible. AJ wondered if she would ever be ready for the fast paced world she would soon be entering?

The following Sunday, AJ didn't want to get up. She knew she stayed in bed far too late, as church services started at eleven and her bedside clock already read eight. She heard the phone, but ignored it. Phone calls were rarely for her. Whenever she wanted to speak with her family it was up to her to make the call and she longed to have them call her, just once.

Surprisingly, Jo called to her to answer the phone. "Good morning," she said, picking up the receiver of the extension in her room.

"AJ, it's Marcia."

"Marcia?"

"I have a copy of the Chicago Tribune and a copy of the New York Times. We've been reading all about you!"

"We?"

"I'm at Daddy's. Listen to this. 'In the opinion of this reporter, Fashions By AJ is an overnight sensation. I predict great things for this company, now in its infancy. Look out fashion world, the new generation has been born.' The papers are full of you. Everybody's buzzing."

AJ laughed. "Everybody? Don't you mean you and your dad?"

"The way this article reads, you've set the fashion industry on its ear. Once we saw the Chicago paper, Daddy ran out and got the one from New York. This is what they say about your show. 'A treat for the eyes was on the menu at a fashion show held in Denver on Wednesday, at a small unknown shop named Jo's. The exclusive designer is known only as AJ and the creations she presented were her first venture into the fashion world. Miss AJ provided the audience with an abbreviated line, which promises great things for the future. Fashions to fit every size and shape of every girl in the country was the dream of JoAnna Bergendahl when she hired an unknown designer known only by the name of "AJ." Taking the fashion world by storm, AJ's designs, JoAnna said, are for women, as we witnessed by seeing the models that presented this unique show. We predict a bright future and expect to see great things from AJ. Anyone in the Crystal Creek or Denver area is encouraged to stop in at Jo's. JoAnna says two more shops will be opening within the next year, one in Las Vegas and the other in Los Angeles. Look for these exclusive shops, if you are planning a trip to these cities."

"That's pretty heavy stuff," AJ commented, at a loss for any other words.

"That's what Daddy thought and he has an idea,"

AJ laughed. Marcia's father always rose up as her champion. She wondered what kind of idea he might have. "You want me to talk to him, right?"

"You bet. It's one reason I called."

AJ waited for Mark to take the phone from Marcia. All the while she couldn't help but wonder what his idea could be. "Hi, Anne," he said.

"Hello, Mr. Bower."

"Look, Honey, I have a proposition for you and if you like it, you better start calling me Mark. As you know, I'm in the textile business. I'm wondering if you would mind if I flew out to see you next week?"

"Mind? Why would I mind? It would be like having family come to see me."

"I want to talk to you and JoAnna about designing some fabric especially for your line."

"An exclusive contract with you?"

"I think it could be a great partnership. No one else would have the same fabrics. We could even copyright the patterns so they couldn't be copied."

"It sounds like a wonderful idea. When can you come out? The ranch is slow right now. We should have no trouble getting you a room."

"I'd like to come out on Tuesday or Wednesday. That wouldn't be too soon would it?"

"Give me a minute to talk to Jo." AJ put down the phone and quickly explained everything.

"I have no problem with it," Jo said. "When he has his flight schedule, have him call me and I'll send Logan to the airport to pick him up," Jo said.

When the conversation ended, AJ couldn't contain her enthusiasm. She could hardly believe she would be seeing Mr. Bower in a couple of days. Adding to her excitement, having an exclusive contract with his company seemed almost too good to be true.

* * *

"So, who is this guy we're supposed to meet at the airport?" Logan asked, as he and AJ drove toward Denver.

"His name is Mark Bower. He's Marcia's father. I told you all of this before." AJ was a bit annoyed with Logan's attitude. "He's coming here with a business proposition for Jo."

"Are you so sure that's the only proposition he has on his mind?"

"So, that's it! You're jealous of Mark! Honestly, Logan, it would be like being propositioned by my own Papa."

"Look, AJ, it wouldn't be the first time someone like him would want to have a fling with someone like you."

"Now you are being silly. Mark is interested in my career, not in my body."

"And just when did he become Mark rather than Mr. Bower?"

AJ laughed. "You *are* jealous! He asked me to call him Mark when we talked about doing business together. I work with you and I don't call you Mr. Prescott."

"That's different, and you know it," Logan said, before falling silent for the remainder of the trip.

When Mark saw AJ, he greeted her with a hug and a kiss on the cheek. "You look wonderful. Your new life must agree with you," he said, holding her at arm's length.

"Yes," she replied, "it certainly does. I'd like you to meet my friend, Logan Prescott."

"Mr. Bower," Logan said coldly, extending his hand.

Mark smiled at the formality. "Please, I'd like you to call me Mark."

"It seems like you want everyone to call you Mark," Logan muttered.

Mark ignored the remark, assuming the young man was perhaps fond of AJ and viewed him as a threat. Changing the subject, he continued, "I'm anxious to meet with JoAnna."

"You have a lot to talk over with her," AJ said absently, thinking about Logan's tone.

"I brought some of the samples. I'm eager for both of you to see them."

AJ put her finger to his lips. "No shoptalk until we get back to the ranch. I want to hear all about Marcia, her apartment, and her new job."

"She's only just moved into her apartment. She said to tell you she's taking pictures of every room so you can see what it looks like. As for her job, she just started on Monday, so there's not much to tell. She is very excited, though. We've talked enough about Marcia. Tell me about your summer. From the reviews in the paper, it must have been a very busy one."

"Where do I start? It seems like I just got here and yet so very much has happened. I've met some wonderful people. I've also learned how to pace myself, as far as work is concerned that is. The show was only the icing on this very exciting cake. I certainly don't know where to start to tell you all about it. It seems as though this has all been waiting for me, as though it was meant to happen."

Mark smiled at her excitement. He could never remember seeing her so excited, so happy. "How do your folks feel about your success?"

"They are very quiet on the subject. I make the phone calls and carry on both sides of the conversation. When it's all over, I feel very empty. They make polite talk about how pleased they are that I'm doing well, but I know they are eager to end the conversations. Have you seen them lately?"

"Not since I moved from New Oslo. The only thing we had in common was you. I don't think your father ever approved of me."

AJ sighed, hurt by the treatment her parents always gave Mark. "Papa doesn't approve of much, and especially not me."

Mark saw the tears in her eyes. He put his arm around her shoulders and comforted her while she cried. When at last the tears subsided, he continued. "I ran into Karl the other day."

"Where?" she asked.

"In the Twin Cities. We were having lunch at the same restaurant."

AJ laughed out loud. "Karl having lunch in a restaurant? That sounds very frivolous to me."

"He was there for a medical conference. He seemed very excited about your new life."

AJ looked at him in dismay. "I don't really think so. Perhaps it is easier for him to pretend to strangers than it is to me. The message I get is one of 'isn't it nice Anne is trying her wings. She will fall on her face, but she is trying'. I don't understand my family. They never call me. It's always me who has to call them. I usually get the excuse that they don't know if I'm at home, but everyone knows I'm in the studio almost every morning."

"What about your brother, Johann? Being a minister ..."

AJ raised her eyebrows. "Being a minister what? Is it supposed to mean he has more compassion? Papa is a minister and he has little compassion for those who choose a path different from his. As far as I know, Johann is very happy with his small country church. He has even met a nice young lady and is planning to be married in the spring."

Mark allowed the subject of AJ's family to drop. He realized how painful it was for her to talk about them. Instead, he turned his attention to Logan. "So Logan, what do you do around the ranch?"

"I'm the riding instructor in the summer and the ski instructor in the winter. Once we get some good powder, I plan to teach AJ to ski."

"That shouldn't be difficult. I taught her how to cross-country. She's an excellent student."

"Everyone knows cross-country isn't really skiing."

Mark laughed at Logan's rude comment. As he did, he couldn't miss the expression on AJ's face.

"I am looking forward to seeing your designs close up. How much longer before we get to the ranch?"

"We should be there in about ten more minutes. We will put together a private showing for you after lunch. The designs were put into the shops over the weekend. You can check them out at the shop in the lodge. Jo has a room ready for you. There are still a few guests left. We don't close down for what, about a week, Logan?"

"More like a week and a half," Logan said. "Jo closes from September 15 to October 15 and again from April 15 to May 15. It gives her a chance to completely redecorate between seasons."

Mark nodded. "It makes good business sense to close down during slow periods. How far does she go with the redecorating?"

"She does a complete make-over," Logan said. "Everything is repainted twice a year. In the fall we get ready for the skiers and in the spring we get ready for the dudes. Somehow I got conned into helping with the painting this year."

"You have my sympathy. My least favorite job in the world is painting."

Mark's ideas proved to be just the touch Fashions By AJ needed. By the end of the week, contracts were drawn up and signed.

"I wish you didn't have to leave so soon," AJ said at the airport, hugging Mark tightly.

"With our new partnership, you will see more of me than you want. You have a brilliant future here. You will never know how proud of you I am."

AJ watched, as he exited the waiting area and disappeared from view. He was her link to home, the only person, it seemed, who cared what happened to her.

Chapter Eight

With the closing down of the lodge for the season, AJ's routine changed. Logan became a permanent fixture in her life. He took her on long rides into the beautiful valleys and canyons gracing the Lazy B.

His attentions seemed so sincere that she forgot his earlier jealousy and overlooked his shallow nature. It flattered her when he prompted AJ to contemplate her future. She listened wide-eyed, when he speculated on her earning power.

Today AJ took extra care in dressing. She could hardly believe the beauty of this mild October Saturday. Logan's invitation to go on a picnic came as a welcome diversion to her daily work routine.

"You look lovely, dear," Jo commented, as she readied herself to go to the Crystal Creek shop for the day. "Where is Logan taking you?"

"He said something about having a picnic in Upper Valley," AJ replied.

"Well, enjoy it while you can. By the end of the month it will probably be filled with snow."

"Snow?" AJ questioned. "How can you talk about snow on a beautiful day like today?"

"You have a lot to learn, AJ. You're in Colorado. The weather can change without warning. I'm surprised it hasn't snowed already. When snow comes, it comes quickly and thank goodness it does. Snow is the one thing which keeps us running in the winter."

AJ watched Jo leave and thought over what she had said about snow. She might come to appreciate the slow season between the summer dudes and the winter snow bunnies. Because of it, Logan's time was his own and he spent much of it with AJ. With the coming of snow, Logan would be busy on the slopes, too busy to spend time with her.

"Are you ready to go?" Logan called from outside.

"Just about," AJ said, as she grabbed the blanket she'd promised to bring.

"You look great," Logan said, as his eyes ran slowly over her body, assessing her from the elastic neckline of her peasant blouse, to her full skirt and boots. "You look good enough to eat," he continued, as he held her coat.

AJ laughed at his statement. "I'd much rather eat the fried chicken the cook packed."

Logan nodded, then pulled her into his arms and kissed her. "The first order of business for today is to teach you how to kiss," he declared, once he released her lips.

"What do you mean?" she asked, pulling back to look into his eyes. Just being close to him left her breathless, made her heart pound with excitement. No one ever thrilled her like Logan did. Considering they'd spent every free minute together since the summer guests left, his response surprised her. What was she doing wrong?

"You kiss like you're blowing up a balloon. We'll start your lessons right now." He put his fingers to her lips and parted them slightly, then covered her open mouth with his own parted lips.

When his tongue entered her mouth, she couldn't help but shudder as a shiver of delight went through her body.

"Isn't it better my way?" he asked, once he released her.

"Anything this delightful must be sinful." In her mind she wished he would kiss her again, and awaken her inner spirit once more.

"Don't look so sad, my love. We'll continue our lessons after lunch," Logan promised, as he helped her into the surrey.

"I didn't know I looked sad." His statement made her wonder if her expression mirrored her trepidation over the new stirrings his kiss prompted. Would she ever be content to stop with just a kiss, when her body screamed for more from him than she was entitled to?

They drove across the pasture then started the climb to the higher level of Upper Valley. AJ could see why Jo didn't allow motorized vehicles in this area. The sweet smell of fall mingled with the songs of the birds. These were the sounds and smells so easily blocked out by the bustle of the modern world.

Once Logan selected the perfect spot for a picnic, AJ spread the blanket while he tied the horse's reins to a branch. Around her, birds sang and at the edge of the clearing she could see a yearling deer watching her intently. It seemed as though God made this spot especially for young lovers. Even the last of the summer flowers lingered in the grass, adding their own colors to the patchwork of perfection. She finished smoothing out the blanket when Logan appeared with a picnic basket.

She watched him expertly use the corkscrew to open a bottle of wine.

"Lesson number two," Logan teased. "You do like sangria, don't you?"

"I have no idea. I've never tasted it," she said, accepting the Dixie cup.

Logan held out his glass, as though offering a toast. "To new experiences and successful lessons," he said, his glass touching AJ's.

The fruity liquid tasted pleasing to her, almost like the punch her mother served to the Ladies Aid Society.

Before she could protest, Logan refilled her glass.

Throughout lunch, she consumed more of the sangria. The slight buzz the wine gave her sent up warning flags, only it was too late to do anything about them.

Logan pulled out slices of chocolate cake from the basket.

"Devil's food?" AJ questioned. "Does the cook know something I should know?"

"Are you suggesting I'm a devil?" Logan asked, putting his hand to her cheek and looking deep into her eyes.

"Then are you telling me you're an angel instead?" she teased. "If you are, I'm afraid your halo has slipped."

"I'm neither devil nor angel," Logan replied. "I'm only a mortal man entranced by a beautiful woman."

To AJ's delight, Logan enfolded her in his arms and kissed her. The disappearance of her earlier inhibitions surprised her. She flicked her tongue into Logan's mouth, teasing and enjoying the sensual feeling her actions produced.

"I think you deserve an A+," Logan whispered, when they parted. "Let's take a walk. There's something I'd like you to see."

AJ allowed him to take her hand and lead her to a small cabin. "Who lives way up here?" she asked, her speech a bit slurred.

"No one. It's called a line shack. The ranch hands use it when they're checking on the cattle. If we're lucky, we'll find something to make a fire with. It's starting to get cold."

AJ couldn't understand why he was concerned about the cold, when the October weather was so beautiful.

Once they were inside and he'd started a fire, Logan turned to face her. He put his hands on her shoulders before moving them to the elastic neckline of her blouse. Once he did, he pushed it down over her shoulders. When her breasts were exposed to him, Logan brushed his fingers against the white mounds before tweaking her nipples between his thumb and forefinger.

"Oh, Logan, we shouldn't be doing this," she said. His fingers kneaded the flesh of her breasts, teasing her nipples to arousal. She closed her eyes, realizing Logan, not the wine now intoxicated her.

He began to lightly kiss her neck, then moved lower until he reached her breasts, pulling one nipple into his mouth. His actions sent silent shock waves throughout her body, driving thoughts of Mama's dire warnings about dangerous young men from her mind.

She became so lost in her pleasure she didn't realize Logan's free hand had slipped to the hemline of her skirt. Not until he parted her legs and slipped his fingers into the warm moist place, guarded by the hair at the juncture of her thighs, did she try to mildly protest.

"Relax, AJ," he whispered, as he lowered her to the cot that sat against one wall of the shack. His fingers worked in a circular motion, touching her point of arousal until she thought she would explode.

When he got up, releasing her body from his weight, it surprised her. She couldn't take her eyes off him as he took off his jeans. His full erection made her gasp. She'd sketched nudes in college, but she'd never seen a man in full arousal. The beauty of his perfect body took her breath away.

Logan again positioned himself over her. Gently he helped her remove her blouse, then unbuttoned her skirt and slipped it off. Lastly he removed her panties, leaving her as naked as himself. "You are so beautiful," he said, as his fingers returned to the area which gave her so much pleasure earlier.

This time he moved his hand and slipped his fingers inside her hidden channel, making her moan with further pleasure. Slowly, he removed his fingers and slid his shaft into the area where he only teased her earlier.

For a moment, the tearing of the membrane, which stood between virginity and womanhood, caused her to cry out. Logan slowed his movement, giving her time to adjust to his lovemaking.

When he increased his motions, the intimacy of the moment overcame her until, lost in his embrace, she gave herself fully.

His complete release caught her by surprise. He lingered within her a bit longer until she felt him begin to shrink.

When he rolled away from her and lay on his side, she opened her eyes and stared at his still swollen member that had driven her to such heights of pleasure.

"Oh, Logan, what have we done?"

"We did what millions of people do every day."

"Only we aren't married."

"Marriage isn't mandatory, to do what we just did.

"It was for me. At least it was until now."

Logan laughed at her comment. "Then you must marry me because I can't imagine going through life without making love to you again."

AJ could hardly believe her ears. She suddenly saw what her father wanted her to see all along. Women needed to be loved. They also needed to be married, to have children. With Logan's proposal, her sister's world held out its hand to AJ. With her work done mainly at home, she could have both worlds rolled into one. She could have a happy and loving marriage to satisfy her father and a rewarding career to satisfy her. Maybe then her father would learn to love her. "Do you really mean it?"

He rolled over on top of her, his hardness against her leg surprising her. "I mean it more than I've ever meant anything in my life. I've loved you since the day you arrived. Let me love you for the rest of our lives."

Her earlier protest dissolved as he again made love to her and sealed their future.

After leaving AJ at the house she shared with Jo, Logan returned to the Lady Jo. After he stabled the horse he made his way back, toward the lodge. As he left the barn, he thought about the afternoon he had just spent in Upper Valley with AJ. He had expected her to be more reluctant. He was lucky she'd never had wine before. It had not taken much for her to become intoxicated enough to forget her inhibitions. The memory of her naked body brought a smile to his lips. Knowing he was the first man to see it, to enjoy it, made this afternoon's conquest even more satisfying. It had been a long time since he made love to a virgin. The very thought of pushing past the thin membrane, of breaking the final barrier which separated the little girl from the woman who matched him stroke for stroke, excited him even now. At his age, there weren't many virgins left. Most of the women who came to him were highly experienced and knew exactly what they wanted. They certainly didn't need to be teased and coaxed.

AJ's suggestion of marriage suited his purposes perfectly. He'd marry AJ; maybe even give her a child. Once she began making the money Jo promised her, he would be able to live off her earnings and finish his novel. As soon as he got published, he'd go his own way and say good-bye to Colorado and AJ.

"Logan, Logan Prescott," a woman called, her voice sounded with a soft drawl.

Logan turned to face her. "You got the right guy. What can I do for you?"

"My friend, Suellen Allen, said you could teach me how to ride," the woman said, dangling a chalet key in front of his face. "I can make it worth your time." She shoved a folded bill into his shirt pocket.

He didn't have to check. He knew his pocket now contained a $100 bill. It was meant as payment for a week of his time both on and off a horse. He'd learned how to satisfy these women and still do his job. Of course if Jo ever found out about his part time employment, she'd fire him.

He assessed the woman who now led the way back to her chalet. She was about thirty-five, more than likely divorced or contemplating it. She definitely wanted sex, the kind of sex he enjoyed the most. No strings, no expectations, no commitment.

AJ eased herself out of the tub of hot scented water. One afternoon with Logan had turned her life in a whole new direction. Although no ring yet graced the third finger of her left hand, she needed to only close her eyes to hear his marriage proposal. The thought of making love to Logan every night spread a fire through her entire body. Especially the area Logan awakened only hours earlier.

After dressing in denim skirt and plaid shirt, she left the bathroom. It didn't surprise her to see Jo waiting in the living room.

"Did you have a good day?" Jo asked.

AJ nodded. "I've never seen a more beautiful area. I still can't believe it will be completely filled with snow soon."

"Well, I can," Jo replied. "For now, let's go down to the lodge and get acquainted with our new guests. I'm starved."

AJ smiled. She'd eaten lunch hours ago, but she remained so full of Logan, she couldn't even consider being hungry.

The lodge buzzed with conversation, as would-be cowboys and cowgirls got to know the people they would see for the next week. The fall guests were definitely different from summer guests. They were all adults, the carefree children of summer having gone back to school over a month ago.

AJ looked around the room, able to easily identify the staff members among the guests. Although she recognized the staffers, she noticed Logan's absence.

"Are you AJ?" a woman asked.

AJ turned to face the woman, automatically smiling at the recognition. "Yes I am," she replied.

"I'd like to get an original design. What do I need to do?"

AJ explained about needing to do an interview and they set a tentative appointment for Monday morning.

As she did, she saw Logan enter the room. At his side, a woman of about thirty-five with brassy red hair seemed to be clinging to his every word. The look on Logan's face told AJ more than any words. She had seen the same look hours earlier after they made love.

"Are you all right?" the woman next to her asked.

"I'm sorry," AJ apologized, realizing she'd inadvertently diverted her attention from her potential client. "I'm afraid I've developed a splitting headache. If you'll excuse me, I'll see you on Monday morning. Just ask any of the staff. They'll bring you up in the surrey."

After she'd excused herself, AJ hurried out of the lodge. She needed to get back to the house, to get away from the lodge, to get away from Logan and the redhead. For a brief time, Logan had persuaded her to dismiss all of the rumors she had heard about him. Seeing the look on his face as he talked to the redhead made her wonder why she ever thought he could make her happy.

"Where do you think you're going?" Logan's voice sounded in the darkness.

"Why do you care?" AJ asked, forcing her tears not to fall.

"I love you, AJ. I told you so this afternoon," Logan said, encircling her arm with his hand. "You promised to marry me."

"I was drunk," AJ snapped, as she turned to face Logan in the light of the full moon.

"What kind of a burr do you have under your saddle?" he asked, still holding her tightly.

"Did you make love to the woman you were just with the way you made love to me this afternoon?"

"What woman?" Logan asked.

"Are there so many you don't remember? I wouldn't doubt it."

"Mrs. Goodwell was inquiring about riding lessons."

"I know all about your lessons, Logan. Now here's a lesson for you. I have a headache and I'm going home. I don't want to see you again. I don't even want to hear your name."

"So that's it," Logan said, a smile spreading across his face. "You're experiencing your first hangover. Your imagination is playing tricks on you. Things will look different in the morning. Now let me get a Jeep and take you home."

"I'm not hung over. As far as the Jeep is concerned, you can forget it. I'll walk back to the house. It will give me a chance to clear my head." She tried to wrench free, but Logan held her fast.

"I won't let you walk back to the house alone. Not only is it dark out but what if something happened? I'd never forgive myself. Believe it or not, I do love you. Now, are we going in and get something to eat or am I going to take you home?"

AJ hung her head, confused about the emotions raging within her. Logan's grip on her arm physically hurt her, but his profession of love emotionally pleased her.

Listening to gossip is sinful, she could hear her mother say from the confines of her mind. *Look for the good in people and don't jump to snap decisions.*

"I don't know," AJ said, her voice low, her mother's words still ringing in her ears. "I want to believe you, but the look on your face when you were with that woman. It's the same look ..."

Logan put his finger to her lips. "I can't help the look on my face, just as I can't control my feelings for you. Give me a chance, AJ. Let me show you what you mean to me."

Logan took her in his arms and kissed her tenderly. Against her will, he again intoxicated her with his being. She relegated all thoughts of her earlier jealousy to the back of her mind as she allowed him to hold her and tease her to arousal.

"A chance," she whispered, when he at last released her. "Yes, I can give you a chance. One chance."

Chapter Nine

Six weeks had passed since AJ allowed Logan to make love to her. Her emotions were in such turmoil she couldn't begin to understand them.

When Logan held her in his arms, she knew she loved him, wanted him. When she sat alone, as she did now, her doubts returned. What she allowed to happen was wrong, was sinful. Nevertheless it gave her great pleasure, but they weren't married, which made it wrong

She glanced down at the sketch on her pad. The original design would only need a few more pencil strokes before she could show it to the guest who ordered it. She smiled at the lines of the dress, pleased to be able to do something well.

A wave of nausea washed over her. It no longer came as an unexpected surprise. A week ago, when it first happened, she dismissed it as a bout with the stomach flu. Now she knew better. With the stomach flu, you didn't feel better when you lost everything. After the second day, she mentally checked her biological calendar. No matter how she figured it, she was late. She was pregnant.

Ever since the onset of the morning sickness, AJ purposely avoided Logan. She even convinced Jo she felt too weak from the flu to go down to the lodge. She wondered if Jo guessed the real reason behind her daily bouts of illness.

She pushed back her chair and hurried to the powder room. After the sickness passed, AJ got to her feet. Usually she felt better by now, but today was different. Today AJ couldn't shake the weakness, the lightheaded feeling which encompassed her being.

You're just feeling sorry for yourself. You've wasted enough time. Get back to work and you'll feel better.

Logan hurried across the expanse separating the bunkhouse from the lodge. The frigid air made him realize he'd have to cancel any scheduled ski lessons. With weather like this even the experienced, diehard skiers would spend the day cozied up to the fire.

Once inside the lodge, he fought the urge to stay in front of the fire for the rest of the day. Instead he intended to seek out Jo. After hanging up his coat on the rack by the door, he saw her heading for the dress shop.

"Jo," he called, hoping to get her attention. "Can I talk to you for a minute?"

"Of course, Logan. What's up? Do you have a problem with a persistent skier?"

"No," Logan said, "I wanted to know if AJ will be coming down today."

"I doubt it," Jo replied. "She's still fighting the flu."

"Is she?" Logan questioned. "Is she fighting the flu or are you giving her an excuse for avoiding me?"

"I told you, she doesn't seem to be able to shake this thing."

"Bull," Logan spat, momentarily forgetting who he was talking to. "Half a dozen staffers have been down with the flu over the past two weeks. They've all been down a day, maybe two at the most. It's been a week. It has to be more than the flu."

"Calm down, Logan," Jo cautioned. "Everyone who contracted the flu has gone to bed for a day or two, everyone except AJ. She could shake this off if she'd just get some rest. Unfortunately, she doesn't listen to advice from me. Maybe you can get her to listen to reason."

Logan nodded, relieved to hear Jo deny his worst fears. After AJ's reaction to Mrs. Goodwell, he had been trying to turn down the women who approached him. If he wanted to have her as his wife, he knew he would be wise to give up his extra curricular activities, at least until they got married.

Damn her anyway. It certainly wasn't him who said no to sex. If he heard her say how sinful they'd been one more time, he thought he'd puke. She didn't understand what going without could do to a man. He just hoped no one found out about the women he hadn't been about to turn down over the past three weeks.

"I'll talk to her, Jo. It's too cold to take anyone out on the slopes today. It will be the perfect time for me to go up to the house and see her. I'm sure I can get her to rest."

"Well, good luck," Jo said, as she returned her attention to her original destination.

Logan watched Jo enter the dress shop, then made his way to the front desk. "Give me the keys for number seven, Katie," he said, once he caught the attention of the on-duty clerk.

"Can't believe you want to take out a Jeep when there are several lonely guests sitting around the fire." Katie nodded toward the group of women, including the one he hadn't been able to refuse last night. Try as he might, he couldn't even remember her name. Of course, it really didn't matter. He'd stopped using names long ago. They only confused matters. Simply using endearments like Honey and Sweetheart made things much easier.

"I've got things to do today," he replied to Katie's statement.

Katie took the keys from the hook by the message board and tossed them to him. He caught them in mid air and winked at her.

"Your business wouldn't be taking you up to Jo's place, would it?"

"What if it is?"

"If it is, I'd say you better give up pleasing the guests and concentrate on AJ. Jo may not know about your nighttime activities, but the rest of the staff isn't blind. The grapevine has it you asked AJ to marry you. She won't stand for you catting around with the guests."

"You know what your problem is, Katie?" Logan asked, annoyed by her comments.

"I didn't know I had one."

"You've got a problem all right," Logan continued. "You listen to too much gossip. The only thing you have right is that I'm going to marry AJ."

Without giving Katie a chance to make a further comment, Logan pocketed the keys and went to retrieve his coat. If Katie knew about the women he had accommodated over the past three weeks, certainly others on the staff knew as well. No matter how hard restraint would be he needed to resist until he could make his way into AJ's bed permanently.

The Jeep seemed as annoyed about starting in the cold, as he'd been at Katie's words. On the third try, the engine finally sprung to life.

After the short drive to Jo's house, Logan stood at the door. He debated about knocking, but decided against it. Jo had built AJ's studio far to the back of the house. A room for the secretary she would someday need separated the studio from the living area. Being so far from the front door, AJ wouldn't hear his knock.

The house represented everything Logan wanted, wealth, security, a place to call his own. For a moment he listened, hoping to hear some sound from the studio. Instead, only silence met his ears.

When he entered the studio, its emptiness surprised him. A floor lamp beside the drawing table augmented the weak winter light coming through the windows.

On the drawing table, an almost finished sketch caught his eye. Having never seen AJ's work, he studied the drawing. AJ's talent radiated from the sketchpad. There could be no doubt about Jo's predictions. AJ would become more than a young woman drawing on a sketchpad. Someday she would be a trademark, a name to be reckoned with.

Behind him a door opened. With the sound, his earlier anger over AJ's absence this past week returned. If AJ did know about the other women, he wanted to have the upper hand from the start.

"Just what the hell is going on?" he asked, as he turned around. Seeing AJ standing in the doorway leading to the bathroom stopped any further words before they could form in his mouth. AJ's face was deathly white and rivulets of sweat rolled down her cheeks. Before she could respond, AJ began to weave back and forth, then collapsed.

Logan hurried to her side and easily picked her up. He carried her to the bedroom to lay her on the bed before returning to the bathroom for a wet cloth and a towel.

Something cool and wet caressed AJ's face. Slowly her mind cleared and she forced her eyes open. Logan sat beside her, his eyes betraying his concern.

"Logan," she said, surprised at the weakness in her voice.

"Don't try to talk, AJ." Logan cautioned. "I'm sorry I snapped at you. Jo said you were sick, but I didn't believe her. I thought you were mad at me. Jo's right, you need to rest so you can get better."

AJ closed her eyes and turned from him. "I'm not sick, Logan. No amount of rest will change what's happened."

"You aren't making any sense, AJ," Logan said. He took her hand and pressed it to his lips. His actions brought tears to her eyes. "How can you say you aren't sick?" he continued, not giving her a chance to explain. "You have no color in your face, you've lost weight, even your eyes tell me you're not well."

"You didn't let me finish Logan. I'll get better, but not right away, and certainly not because I get some rest. In another few weeks the sickness should end. It will take another six months or so for it to be over with."

Logan put his finger to her lips. "Are you trying to tell me you're pregnant?"

AJ couldn't bring herself to say the words. Instead she nodded, mutely, allowing her tears to fall.

"I don't know why you're crying. This is wonderful news," Logan said.

"No, it's not," she managed to say. "I'm not married. It's sinful."

Logan enfolded her in his arms. "We'll be married, Honey, just as soon as we can arrange it."

For a moment her fears ceased. Logan did love her and he would give her child a name, his name.

Telling Jo proved to be the hardest thing AJ ever did. Logan stayed by her side, giving her strength when she thought she might falter.

Although Jo didn't approve of their reason to get married, she did lend her support to their decision. "You will continue to stay with me," she said, when they finished telling her. "The baby will be a welcome addition to the family."

"We couldn't impose on you, Jo," AJ protested.

"Who said it would be an imposition? It only makes sense for you to be close to the studio. Where else would you stay?"

"Jo's right, AJ," Logan agreed. "You need to be close to your work."

"I won't hear any more arguments," Jo said. "You look tired, AJ. I think you should rest."

"Not until I call my parents," AJ said. "I have to tell them."

"Why not wait?" Logan rationalized, putting his arm around her shoulders.

"I can't," AJ replied. "If I wait, it will only be harder."

Logan held AJ's hand tightly as she waited for her mother to answer the phone. When she announced her impending marriage, the reply echoed despair. "Oh, Anne, it is so sudden."

"I'm pregnant, Mama," AJ said, the words burning on her tongue like a bitter pill.

"No, not my daughter," Solveig cried, her voice belying disbelief.

"Yes, Mama, your daughter. It just happened. We got carried away. Logan loves me. He wants to marry me. The child will have a name," AJ pleaded. "Please, I want you and Papa to come for the wedding." Her request met with a muffled argument between her parents.

Without saying hello, her father came on the line. "So, as soon as you were out of my house, you went whoring after a man. You've received what you deserve, Anne. Your Mama and I will not be at your wedding. You have shamed us. We no longer have a younger daughter."

"But Papa" she said only the two words before her father broke the connection.

No matter what Jo and Logan said, AJ knew she would be unable to call her brothers and sister. She couldn't stand to hear the condemnation in their voices as well.

Within a week, Jo planned the wedding. AJ had sunk so deeply into depression she wanted no part of the plans.

On the morning of the wedding, AJ dressed in a pale green suit with a cream-colored silk blouse and cream accessories. As she waited in the small office of the church, a knock at the door surprised her.

"Come in," she said, expecting to see Jo enter the room.

"Are you decent?" Mark Bower's voice called.

AJ turned to see Mark and Marcia standing in the doorway.

Marcia hurried to AJ's side, hugging her tightly. "Jo called me. She wanted to send plane tickets, but I said no. Daddy and I wanted to be here. I called your mother. She said they weren't coming. I couldn't believe it."

"Come now, can't you just hear Papa damning me to hell? 'And the sins of the mother shall be visited upon the child even unto the tenth generation.'"

"You're misquoting," Mark said, hugging her, as Marcia did only moments earlier.

"I don't care. They've washed their hands of me. I've shamed them."

"Well, you haven't shamed us," Mark continued. "I wondered how long you would be able to resist Logan's charms."

"I don't even know if I love him," AJ lamented, hanging her head to avoid Mark's eyes. "We experienced a beautiful moment in a hidden mountain valley. I'd call it passion, perhaps even lust, but I don't know if I can ever call it love. I honestly think he's more excited about this wedding and the baby than I am. I hardly know him. I don't know if I want to be married to him for the rest of my life, but I have no other choice. My child needs a father, as well as a name."

"It will come. I promise you, Honey, it will come in time. Jo asked me to give the bride away and she asked Marcia to be your maid of honor. It is all right with you, isn't it?"

"It's very all right with me," AJ said, managing a genuine smile for the first time in weeks. "I thought Jo planned to be my matron of honor."

Marcia giggled. "She said she wanted to play mother of the bride and cry when you come down the aisle."

After the wedding, AJ's life changed very little. Her days were filled with work in her studio and time at the shop in the lodge. The guests were thrilled to meet the designer and many booked appointments for personal designs. If it weren't for the changes in her body and Logan sharing her bed at night, she would have hardly known she was married.

Just over three months into the marriage, she found Logan's wedding ring on the dresser. She saw the looks he received from the female guests and wondered why he left this obvious symbol of their vows for her to find.

"I found your ring on the dresser this morning," she said that evening when they went to bed. Did you forget it?"

Logan looked surprised by her accusation. "No, I didn't forget it. With the cold weather it's too large. I don't want to lose it."

He made love to her, as he usually did, but somehow she knew the rumors were true. Logan cared for Logan. Her feelings meant nothing.

With the passing months, AJ's body swelled with pregnancy while Logan's manhood swelled for each new woman who crossed his path. He began to spend more and more time with the snow bunnies in the lodge. His blatant infidelity meant he was spending less and less time on the slopes.

"I'm afraid I'm going to have to replace Logan," Jo said one morning while she and AJ lingered over coffee. "I can't expect Tom to carry the load alone."

"I understand, Jo. I'm sure Logan will appreciate having more time to work on his book. I'll pay his way."

"That's not what I meant, AJ. There's more than enough money to care for both of you. If Logan is what you want"

"He's not what I want, Jo, he's what I need. It's bad enough I had to get married. If I divorce Logan, it will mean the end for me with my family. Even if Papa won't let me talk to Mama, at least the boys and Kristin still talk to me. I can't jeopardize those relationships."

On a Saturday in early July AJ's labor began. After looking all over the ranch for Logan, Jo finally took AJ to the hospital herself.

"We can't leave yet. What if Logan comes back and finds me gone?" AJ pleaded.

"Everyone knows we left for the hospital. They'll send him to town," Jo assured her.

After twenty-two hours of labor, Elizabeth JoAnna was born. The birth left AJ exhausted and alone. Although Jo stayed by her side, it wasn't the same. She needed Logan to share in the birth of their daughter.

Elizabeth, dubbed Libby at birth, was two days old before Logan even knew of her birth.

"Where were you?" AJ demanded when Logan finally appeared at the hospital. "How could you take off like that and not let me know where you were? How could you miss your own daughter's birth?"

"I told you about the writing seminar in Denver. You said you had another two weeks to go."

"Two weeks can mean anytime, Logan, and no, you didn't tell me about Denver. Was she a blonde or a brunette?"

"Honey," he said, taking her hand, "how could you say such a thing? I was at the seminar for our future. I learned so much and made such good contacts. I'm sorry I wasn't here for you, but I promise this weekend will open doors for us. You'll see."

"I'm sure I will, especially when I get the bill for everything you charged to my credit card."

Logan stayed with her, professing his love for her and Libby until, at last, AJ relented and forgave him whatever sins he committed.

Two days later, they brought Libby home. It seemed as though Libby's birth worked some miraculous change in Logan.

He became attentive to AJ and played proud Papa to Libby. The change made AJ feel as though she had imagined Logan's affairs.

Libby's christening became the one thing Logan surprisingly seemed eager to plan. AJ knew she wanted Libby christened, but she planned nothing elaborate. She thought she would just invite Logan's parents, Marcia and Mark, and Jo, but Logan wanted to ask several friends as well.

"This isn't a circus, Logan. It's Libby's dedication to God. Why do you want to invite so many people?"

"Presents, AJ. Everyone gives christening gifts. I've given enough over the years. It's time I--I mean Libby, gets something back."

"Is money the only thing you care about? I won't use Libby as a gimme. She is too young to know what is going on now, but in the years to come, I don't want her to think everyone should give her things."

Logan's eyes flashed angrily. "Well, I can tell you one thing, don't plan on asking my parents, they won't come."

"Why not?" AJ asked. "Libby is their grandchild. They're not like my parents. At least they still talk to you"

"We don't have christenings in our family, AJ, I'm Jewish!"

AJ couldn't believe her ears. Why hadn't he told her this before? "You're what?" she finally managed to exclaim.

"I'm Jewish. Why do you think my folks have been so distant? They don't approve of having a Gentile as a daughter-in-law."

Logan's words hurt her so much she began to cry. "Why didn't you tell me?"

"Would it have made any difference? Would you have been any less willing to go to bed with me? Am I any less of a man to you because I am a Jew?"

AJ stood, speechless as Logan turned on his heel and left the house. Logan Prescott didn't sound like a Jewish name, how could she have known? His revelation left her devastated. Why didn't he tell her before of his upbringing? It wouldn't have mattered, but at least it wouldn't have been such a shock. Libby's christening meant nothing more to Logan than the present's people would bring.

"I am going ahead with the christening, Logan," she screamed after him. "Do you hear me? I am dedicating Libby to my Lord, Jesus Christ. I am not doing it for the presents or any other earthly reason. I am doing this for Libby!" AJ stood alone in the doorway, angry, hurt, betrayed as she watched Logan spin the wheels of the Volkswagen in the gravel.

With her emotions churning, she went back into the house. She needed someone to talk to, but with Jo at the Denver shop, the only other person in the house was Libby. She stood, for a moment, looking at Libby's silky dark hair and wondered whether it mattered if Logan was Jewish. He agreed to be married by a minister, he was allowing her to have Libby christened therefore he didn't practice his religion as an Orthodox Jew. She would apologize to Logan as soon as he came home.

The ringing of the phone brought her back to the present. "Fashions By AJ" she answered.

"AJ?" A woman's voice sounded on the other end of the line. She wondered which of Logan's conquests would be so bold as to call her by her name. "This is Logan's mother," the woman continued. "Is he there?"

Having never spoken to Logan's mother, she couldn't have expected to recognize her voice. She thought she caught something in her mother-in-law's tone, but she couldn't be certain.

"Mrs. Prescott," she managed to say. "It's good to finally get to talk to you. I am sorry but Logan isn't here right now. I can have him call you when he returns, though." She concentrated on trying to be polite, but hadn't Logan told her his mother hated her?

"No--no," Logan's mother sniffed. "I'll call him later."

AJ couldn't help the feeling of something being terribly wrong. "Are you crying?"

The woman on the other end of the wire began to sob. "I shouldn't trouble you."

"Of course, you should," AJ replied sympathetically.

Mrs. Prescott sounded as though she'd begun to relax and as she did, she told AJ a shocking story. "You see, I called to tell Logan that-that his father and I are getting a divorce."

"A divorce?" AJ echoed. "Why?" She had trouble comprehending the need for a divorce in a couple married as long as the Prescott's. Wasn't divorce for young couples that rushed into marriage without thinking, the way she and Logan had? She couldn't imagine anyone with such a long-standing marriage taking such a drastic measure.

"Aaron has been cheating on me for years," her mother-in-law confessed, obviously relieved to have someone to talk with. "This time the girl is pregnant and he wants to marry her. It's time I quit fooling myself. He'll never change and I can't go on forgiving him. I'm leaving for London on Thursday. I have a friend there and I'm going to stay with her until after the holidays. I need to get away and put my life back together."

AJ wondered if she should say anything about the christening. Not caring what kind of an impression she made, AJ plunged ahead. She was determined to show her mother-in-law, no matter what, that Libby's christening would be an important day. "I'm sorry to hear you're leaving the country. As it is, I planned to call you later. I know you're Jewish, but I'm having Libby christened on the second Sunday in September."

"I'm what?" Marge Prescott echoed, her voice hardly audible. "Where did you ever get the idea I'm Jewish?"

"From Logan," AJ replied, wondering if she were out of line mentioning what Logan just told her.

"I think we need to talk, dear," Marge said. "Logan's father is Jewish, but I'm not. Logan was raised in both the Jewish and the Christian faiths and was allowed to make his own decisions. I wish I could attend Libby's christening, but my plans are made. I'll be there in spirit, though."

AJ choked back her own tears. She had, again, allowed Logan to deceive her. "I can see now, it was his way of hurting me. We were having a fight."

"Do you fight often, AJ?" Marge asked.

"It's hard to fight when Logan isn't here. I guess he's his father's son," AJ confessed, trying to make light of the situation.

"Don't make the mistake I did, AJ. Divorce him before he hurts you even more."

"I-I can't. I don't believe in divorce and Libby needs a father. I can't deprive her of Logan. In his own way, he loves her very much."

"Just keep what I've said in mind," Marge continued. "I'll call Logan later and give him my address in London."

AJ ended the conversation then realized how much she missed her own parents. She knew her father would never forgive her, but hopefully, he wouldn't deny Libby her grandparents. She wanted her father to dedicate Libby to God.

The first call she placed to New Oslo went unanswered. Her father answered the second call an hour later.

"Papa, it's Anne," she said, feeling like a little girl again. After her last call, she was almost afraid of her father's reaction.

"Anne?"

"Yes, Papa, Anne. I'm having Elizabeth christened. I want you to perform the service. I want ..."

"You — *you* want, Anne? It seems like it's always what *you* want. As I recall, you have Elizabeth because of what *you* wanted. My schedule is far too busy and the cost of coming to Colorado is much too high."

"Please, Papa, I'll send tickets to you and Mama. It won't cost you anything. I need you here."

"I told you, my schedule at the church is too busy. Perhaps you can find a pastor there who is more forgiving of an illegitimate child. If I were to perform the service I would be accepting your lifestyle and I can't approve of your sins. You certainly can understand my position."

"I know Papa. It was foolish of me to ask. Give Mama my love. I-I love you."

Her words brought only a polite good-bye from her father. His words rang in her ears, preceding bitter tears and heart wrenching sobs. Only Libby's hungry cries made her compose herself and attend to the duties at hand.

When at last Libby slept peacefully in her cradle, oblivious to the turmoil her birth caused, AJ placed a call to Mark.

"Why AJ, what a surprise," Mark said, when he heard her voice.

"I'm having Libby christened the second Sunday in September. Can you and Marcia come?"

"I'm honored you asked. We wouldn't miss it. As a matter of fact, I was just about to call you. Would it be an inconvenience if I came out a week early?"

"You an inconvenience? Never!" AJ could feel the tension beginning to drain from her voice as well as her body. For the first time all day she felt lighthearted and happy.

When Logan returned to the house, he found Libby sleeping peacefully in her cradle and AJ napping on the couch beside her. "AJ," he whispered, as he lightly touched her arm.

She opened her eyes, surprised at being awakened. "Honey, I'm sorry." As though the words would erase the harsh ones spoken earlier, he took her in his arms. "You were right. I am being selfish. We'll call my folks and yours. We'll make Libby's christening a family affair, just like you want."

"No, Logan," she said sadly. "It won't work." He listened as she went on to relate the conversations with his mother as well as her father. "At least Mark and Marcia will be able to come. They understand how important this day is for Libby."

"And for you," Logan added.

A week before the christening, AJ left Libby with Logan and drove to the Denver airport to meet Mark.

"It's so good to see you," she said, as he entered the waiting area.

Mark held her at arm's length. By the look on his face she knew her appearance shocked him.

"You look tired. Are you working too hard?" he asked.

"No, just not sleeping well. I'm having trouble coming to grips with Papa's feelings. I don't think I'm a terrible person. Why does my own papa hate me?"

Mark took her in his arms and held her while she cried. "He doesn't hate you, AJ, he just doesn't understand you. Someday he'll realize what he's missed. I only pray it isn't too late."

Once they collected Mark's luggage, they headed for AJ's car. "Marcia's bringing out a surprise," Mark teased, as AJ pulled out onto the highway.

"A surprise, what kind of a surprise? Does she have someone special in her life I don't know about?"

"No, but I do. I've met a woman. Her name is Norma Collins and she's a widow. We plan to be married on Saturday, right here in Crystal Creek. We've contacted your minister and he agreed. We decided we wanted both of my girls at our wedding."

"What wonderful news, but what about her family?"

"Her daughter, Jenny, is in Germany with her husband and her son, Paul, is stationed in Alaska with the Air Force. It

124

doesn't matter when or where we get married, they wouldn't be able to attend."

"I wish you would have told me earlier," AJ said. "I could have designed something special for the wedding."

"I suggested it, but you have to know Norma. She wants to buy something off the rack once she gets here. I showed her the fall collection and she made her choice. Now we just have to see if you have it in a size twelve."

Once they returned to the ranch, AJ checked the selection Norma made. With one phone call, she arranged to have the dress made up in pale pink brocade and began looking for accessories. She considered this was the least she could do for the woman Mark considered special.

Jo arrived back at the house by dinnertime. Logan gave them some excuse about checking something at the lodge and left as soon as Mark arrived, leaving AJ with plenty of time alone with her old friend.

"I saw Logan at the lodge," Jo said, as she put her bag on the buffet.

"I know. You don't have to tell me about him romancing some lovely young guest," AJ replied nonchalantly.

"Don't you care?" Mark asked, his bewilderment at her statement showing in his eyes.

"Of course I do, but I can't change him. What no one seems to understand is Logan cares for Logan. Period. I'm nothing more than a means to an end for him. He's just like Papa. I'm his dirty linen, something to be ashamed of, someone to be shunned." She turned and ran from the room.

Mark's week of rest passed all too quickly. Friday morning he joined AJ, Logan, and Jo at the house for breakfast. "I wish I never had to leave here," he said as they sat down to eat. "You know, if things continue to prosper for you, the way they have this past year, I may have to open another plant to accommodate your orders. How many new shops are you planning to open this winter?"

Jo thought for a minute. "Let's see, there's Dallas, Seattle, San Francisco and Reno. Those are the ones I've planned. I've also received requests from Phoenix, Tucson, Portland, and Santa Fe. There will be at least four, if not eight by this time next year. Requests are coming in faster than I can reply. I'm considering leasing the franchise on the condition they only handle Fashions By AJ. I suggested it to the shops in Las Vegas and Los Angeles and they are receptive to the idea. It certainly would take a load off my shoulders. Lord knows I have my hands full with the ranch, the lodge, the Crystal Creek shop, and the Denver shop."

"It sounds like a good move to me. Maybe I should start looking for some land for another plant closer by."

"Well, it looks like everyone has good news this morning," Logan said, joining the conversation. "My father is coming for the christening and he's bringing Tammy."

"He's what?" AJ exclaimed, almost choking on her eggs.

"He's coming for the christening. I thought it would make you happy."

"It does. It's just a surprise. We'll have to get them a cottage. When do they arrive?"

"Their plane gets in this afternoon, about the same time as Marcia's." Logan smiled broadly, as he excused himself from the table. No one missed how much he enjoyed watching AJ chafe against his words.

AJ sat, almost in shock, as he left the house. "Just what am I supposed to do with Aaron Prescott and his pregnant bimbo?"

"You'll smile and make them welcome," Mark said. "Marcia and I understand what Logan is. We've read between the lines of your letters for a year now. He only wants to make you uncomfortable. Don't let him get to you. Show him the strength I know you have."

Later in the afternoon, AJ left Libby with the nurse she hired for when she went back to work. Although not comfortable leaving Libby with Logan, the nurse worried her even more. At least she knew Logan, knew his faults. This woman came to her as a virtual stranger. Even though she presented excellent references, AJ couldn't help but be apprehensive.

They got to the airport about a half an hour before Marcia's flight arrived. Although she tried, AJ couldn't hide the case of nerves she now experienced. She wanted to make a good impression on Mark's future wife, but how could she ever explain Aaron's appearance with his pregnant girlfriend?

AJ waited anxiously for Marcia and Norma to enter the waiting area. Once they did, they both hurried to greet Mark and AJ. Mark made hasty introductions before the flight from New York was announced.

AJ felt her stomach churn as Logan scanned the passengers when they came through the door.

She found no problem in identifying Aaron Prescott. His dark hair was streaked with gray, his blue eyes twinkled and his smile reminded AJ of a roving playboy. He was tanned, as though he spent all his time on the beach and wore a large diamond ring on the third finger of his right hand.

Beside Aaron stood Tammy, clinging to his arm as though afraid she might lose him if she let go. She appeared to be little more than a child. AJ knew her age to be twenty, although she looked more like sixteen. Surprisingly, her pregnancy barely showed.

"You must be AJ," Aaron said, hugging her tightly. "I've been looking forward to meeting you."

"You must be Tammy," AJ said, turning her attention from her father-in-law to the girl at his side. The calmness of her voice surprised her as she gave Tammy a friendly hug.

"I could hardly wait to meet you," Tammy said, in the thickest Southern drawl AJ ever heard.

"I've never met a lady minister before. Daddy just couldn't believe it when I told him Sweet-ums had a minister for a daughter-in-law."

"But I'm ..." AJ began, only to be interrupted by Aaron.

"I don't know where you got such an idea, Tammy," Aaron said, his words sounded almost accusatory.

AJ recognized the tone. She'd heard Logan use it time and again to put her in her place. AJ could tell Tammy was embarrassed and close to tears. "It's an easy mistake," she said, squeezing Tammy's hand. "My papa is a Lutheran minister and so is my brother, Johann. I'm just a fashion designer, though I doubt Fashions By AJ has hit New York yet. Now, let's go and claim everyone's luggage. I'm certain it's been an exhausting trip and we have a big weekend ahead of us."

Logan took over making the introductions. He even went so far as to explain about how Mark and Norma's wedding would be held the next evening.

Against her better judgment, AJ liked Tammy. AJ found the girl young and far too trusting. To add to that the girl talked far too much. It bothered AJ. But she knew if Tammy had any thoughts that Aaron would marry her, she was mistaken. He used her pregnancy to end his marriage to Marge, although why he wanted out at this particular time left AJ in a quandary.

The luggage rode around on the carousel and AJ stood back, surveying the group. Mark, Norma and Marcia seemed so perfect, so happy. Aaron and Logan were so imperfect, so unable to handle responsibility. Tammy was young, so trusting, so vulnerable. Where did AJ fit in? She wasn't perfect or happy, imperfect or irresponsible, trusting or vulnerable. Even with this many people around, she again became a child, scared, lonely and out of place. She fit in much better in her studio, on the phone, eating, drinking, and breathing fashion design.

All too quickly it was over. Marcia returned to Duluth late Sunday evening. Early on Monday, Mark and Norma left for two weeks in Hawaii. Only Aaron and Tammy remained as AJ returned to work.

Jo left for the Crystal Creek shop, Logan busied himself with Aaron and Tammy, Libby and her nurse were content in the nursery, and AJ sat at her desk reading over the orders and contracts which had piled up over the past week.

The feeling of being watched prompted AJ to put down her papers and look toward the door. It surprised her to see Aaron watching her intently.

"I'm sorry, I didn't hear you come in," AJ said, standing to extend her hands.

"I wanted to see you in your element. You look very professional," Aaron commented.

"Thank you, but I'm certain you didn't come here to see how professional I look."

"You're very perceptive, AJ. You don't like me and I can understand why. You're married to my son and my son is like me in every way. I've caused Marge a lot of pain over the years. Getting Tammy pregnant was an easy way to give her the freedom she deserved. Get out while you can. Don't let Logan ruin your life."

"I don't understand you, Aaron. Why are you warning me? Why aren't you trying to make things up to Marge?"

"I've tried to make things up before. We've split and reconciled numerous times. I'm like an alcoholic, only my addiction is to women. Unfortunately, my son has the same addiction. He'll ruin you, drain your emotions and break your heart."

"I know you're right, but I married for better for worse, for richer or poorer, until death do us part. If this marriage is ended by divorce, it won't be by my hand."

Aaron shook his head. "You've got guts, AJ. I admire you. I promise I'll do everything I can to make things easier for you. I'm proud to call you my daughter."

AJ walked around the desk and hugged Aaron. He understood, unlike her father. He didn't look only at her mistake. He worried about her future as well as Libby's.

Chapter Ten

AJ sat at her desk, looking at her calendar. It was the end of May 1974. Where had the time gone? Five years had slipped away virtually unnoticed. Libby would start school in September.

Her marriage was no more a marriage now than it had been at Libby's christening. Logan still had his flings. She still had her work.

So much had changed in those years. There were now more Jo's Dress Shops than AJ could even begin to count. Franchises had sprung up all over the western states. Plans were in the works for a mail order line, even though AJ knew it would be a long time in coming. Fashions By AJ was in demand.

True to his word, Mark opened a plant between Crystal Creek and Denver. Although he and Norma kept their primary residence in Minneapolis, they built a beautiful vacation home near the plant. For AJ it was like having family close to her. She saw him often and accepted his unconditional love.

As for Marcia, she married and now lived in Spokane. She taught school for three years, but her husband, whom she met on a European tour, was wealthy enough to indulge her every desire. She had opened a Jo's Dress Shop franchise less than a year ago. From the figures AJ had seen, she knew Marcia's shop was doing well.

The ranch, as well as the lodge, prospered, summer and winter. Logan no longer worked for a living. He was content staying in Jo's home, living off AJ's earnings, pursuing his affairs and working on his book. His unemployment did give him the opportunity to care for Libby while AJ worked, and for that she was grateful.

Things had changed on the east coast as well. Aaron had never married Tammy. It was the one thing she admired her father-in-law for doing. He was aware of his weakness and decided to spare the girl the agony of coping with a cheating husband.

Tammy returned to Memphis just a month after her daughter, April had been born. When the child was less than a year old, Tammy met and married a nice young man who adopted her baby. The turn of events had not surprised AJ. She predicted them and anticipated them.

As for Marge, she had begun a new life by moving from Vermont to New York and was working as a receptionist at the UN. On her summer visits to the Lady Jo, she told AJ how exciting she found her work and how many interesting people she met.

While Marge visited in the summer and Aaron in the winter, AJ never saw her parents. She still called her family once a month, but that, too, was disappointing. Just once, she wished they would initiate the calls. Other than their conversations, the only word she had from them was in the form of polite cards with short notes at Christmas, birthdays and her anniversary. Was this what it had come to? Why did her own brothers and sister seem to have no time for her?

She thought of her graduation from college, when they had presented her with the yellow Volkswagen, which had since been replaced by a white Lincoln Continental. Logan still drove the bug. "It's a good little car," he told her. "It works good enough for the running I have to do." She often thought how ironic it was that he called it his "running," since that was exactly what he was doing, running around with any woman who would have him.

Unexpectedly, Logan burst into her studio and shattered her thoughts. "I've got great news."

"News? What kind of news?" AJ asked, looking up into his eyes, which sparkled with excitement.

"Remember the publisher who wanted to read the first three chapters of my book? He wants me to come to New York and bring the entire manuscript with me. He's sent me an advance and insists I sign a contract, all based on the first three chapters. I guess he saw my talent."

AJ got to her feet and gave Logan a congratulatory hug. "That's wonderful, Logan. You've worked hard for this."

"I want to take Libby to New York with me."

"To New York?" AJ echoed. "She's just a baby! What would she do in New York?"

Logan patted her hand reassuringly. "She's a very grown up five year old. She'll love it. We'll be staying with my mother, so she won't be coming out this summer. I know she'll want to have Libby all to herself for a while."

"The summer, the whole summer? Are you planning to take Libby away for that long?"

"Well, why not?"

AJ seemed to be in shock. "I don't know if I can get away for much more than two weeks."

"You won't have to get away. You won't be going. It would be just Libby and me."

"Oh, just Libby and you. I thought I was your wife, I thought-oh, never mind."

"You are my wife, but there would be little for you to do there and I will be tied up with editors. We wouldn't have any time together."

Reluctantly, she agreed to the trip. She rationalized it in her mind with the realization that Logan's parents wanted to be part of Libby's life. She wished her own family would be as excited to play grandma and grandpa to Libby.

The next two weeks were rushed. AJ spent time scrutinizing Libby's wardrobe, choosing and rejecting outfit after outfit. At last their suitcases were packed and AJ drove Libby and Logan to the airport.

"What will you do without us, Mommy?" Libby asked, as they waited for their flight.

"I'll be just fine, Sweetie," AJ replied, not at all certain it was the truth. "Jo and I are going to take a trip and visit some of the shops. I'll call you, though, just like I promised."

The explanation seemed to calm Libby's fears. AJ knew her daughter worried about her mother being terribly lonely without her, but since AJ, too, was taking a vacation, she was content.

AJ stood at the window and waved until the plane disappeared in the brilliant blue Colorado sky. Her heart ached. She wished Logan had insisted she join them, if only for the first week. Was the barrier between Logan and herself due to something she had done, something she could have avoided? Had she ever loved him or was marriage, for her just, a convenient solution to the problem of her pregnancy?

Jo's suggestion that they, too, take a vacation seemed to help. Being away from the ranch and the studio for a few days would be just the thing to take her mind off the fact Libby would be so far away.

AJ's Lincoln sat in the lot. As she slipped behind the wheel, she wished she were in her old VW. Of course, it no longer belonged to her. Logan had taken it away. The bug had become his means of escape from their life together.

The Lincoln seemed very large and lonely. For the first time since Libby's birth, they wouldn't be sleeping under the same roof. Libby would be two thousand miles away, sleeping in a strange bed, seeing new sights, enjoying her summer in New York.

AJ pointed the car toward the Lady Jo. She knew she should have stopped at the Denver shop, but she was in no mood to see anyone. Tears blurred her vision as the car wound its way home. By the time she reached the Lazy B she was mentally and physically exhausted.

"Are you all right AJ?" Jo asked, concerned by her appearance.

"I'm scared, Jo. A whole summer, Libby will be gone for a whole summer. What if she doesn't want to come home?"

"Don't be silly. Logan will be coming home. She'll be ready to come back as well."

AJ didn't want to upset Jo, so she said nothing more on the subject.

"How's the new line coming?" Jo asked, branching off in a different direction.

"It's just about finished. By the end of the week I should have it ready for the pattern makers."

"Good. I have reservations for us at the MGM Grand in Las Vegas for next Monday night."

"Las Vegas? I thought we were going to Reno," AJ said, a bit surprised at the change in their plans.

"We are, but you need to relax for a while first. I thought Las Vegas would be the perfect place. Reno will be a business trip and you need some time for yourself before we get there."

AJ loved the MGM Grand, the shows, the gambling and the glamour. It almost made her believe she was like all of the other tourists.

On their third day, she decided to go sightseeing. Jo opted to stay at the hotel and rest. "I've seen it all before, but you go out and enjoy yourself. There's a lot to see. I'll meet you at the pool at five."

AJ donned a pair of shorts, a crisp white blouse, white tennis shoes and a pair of sunglasses for her venture into the make-believe world of Las Vegas. After she had walked the entire length of the strip, she boarded a bus for the downtown area.

The older streets bustled and AJ walked past the casinos, entranced by the lights that flashed even in the bright daylight. She was surprised to find herself in front of a small shop with a sign reading, Jo's Lucky Lady. Unable to resist seeing a shop different from those at home, she entered the building. She smiled as one by one she browsed through the familiar designs.

She picked out a blue pantsuit and held it up to check the sizing when she heard a strangely familiar voice behind her. "You're AJ, aren't you?"

She turned, surprised to be recognized. She hadn't traveled, and had granted only a few interviews over the past six years. "Why, yes, but how did you know?"

"I'm sure you don't remember me. When you first came to the Lady Jo, my husband and I were staying there. As a matter of fact, I met you on your first night there, at dinner."

AJ smiled at the memory. She had been so young, so full of wonderful plans. "The lady from Iowa. You never came back for your original design."

"I could never afford one, but I have been back to the Lady Jo every year and purchased an outfit each time. I do wish you'd open a shop in Des Moines."

"Why don't you buy a franchise? Jo is looking for someone to open a shop in the Midwest."

Before the woman could answer, several people began to gather around them. "Are you really AJ?" someone asked.

"Guilty as charged."

"This is wonderful. Irene! Irene! Come over here."

AJ protested. "I'm on vacation!"

A tall woman in her late forties came over to her. "I'm Irene Bjusan. I opened this shop for Jo in 1963 and purchased the franchise two years ago. It's good to finally meet you. You have to admit, you are a bit of a mystery."

AJ relaxed. She liked the woman's warm nature. "It's true, that I don't get out much."

"We must do something special. Would you mind if we put on an impromptu fashion show in your honor?"

"Well I--I, sure, why not? It sounds like fun. As a matter of fact, Jo is here as well."

"She is?" Irene's face lit up. "I haven't seen her since I bought the franchise. I've talked to her by phone, but it would be good to see her again. I'll plan the show for tomorrow afternoon."

AJ arrived back at the hotel to meet Jo by five. She had to admit, she was just a bit overwhelmed by the reception she'd received at the shop.

When she related the story of the upcoming show Jo began to laugh. "What happened to your relaxing vacation, AJ?"

"I don't know. One minute I was on the bus heading downtown and then next I was in Jo's Lucky Lady. I thought I could just look around and not be recognized. Boy, was I wrong."

"The curse of being famous. The show certainly won't hurt us. We should make arrangements for shows in Reno, Seattle and at Marcia's shop in Spokane."

The next afternoon, when the show as over, AJ was surprised to be met by reporters.

"If I remember correctly, AJ, you were married shortly after your first show. Is your husband with you?"

AJ thought for a moment before answering. *My husband?* She asked herself. She wondered if she should tell the truth or a believable lie. She finally said, "My husband, Logan, is in New York with our daughter, Libby. He's a writer and he's there to discuss a contract with his publisher. He thought this would be a good time for me to take a vacation. His parents live in New York and are enjoying the time with Libby."

AJ cringed. She hadn't really lied. Logan and Libby were in New York, but it certainly wasn't because she needed a vacation. They were there because Logan wanted to get away from her, to hurt her by taking Libby away for an entire summer. She wanted to cry, but instead put on the face the reporters expected, the face of a successful designer, the face of a happy tourist, the face of someone enjoying a well-deserved vacation.

"Are you here alone?"

"No, Jo Bergendahl is with me. This is both a business and a pleasure trip. We're going to be stopping at several of the shops. From here we will be going to Reno, Seattle and Spokane."

"Will you be doing shows at the other shops?"

"Yes. We thought Irene had such a good idea, we called ahead and set up the shows in advance."

"How many shops do you have now?" another reporter asked, changing the subject.

"You'd better ask Jo. I'm afraid I've lost count."

AJ's comment brought a laugh as Jo took over answering the questions. "We have twenty-seven, with more proposals coming in every day from people who want to buy franchises. As of now, we only have shops in the western states, but we're anxious to break into the Midwestern and Eastern markets. It's hard to believe, but it was only six years ago when AJ joined me. At the time she was a newcomer, and an unknown. It's because of her designs the Jo's franchises have done so well. I'm very proud of her accomplishments."

The shows in Reno and Seattle were as successful as the one in Las Vegas. By the time they arrived at Marcia's home, the strain on AJ was evident.

"It sounds like you two have had a hectic vacation," Marcia said, when they arrived at the house. "I'm beginning to wish I hadn't planned the show here. I've never seen you look so tired."

"I'm fine," AJ replied. "Just lead me to a bed and I'll be good as new in the morning."

Once AJ retired, Jo and Marcia sat up and talked over a glass of wine. "How long has she been this rundown?" Marcia asked.

"Ever since Logan told her he wanted to take Libby to New York. If you ask me, it's the beginning of the end for the two of them."

"Why hasn't she divorced him before this? I certainly wouldn't put up with his catting around."

"You know the answer as well as I do," Jo replied. "She's so worried about what her family will think that she just hangs on. If they knew the hell she's been through, they'd probably understand, but she doesn't want to take the chance."

At last it was time to go back home. As they drove from Spokane to the Lady Jo, they reviewed the success of the trip.

"While we were doing the show at Marcia's, I came up with an idea for a new line," AJ commented.

"What kind of line?"

"One for women over size sixteen. I saw several larger women in the audience and one of them approached me with the idea. I hadn't given it much thought, but these women seem to be forgotten. It's as though if you're larger than a sixteen you shouldn't be fashionable."

AJ could see the wheels turning in Jo's mind, as she contemplated the suggestion. "It's an exciting idea. The market for larger clothes is a virgin one all right. There certainly is money to be made in it."

"You know money isn't a concern to me."

"Yes, but it's an important consideration, none the less."

Being only July, AJ dived into the new project with gusto. As she hoped it would, the work took her mind off the two months still stretching ahead of her without Libby.

During her first week home, she spent much of her time in town, getting to know people she had only carried on a nodding acquaintance with at church.

Julia Parquist was a young wife and mother, not much older than herself. She seemed pleasantly surprised to find AJ on her porch when she opened the door.

"I realize we don't know each other well," AJ began when Julia invited her in for coffee.

"No," Julia said, "we don't, therefore, I must assume this isn't a social call."

AJ smiled at the comment and ached for the normal life Julia's house represented. As she looked around, she saw pictures of Julia and her husband, of the children, of older couples she assumed to be their parents. For all of her success, she longed for someone to look at her as lovingly as Julia's husband did in the picture on the piano.

"This is a business call, Julia. I've just returned from a trip. While I was gone, I came up with an idea for a new line. The only thing is, I need your help. I need you and perhaps five of your friends as models and advisors."

Julia began to laugh as she looked down at her ample figure. "Are you sure you haven't had too much sun? I'm hardly what you'd call a model. I've been in your shop and to be frank, I'd never be able to fit into your clothes."

"But you'd like to, right?"

Julia nodded.

"That's what I thought. When I first came to the Lady Jo, JoAnna told me Fashions By AJ was for robust women. What I seem to have overlooked is that roust women do come larger than a size sixteen. I'd like to plan a line for those size women. What I need from you is input. It's one thing for me to consider the project, but I'm not certain my ideas are what you might actually wear.

Julia smiled, obviously flattered by AJ's proposal. With little prompting, she agreed to meet with AJ the next morning at the studio.

At nine the next morning, six rather large women dominated the conference table in AJ's studio. At her insistence, Jo sat in on the session with them. As usual during a designing session, AJ's tape recorder sat on the desk, ready to capture every word.

As the women talked about their lives, their husbands, their children, their expectations, AJ couldn't help the feeling of sadness, which overwhelmed her. For all of her success, her wealth, she desperately wanted what these women were describing. They had husbands who loved them. Would she ever be able to say Logan loved her?

One of the women started a discussion of what her husband's expectations were as far as her involvement in this project. It made AJ wonder what Logan's expectations were. What was he looking for in New York, a blond, a brunette or a redhead?

By the middle of August, the new line was taking shape. AJ had, in six weeks created twelve designs and sent them to the pattern makers. She hadn't been so excited about anything since before her marriage to Logan.

"I've decided to redecorate Libby's room," she announced one morning at breakfast.

Like every other project she started, she attacked this one with gusto. She purchased new furniture, complete with the canopy bed Libby had begged her to get. She painted the walls a subdued shade of pink and added pink and white carpeting, finishing the project with white eyelet curtains, bedspread and canopy

"It's done," she declared, standing in the doorway, a picture of a large-eyed child with a puppy staring at her from the opposite wall. "Do you think she'll like it?"

"She'll love it," Jo replied. "Why would you even ask such a question? You get cleaned up and we'll go down to the lodge for dinner."

They were just going out the door when the phone rang. It was AJ who turned back to answer the persistent ringing.

"AJ, it's me, Logan," he greeted her.

"You don't have to tell me who you are. You haven't been gone long enough for me to forget your voice," she replied, sounding more annoyed than she meant to sound.

"Don't be so defensive."

"Defensive? Not I."

"I'm not coming home with Libby," he began.

"What are you saying? Are you insinuating you're going to take my baby away from me?" she asked before he could finish.

"I have no plans to take her away from you. I have to stay here. My editor wants me to do some more work on the book and ..."

"And just how do you plan to get Libby back to me?"

"My mother will be bringing her home." Logan paused for a long moment. "I want a divorce, AJ."

142

"A divorce?" she echoed.

"Are you having trouble hearing me? I said I want a divorce. You and I both know our marriage has been one of convenience. Don't you realize by now that it was all planned? I needed your help, as well as your money, to get my book published. If I had had to support us, I'd never have found time to write. My hat is off to you."

"I suppose it is, and your pants as well, at least with all of your other women."

"Go ahead and file"

"No, Logan. I won't be the one to file for divorce."

"Why not? God knows you have grounds."

"I may have grounds, but this marriage won't end by my hand. You know if I get a divorce it will break all ties with my family. I won't initiate it, but I also don't plan to contest it, but you'll have to be the one to file."

"Whatever you say," Logan said, sounding relieved by the knowledge she wouldn't fight him. "There are a few things I want."

"I'm sure there are. How much do you want me to send you this time?"

"I don't want your money"

"That's a switch."

"Don't, AJ. Don't make this any harder than it already is. I want Libby as much as possible."

"No, Logan, she's mine."

As though he hadn't heard her, he continued. "I want her December twenty-sixth to New Years Day. You can have her for Christmas and Christmas Eve. I want her for spring vacation. You can have her for Easter day. I want her every other Thanksgiving, and I want her for a month in the summer."

"You seem to want a lot. What do I get in return?"

"I'll send you a hundred dollars a month in child support. I'm being more than generous considering you certainly don't need the money. In addition I'll pay all of her traveling expenses."

"And just how do you expect to get her to New York?"

"She's old enough to fly alone."

"Alone!"

"As a ward of the airlines. They're very strict. I've checked it all out."

"I'm certain you have. Just answer one question for me. Will your girlfriend be there when Libby comes to visit?"

"It may be hard for you to believe, but right now there is no one. My girlfriend, as you call her, is the one mistress I've had for years, my book."

"Whatever you say, Logan. Whatever you say." The fight, along with AJ's spirit seemed to suddenly disappear.

"My mother and Libby will be arriving at noon tomorrow. You will be there to meet them, won't you?"

"You must think I'm terrible. Of course I'll meet their plane." Without saying good-bye, she slammed down the receiver.

She stared at the phone for a moment. When she turned back toward Jo, she didn't try to hide the tears flowing down her cheeks.

"Did I hear you right? Is Logan divorcing you?"

"He doesn't need me anymore."

"On what grounds?"

"I really don't care."

"Beat him to it, be the one to file first. You can use his desertion and infidelity as grounds."

"No. If I file, I'd be as bad as he. To me, marriage is sacred. It's forever. Now it's over."

"It was over two months after it started. You know it and so do I."

AJ nodded and picked up the receiver. "I have to call my family. I don't want to do this."

"Then don't. We'll go down and get some dinner. There's plenty of time to call, later."

"No. Logan wants this so badly, he'll file Monday morning. I'm sure he'll make no secret of the fact I'm his wife. The newspapers will have a field day with it."

AJ caught a glimpse of Jo shaking her head before she turned back to the phone. She knew she couldn't call her parents or Johann. The easiest one to talk to would be Karl.

It was Karl's wife, Janet, who answered. "Hi, Janet, it's Anne. Is Karl there?"

Karl looked up when Janet turned away from the phone. "It's Anne," she whispered, her hand covering the mouthpiece of the phone. "She sounds strange."

"Hi, Sis, what's up?" he greeted her.

"I thought I should tell you, before this news hits the papers, that is."

"Anne, what is it? What are you talking about? You aren't making any sense. Are you drunk?"

AJ ignored his last question. "I trust you'll tell everyone. It wasn't my fault."

The tone of her voice concerned him. "What are you saying, Anne?"

"Logan is divorcing me." Her voice was flat, as though the announcement was not unexpected.

"Divorcing you? Why? What have you done?"

"Done? I haven't done anything. I haven't had a marriage. Within two months of the wedding he was romancing every woman who crossed his path. I've put up with it, been hurt by it, but not as badly as I have been hurt by Papa's condemnation.

It was bad enough that I was pregnant with Libby when I got married. The disgrace of a divorce is more than he will be able to forgive."

"You aren't filing for divorce against him?"

"No. I told him I wouldn't end this marriage. I wanted it to work."

"Is he the one who is filing?"

"Yes. He took Libby to New York for the summer."

"I know. I read about your interview in Las Vegas. It was in the papers here. You certainly do get around."

"Yes, I do, considering this is the first vacation I've taken since I started, since I married Logan. I know you all think I'm on a permanent vacation, but I'm not. I'm on a permanent merry-go-round I have endless duties and obligations. I'm a well-respected designer. I've done it all while putting up with a husband who married me because I had enough money to support him while he wrote his marvelous book. You should read it. He's calling it Lost Innocence. At least it's a subject he's an expert on."

"I'm not condemning you," Karl said.

"Why not? Papa will and so will Johann. Kristin will shake her head and say, 'poor Anne, couldn't hold onto her husband.' But then Kristin doesn't live in the real world, does she? She has her own little world with her farm, her husband and her children and let's not forget her church. For her that's enough and that's all she expects from me. She's just like the rest of you. None of you have any idea of what my life is like. You don't even care."

"We do care. I'm worried about you. I just didn't know."

"You didn't know because I never let any of you know. I was too ashamed. My life is a mess. Somewhere in there are Papa and Mama, you, Kristin, and Johann. As if that's not enough there is also Logan and Libby, Jo and the Lady Jo, the Lazy B, Fashions By AJ and Marcia and Mark."

"Mark?"

"Now I know you don't listen to me when I talk to you. You don't listen to me at all. Mark Bower is Marcia's father. He believed in me enough to offer me an exclusive line of fabric from his textile plant. The only fabrics used in my designs are Bower Textiles. No, I don't call him Mr. Bower anymore. I'm a big girl now. He's not just my friend's father he's also my business partner. I have to go. I have a lot to do before Libby comes home on Monday."

"Anne, please wait. Don't hang up yet. Is there anything I can do?"

"I think it's a bit late. Anne died six years ago. AJ has replaced her. I've done quite well up until now without help from you, and I'll continue to take care of myself in the future."

Before Karl could say anything more, the receiver on the other end of the line clicked in his ear. Hanging up the phone, he returned to the living room. Without saying a word, he slumped into his easy chair.

Were they being unfair to Anne? She had been the one to follow a different road from the rest of them. He certainly hadn't known how to react to her accomplishments, her fame, if that was the right word.

"What's wrong?" Janet finally asked.

"Anne and Logan are getting a divorce. She asked me to tell the family. I think we should leave for New Oslo right away. I'll call Kristin and Johann and ask them to meet us at the parsonage."

Karl got up and started toward the kitchen to make the calls. Only Janet's persistent questions stopped him. "I don't understand. I thought Anne and Logan were happy. What could have caused such a rift?"

"I need time to digest everything she said. It's already getting late. You go next door and get one of the girls to babysit while I make the calls."

As they drove toward the New Oslo parsonage, Karl knew Janet was uneasy not knowing what was going on. He also knew he would only want to go over the conversation with Anne once. Her condemnation of the family was hard to accept.

When they pulled into the driveway, Kristin and Lars as well as Johann and Sharon were already parked in front of the house.

"What's wrong, Karl?" Kristin asked. "Karl?" she again questioned when her first inquiry met with silence.

"I'll tell you when I tell Mama and Papa." Karl knew his voice sounded stern.

The door opened and Karl noticed the look of surprise on his father's face. He too, seemed puzzled by a late night visit from his three oldest children.

"What brings you here so late on a Saturday evening?" he asked once they were all in the parlor.

John and Kristin both looked at Karl. The moment he had dreaded ever since he hung up from talking to Anne had finally arrived.

"I've had a call from Anne. I thought I should tell everyone about it at one time."

"Is she ill?" his mother asked, concern sounding in her voice.

"No, Mama, she's not sick, not physically." Karl went on to relay Anne's disturbing news.

"I could have told you something like this would happen," his father declared when Karl finally finished. "She always was wild."

As Anne had so aptly predicted, Kristin merely shook her head, while Johann tended to agree with their father. For the first time, Karl understood what Anne meant. The only sympathetic sound in the room was his mother's soft weeping.

"We must do something to help her," she pleaded.

"No, Mama," Karl said, putting his arm around her shoulders. "I think we're too late. When I offered my help, she said she didn't want it. We'll just have to give her time."

Chapter Eleven

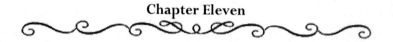

Libby squirmed in the seat next to her grandmother. "Why isn't Daddy coming with us?" she asked.

"You remember," Marge began. "Daddy has business in New York and you have to start school soon."

As though she hadn't heard her grandmother's words, she continued. "I wish daddy was coming home with us."

Marge wondered how AJ would explain why Logan decided to stay in New York permanently to their daughter. Logan left the burden to AJ, telling Libby only that he needed to stay in New York for a short while.

When Libby questioned the fact Marge and Aaron no longer lived together, Marge simply told her she and Grandpa weren't married anymore. Libby easily accepted the fact Grandpa lived there and Grandma lived here.

"My Daddy isn't coming home at all, is he?" Libby's question caught Marge completely off guard. "He's going to be like Grandpa and will never live with us again."

"Yes, Darling, he's going to be like Grandpa." Marge wanted to pull the child onto her lap and comfort her, but the flight was rough and the Fasten Seat Belt sign remained on.

"Why doesn't Daddy want to live with us anymore?" Libby continued.

"Well," Marge began, thoughtfully, "your Daddy's work is in New York and your Mommy's work is in Crystal Creek."

"It's because of Amy, isn't it?"

"Who?" Marge questioned, unfamiliar with the name.

"Amy, Daddy's friend. Amy and Daddy took me to the zoo one day."

Marge stared at the child in disbelief. Under her breath, she damned her son. How could he take his daughter to the zoo with his newest companion? "No, it doesn't have anything to do with Amy. I wouldn't say anything to your Mommy about Amy, though."

"Mommy knows about Daddy's girlfriends. That's why Daddy is going away, isn't it, because of his girlfriends?"

"In a way. He doesn't want to hurt your Mommy anymore."

"I won't say anything to Mommy about Amy," Libby promised, as she nestled her head against Marge's side.

Marge glanced at her watch. It read 1:45 New York time. In fifteen minutes they would be landing in Denver and she would have to face her daughter-in-law.

After they landed, Marge collected their carryon luggage and handing Libby her small bag, took her hand.

AJ spotted Marge and Libby the minute they entered the waiting area. As soon as she caught Marge's eye, she began to wave excitedly.

"Oh, Jo, look how she's grown. She's gotten so tall over the summer," AJ exclaimed.

When they entered the waiting area, Libby broke away from her grandmother and ran toward AJ's outstretched arms.

"Oh, Mommy, I'm so glad to be home. I did so much in New York. I have so much to tell you. I saw the zoo, the Empire State Building, Rockefeller Center, Grandpa took me to a show there, and I saw the UN and oh, Mommy, I missed you so very much!"

"I'm so happy to have you home," AJ said, hugging Libby tightly. "Jo and I are going to take you and Grandma out to lunch and you can tell us all about your summer."

"Daddy's not coming home," Libby whispered in AJ's ear, as though it were some big secret only the two of them could share.

"I know, Sweetie," AJ answered, trying not to let any tears begin to fall.

"He's going to get a house like Grandpa's. Grandpa has a house and Grandma has a house. Grandma says Daddy's getting a house so he doesn't hurt you anymore."

What a beautiful explanation. An explanation so simple, even a child could understand it. Daddy doesn't want to hurt Mommy anymore.

AJ watched as Libby went to embrace Jo. She hardly realized Marge stood in front of her.

"I'm so very sorry, AJ," Marge said. "For your sake I prayed that Logan would be different from his father. Yours as well as Libby's."

"I know, Marge, but he isn't. I've known it for a long time. Thank you for bringing Libby home safely."

Before Marge could answer, Libby began tugging on AJ's skirt for attention. "Grandma took me shopping and we bought so many new clothes for school, that we had to buy a new suitcase to bring them all home in."

"Marge," AJ said sternly, glaring at her mother-in-law.

"It's a grandmother's duty to spoil her only grandchild."

AJ softened, wishing her own mother would someday spoil Libby. "It sounds like you spoiled her rotten."

"Let me do it, AJ. I enjoy it so very much. We had a wonderful summer, but I am going to miss coming out here. On the other hand, I am going to love having Libby visit me in New

York. I have so many wonderful plans. I know I shouldn't plan so far ahead, but I'm loving every minute of it."

"Whatever you say, Marge," AJ said with a sigh. Turning her attention to Libby, she said, "Come on, Sweetie. We'll get your luggage and then go out to lunch."

Libby grinned broadly. AJ knew Libby liked going out to lunch, being treated like a grown up.

As they waited for their luggage, Marge took Jo aside. "How is AJ taking this? I told Logan he should come here and tell her in person, but he thought this was better."

"It wasn't easy. She called her family. I worried about it, but she thought it was something she must do. She doesn't think she'll hear from them again. She's decided to cut the phone calls and just send letters from now on. After she told her brother, not one of them even called her. I couldn't believe it. She wouldn't even go to dinner with me last night. She just locked herself in the studio and sketched all night long. I don't think she even slept. She looked so tired this morning. When I suggested I drive to the airport, she didn't even argue with me. The fight has gone out of her."

"It's a shame," Marge said. "The saddest thing is Logan's exhilaration at the thought of divorce."

After they collected the luggage, they made their way to Jo's Cadillac. Once seated in the back with Libby, AJ asked the question she thought she should ask. "How's Logan?"

"Don't AJ," Marge said. "It's over. Close this chapter and go on with your life."

"How can I? I thought I loved him. How can I close it with Libby here to remind me of him?"

"The only thing I can tell you is to try," Marge said. "You must for Libby's sake."

AJ nodded and hugged her daughter tightly. She knew Marge was right. She also knew that saying Logan no longer dominated her thoughts and going on with her life were two different things.

By the time Marge returned to New York, a week later, plans for the start of school, overshadowed Logan's departure from their lives.

Monday finally came. AJ knew that not taking the school bus with the other children who lived at the ranch disappointed Libby. As they drove to Crystal Creek together, Libby remained unnaturally quite.

For AJ, the drive to school brought back memories of her mother walking to school with her on her first day. She remembered feeling so proud walking beside her mother, finally being able to go to school like her brothers and sister. Karl and Johann were in high school, but Kristin was still in elementary school so she would walk with her every day. Before they left the house, their mother had taken the mandatory picture of them in their new clothes.

That was the day she first met Marcia. She could still see the little girl standing shyly alone with no mother to fuss over her on her first day. While AJ's mother pushed her toward the children she knew, AJ remembered being drawn to Marcia. Now so many years had passed. So much had happened in both their lives. AJ couldn't help but wonder if Marcia harbored the same memories of that day so long ago.

"There's the school," Libby squealed breaking into AJ's thoughts. "Look at all the kids!"

AJ smiled at Libby's excitement. After she convinced herself that Libby was comfortably settled, she gave her a hug. "I'll be back to pick you up at noon. Then we'll meet Jo for lunch. She's in town and will be anxious to hear about your day."

"Can I call Daddy?"

AJ cringed. It was still hard to hear Libby talk about Logan, but to know he no longer existed in AJ's life or shared her bed.

"Of course you can. Daddy will be so excited about your first day of school." It wasn't easy for AJ to sound excited about Logan, but she refused to destroy him in Libby's eyes. "By the time we get home, it will be after five in New York. Daddy will be home by then to talk to you."

At noon, AJ met Libby at school, after making the arrangements for her to ride the bus with the other children from the ranch.

"Jo's going to meet us downtown for lunch," AJ said, as her bubbly daughter got into the car. "Did you have a good day at school?"

"Oh, yes, Mommy. My teacher is Miss Harris, my room number is 102 and my new friend is Shelly."

AJ listened as Libby chattered on about how she would be learning to read and write. She remembered, again, her own first day of school. She remembered being every bit as excited as Libby, but her excitement had been overshadowed by Kristin's announcement that the teacher had placed her in an accelerated reading class. She had taken her lead from her brothers, who sat quietly at the supper table, answering yes and no unenthusiastically to questions about school.

AJ knew their lunch with Jo would be the perfect climax to Libby's first day in school. Jo chose Libby's favorite restaurant, a small cafe close to the shop. She had called ahead and ordered Libby's favorite lunch and even the waitress listened intently to Libby's description of her first morning of kindergarten.

As they ate their lunch, AJ read the list of supplies Libby would need for class.

"From the look of this list," she finally said, "Miss Libby and I will need to go shopping. Crayons, big pencils, tennis shoes, paste, scissors, blanket, painting smock and five cents a day for milk."

"Miss Harris says our mommies can make us painting smocks from our daddy's old shirts. Do we have one of Daddy's old shirts?"

AJ swallowed hard, remembering how she and Marge had packed Logan's clothes to send them to New York. Before she could say anything, Jo answered Libby's question.

"I think we can stop over at the factory this afternoon and find some scrap fabric to make one for you.

Although school became routine, Libby's enthusiasm stayed at a peak. Each day brought added excitement with every new accomplishment. It was as though Libby couldn't get enough of school. She was already printing her name, memorizing her phone number and address, and with AJ's prompting, learning to read her first very simple books. AJ and Jo found their refrigerator decorated with finger paintings, crayon drawings and laboriously printed notes that read, I Love Mommy – I Love Jo.

All too soon, Christmas arrived. On Christmas Eve, they attended church. When Libby at last slept peacefully, AJ and Jo played Santa.

Christmas day was very difficult for AJ. While Libby played with her new toys and drew pictures on the sketchpad she had asked Santa to bring her, AJ thought of the next day's flight to New York.

"Do you have your presents for Grandma and Grandpa and Daddy?" AJ asked, as she parked the car in the airport lot.

"Yes, Mommy, remember you put them in my suitcase."

"Well, then, I guess we're ready to put you on the plane."

At the desk AJ presented Libby's ticket. "Libby is traveling alone. I'm her mother, Anne Prescott."

The woman checked her records. "I must see some identification, Mrs. Prescott."

AJ produced her driver's license.

"Who is picking her up in New York?" the woman questioned, satisfied with AJ's identification.

"Either her grandmother, Marjorie Prescott, or her father, Logan Prescott."

Before they started boarding the plane, a flight attendant came over to where they were sitting. "Are you Libby?"

Libby nodded, unusually quiet.

"My name is Jennifer and we'll be going to New York together. I've ordered a special meal for you. Do you like hamburgers?"

Again Libby nodded, seeming a bit apprehensive. AJ took advantage of the lull to put her own fears to rest. "You won't give her to anyone but her grandmother or her father, will you?"

"Not without the proper identification. It will be the same on the return, Mrs. Prescott. You will need identification to pick up your daughter."

When at last it was time for Libby to board the plane, Jennifer took her hand and they walked down the stairs and out to the waiting aircraft. As AJ watched, she wondered if she would ever be able to do this on a permanent basis. Would she ever feel comfortable sending her child off to New York alone?

* * *

By summer taking Libby to the airport to go to New York was becoming routine. Christmas vacation had gone smoothly as had spring break. Now AJ was preparing to send her daughter away for an entire month.

Marge had outlined their plans, which included an excursion to Vermont and a shopping trip to buy school clothes.

Logan's book had just hit the stands and a life-size poster of him stood next to a rack of books in the gift shop. Lost Innocence screamed at her from the display. She was pleased no one knew her as Anne Prescott. With Logan using his own name rather than a pseudonym, it would have been very embarrassing.

"Are you and Jo going to take a vacation this summer?" Libby asked, as they waited for the flight.

"No, the franchise owners are coming to the ranch for a conference. It's something new we're going to try. Aunt Marcia will be there."

"Are you a summer kid?" a boy of about ten asked, when he approached them.

"Am I a what?" Libby asked.

"A summer kid. If you're sitting here, you must be going to New York. Are you going out to see somebody?"

"My Daddy," Libby replied.

"I go out to see my mom every summer. I'm a summer kid."

"Elliott," a man said, as he entered the area and handed the boy a soda. "You shouldn't be bothering these people."

"I'm not bothering anyone, Dad. I just wanted to know if she is a summer kid, like me?"

"I must apologize for my son, the name is Lanners, Garrett Lanners."

AJ looked intently at the man who stood in front of her. He was tall, at least six-feet, his hair was dark brown with just a hint of gray at the temples, and his eyes were hazel. For some reason, she felt at ease talking to him.

"My name is Anne, Anne Prescott," she replied. For today she didn't want to be anyone famous. She wanted to be a woman named Anne who had met a fascinating man.

"No, Mommy," Libby blurted, "Your name is AJ."

It seemed the remark made no impression on either Garrett or Elliott. Relieved, she continued, "Yes Elliott, I guess Libby is a summer kid. I think it's a neat name. How did you come up with it?"

"When I first started going to New York to see my mom, a kid on the plane said he was a summer's child. I liked it, but decided I didn't want to be called a child. I've used it ever since."

"Do you go to New York often?" AJ questioned.

"Christmas and spring break, as well as summer."

"I get to go at Thanksgiving, every other year," Libby said, not wanting to be left out of the conversation.

"I don't go then. I like to ski too much. I don't have a lot of choice about the other times, but I told Mom I wanted to spend Thanksgiving on the slopes and she understood."

When at last the children boarded the plane, Garrett turned to AJ. "You haven't been sending her off long, have you?"

"I didn't think it was that obvious. The first time was at Christmas."

"How old is she?"

"She'll celebrate her sixth birthday in New York."

Garrett shook his head sympathetically. "Six seems too young for them to be flying alone, but then, Elliott was the same age when he started going to see Susan. Maybe you've heard of my wife, Susan Elliott."

"Wife?" AJ asked, trying not to allow either her surprise or her disappointment to sound in her voice.

"My ex-wife," he corrected himself. "She's in that soap opera, He Loves Me, He Loves Me Not. She plays Jessica Lane."

"I don't watch many soap operas. I just can't find the time."

Garrett laughed. "I guess a single parent doesn't have much time for things like that. I just watch it to get a glimpse of Susan."

"Are you still in love with her?" She regretted the question as soon as she put voice to it.

"No, but old habits are hard to break. You'll see, Anne, it does get easier. So what does your ex do in New York?"

"He's a writer. I'm sure you've seen his book Lost Innocence."

"He's that Prescott? A lot of my clients are talking about it, although I haven't taken the time to read it."

"Clients? What do you do?"

"I'm a freelance business manager."

"What's that?"

"I handle small businesses that need a manager but can't afford one on a full-time basis. I have my office in my home. I decided it was best when Susan left. But, enough about me. I'd like to hear about you. Would you join me for lunch?"

AJ hesitated only a moment. "Sure, why not? I'm not due back for anything today and I don't have to pick Jo up until six."

"Joe?" Garrett questioned.

AJ knew he must think Jo was of the masculine persuasion. "JoAnna Bergendahl," she said. "She owns Jo's Dress Shops and"

"And The Lady Jo Ranch," Garrett finished the sentence for her. "So that makes you Fashions By AJ."

She blushed at the recognition. "It's just AJ-no, it's just Anne. It's been a long time since I've been Anne. Just for today, that's who I am."

"Well, Anne, we'll take my car."

Together they walked to the parking lot and stopped in front of a battered VW. "Your chariot awaits, My Lady," Garrett said, as he opened the door for her.

AJ smiled, remembering her own VW. "When I was Anne, I had a car just like this one. I feel like a kid again."

Garrett took her hand and looked into her light blue eyes. He didn't know her, and yet he felt that he'd known her all his life. He hadn't dated since Susan left. He just didn't think it was fair to Elliott. Until today, he had still considered himself to be in love with Susan, but when Anne asked him the question, he suddenly knew that it no longer mattered. He'd loved Susan, beautiful, willful Susan. Her leaving had hurt him deeply. He couldn't believe he'd met Anne less than an hour ago and was suddenly able to put Susan into perceptive. He wanted to get to know Anne much better. He certainly didn't believe in love at first sight, but he knew this was the closest he would ever come to it.

"It hasn't been easy, has it?" he asked, once they were both in the car.

"No, it hasn't. I've grown up a lot in the last seven years."

"Seven years ago I thought my world revolved around Susan. I guess I've done a lot of growing up since then myself."

It took little effort for Garrett to read Anne's thoughts. It was evident she was uncomfortable with the dating scene. The look in her eyes told him she was a very private person. He could almost see her fighting with the decision not to bolt and run away from this strange man who had just asked her out.

"I hope you like this place," he said, once they arrived at the restaurant. He liked coming to this particular place. It was small and relatively unknown in the city. Tucked away in a quiet corner, it looked like it belonged in an old world Norwegian village rather than in Denver. "These people are one of my many clients," he remarked, once they were inside and seated at a table next to the massive stone fireplace. "The food here is wonderful."

He especially liked sitting at this table. The mural of a Norwegian fjord, on the opposite wall, always made him feel as though he was on vacation.

"We'll have the special, Pat," he said, waving aside the menu when the waitress approached their table.

When the girl left, Anne began to protest. "I didn't see a menu."

"Trust me, Anne, what I ordered will be to your liking. Just tell yourself that today you're Anne. For one day, you're not a successful woman, but a very beautiful girl who deserves to be pampered."

Her smile relaxed him. "I'll warn you, I won't know how to act. I can't ever remember being pampered."

"Then today you're in for a treat." Before he could continue, the waitress interrupted him by bringing side salads with a house dressing and a basket of hot homemade rolls to the table.

He watched as Anne tentatively tasted her salad, and was relieved when she seemed to relish its distinct flavor.

AJ relaxed. She decided if Garrett were the Big Bad Wolf, she wouldn't mind being Little Red Riding Hood for the afternoon. He treated her the way she had always wanted to be treated, like she was someone special. Logan's attentions were always because he needed or wanted something, usually money.

She had to admit, the flavor of the dressing was wonderful and wondered if she could possibly figure out the recipe to give to the cook at the ranch.

"What is this?" she asked, as a wooden plate was set in front of her.

"It's plank steak," Garrett explained. "The steak is broiled on a piece of wood. Just before it's done, they pipe on potatoes, add tomatoes, and put it back under the broiler. The owners are from Norway and it was the specialty in the restaurant where they worked in Oslo."

"My parents are from Norway, but I've never had anything like this before."

She tasted the potatoes and the slight hint of nutmeg brought a lump to her throat. It had been years since she tasted potatoes like these. Memories of her Papa and Mama flooded her mind and she felt momentarily sad.

"Is something wrong?" Garrett inquired.

"No. It's just-just nothing." She didn't know if she could explain this alien feeling of homesickness.

"It's more than nothing." He reached across the table and took her hand in his. "Do you want to talk about it?"

Her first thought was to say no, but before she could voice it, other words tumbled from her mouth. "It's been a long time since I've tasted potatoes like these. I'd forgotten how much I missed them."

"You don't see your folks much, do you?"

"Not since I came to Colorado. I'm afraid I'm a disappointment to my family."

"A successful woman like you, how could you be a disappointment to anyone? I'd think they'd be very proud of your achievements."

"You don't know my Papa. He's a Lutheran minister and I wasn't the perfect pastor's daughter. Papa said I was wild. Maybe he was right. My friends weren't the farm kids who went to our church. They were the kids from town, who I met in school. I wanted to be someone special and I went to college. I didn't get married like my sister, Kristin, and when I did, I was pregnant. My parents have never even seen Libby."

Without realizing it, AJ had hung her head to avoid his accusatory gaze. To her surprise, Garrett put his finger under her chin and raised her head so he could look into her eyes.

"I'm sorry. Your parents certainly don't know what they're missing. I hardly know you, and yet I realize what a special young woman you are."

AJ could feel her spirit lighten as the table talk turned to raising a child alone. How good it seemed to talk about things normal people discussed.

For that afternoon, AJ didn't exist, didn't matter. Garrett didn't care that her papa thought she was a slut or her husband no longer loved her. Her fame didn't seem to bother him and he didn't notice the fact she was unlovable.

All too soon their lunch was over. As they drove toward the airport, she couldn't help feeling sad over the fact the day was ending. Garrett Lanners would disappear from her life and Anne would again become a part of her past. She didn't want it to end. Like Cinderella, her midnight was fast approaching and her coach would, again, become a pumpkin. As much as she enjoyed the day, she knew she could never be Anne again.

"Can I see you again?" Garrett asked, once he parked his bug next to her Lincoln.

"I'd like that," she replied. *If I'm dreaming, don't let me wake up.*

"Tomorrow?"

His question shattered the dream. Tomorrow she would be back at the ranch. Tomorrow she wouldn't be Anne. AJ would be back

"I'll be in Crystal Creek tomorrow. I'm afraid I won't be coming back to Denver until Libby comes back next month."

"Then I'll come to you. Crystal Creek isn't that far away. Can I come out and see you tomorrow?"

AJ smiled. For the first time someone wanted her for herself. "Tomorrow would be perfect. Come out early and I'll have one of the hands get us a pair of horses and we can go for a ride. I know a perfect place for riding. It's one the tourists never get to see."

AJ was surprised when Garrett took her in his arms and kissed her tenderly. "Until tomorrow," he said, as he held open the car door for her.

As she drove back toward the ranch, she wondered why she suggested riding up to the secluded valley where Logan first made love to her. She certainly didn't expect to give herself to Garrett Lanners the way she had with Logan. The answer rang loud and clear in her mind. No matter what had happened in

Upper Valley in the past, it was still the most beautiful place on the ranch. It was something she wanted to share with Garrett.

Chapter Twelve

Five years later:

Garrett Lanners seemed sincere, but AJ was vulnerable, just coming out of her involvement with Logan. The thought of AJ and Garrett together caused Jo to be skeptical. She wasn't at all sure AJ could handle another relationship, no matter how sincere the man appeared.

When he came out to the Lady Jo, the day after meeting AJ at the airport, Jo questioned him closely. She'd never heard of a freelance business manager before. The more she heard about the job, it sounded like a novel idea.

To her amazement, she, like AJ, came to enjoy his company and look forward to his visits to the ranch. As far as she knew, he'd never been out of line with AJ.

"I'm taking on a partner," he announced one Sunday when he and Elliott came to visit. Five years had passed since Garrett had entered their lives.

"A partner?" AJ questioned.

"A young man who thinks my business is a good idea has asked to join me."

Jo noticed a hint of something in Garrett's voice, but she wasn't able to decide what he meant. Could it be he was trying to tell them he wanted to take his career in a different direction?

* * *

For the first time since she'd known him, it was Jo who sought Garret out. The unusually mild December weather made the trip from Crystal Creek to Denver an easy one. She hoped her meeting with Garret would go as smoothly.

"Why, Jo, what are you doing here? You're the last person I ever expected to see standing on my doorstep," he greeted her.

"I'm getting some mixed messages from you and I'd like to clarify a few things."

"Mixed messages? I don't understand."

"You've taken on a partner and yet it doesn't seem as though your business has grown enough to warrant one. Are you looking to move on or up?"

"To be honest about it, I'm putting out feelers. I just couldn't leave my clients in the lurch, so I took on a partner. I'm hoping he can buy me out. He says he has the capital. All that's left is for me to find a position I'd be comfortable in. I'm getting too old to handle this many accounts. I'd like to work for one company. Elliott is old enough. He certainly doesn't need me at home on a full time basis."

"I thought you might be considering something of this nature. I'd like to offer you a job."

"You? But you have a business manager."

"Cal Prisk? He's retiring the first of March. I've known it was coming, but he gave me the official notice yesterday. He turned sixty-five last year and wants to do some traveling. I don't blame him. I'm beginning to feel the same way myself."

"Come on Jo, you aren't old."

"I'll be fifty next year, still in my prime, but I'd like to feel secure, if you know what I mean. I trust you. Don't think I go on my intuition, because I don't. I've checked you out. More important, AJ trusts you. Don't kid yourself. It's a lot of hard work. There's Fashions By AJ, the Jo's franchises, The Lady Jo,

The Lazy B and the three shops I own outright. So what do you say?"

"I say I'd like to do it."

Garrett extended his hand. Although Jo shook it, she knew she must make certain he realized what taking the job would mean. "Don't say yes so fast. It will mean leaving Denver and moving to Crystal Creek."

"I don't see any problem with the move."

"I'm only thinking of Elliott. He'll be fifteen in another month. Next fall he'll start high school. How will he react?"

"Quite well, I think. We've done a lot of talking about it. He's the main reason I've been considering the change. He's tired of the crazy hours. Clients call me at all hours of the day and night. In a business, I'd have real hours, but with freelance, it's hard. He also wants to get out of Denver."

Garrett's statement puzzled her. "Why? Denver is his home. He's always lived here."

"He says it's getting too big. He's been talking about Crystal Creek ever since I started seeing Anne. He likes the town, as well as the Lady Jo."

"Other than Anne and the Lady Jo, why Crystal Creek? Why not any one of a dozen small towns?"

Garrett laughed then began to explain. "Elliott is an avid skier. Crystal Creek has one of the best high school ski teams in the state. He wants to be part of it."

The way the meeting had gone pleased Jo. "With Cal retiring in the middle of the school year, I thought there might be a problem, but the new semester starts February first and if you can be ready to start that soon, I know Cal would appreciate it. As much as I'd like to have you out at the ranch, I'm sure you'd be more comfortable in an apartment in town."

"You must have been pretty sure I'd say yes, checking out the school and all. You know I'd like to be at the ranch and close to Anne, but the time isn't right. We'll find an apartment."

"What about this house?"

"It goes with the business. As you can see, I'm prepared to move quickly for the right position."

Jo finally left Garrett's house and stopped by the Denver shop before returning to the ranch.

She found AJ sitting in her studio, taking advantage of the last light of the afternoon. "Time to knock off for the day," she said, entering the studio.

"Guess it is," AJ replied, stretching her tired muscles. "Where have you been all day?"

"Denver, I had some business to attend to. You get freshened up. I'll tell you all about it over dinner at the lodge."

AJ knew better than to press Jo for an answer. If she wanted to tell AJ something over dinner, the discussion would take place no sooner nor in any other place.

"I thought you didn't like Garrett," AJ declared when Jo broke the news.

"There's a lot about me you don't know. One of those things is that I do like Garrett. I was worried when you first started seeing him. I didn't want him to hurt you the way Logan did."

In AJ's mind, she could envision helping Garrett find and furnish an apartment. It would be fun looking for just the right things to make a strange place seem like home for Garrett and Elliott.

"Answer me one thing, AJ," Jo said, breaking into AJ's thoughts. "How involved are you and Garrett?"

"Come on, Jo, we're just friends, you know that."

"Do I? He loves you and I think you feel the same way."

"I don't think I'm capable of love. Logan saw to that. I care deeply for Garrett, but I want my life to settle down before I explore those feelings."

"Don't wait, AJ. Let yourself discover your feelings. Don't let happiness slip away."

AJ knew Jo made sense. Allowing herself to care for Garrett seemed only natural. Ever since they'd met, Libby and Elliott insisted on traveling together. They became like brother and sister. It seemed as though everyone but AJ sensed the bond which was forming. She remembered a strange conversation she had engaged in with Libby, just before she and Elliott had left for New York on the day after Christmas.

"I find it so hard to understand Elliott," AJ had commented.

"Why, Mom?"

"I don't know. He's so much older than you and yet the two of you get along so well."

"We're friends. Garrett's older than you are and you have no trouble getting along with him."

"All right, Miss Smarty, I'll buy that. You and Elliott are friends and I'm glad you have him as your friend."

Libby seemed pleased with her mother's approval. "His grandma is neat too. She's a lot like Grandma Prescott."

"Why is it you never talk about Elliott's mother?"

"The same reason I don't talk about Daddy much. Face it Mom, we don't go to New York to see Daddy or Susan. We go to see our grandparents. Oh, they're around, but they're too busy with their lives to be concerned with us."

"Have they gotten together?"

"I doubt it. Susan is too old for Daddy. His girlfriends are all much younger."

"Are you with me or a million miles away?" Jo asked, dissolving AJ's memories.

"A million miles away. I was thinking about Libby and Elliott, and how good it will be for them to be closer together."

As the days passed, AJ wondered how Garrett would adjust to the world of fashion. She knew he had some retail experience, but it had been with sporting goods and hardware stores. Would he be able to cope with the complicated world of franchises? Cal Prisk seemed to have had difficulty with it, even though he had grown with the projects.

The transition between Cal and Garrett went surprisingly smooth. Garrett and Elliott found a small apartment within walking distance of the junior high school and were settling in.

It was a beautiful March Saturday and as usual Elliott and Libby spent the day on the slopes. Together they boarded the lift for the ride to the top of the run. The two of them skied well together as both were adept at the sport.

"Are you really going to be skiing with the high school team next year?" Libby asked eagerly. She hadn't seen him since he tried out with the coach on Wednesday. She'd waited to ask the question until they were alone, just in case the news wasn't encouraging.

"I think so. The coach seemed impressed. I won't know until next fall, but he sounded positive."

"I just know you'll make it," she reassured him.

For a moment she sat quietly taking in the panorama that was still new and breathtaking, even though she'd seen it almost every day of her life.

"Do you think your dad and my mom…" Libby left the rest of the sentence unspoken.

"I know my dad would like it."

"He hasn't asked her."

"He says she's not ready yet. He thinks she's still hurting from what your dad did to her."

Libby nodded. She, like Elliott, loved both of her parents, but she knew what had led up to the divorce, even if she didn't fully understand it. Her father had indeed hurt her mother and the hurt would take a long time to heal.

"So, are you ready to leave for New York next week?" Elliott asked, changing the subject.

"I guess so," she replied, as they got off the lift. "Daddy's all excited about me coming. He says he has someone new he wants me to meet. He always has someone new he wants me to meet."

Elliott laughed at her comment. "Come on, Squirt, I'll race you down the run," he called as he pushed off, leaving her behind.

* * *

AJ and Garrett sat in front of the fire at the lodge. She took a sip of her hot chocolate and looked up to see Garrett watching her intently.

"Would you like to go skiing tomorrow?" Garrett asked. "It seems a shame to waste such good powder."

"You know I don't downhill."

"Right, but you do cross country and there's some great skiing up by the house."

"How do you know I cross country?"

"I do my homework. Mark told me."

AJ laughed. "I should have known. It's been years since I've done any skiing at all. I'd probably fall off and break my neck."

Garrett looked deeply into her eyes. "I'd never let anything happen to you. Oh, hell, I can't beat around the bush anymore. I love you Anne, I have since we first met. I want you to be my wife."

"Are you serious? Do you really want to marry me?"

"I've never been more serious in my life."

AJ's heart beat wildly. She could hardly believe what was happening to her. Jo's comment about not letting love and happiness slip away from her mingled with Garrett's proposal. "Oh, Garrett, I love you too. Yes, yes, yes! I'd be proud to marry you, whenever you say."

For a moment, it was as though he hadn't comprehended what she said. After a brief hesitation, he took her in his arms. He had kissed her in the past, but never with the feeling of this moment.

"Summer?" he asked. "We'll have a summer wedding, just before the kids go to New York. When they leave, we'll plan a honeymoon to end all honeymoons."

"It would mean a lot of work. I'd need to have the fall line finished by the end of April, but I think I can do it. Oh, yes, yes, a June wedding would be perfect!."

Garrett reached into his pocket and produced a blue, velvet box. Nestled inside was a beautiful two carat, pear shaped, diamond engagement ring.

"Oh, Garrett, it's beautiful," she sighed.

"You never had an engagement ring from Logan, did you?"

The mention of Logan should have tainted the moment, but she wouldn't allow it. "No. All he ever gave me was a plain gold band." As she thought back on it, she realized her wedding ring was the only thing in their marriage she hadn't paid for.

"I don't intend there to be anything simple about our lives together. For you it will be only the best, only what you deserve."

He took the ring from the box and slipped it onto her finger. The diamond seemed to come alive and glow in the firelight.

"You must have been certain I'd say yes."

Garrett laughed. "The only thing certain about this whole thing is my love for you. I've carried it around in my pocket for weeks. All I could think about was the possibility you'd say no, and I'd be stuck with this ring. I'd decided to wait for just the right moment. I'd planned to ply you with wine or maybe catch you off guard."

"You certainly did catch me off guard, but you would have never needed to get me drunk for me to say yes to you."

He took her in his arms again. This time, the kiss was even more passionate than before. AJ knew she should have been embarrassed to be seen kissing Garrett in front of the few guests who remained at the lodge, but she didn't care.

At dinner, Jo and the children joined them. Garrett ordered champagne and AJ knew Jo had an inkling something was afoot.

"Anne and I have an announcement to make," Garrett began. "This afternoon, she agreed to marry me in June, just before Libby and Elliott go to New York for the summer."

Jo beamed. "I'm so happy for the two of you."

"It will mean a lot of work. I'll have to have the fall line completed two months early, but it will be worth it."

"You can count on all of us to help you, Mom," Libby suggested. AJ marveled at how wise she sounded, considering she was only nine. She wouldn't turn ten until she was in New York with her father for the summer.

"Good, because we'll need it," Garrett admitted. "Besides getting the fall line finished, Anne and I will have to find a place to live."

"Don't jump into anything," Jo said. "We have a spare bedroom at the house for Elliott. You'd be close to the ranch, AJ would be at her studio, and you could take your time selecting just the right place."

Garrett shook his head and AJ took the action as one of disbelief rather than refusal. "I'm afraid it would be a terrible imposition on you, Jo."

"No imposition at all. Besides, it will only be temporary until you have the time to decide what you really want. There's a lot of land, perhaps you could even build your own house just the way you want it."

AJ couldn't help but smile. Up until now, she hadn't thought about the ramifications of her marriage. Everything seemed to have happened so quickly, she forgot about things like moving away from Jo's house. Somehow, she would have to convince Garrett to stay in the one place she felt at home.

Chapter Thirteen

It was a bright Saturday in early May. With the fall line finally completed and in the hands of the pattern makers, AJ began planning her wedding.

As they finished the breakfast dishes, Jo and AJ discussed their plans for the day. "I have a full day at the Crystal Creek shop planned," Jo said. "Are you meeting Garrett?"

"Not until lunch. Libby and I have some shopping to do for the wedding and I have an appointment to get my hair done at twelve. We're meeting Garrett and Elliott at one. They're going shopping with us this afternoon and then bringing us home."

"Well, if we're all ready, I guess we should get going. Betty has a wedding today, so I told Cory I'd be there to help her open the shop."

As they pulled out of the driveway, AJ engrossed herself in some correspondence, which had piled up over the past month. As usual Libby curled up in the back seat with a book she needed to finish by Monday for school.

My family, my wonderful family, Jo thought to herself. She prayed things wouldn't change with AJ's wedding and had voiced her opinions to Garrett only yesterday. He had assured her things would remain the same for as long as she wanted them to. It pleased her that the talk of AJ and Garrett moving out of the house had ceased.

She immersed herself in the beauty of the day. This, she decided, was her favorite time of the year. Here and there, stubborn patches of snow clung to the side of the road, while the trees budded and a warm southerly breeze promised summer to be just around the corner.

The pain came on so suddenly, so intense, there was no time to scream, no time to safely stop the car, no time to say good-bye. There was only severe pain and then the blackness of death.

AJ's correspondence had become like a jealous child, clamoring for her attention. She could turn it over to her secretary, Pam, but then she would lose touch with the people who purchased her clothes, the people who made her successful.

She picked up the letters and began to read them, soon becoming lost in their words.

Dear AJ,

I've worn your designs for three years now and was thrilled when you brought out a line designed especially for teens and priced for their budgets.

Dear AJ,

Imagine my surprise when your new shop opened in St. Louis and I found an entire section for big women. For the first time, I'm able to buy clothes off the racks and not pay three prices for them.

Dear AJ,

When I left Los Angeles and moved to Little Rock, I knew I'd have to make sacrifices. I was certain Fashions By AJ

would be one of them. What a wonderful
surprise when my mom sent me your
catalog. When asked where I buy my
clothes, I share my fashion secret. Hopefully,
Little Rock will have a shop soon. Until
then, I'll keep the mailman busy with my
orders.

AJ closed her eyes and said a silent prayer of thanks for her
success. As always, when she thanked God, she promised to
answer each letter personally. *It's only right, God. It's the way you'd
want me to run my business. I promise, I'll never forget the people who
are responsible for my success.*

When she formed the Amen in her mind, she opened her
eyes in time to see the car go over the embankment. The impact,
when they struck the pine tree, threw AJ into the windshield and
the bliss of unconsciousness.

Libby became aware of the voices of several men. She lay
on the floor of the back seat of Jo's car. Her arm hurt and
something sticky was running down her face.

"Mom, Mom!" she cried, but received no answer.

Panic overtook her and she began to scream for help at the
top of her lungs.

"Someone's alive in there," she heard a man say. "Are you
hurt?"

"Yes, my arm hurts and so does my head. Why won't my
mom answer me?"

"She can't hear you. I think she's unconscious. Don't move,
help is coming. What's your name?"

"It's Libby," she replied, starting to cry. "Please help my
mom and Jo."

"My God, Pete, look at the license plate. That's JoAnna
Bergendahl and AJ in there."

Libby relaxed. Even though she couldn't control her tears, she felt relieved. These men knew who they were. They knew her mom and Jo were special people. They would help to get them out. Sirens were screaming from behind her and she knew more help would be there soon.

Someone used a crowbar and pried open the back door. Libby held her breath as the men pulled her from the car and put her on the gurney.

"Do you know where you are Libby?" the man who placed the brace on her neck asked.

"I'm somewhere between the Lady Jo and Crystal Creek. What a silly question. I want my mom."

"I know you do. They're getting her out now. We're going to take you to the hospital so they can take care of you. As soon as we can, we'll bring in your mom and Mrs. Bergendahl."

Libby fought the urge to drift off to sleep, as the siren began to wail and the ambulance sped off toward Crystal Creek. "Someone should call Garrett."

"Garrett?" the man monitoring her questioned.

"Garrett Lanners. He's Jo's business manager and he's going to marry my mom. Please call him. His number is ..." Although she knew the number as well as she knew her own, now she couldn't remember it. Tears of frustration ran down her cheeks, making it impossible for her to speak.

"It's all right, Libby. We'll radio the hospital and they'll get hold of him."

* * *

Garrett and Elliott sat at the breakfast table. "Dad, can I go to the mall with the guys before we have to meet Anne and Libby?"

Before Garrett could reply, the phone rang. "I'll get it," Elliott said, getting to his feet. "It's probably Tom."

Elliott picked up the phone. "Hello-yes, this is the Lanners' residence-No, this is his son. I'll get him. Dad, it's for you."

Garrett took the phone and could hardly believe what he was hearing. It wasn't possible!. Anne, Libby and Jo couldn't have been in an accident, and yet he was being summoned to the hospital. Libby had asked for him. No one knew anything about Anne's and Jo's conditions. He had to be there, had to be at Libby's side. What if Anne and Jo were dead?

"Do you want me to go with you, Dad? I could stay with Libby while you're with Anne."

Garrett nodded. He needed his son with him. They grabbed their jackets and rushed to the hospital. His heart pounded wildly when they pulled into the parking area right behind an ambulance. Was this the one with Libby or was its passenger Anne or Jo? He had no idea where the accident had occurred or how long it would take to transport them to the hospital.

Slamming the car door, he ran toward the emergency entrance with Elliott close behind.

"I'm Garrett Lanners," he said to the woman at the desk. "Someone called me regarding the accident with Anne, I mean AJ, and Jo Bergendahl."

"I called you." He turned to see a young doctor standing behind him. "I've been waiting for you. I've been in contact with the paramedics. They just brought in the child. She has facial cuts, a broken collar bone and a compound fracture of her right arm."

"What about her mother and Mrs. Bergendahl?" Garrett asked, almost afraid of the answer.

"We just received word they are out of the vehicle, but they haven't determined their condition as of yet. I am sorry."

Garrett nodded. Sorry? Wasn't there more to say than *sorry*? "Can we see Libby now?" Elliott asked.

"We will need parental permission to treat the child. Can you reach her father?"

"If that isn't the most asinine thing I've ever heard! God only knows what shape her mother is in, and her father lives in New York. I have power of attorney for her mother. Can't I give permission?"

The young doctor shook his head. "I suppose you could. It's just that I'd feel better having her father's consent, but I have to start treatment. You will contact her father, won't you?"

Garrett nodded. "I'll call New York as soon as I see Libby. He'll want to know if I've seen her."

They were taken into an examination room with four curtained areas. Behind the second curtain, Libby lay on a bed. She looked so small and helpless. Garrett wanted to cry. Instead, he put on his brightest smile to put her at ease. It was Elliott who took command of the situation.

"Hi, Lib," he said, sounding falsely cheerful.

"Elliott, Garrett, I was afraid they wouldn't find you, afraid you wouldn't come." Her voice sounded strange and Garrett knew it was from whatever she'd been given for the pain.

"You know we wouldn't be anywhere else," Garrett replied, taking hold of her left hand.

"Mom?"

"I don't know, Champ. They haven't brought her in yet. We can't stay long. I have to call your dad. They're going to take you upstairs now. When you wake up, we'll be there and tell you all about your mom."

Libby closed her eyes, giving into the sedative. Garrett watched her closely. She was a strong little girl, just as Elliott was a strong young man. He envied them the strength of youth. At his age, strength was but an outward appearance. Within, the strength was more like a bowl of quivering Jel-o. What if he lost Anne? It would mean losing Libby as well. She would be sent to

New York. He thought of her as a daughter. He'd hoped to make it official in a month. Now what would happen to them?

"Come on, Dad. We'd better go out to the waiting room. You've got to call Libby's dad."

Garrett nodded his answer, allowing Elliott to lead the way out of the room. Once they reached the waiting room, Elliott took a seat across from the bank of phones, giving Garrett the proper amount of privacy.

"I'd like the number for Logan Prescott in New York, please."

It seemed to take forever for the operator to reply. "I'm sorry sir, that number is unlisted."

Garrett thought of several obscenities, but left them all unspoken. "What about a listing for Marjorie Prescott?"

"Yes, sir, we do have a listing for her. One moment please."

Garrett waited until the automated voice on the other end of the line gave him the number. After writing it down, he placed the call on his credit card.

"Hello," a woman answered.

"Mrs. Prescott, you don't know me. My name is Garrett Lanners ..." before he could continue, Marge interrupted.

"Elliott's father?"

"Yes, but there's no time for that now. I need to find your son. There's been an accident."

"Accident? Libby? Oh, dear, Logan is here helping me with some painting. I'll get him-just a minute." The woman seemed on the verge of hysteria.

For Garrett, the minute seemed to drag until Logan finally answered the phone. "What the hell happened out there, Lanners? Where is AJ? Why isn't she calling? What's going on with my daughter?"

Garrett wanted to be calm, but he was so worried about Anne, Logan's words were the final blow. "In case you're interested, Anne and Libby were in an accident with Jo. So far, they've only brought Libby to the hospital. She has some broken bones and some cuts, but she'll be all right. They've taken her up for treatment."

"Treatment? On who's say so? If AJ isn't there, who gave them permission?"

"I did. I have power of attorney for both Jo and Anne."

"Maybe you have power of attorney for AJ but not for Libby. The way I see it, you have no right to..."

"Maybe I don't but I refuse to let her suffer because if it. When we finish talking, you can make the proper arrangements here. In the meantime, I thought it was best if she were able to get the treatment she needs."

"In this case I guess you're right. I'll talk to the people in charge, but don't think I'll let you get away with taking over everything out there."

"I don't see why you would be concerned with anything but your daughter and she's being well cared for, even if I had to bend the law to get it done. I love Ann and Libby very much. Right now Libby is in surgery and Anne could be dead for all I know."

A long pause on the other end of the line told Garrett his words had shocked and sobered Logan. "I'm sorry I jumped on you. Tell Libby I'll be there as soon as possible. Her grandmother and I will be taking the first flight we can get. In the meantime, I'll call the hospital and see what I have to do to straighten out all of the paperwork."

Garrett ended the conversation. He had never met Logan Prescott, never expected to meet him and now he would be arriving in Crystal Creek within a matter of hours.

"Is he coming out here, Dad?" Elliott asked, when he came over to where Garrett stood.

Garrett nodded. "It's only right, especially if ..."

"Don't Dad. Anne isn't dead. You can't think that way."

"Mr. Lanners," the doctor he'd spoken with earlier said as he entered the waiting room. "They just called saying Mrs. Bergendahl and Mrs. Prescott will be arriving in about two minutes."

Garrett pushed past the doctor. He needed to be there when they brought them in. He had to see them for himself.

"Mr. Lanners, you can't ..."

He didn't listen, but stopped short when the paramedics rushed in with a gurney. Anne lay on it, her face covered with blood, her hair matted, her skin almost deathly white.

"Mrs. Bergendahl is dead. They've taken her to the morgue for an autopsy, since she was dead at the scene. From the lack of blood from the impact, we're assuming it was a heart attack, but we won't know for certain until the results are in from the autopsy. As for Mrs. Prescott, she has internal injuries and a possible broken pelvis. We need to get her to surgery right away. There's a waiting room on the second floor. We'll contact you there."

Garrett wanted to go into the room where they had taken Anne, but the doctor escorted him to the area where Elliott waited for him.

"Dad," Elliot said, as Garrett slumped into the chair next to his son. "What happened?"

"They're taking Anne to surgery. They want us to go upstairs to the waiting room there."

"What about Jo?"

Garrett shook his head, unable to hold back his emotions. He knew he should be strong for his son, but he couldn't stem the flow of his tears. "She's dead."

Elliott put his hand under Garrett's arm and helped him to his feet. "We'll go upstairs, then I'll get you some coffee."

Garrett agreed, and followed his son. Once Elliott left for the cafeteria Garrett sat in the waiting room alone. He knew no one would be coming to tell them the outcome of either Libby or Anne's surgery for several hours, but he wanted to be accessible.

Libby's tear-filled, pleading eyes and Anne's blood smeared face haunted him. This couldn't be happening and yet he was living it. *Dear God,* he silently prayed. *Let it pass. Don't let me lose her.*

"Garrett?"

He jumped at the sound of his name and turned to see Ken Aubry, Jo's lawyer, standing behind him. "I'm glad to see you," he said, standing to shake Ken's hand. "How did you know?"

"Your son called me. He didn't know much, but he thought you needed someone to talk to."

"Guess I do. I've discovered he's quite a grown up young man today."

"Tell me, what's going on?"

"It's a nightmare, Ken. Libby's upstairs in surgery. She's not hurt too badly, broken bones, cuts and bruises. I did contact Logan, he's coming out. Jo's dead. I conned the hospital into thinking I had power of attorney for all of them. Once I talked to Logan, he pointed out I had no right to give permission to have Libby treated. I guess I wasn't thinking straight. I just wanted to get Libby taken care of. Logan was going to call and get it straightened out."

"And AJ?"

The question tore Garrett apart.

"They took her to surgery. She has internal bleeding, broken pelvis, head injuries. God only knows what else. She looked like hell when they brought her in. Her face was smeared with blood, her hair matted with it." Garrett's voice trailed off.

"I can probably tell you what that autopsy will find," Ken said, taking advantage of Garrett's silence. "She suffered a massive heart attack."

"How did you know? The doctors thought as much, but they couldn't be certain until the autopsy report."

"She was in my office yesterday and wrote a new will. She'd just left the doctor's office because she had chest pains. He recommended open-heart surgery. I don't think I'm violating any lawyer/client privilege here, considering she'd dead. She wanted some time to think about it and promised to give him her answer on Monday. She wasn't well."

Garrett stared at Ken in disbelief. "Did Anne know?"

"As far as I know, I was the only one, other than the doctor, to have that information. We have to focus on AJ and Libby right now. They're the future of this business. I know, I wrote the will."

They sat, silently, for a moment, each lost in thought.

"Here's your coffee, Dad," Elliot said, as he entered the room. "Mr. Aubry, I didn't expect you so soon. Would you like me to get you a cup too?"

"Thank you, Elliott. I would like a cup of coffee," Ken replied.

Elliott was just leaving when a doctor came in. "Mr. Lanners?" Garrett jumped to his feet and acknowledged the man. "I came to tell you the Prescott girl is in recovery. Everything went well. I also checked on Mrs. Prescott for you. Her surgery will take about three to four hours, barring complications."

"How long before we can see Libby?"

"About forty-five minutes. In the meantime, there are several reporters downstairs. Do you want to make a statement?"

"How in the hell did they get it this fast? My God, they're nothing more than vultures!"

"Calm down," Ken said. "I'm sure it was on the scanner. Jo's license plate is a dead giveaway. After I had the call from Elliott, I called the sheriff's office. It all makes sense. Jo was driving when she had the attack. She probably never even knew what happened. I'll go down and set up a place where you can hold a press conference. You'll have to give some sort of a statement."

Garrett nodded. Ken was right. He hoped he could get through it without breaking down. He had to remain strong for Libby and Anne.

Chapter Fourteen

Karl Jorgenson pulled into the driveway of his home just as the mailman was depositing mail in the box on the house. In the seat beside him, nine-year-old Michael squirmed. They had just returned from Little League try-outs.

Karl was anxious to get home. It was a special day. He had promised Janet they'd do something to celebrate their twelfth anniversary tonight.

"Good morning, Dr. Jorgenson," the postman called as he came down the steps from the porch.

"Good morning," Karl returned the greeting. The man had him at a disadvantage. He knew Karl's name because he delivered the mail, but to him, the man was just a uniform.

Before going into the house, he picked up the mail. Anne's delicate handwriting graced one of the envelopes. *Dear Anne, she never forgets an anniversary, birthday, or Christmas.* He wondered how she was doing. Maybe he'd surprise her with a call. They hadn't talked on the phone in months. Or was it years? They'd spoken once or twice since the call about the divorce, but she'd made it perfectly clear she didn't want to call, nor did she want him calling her. Her notes said little. He knew more about her from reading the fashion section of the Chicago papers. Luckily, she did send pictures. The pictures worried him. Libby was a beautiful child, while Anne, looked tired and thin.

As he shuffled through the remainder of the mail, he put Anne to the back of his mind. He noticed cards from Kristin and Lars as well as from Johann and Sharon and his parents.

"Hey, Dad, can I go over to Billy's to play?" Michael asked when he entered the kitchen.

"As soon as you grab some lunch," Karl said, tossing the mail on the counter.

"Aw gee, Dad, I don't want to wait all day. Mom's not here yet."

"I'll fix you a sandwich. Mom said she was leaving some spreads for us."

"Why isn't Mom here? I wanted her to see which team drafted me."

"You know she had to take your sister to dance class. We'll make your games, don't worry about it."

"Sure, but it won't be the same."

Karl tousled his son's hair. "What do you want, tuna or egg salad?"

"Egg."

Karl quickly fixed the sandwich and put it on a plate.

"Can I watch TV?"

"There's not much on." Karl looked at the clock. "Don't suppose you'd be interested in a golf tournament?"

"Aw, Dad," Michael said, biting into his sandwich. "That's no fun."

"Well, it is for me."

Before making his own lunch, he turned on the kitchen television. The set warmed up and he saw the golf course in Atlanta flash on the screen. The announcer droned on about the statistics of each player and their chances of winning today's tournament, while Karl spread tuna onto a slice of wheat bread.

The words *Special Bulletin* came across the screen and the scene shifted from the golf course to a newsroom. He hated the words *Special Bulletin*. They always meant trouble. Wasn't it enough they'd just gotten out of Viet Nam? What had the government decided to get them into now?

"We interrupt this program to bring you a special bulletin. This morning, just outside of Crystal Creek, Colorado, a car carrying JoAnna Bergendahl, owner of Jo's dress shops, The Lady Jo Ranch, and Fashions By AJ; Mrs. AJ Prescott, head designer for Fashions by AJ, and Mrs. Prescott's daughter, Elizabeth, were involved in a traffic accident. We take you to a live press conference given by a spokesman for the family, Garrett Lanners, at the Crystal Creek hospital."

Michael came in from the living room, carrying his empty plate. "Can I go over to Billy's now."

"Ssh, I want to hear this."

"What's so great about an old golf match?"

"It's more than that," Karl said, as pictures of Anne and JoAnna flashed on the screen.

"Hey, that's Aunt Anne!. Why is she on TV? Is she someone famous or something?"

"Something like that. I'll explain later. You go out and play."

Karl turned back to the set in time to see a man, who he judged to be in his late thirties, enter a room filled with reporters.

"Ladies and gentleman," the man began. "I'll make this brief. Early this morning, JoAnna Bergendahl, AJ Prescott and AJ's daughter Libby were on their way to Crystal Creek when they were involved in an accident. Mrs. Bergendahl was pronounced dead at the scene. AJ's condition is critical at this point. She has been taken to surgery and I won't have any word on her progress for several hours. As for Libby, she is in recovery and her condition is good. She has minor cuts and bruises as well as a broken arm and collarbone."

"Mr. Lanners, what was the cause of the accident?"

"It hasn't been officially determined yet, but the doctors are going on the assumption Mrs. Bergendahl suffered a heart attack while she was driving. She was dead at the scene. Thank God there wasn't another car involved."

"Then it wasn't an alcohol-related accident?"

Garrett seemed ready to lose his temper. "It was nine in the morning, for God's sake!"

"Is it true that you and AJ are ..."

Garrett interrupted the reporter. "I won't dignify that with an answer. This is neither the time nor the place to discuss AJ's personal life. I'll take no more questions. This press conference is over."

When the man left the room, the golf tournament resumed. The look in the man's eyes, the quiver in his voice, made Karl wonder about the question he hadn't answered. Was he in love with Anne and if he was, who was he, and how well did he know her?

Karl was ready to reach for the phone when it rang, startling him.

"Karl, its Johann," the voice on the other end of the line said before he could answer. "Have you been watching the golf match?"

"Yes."

"How bad do you think it is?"

"They said critical."

"You're the doctor, just what does critical mean?"

"It could mean anything, from they aren't certain how she is, so they're waiting for her to get out of surgery before they make any comment, or..."

"What do you think we ought to do?"

"I don't know if we ought to do anything. I'm just getting ready to call out there and talk to Lanners, the family spokesman, whatever that means. Have you ever heard of him?"

"I think Anne might have mentioned him in a letter, but I'm not sure."

"Well, whoever he is I intend to talk to him. Stay by the phone. I'll call you back after I call out there."

* * *

Feeling drained, Garrett returned to the surgical waiting room. He knew how close he'd come to breaking down during the interview. It was all too much, too fast.

He found Ken waiting for him. "I watched the press conference on TV. You did well."

"The last question was uncalled for," Garrett said, unable to keep the anger from his voice.

"People want to know. AJ is big news. Once the two of you are married, you'll be big news as well."

"I understand, but it's not the right time. They haven't been down to say anything yet, have they?"

"Calm down, Garrett. They said three to four hours. They did come to tell us Libby's been taken to her room. Elliott went up to be with her."

"I'll go up too, in a minute," Garrett commented, sinking into a chair and taking a sip of the cold coffee he left earlier.

"There's a call for you, Mr. Lanners," the volunteer at the waiting room desk told him.

Without thinking of the ramifications of today's press conference, he picked up the phone.

"This is Garrett Lanners."

"I want to know about AJ Prescott," the man on the other end of the line demanded. Garrett wondered if he detected a slight hint of a accent.

"You and half a million other people," he replied flatly, wishing he'd declined the call. "Why should I tell you anything?"

"I'm her brother."

"Well, how nice for you," Garrett snapped.

"Look, Lanners, I want to know about my sister's condition."

"If you're her brother prove it to me. I don't know you from Adam."

"The AJ stands for Anne Jorgenson."

"If you are her brother, which one are you?" Garrett knew the question was an important one. No one but a close friend or a family member would know the answer.

"I'm the doctor, Karl."

"One more question. What town are you from in Norway and where is it located?"

"We're from Kinsarvik on the Hardanger Fjord."

"OK, so you're her brother. There's not much more I can tell you. If you heard the press conference ..."

"Why weren't we called?" Karl interrupted. "Why did we have to hear about this on television?"

"You weren't called because I had no idea how to reach you, and you weren't called because Anne probably doesn't want you here. As for before the press conference, we haven't had a lot of time to think out here. I've been concerned about Libby as well as Anne."

"I'd like an answer to the question you wouldn't answer for the press. How close are you to my sister?"

"Apparently closer than you are," Garrett said. "We're planning to be married."

"How long have you known her?"

"Five years."

"Then you're her lover?"

Garrett couldn't help but laugh at the question. "I don't know why you feel you're entitled to an answer to that question, but Anne and I aren't lovers. I'm her friend. I'd give my eyeteeth to be her lover, but not until we're married. You see, she's not as wicked as you and your family seem to think she is. She's a very successful woman, but between your family and her ex-husband, she's been terribly hurt. It's taken me five years to get past her hurt. To get her to even consent to marry me was hard. She has this misconception that she's unlovable."

"I'd like to come out there," Karl's voice had softened, his accusations ceased.

"I don't think it's a wise idea."

"Why?"

"Because I honestly don't know what shape she'll be in after surgery. I don't know what they'll find. I don't even know if she'll be alive. She was thrown into the windshield. When they brought her in, her face was red with blood. They think she has a broken pelvis. From what I can ascertain, it means she'll be in a wheelchair for a while and will require physical therapy to learn to walk again. You'd know more about it than I would. They also told me she's bleeding internally and if they can't stop it, I'll lose her. I'm sorry, Doctor. I'm not in a very good mood, but I will keep you informed, if that's what you want. Good-bye."

Karl listened to the click on the other end of the line. The man was right. What gave him the right to demand information about his sister? When Anne had quit calling, he hadn't made the effort to call her. He knew Johann and Kristin hadn't. They'd all been content with short notes. Anne was too far away and their lives were too complicated.

He stood there for a minute then depressed the button on the phone. When he again had a dial tone, he called Johann.

"What did you find out?"

"We're not needed out there."

"What do you mean not needed? We're her family."

"Are we? You know as well as I do that we let her down. When she stopped calling, did you ever call her? Did you ever call out there just to hear her voice? I didn't. I was comfortable knowing she was paying the long distance phone bills. I told myself I had such a good life that I didn't want to hear how miserable she was. I wanted to think she'd brought her troubles on herself."

"Well, didn't she? She was the one who was pregnant when she got married."

"Listen to yourself, Johann. You sound like Papa. Haven't you ever had a young couple in your office that went too far and had to get married? Did you deny them? What have you told women whose husbands are cheating on them and have been for years?"

Karl's questions met with silence. "So what did Lanners have to say?" Johann finally asked.

"Nothing more than he did at the press conference. He did say he'd keep in touch."

"So what is he to her?"

"He plans to marry her."

"He looks so old. He's too old for her, if you ask me."

"Are you thinking of the AJ of today, or the Anne who left here? We haven't seen her in twelve years. She's thirty-four years old, not twenty-two."

"She hasn't made the effort to come home," Johann continued, smug in his complacency.

"We haven't made the effort to go out there. I was able to travel over ten thousand miles to Norway, but I didn't think to go less than a thousand miles to Crystal Creek. Maybe if I had, I wouldn't be feeling like such an ass right now."

"Has he known her long?"

Karl couldn't believe the way Johann was acting. It seemed as though he wasn't listening to anything Karl had said. "They've known each other for five years. He seems like an interesting man. I'd like to get to know him." He paused for a moment, collecting his thoughts. "You're better at breaking bad news than I am. Why don't you talk to Kristin and the folks? I'll tell Janet."

"You're going out there, aren't you?"

"I don't know. I feel I should, but then again, I think I should honor her wishes. Lanners says she won't want us there. I don't know what to do."

* * *

Garrett hung up the phone and turned to face Ken. "Anne's wonderful family," he said aloud. "Suddenly, they're all concerned."

"Don't be too harsh on them," Ken warned.

"Harsh? Where were they when she got the divorce? Where were they when she needed them?"

"It was AJ who cut the ties."

Garrett shook his head. "I don't buy your explanation. If you had a sister who cut the ties, would you stand by and let it happen?"

"I've never been put in such a position. If it were to happen, I don't know what I'd do. People today lead very busy lives, Garrett, so accept it. The man you talked to is a doctor. Her brother Johann is a pastor. They're busy men with busy lives. Her sister is a farmer's wife with five children, another busy life. AJ's life is far from quiet. They've drifted apart. It's sad, but it happens."

"I don't want to accept it, not for Anne, and not for Libby."

Ken shook his head. "While you were on the phone, I contacted the switchboard. They won't be sending up any more calls."

"Thanks. The next one might be even worse than this one was. Did you get Libby's room number? I think I'd like to hide out there for a while."

Ken reached into his pocket. From it, he pulled out a piece of paper with the number of a room on the fifth floor written on it.

Garret left the room, and checked his watch. It was only one in the afternoon and yet so much had happened. He wondered if he had handled the call from Karl Jorgenson correctly. He certainly hoped so.

He made his way toward Libby's room at the end of the hall in the pediatrics ward. "Hi, Champ," he said when he entered the room.

"Hi, Garrett. Elliott's been here with me. He said you were on TV and everything."

"People want to know about you and your mom ..."

"And Jo," she said, finishing what he left unsaid.

"What happened, Libby?"

"I don't know. One minute we were driving along and I was reading. The next thing I knew I woke up on the floor and my arm hurt. Is my mom dead?"

"No, Champ, she's upstairs in surgery right now.

"And Jo?"

He dreaded the question. He couldn't lie to the child. "Jo didn't make it."

There were no screams, no hysterical tears. Perhaps it was the medication they'd given her that numbed her feelings. Only silent tears marked her grief.

Elliott and Garrett stayed with Libby until she slipped into a peaceful sleep with the aid of the medication the nurse gave her.

"Come on, Elliott. We'll go down to the cafeteria and get something to eat. You haven't had lunch and neither have I."

They went through the cafeteria line and each halfheartedly took a salad. Ken saw them and waved them over to a large table where Garrett recognized people from the ranch, Fashions, and the shops. The people who had gathered were there to share their grief and concern. It was easier to be with people who shared their thoughts, than to be alone and not knowing what happened. What they sought was support and answers as to how they should handle the days ahead.

"We've been talking about what to do," Ken explained, when Garrett and Elliott joined them. "We're putting in more lines at the lodge and closing down the shops, the factory and AJ's office. Pam will be moving down to the lodge to help with the phones."

Garrett nodded. It pleased him to have someone other than himself making the decisions.

At the other end of the table, he saw Jo's friend, Collette and her husband. "I'm so sorry, Collette, so very sorry," he said, feeling he must express sympathy to someone and with Jo having no family, he thought it should be Collette. He went over to her wheelchair to embrace her.

Collette nodded. "We both believe in fate. It was her time and I'm certain she accepted it well."

Looking for answers, which he was certain didn't exist, he continued. "Did anyone, other than Ken, know how sick she was?"

Around the table, people shook their heads. It was Collette who spoke up. "I knew she wasn't feeling well the last time I saw her."

"Why did she keep it a secret?"

A strange smile crossed Collette's lips. "For AJ. She would have made Jo quit working and insist she relax. It would have killed her. It's better this way. I've known her for years. She needed to work. It made her happy."

"I guess I can understand her reasoning," Garrett replied. Changing the subject, he continued. "Did anyone call Mark?"

"I did," AJ's secretary, Pam, assured him. "He said he'd call Marcia. I'm certain they'll be here as soon as Marcia's plane gets in."

Relief flooded Garrett. The pressure of having to contact key people had been taken from him. "Libby's father and grandmother will be arriving."

"I don't look forward to seeing him," Ken commented.

"It's all academic. These are things that have to be done. Right now we need to form a battle plan. Closing things down is only a temporary measure. It won't change what's happened. We'll open everything again the first of next week."

"I sent wires to all of the franchises as soon as I heard," Pam said.

"What would we do without you?" Garrett said, pleased to know someone could take charge. "I hadn't even thought of the franchises."

They talked on for a while, oblivious to the news-hungry reporters who sat two tables away.

At last, the doctor whom Garrett had spoken with earlier entered the room and asked Garrett to accompany him to a small conference area.

"She's out of surgery," the doctor began when they sat down.

"Head injuries?" Garrett asked.

"They weren't as bad as we first anticipated. There's always a lot of bleeding with a head wound. She has a concussion, but it's not serious. She has several stitches in her face, but plastic surgery will take care of them. It's her eyes we're worried about."

"Her eyes?" Garrett echoed.

"We took over a hundred and fifty shards of glass from her eyes. As far as we can tell, there will be no permanent damage. We won't know until we can do a more extensive examination. It won't take place until she's awake. We want her to rest her eyes until Monday.

"As for the broken pelvis, it will heal. She will be in a wheelchair for a while and will require physical therapy. She won't be back to full strength for several months."

Garrett thought of the designs just finished and sent to the pattern makers as well as the partially completed spring line that sat on Anne's drawing table.

"She'll be back in her room in about an hour. She'll need you there."

"Try and keep me away," Garrett replied.

The doctor continued to describe the internal injuries and the surgery required to correct them, but Garrett hardly listened. The words were beyond him as he worried about her eyesight. If she couldn't see, he knew she wouldn't want to live. Her eyes were her life.

"She'll be groggy," the doctor cautioned. "She won't make much sense. This won't sink in until much later. Try not to worry. Everything looks good, very good."

Garrett thanked the doctor and returned to the cafeteria dining room. Everyone, including the reporters, turned to look at him. Giving the thumbs up signal, he smiled. Not a jubilant smile but a smile of reassurance.

"The surgery went well," he said, taking his seat at the table. "The doctor says she'll be all right, but it will take a while."

Lowering his voice so only the people at the table could hear, he continued. "There's only one problem. They don't know about her sight."

"Her sight?" Pam half whispered, her voice echoing Garrett's words.

"There was a lot of shattered glass in her eyes. They're sure they got it all, but they won't be positive until the bandages come off on Monday."

Garrett watched the people around him, aware of the myriad reactions from those seated at the table. Ken was the first to say anything. "What can we say? She's alive and since we won't know anything until Monday, there's no sense in getting into a panic over this."

"You're right," Garrett said. "I have a call to make and then I have to go up to her room." Nodding toward the reporters, he turned to Ken. "Can you take care of things here?"

"Sure Garrett. Are you calling her brother?"

"I am if I can find his number. It was the one thing I neglected to get when I talked to him."

"I have it here," Pam said, producing the small address book he'd seen on AJ's desk.

Garrett opened the book to the "J" section. Dr. Karl Jorgenson, 532 Maple Street, St. Peter, Minnesota. On the line beneath the address she'd listed a phone number.

The phone on the other end rang only once before it was answered.

"Dr. Jorgenson, this is Garrett Lanners," he began. "I told you I'd call. Anne came through surgery well."

A sigh of relief came from the other end of the line. "Thank God!"

"They told me all of the details, because I didn't understand most of what they said. I was more worried about what they told me earlier. They don't know if she'll ever be able to see again."

"Her eyes?"

For the second time he repeated the story the doctor told him minutes earlier. "I thought you should know," he concluded.

"Thank you. I appreciate you being honest with me."

"I'll keep in touch with you. There's no sense in calling out here. The switchboard is transferring no calls to us, the lodge is giving out no information, and Anne's office is closed. You'll get no information from anyone but me. Just tell me when it's a good time to contact you. I won't call again before Monday. There would be no sense in it since I won't know anything."

"You can call abut six in the evening, your time. I'm always home by then."

Garrett ended the conversation and wondered if he should have insisted someone from Anne's family come out to be with her. As he thought about it more, he decided he'd been right to go with his original plan. Anne's family was here, seated in the cafeteria. The ones in Minnesota merely shared here genes, not her love.

He arrived at her third floor room just as they were wheeling her into the private room at the end of the corridor. Just seeing her scared him. Her face was held together with stitches, blood clung to her hair and neck, and her eyes were swathed in bandages.

"Anne," he whispered, once she was moved into a bed.

"Garrett?"

"I'm right here beside you."

"I can't see. They've got something over my eyes."

"They removed some glass from your eyes. They want to keep them covered to rest them. It's a necessary precaution. On Monday, they'll be taking off the bandages."

She seemed to accept his explanation without question. "Libby?"

"She's just fine. I saw her a little while ago. She's sleeping now."

"Are you sure?"

"Positive. She has a broken arm and a broken collarbone. Her father and grandmother will be here soon."

"You called Logan?"

"I had to. He needed to give permission for her to be treated. I expect him around seven."

"Seven? What time is it now?"

"It's about five thirty."

"What happened? What happened to Jo?"

Garrett swallowed the lump in his throat. Somehow telling Anne what happened was harder than telling Libby. Maybe it was because he couldn't see her eyes, couldn't judge her reaction. "She didn't make it."

"This can't be happening. What about the business? What about our wedding?"

"Don't worry about a thing. All of the people who love you and who are involved in the business are here. Everything will continue to run smoothly. As for the wedding, we may have to postpone it for a while. We certainly won't be canceling it. You need to rest, so try and get some sleep. I'll be right here."

"You said something about people being here. Who are they?"

"No one you would disapprove of. I did talk to your brother, Karl. He called here right after he heard about it on television. He wants to come out."

"No, I don't want them here."

"I thought that would be your reaction. I told him not to come. I don't think he was very happy with me. If you want him here, I'm certain he'll come."

"No, no, no …" Her voice trailed off.

"You go back to sleep. I'll handle things here."

"You talk to Logan. Tell him she's mine. He can't have her. She's mine."

"I won't let anything happen to Libby."

"She's mine. Do you hear me? She's mine." She paused for a moment, as though she were suddenly disoriented. "Jo? Jo's dead?"

"Yes."

"I want to sleep. I want to sleep and make it all go away."

"That's just what you should do. We'll take care of everything."

When Garrett knew Anne was sleeping soundly, he left the room. For the first time since he'd received the phone call, he cried.

"Libby's dad is here. He wants to talk to you."

Garrett looked up to see Elliott standing in front of him. He made no attempt to wipe his eyes. He saw no shame in crying.

"I'll be there in just a minute. I'll meet you in the cafeteria."

When Elliott left, Garrett stepped back into Anne's room. The figure in the bed looked small and helpless. He was certain she was convinced her sight was gone. He had told her Jo was gone. He certainly wouldn't let Libby be taken from her as well. "I'll tell him, Anne, I'll tell Logan that Libby is yours."

He steeled himself for the meeting he'd dreaded all day. He knew enough about Logan Prescott to know they would never be friends.

They were waiting for him in the cafeteria. He saw them sitting at a table by the window with Elliott. He also noted several reporters who were still lingering. The people he'd been with earlier had more or less disappeared. Only Pam and Ken remained.

He recognized Logan immediately. He looked exactly like the publicity pictures. With him was an attractive older lady that Garrett assumed was Logan's mother. "Mrs. Prescott, Logan I hope you had a good flight. I'm Garrett Lanners."

Logan got to his feet and extended his hand. "I want to thank you for calling. Your son has been very helpful in filling us in on Libby. I wanted to talk to you before we go up and see her."

"There's not much to talk about."

"I think there is. There's AJ. What kind of shape is she in?"

"Right now she's sleeping."

"That's not what I asked you. I want to know what kind of physical shape she's in and where I stand legally?"

"Legally? Right now nothing has changed. Anne has custody of Libby and you have visitation rights."

"That's what I mean. With AJ's condition, well, you know, I want to take my daughter to New York permanently."

"Not in a million years," Garrett said, checking his temper. "I agree that Libby should go back to New York with you for the summer. It will give Anne time to recover from her injuries."

Marge put her hand on Logan's arm. From the look on her face, Garrett realized she didn't agree with her son. "How badly is AJ injured?"

For the third time, Garrett related the story of Anne's injuries. As he did, he saw tears pooling in the older woman's eyes.

"Oh, dear Lord," Marge said, shaking her head as though the gesture would soften Garrett's words. "We heard about Jo on the car radio on the way here from the airport. They seemed to have no word on AJ's condition."

"We haven't released anything more to the press. I hope you're prepared to stay."

"We are," Logan snapped. "We'll stay as long as it takes."

"I found rooms for you in town," Pam advised them, when she joined the group.

"In town? Why not at the ranch? Are you too cheap to part with a couple of rooms for the time we're here?"

"It has nothing to do with finances," Pam continued. "The company is taking care of your expenses while you're here. We just thought it would be best if you were in town and close to the hospital. We didn't want to inconvenience you. We also thought you would be comfortable in a more private setting. The ranch will be chaotic."

"Thank you for your concern," Marge said, giving Pam a hug. Turning to Garrett, she continued. "Can we see Libby now?"

"Of course you can. I'll go with you."

"I don't need you going with me," Logan barked. "In case you've forgotten, Libby is *my* daughter."

"Logan!" Marge's voice sounded with admonishment. "Let Garrett come with us. The child is frightened enough. She's just lost Jo, her mother is very ill, and she's been hurt. Garrett will represent the familiar to her."

Garrett didn't care if Logan wanted him to go with them or not, as he led the way to Libby's room. Behind him, he could hear Logan talking to Elliott.

"So, I hear your old man is going to marry my ex-wife." Garrett couldn't believe Logan would bring up such a thing at a time like this.

"Why not?" Elliott replied. "He loves her."

"He loved her before, will he love her now? What if she loses her sight?"

Garrett wanted to turn around and say something, but instead he held his temper in check. Elliott was handling himself very well.

"It won't make any difference," Elliott defended him.

"She won't be rich if she doesn't have *Fashions* behind her."

"I don't think my dad cares if she's rich or poor. As for *Fashions*, she'll always have it. She's going to be just fine. The doctors know what they're doing. She won't lose her sight."

"What do you know? You're nothing more than a smart-ass kid."

Garrett could hold his tongue no longer. "I understand how you feel about Anne. She was your meal ticket when you needed one, but she's more than that to me. If you've got a problem with our relationship, come to me with it. Don't lay your guilt trip on my son. He's the innocent party here. Do I make myself clear?"

"Perfectly. I wasn't laying anything on the kid. I thought he should know how things are in the real world."

"Maybe they're like that in your world, but they aren't in mine. I take love and marriage very seriously."

"Oh, like you did with your ex-wife? I don't see her here holding your hand. She saw through you and followed her dream to bigger and better things. You'll do the same once you realize AJ is destined to be little more than an emotional and physical cripple."

Garrett knew he would have hit Logan if Elliott and Marge hadn't been there. Instead, he turned and entered Libby's room. He was pleased to see her sitting up in bed and eating ice cream.

"Hi, Champ. I'm back."

"Have you seen Mom?"

"I sure have. She can hardly wait to see you. Right now, I have someone else who wants to see you. Your dad and grandma are here."

"From New York?"

"Why sure, where else would they come from? Come on Champ give me credit. Didn't you think I'd call them?"

"Oh, Garrett, of course I did. I just didn't expect them to come. Daddy hasn't been in Colorado since ..."

"I know, but things are different now. They're very worried about you. I bet your grandma would like to help you with that ice cream. It looks like you're having a hard time trying to eat it left handed."

"Are you going back down to see Mom?"

"No. She's sleeping. Now, you be good and do what they tell you. I won't be back until tomorrow. Your dad and grandma need some time with you."

"Is Mom really OK?"

"She came through with flying colors. When this is all over, you and I are going to teach her to downhill."

"Really? Mom's never gone downhill skiing before."

"Your mom's going to do a lot of things she's never done before. She's going to take on another designer and get more rest. She's even going to take a vacation. As a matter of fact, we all are."

Logan entered the room, just as Garrett kissed Libby on the cheek.

"I'll be back tomorrow. Until then, you remember what I told you."

"I know. Do what the doctors tell me and don't worry about Mom."

Garrett smiled then exchanged glances with Logan. Without saying more, he left the room, watching only briefly as Libby hugged her father and grandmother.

"So, now what, Dad?" Elliott asked.

"Anne's sleeping. She probably will be out of it for the rest of the night. They have her heavily sedated. As soon as Mark and Marcia get here, we'll go home and get some rest ourselves."

"Sounds good to me. Do you think Libby's dad will try to get her permanently?"

"He may try, but it won't happen. If Logan pushes the issue, Ken and AJ, will make the judge see it's in Libby's best interest to stay here, where she belongs."

"He's a strange man, Dad. I don't like him. He thinks if Anne loses her sight, you won't marry her. He thinks she'll lose everything."

"He had no right to say those things to you," Garrett said, feeling the anger again rise in him.

He was still seething when they returned to the cafeteria and saw Mark, Norma, and Marcia sitting at a table with Ken and Pam. Marcia hugged him tightly, unable to control her tears.

Again, Garrett repeated the details of the accident and Anne's condition. When he finished, he turned to Ken.

"We have to do something about Logan. He wants to take Libby, permanently."

"Permanently?" Marcia questioned. "He can't, can he?"

"Not with his track record," Ken replied. "I'll see to it nothing like that happens. For now, I think we all need to get out of here and get some rest. The next few days will be difficult."

Chapter Fifteen

The world into which AJ awakened was becoming comforting. As long as she stayed in total darkness with the bandages keeping out the light, she had nothing to face, no decisions to make. With the bandages covering her eyes, she didn't have to think about Jo's death, didn't have to cope with the reality of losing her sight.

As much as she wanted to see Libby, she purposely postponed the meeting until she knew the condition of her eyes. To her surprise, Garrett agreed with her. Could there be something he wasn't telling her?

She knew she'd awakened to morning, at least she hoped she judged the time right. Someone moved around in the room and she assumed it to be Rita Sullivan, the private day nurse Garrett insisted on hiring.

"Rita, is that you?" she asked.

"You're becoming very perceptive, AJ. Good morning."

"What time is it?"

"Seven fifteen."

"When will the doctor be in?"

"In about forty-five minutes."

AJ said nothing more. She had forty-five minutes of security, forty-five minutes until she knew the truth about her sight.

Sunday seemed like a blur as she slipped in and out of consciousness, in and out of sleep induced by the pain-killing injections she'd been given. Garrett and Elliott had been with her throughout the day. She remembered talking to Marge, Mark, Norma and Marcia, remembered them telling her they would stay as long as necessary. She wondered what they meant. Nothing would ever be the same again, so why should they be willing to stay?

Garrett had been so comforting, so reassuring, but if she couldn't see, if she was terribly scarred, would he still love her? How could she survive if he drifted out of her life, leaving her totally and utterly alone?

She put her hand to her face. "How many stitches are there, Rita?"

"A lot. Plastic surgery will take care of them. You know that's what the doctors told you."

"The doctors tell me a lot of things. I don't know if I believe any of it."

"Believe all of it. Everyone has been up front with you about everything."

"I'm certain they have, but I'm so terribly afraid."

"Afraid?" Garrett repeated her word, and she realized he had entered the room. "I never thought I would hear you say such a thing. How are you this morning?"

"Anxious about having the bandages removed. What about you? Are you getting any sleep?"

"Don't worry about me. I'm doing great. I just dropped Elliott off at school. He wanted to be here, but I told him it was best to get his mind on other things."

"What about the office, the shops?"

"With the exception of the Lady Jo, everything is closed for a few days. With the amount of calls coming in, most of the key personnel are handling the switchboard there. We're installing four more temporary lines to handle it this morning."

Garrett paused for a moment. "I have something for you."

She felt him lay something heavy on her stomach and reached out to touch the stack of papers. "What is all this?"

"Telegrams from all over the country."

"I don't think I'll be able to read any telegrams." The thought of all the wonderful people who had sent them caused her to cry. What good would they do if she couldn't see to read them?. In despair, she turned her face from his voice.

"You don't know that."

"Do you?"

"I don't know either, but I can't imagine God taking your sight."

She wondered if he could feel her tremble and would realize her fear.

Changing the subject, he said, "There's a breakfast tray here. Can I help you with something? You haven't had anything to eat in two days. Try to eat a little."

"I don't imagine there's any coffee on that tray, is there?"

"Coffee wouldn't be good for you. There's some milk. It will ..."

"Be good for me?" she finished his sentence. "You know I loathe milk."

"Take a sip anyway. It's good for you."

She could hear him tear the paper from the straw and assumed he'd put it into the glass.

"Now, give this a try," he said, touching her lips with the straw.

In an attempt to appease Garrett, she took a sip. The cold and creamy tasting milk slid down her throat, surprising her. It actually tasted good.

"Do you want some more?"

"Let me see how this sets, first. When they take off the bandages, will Libby be able to come and see me?"

"Now you're changing the subject, but yes it's all arranged."

"Will all of my stitches frighten her?"

"No. She has stitches in her face, too. You'll both require plastic surgery, minor stuff."

"You and your minor stuff," AJ teased. His laughter put her at ease. If he was laughing, maybe everything would be all right. "So, where do we go from here?"

"Nowhere, until the bandages come off."

"What do you mean? What's going to happen when I go home?"

"You'll be in a wheelchair and you'll do a lot of physical therapy to get back the use of your legs. They say it will be two, maybe three, months before you'll be able to walk without assistance."

"What do you mean by assistance?"

"You'll use a walker."

AJ wrinkled her nose. "I guess you'll just have to start calling me 'Granny'." She hoped her voice sounded lighter than she felt.

"By that time," Garrett continued, "Libby will be back from New York."

She made no move to disguise her fears. "Back from New York?"

"She's going back with Logan and Marge. Logan is making the arrangements at school this morning."

"How long? How long will she be gone?"

"She'll be going back with them now and will finish the school year out there. Then at the end of the summer, she'll be back home."

"She can't go. He wants to take her away from me."

"Not a chance. You're not an unfit mother. Her going there will work out perfectly. It will give you time to heal. By the time she comes home, you'll be back on your feet."

AJ could feel the fight drain from her body. "Whatever you say. It doesn't seem like I have much choice in the matter."

She heard footsteps and instinctively turned her face toward the door.

"Good morning, AJ," Dr. Henley said. "It's time for the moment of truth."

"I don't know if I want to do this."

"Of course, you do."

Gently he began cutting away the bandages. "We're going to darken the room. Your eyes will be very sensitive to the light."

She touched his hand to stop him. "Before you go any further, there are some things I need to know. Garret says you removed a lot of glass from my eyes. How much was there?"

"About a hundred and fifty shards in each eye. There were some cuts, that's why we covered your eyes. We were able to repair the damage, but you needed time for it to heal before you tried to use your eyes. At the worst, you'll need to wear glasses."

"I can accept that. Are you certain I won't be blind?"

"Positive."

She put her hand back on the bed, allowing him to continue his work. Feeling the pressure of the bandages lessen, she held her breath. Now all that was left were the gauze pads, which covered her eyes. She felt the coolness of the air when first one pad and then the other was removed.

"Open your eyes, AJ," Dr. Henley instructed.

"I'm scared."

"I'm right here, Honey," Garrett said, taking her hand in his.

Slowly, she opened her eyes. "It's a little blurry, but I can tell you're a redhead, Doctor."

The tension was relieved. The longer her eyes were uncovered, the clearer things became. She could see Garrett smiling at her and realized it was the most beautiful sight in the world.

The doctor then took a small flashlight and looked into her eyes. "That's what I wanted to hear," he said. "I don't see any permanent damage. I'm giving you these dark glasses. The light will be an irritant for a while." He placed the glasses over her eyes.

"I want a mirror."

Rita handed her a compact and she looked at her reflection. "I don't think I'll be winning any beauty pageants, but it's not as bad as I anticipated. You must have learned to embroider at your mother's knee, Doctor. I could use you at the factory."

"Don't praise me for your stitches. A plastic surgeon worked on your face, while I concentrated on your eyes. The stitching is good. The scarring should be minor. I wouldn't even consider plastic surgery for a year, if I were you."

AJ nodded. She wasn't pleased with her appearance, but it didn't appall her either.

"I think there's someone here to see you, Honey," Garrett said.

"Libby?"

"I'll go and get her." Garrett turned and went to the door. Once he held it open, a nurse wheeled Libby into the room.

AJ watched as her daughter's frown turned into a wide smile. "Oh, Mom, I'm so glad to see you."

AJ touched Libby's cast. "You'll never know how good it is to say I'm glad to see you."

"You can see?"

"You bet I can. These doctors did a great job. Garrett tells me you're going to New York with your Dad and Grandma."

"Daddy says I'll be finishing the school year in New York, but I'll be back before school starts next fall. I don't want to leave you." Tears rolled down Libby's cheeks as she got out of the chair and hugged her mother tightly.

"I'll be just fine and your Grandma will have a wonderful time spoiling you rotten."

They allowed Libby and AJ a few minutes alone. Then, as though he could read her mind, Garrett insisted AJ needed to rest and so did Libby. Although she didn't want to let her daughter out of her sight, AJ knew they were both tiring.

"I'm going to let you get some rest," Garrett said, as he kissed her on the cheek. "I have a meeting with Ken in the cafeteria in half an hour. I'll be back later."

Garrett anticipated an argument from AJ, but when none came, he left the room. As he did, he realized he needed to rest more than AJ. She had been sedated. She didn't have to worry about the things that weighed heavily on his mind.

At the cafeteria, he chose toast and coffee then went to a corner table where he could be alone.

"Mr. Lanners," someone said from behind him. When he turned, he was surprised to see Libby's doctor, Tina MacArthur.

"Have a seat, Doctor. Is something wrong?"

"Nothing is wrong," she assured him. "I just came from a meeting with Libby's father. He suggested I speak with you as well. Under normal circumstances, I would be releasing Libby today, but as we both know, these are not normal circumstances. Even though she could go home, she has no home to go to. Her life has been turned upside-down. Libby's father and I are in agreement on this. It would be in Libby's best interests if she could put this all behind her for a while."

Garrett nodded. He agreed with Dr. Mac Arthur, but he'd hoped to postpone the inevitable. "How soon before he plans to take her back to New York?"

"They'd like to leave tonight, especially since Libby was able to see her mother this morning."

"I knew they'd be leaving soon, I just didn't expect it to be today. There's so much we need to do. We'll just have to work a little faster. Mrs. Bergendahl's will has to be read and since Libby is mentioned, it will have to be done today. Do you see any problem with Libby being there?"

"No. She's accepted what has happened very well. I do believe she will recover much quicker if she is away from here for a while, though."

"I agree. It will be difficult for her mother, but she knows it is for the best."

Garrett refilled his coffee. He reenacted this morning's events in his mind, while he waited for Ken to arrive.

Ken, like everyone else, was concerned about AJ and eager for information about AJ's condition. When Garrett told him about her sight, a broad smile crossed his lips. It quickly disappeared when he learned of Logan's plans to leave for New York in a matter of hours.

"Do you have the will with you?" Garrett asked.

"No, but I can have it delivered here. Look, you said Dr. MacArthur told you Libby was up to this, but what about AJ?"

"She'll have to be," Garrett sighed. "Logan isn't giving us any other options."

Garrett and Ken tentatively entered AJ's room. Behind the dark glasses, it was hard to tell if she was awake or asleep.

"I'm not sleeping," she said, breaking the silence. "Is something wrong?"

"No," Ken said, as he bent to kiss her cheek.

"Don't give me a snow job, Ken. The only reason the two of you would show up here together is trouble. So, what is it?"

"I just had a meeting with Libby's doctor," Garrett explained. "She feels Libby should be released and sent to New York. She thinks ..."

"She thinks?" AJ interrupted. "Don't you mean Logan thinks?"

"Logan only asked when Libby could be discharged. It was Dr. MacArthur who felt it was best for Libby to put this behind her. She feels New York would be familiar surroundings, and yet far enough away from the reality of what happened here for her to heal."

"I don't like it, but it does make sense. There are too many bad memories for her here."

"We want to read Jo's will this morning," Ken advised her.

Garrett watched AJ's reaction, closely. He didn't miss seeing her tense, and knew reading Jo's will would bring the reality home.

"Whatever you say," she said, with a sigh.

"We've already called upstairs to have Libby brought down. We'd wait until you were stronger, but Logan and Marge are taking her to New York this evening. It's important for Libby to be here. I doubt if you knew it, but Libby is one of the heirs to Jo's estate."

Within minutes, Logan appeared with Libby. Garrett knew it was the first time AJ had seen him in six years. He had no doubt the encounter would bring back painful memories of their life together.

"I hear you're taking Libby to New York, tonight," she greeted him. "What about her arm, her stitches?"

"We've been given the names of good doctors in New York and have already contacted them."

"It's only until the end of the summer, Logan," she warned.

Garrett recognized the tone in her voice. He'd heard it when she talked with shippers who didn't get her products to their destinations on time.

"Mother and I have already been to Libby's school to explain things. When we talked to the principal this morning, she assured us Libby could finish the year by mail. We'll make certain her assignments are done on time.

It was Ken who interrupted their exchange. "This will be short. I know it's soon, but Jo's holdings are too large to be in limbo for any length of time."

Garrett watched as AJ nodded and seemed to listen intently, as Ken continued.

"Jo was in my office on Friday and rewrote her will. She also addressed this letter to you and Libby."

Before he began to read the letter, he, like Garrett, tried to read the expression behind AJ's dark glasses.

Slowly, he began to disclose the contents of the letter Jo left for AJ and Libby.

"To my dear AJ and Libby,

If you're reading this letter, I'm no longer with you. Please forgive me for not telling you, but I needed to continue my life without the threat of your sympathy. I love you both and although I know you will be sad at first, I want you to remember all of our good times. Please do not plan a big funeral. I want to be cremated and have my ashes scattered, as I scattered Paul's ashes, on the ranch. In that way, I will be free to watch over those I love for eternity."

If Libby understood the words, the only expression that confirmed her comprehension was a single tear rolling down her cheek.

AJ, on the other hand, wept openly. Garrett knew the tears would sting her already sensitive eyes, but he was aware they were cleansing for her.

"Jo never liked saying good-bye," she whispered, clutching his hand tightly.

Ken waited until AJ was more composed then began to read the will.

> "I, JoAnna Clarke Bergendahl, being of sound mind, do hereby set my hand to this, my last will and testament. To AJ, I leave control of the franchises, the Jo's dress shops at the lodge, in town, and in Denver, as well as full ownership of Fashions By AJ.
>
> "To Elizabeth JoAnna Prescott, I leave the Lazy B Ranch as well as the Lady Jo. Both enterprises are to be administered by Garrett Lanners until Libby reaches the age of twenty-five, or until Garrett sees fit to relinquish his guardianship."

"That can't be right!" Logan shouted. "I'm Libby's father, what right does Lanners have to oversee her future?"

"Look Logan," Ken countered. "The only reason we allowed you here was because of Libby. You're her father and AJ thought you should know what the will contained. You have AJ to thank for being so generous. I told her you had no right to be here whatsoever. Garrett is Jo's choice. He's the executor of the estate. Had Jo lived longer, Garret would have been Libby's step-father long before the reading of this will was ever necessary."

"It galls me to see some gold-digging bastard getting rich off my daughter. For all I know, she'll have nothing when she comes of age."

"Stop it, Logan!" AJ shouted. "Stop it! I'll not have you talking that way." It was evident to everyone in the room she was becoming overwrought.

"Please, Daddy," Libby pleaded, "Garrett ..."

"Shut up. Everybody just shut up!" Logan said. "I didn't mean ..."

Garrett put his hand on Logan's arm and without saying anything, pushed him toward the door. Once outside, he pinned Logan against the wall.

"Look, Logan, if Anne wanted to she could get a court order to restrain you from taking Libby to New York tonight. She does have custody. I know, for a fact, that she wouldn't do something like that for fear of hurting Libby. If she even tried, I would probably tell her not to do it. I love Libby like my own daughter. There's no way anyone associated with Anne would ever want to hurt her daughter. It's not because she has suddenly become a very wealthy little girl, but because she's Libby."

When he paused to take a breath, Logan took the opportunity to speak up. "Don't give me your bullshit. You're using AJ just like I used her. She's wealthy a woman. She can support you well ..."

Before he could finish, Garrett's fist connected with Logan's jaw. The unexpected blow dropped Logan to his knees.

"You'll be sorry you did that, Lanners." Logan threatened.

"Don't even think about it," Garrett warned. "It's your word against mine. If you go too far and even consider hurting AJ, I'll ruin you. That's not a threat, it's a promise."

They were so engrossed in their confrontation neither had seen the doctor hurrying into AJ's room, nor the security guard who now stood behind them.

"Is there a problem, Mr. Lanners?" he asked.

"No problem at all," Garret replied. "Mr. Prescott tripped on an untied shoelace. He'll be just fine." He reached down to help Logan to his feet. "Isn't that right, Logan?"

"Yes, Mr. Lanners is right," Logan agreed.

"Whatever you say," the guard said, taking note of Logan's slip-on tennis shoes.

Garrett returned to AJ's room, surprised to see Libby was gone. They'd only been down the hall a short way, but he'd seen no one wheel her out. Rita, too, was gone, although Ken stood silently by the door, while a doctor bent over AJ's bed.

"Rita took Libby back to her room," Ken said, his tone hushed. "What happened with Logan?"

"I decked him, but that's off the record. Officially, he tripped on his shoelace. What are they doing to Anne?"

"They're sedating her."

The doctor turned toward Garrett and motioned him to come over. "Mrs. Prescott wants to see you."

"Garrett," AJ's words were already slurred as the sedative took hold. "What happened?"

"Nothing, Honey. Logan was understandably concerned about Libby's future. He knows she'll be taken care of."

AJ nodded and gave into the sedation, slipping off to sleep. When he was certain she slept soundly, Garrett left her room.

"Now what?" Ken asked.

"I'm going to see Libby. I'll talk to you later."

Garrett left Ken standing in the hallway, as he made his way to the elevators. When the door opened on the fifth floor, he met Rita.

"Are you going to see Libby?"

He nodded his answer.

"Her father is with her. What happened?"

"He tripped on his shoelace. What did he tell Libby?"

"He said he tripped on his shoelace."

Garrett laughed. "Good. Is she terribly upset?"

"A bit, but not enough to worry about. She's too young to understand all that went on today. I'm going back down to AJ now."

"Why don't you grab some lunch first? She's been sedated. She won't need you for a while."

Without waiting for an answer, he made his way to Libby's room. Marge answered his knock. By her look, he knew she wondered what his presence meant.

"I'd like to see Libby," he said.

Marge nodded, opening the door to admit him to the room.

"Oh, Garrett," Libby cried. "I didn't think you would come. I thought maybe Daddy wouldn't let you."

"Give us more credit than that, Champ. I wouldn't miss saying good-bye. As for your Dad, he told me to come up, since I won't be seeing you until the end of the summer."

"Will Mom be all right?"

"I promise she will. It was a difficult meeting. By the time you get back from New York, she'll be just fine."

"You and Daddy were fighting, weren't you?"

"We had a minor disagreement," Garrett assured her, his eyes meeting Logan's. "We're both tired. Your dad is only worried about your future. I can't blame him. He hardly knows me. We understand each other much better now, don't we Logan?"

"Yes, Libby," Logan replied, "we do. Garrett assures me you'll be well cared for."

"Now look, Champ," Garrett continued. "Your mom will need you to be strong. She'll call often, but she needs you to keep up your schoolwork and get better yourself. When you come back we'll do some heavy-duty wedding planning. You have a good trip. Elliott will be there in a month and you'll get together."

After kissing Libby's cheek, Garrett turned and left the room. It was the hardest thing he'd had to do in a long time. He certainly didn't want Libby going to New York with Logan, but he knew he had no choice in the matter.

Chapter Sixteen

Karl Jorgenson finished his rounds. It had been a difficult morning. Every patient he'd seen reminded him of Anne. Ever since he'd seen the press conference on television, she'd been on his mind.

Guilt. It's guilt that I haven't kept in touch the way I should have. I always rationalized it by saying I was busy but it was a rotten excuse.

Janet tried to lessen his guilt by telling him he wasn't alone with his neglect. They had all participated equally, had all seemed content to drift apart.

Together, they had scanned the stack of letters Janet saved from Anne. Unfortunately, he'd found little of what he was looking for. There had been one mention of Garrett Lanners, in a letter dated two years earlier. No wonder he didn't recognize the name when he heard it.

> *You'll be pleased to know,* she had written, *I've met a man and we've become very good friends. I don't know if I'll ever remarry. Garrett at least gives me someone to talk to who understands what it's like to raise a child alone. He has been raising his son, Elliott, by himself for several years. He's been a godsend.*

So few words, he thought, *and this was the man she was in love with, the man she planned to marry. I hardly knew Garrett Lanners existed.*

Garrett's words bothered him as well. *I don't think she wants you here.*

How does he know if Anne wants me there or not? Who died and made him God? What about Anne's sight? Seven o'clock tonight was a long way off. I want to know about her sight now. I won't get any information from the hospital. Garrett assured me of that much on Saturday.

On Sunday, they had driven to New Oslo, where the entire family met at the parsonage. His father's reaction saddened him. It was as though the accident happened to someone he hardly knew.

It's tragic, a real shame, he remembered Papa saying. At the time Karl did his best to keep his anger in check. Now he wondered if Anne's pregnancy affected Papa so badly or if it was her independence?

His mother had cried, but then she had cried about the divorce. Lately, she cried about a lot of things.

"So, are you going out there?" Johann had asked.

At the time, he couldn't answer his brother. He didn't know if he could or should go to see his youngest sister.

Kristen, too, cried, but as she had said, there was little she could do. He was still angry when he remembered her words. "The kids are so small and May is such a busy month on the farm. Besides, Anne never seems to want anything to do with us."

Karl was glad he had held his tongue. It made things easier, relations less strained. Anne had been right six years ago when she said Kristen didn't live in the real world. For her, reality was Lars, the children, the farm, and the church. Anne's life was too complicated, too far away, to be included in anything the family considered important.

He remained troubled as he drove from the hospital to his office. As usual his nurse greeted him.

"When Dr. Martin comes in, I'd like to talk to him," he said, when he stopped at her desk.

"Certainly, Doctor," she replied. "Is something wrong?"

"Yes, I'm afraid there is." He knew he should let it drop there, but he needed to talk to someone. "Over the weekend, I had word my sister was in a car accident. I've been debating going to be with her."

"I'm so sorry." Her concern, he knew, was genuine. She had been with him for ten years and they had a good working relationship. Without having to be asked, she added, "your schedule is very light this week. If you decide to go, I should have no trouble clearing it for you."

After thanking her, he entered his office. He looked at the papers on his desk, but found he couldn't concentrate on them. Instead, he called the travel agent and made reservations to Crystal Creek. He was staring into space when Jeff Martin entered the room.

"What's wrong, Karl? You look like hell," he said.

"I haven't had a very good weekend. On Saturday, I had word my sister was in a car accident."

"Kristen?"

"No, my youngest sister, Anne," he said. He'd momentarily forgotten Jeff met his family two years ago when he and Janet put on a tenth anniversary party, including family and friends.

"I thought there was just the three of you," Jeff's voice sounded bewildered.

"Most people do."

"I'm very sorry. Where did the accident happen?"

"Crystal Creek, Colorado." He paused, wondering if he should say more. "You see, my sister goes by the name of AJ."

"My God, I heard about that accident. The news has been full of it all weekend. How is she?"

"You know as much as I do. I'm supposed to wait until tonight for a phone call from the family spokesman, Garrett Lanners. I don't even know if Anne will see again."

Jeff nodded. "The press is making a big thing about a fashion designer without her sight. I'm still in a state of shock. I didn't ever think she could possibly be your sister."

"No one does. She left home a long time ago. We haven't been particularly close."

"If she was my sister, I'd be screaming it from the rooftops. All I ever hear is how much my wife would like one of her designs."

Karl had never thought of telling people about Anne being his sister. It was as though for the past twelve years she had been rebellious, wild, as Papa said. Her pregnancy and divorce had shamed them all.

"From what I've read, she has quite a mail order business. I'll try to get you a catalog while I'm there."

"From what you've read!" Jeff echoed. "I can't believe you'd say such a thing! Your family is so close ..." He said no more, as though at a loss for words.

"I'm flying out there today. I called the travel agent and was able to get a flight at noon to Denver and then a commuter flight to Crystal Creek. I'll be getting in at about three and going straight to the hospital."

"Look," Jeff said, "I have a friend in Mankato who has a private plane. Let me see if he can get you to Minneapolis. It would save at least an hour and a half on the road."

Karl waited while Jeff called his friend and confirmed he could leave at ten thirty. It would give him an hour and a half to get home and have Janet drive him to Mankato.

Before leaving, he called home. "I've decided to go to Crystal Creek," he announced when Janet answered the phone.

"I thought you might. I've already packed a bag for you. Are you going to ask Johann to go with you?"

"No. If she's going to reject anyone let it be me. I just have to go out there and see for myself what's going on."

"I understand, but will the rest of the family?"

"At this point I don't care if they do or not. I'll be home in about twenty minutes. I have someone flying me from Mankato to Minneapolis, so be ready to take me to the airport."

The flights were smooth and uneventful. The planes were relatively empty, allowing Karl to be alone with his thoughts without the benefit of a seatmate who would require him to participate in trivial conversation.

At last he arrived in Crystal Creek. As he drove from the airport to the hotel, he was awed by Colorado's natural beauty. For the first time, he understood Anne's love for this country. He thought of the mountains of Norway. They held their own beauty, their own magnetic pull, but they couldn't rival the panorama spreading before him now.

Once he checked in at the hotel, he went directly to the hospital. It was a small hospital, like the one he was accustomed to at home. He liked the family atmosphere of a smaller facility.

"May I help you?" the young woman at the reception desk asked.

"Yes. I'd like the room number for Mrs. Prescott, please."

"May I have your name?"

"My name?"

"Yes, Sir, your name."

He wondered what his name had to do with anything. "It's Jorgenson, Karl Jorgenson."

The girl looked at a typewritten sheet taped to the desk. "I'm sorry, I don't find your name on my list, Sir."

"List?"

"The list of people authorized to see Mrs. Prescott."

"Perhaps I didn't make myself quite clear. My name is Dr. Karl Jorgenson," he heavily emphasized the word doctor.

"I'm sorry Doctor, but your name is not on my list."

"What in the hell are you talking about? What is this damned list?"

The woman was obviously becoming frustrated. "The approved list of people authorized to see Mrs. Prescott, as well as the approved list of authorized personnel."

"Just who approves this list?"

"Mr. Lanners and Mr. Aubrey. I've just double checked both lists and your name does not appear on either of them."

"If that isn't a line of crap. I want her room number and I want it now!."

"The young lady told you she's not authorized to give you that information. Now just who in the hell are you, anyway?"

Karl turned to face the person who was speaking to him. It didn't surprise him to see Garrett Lanners standing behind him.

"I'm Karl Jorgenson."

"You amaze me, Doctor," Garrett said, shaking his head. "What is there about the word 'no' you don't understand? I told you, Anne doesn't want to see you."

"Yes, you told me, but Anne didn't. I want to hear it from her."

"I can't let you see her, just now. It's been a very trying day."

"Her eyes?" Karl questioned.

"Come with me to the cafeteria, where we can talk. I could use a cup of coffee and I'm certain you could as well. I'll tell you what's been going on with Anne. I'd rather not talk about things here in the lobby."

Once at a secluded table in the cafeteria, Karl again inquired about Anne's eyes.

"She has her sight. What's left is the healing process. This just isn't the best time for you to see her, at least not today."

"What do you mean not today?"

"She was very worried. The positive results came as a relief. Then Logan decided it was best to take Libby back to New York tonight. I don't know how he did it, but he got her doctor to agree with him."

"Maybe he's right," Karl said, trying to see things from a physician's point of view. "It's best she recuperate in familiar surroundings. Thank goodness she has a place to go where she won't be reminded of what happened to Jo and her mother."

"I guess I'm dense, but I think it would be better for her to be here. Unfortunately I was outnumbered."

"As an outsider, I can see both sides. Had I been her doctor, it would have been a hard decision to make. How did Anne take it?"

"She accepted it. I think she felt it was inevitable and was too tired to fight it." Garrett paused and took a drink of his coffee. "Her lawyer, Ken Aubrey, decided he should read the will before Libby left."

"Why? Libby is just a child."

"Anne and Libby were Jo's primary beneficiaries. She left everything to do with the fashion industry to Anne and the ranches to Libby. Since I'm the executor of the will, it was Jo's decision that I should administer Libby's assets until she reaches the age of twenty-five. Unfortunately, your former brother-in-law didn't agree with Jo's wishes. He'd anticipated Libby's inheritance, but at the same time, he thought he should be the one to oversee it, perhaps even skim off the top for all I know. I don't understand Logan Prescott. I'd hoped I'd never have to deal with him again. Unfortunately, there was a scene. Things were said and done which I'm not proud of being a party to."

"And Anne?"

"They sedated her. They assure me they'll keep her sedated until morning. As for Libby, I'm sure she's on a plane to New York by now."

Karl felt almost close to the man who sat across the table from him. "You do care for them, don't you?"

"I told you as much on Saturday. I'm going to marry Anne and be a father to Libby."

"What if she would have been blind?" Karl considered the question necessary, yet he asked it almost hesitantly.

"It wouldn't have made any difference. You see, I didn't meet and fall in love with AJ. The woman I want is Anne."

Garrett's comment confused Karl. "I meant to ask you about that. No one calls her Anne, but us."

"We were in the Denver airport. I was taking my son to fly to New York to be with his mother. Anne was taking Libby to go to the same city to be with Logan. When I asked her name, she said it was Anne, for today it's Anne. Libby said something about AJ, but I didn't pay much attention. I had met a very frightened young woman by the name of Anne. I hesitate to say it was love at first sight, but that's just about what it was. It took a long time to get past her hurts and fears, to get her to understand just how special I consider her. I've never called her AJ and she's never asked me to. AJ belongs to her customers and her franchises as well as the public. Anne belongs to me. Anne can be herself with me, and I don't think she's been herself with anyone but Jo since she became AJ."

"I've been having some very judgmental thoughts about you, Lanners. I couldn't understand why Anne never mentioned you in her letters. I found one mention in a letter of two years ago."

"There's a lot about Anne you don't know," Garrett said, sadly. "The hurt, the sense of abandonment by her family, the person she is, are all things she keeps very deeply hidden. She works too hard, doesn't get enough rest, and pushes for deadlines. Maybe that's what I love about her. I know it's something I can change. I hope I can make her see things my way."

"How does she feel?"

"I don't know. I do know she accepted my proposal, and she says she loves me. I've known how much she means to me for years and this accident only strengthened my love. When I thought I might lose her, it devastated me. Life without her would be difficult, if not impossible."

Across the room, Karl saw a young man who resembled Garrett enter the room.

"Dad," he said, coming toward the table.

Garrett motioned for the boy to join them. "Elliott, this is Anne's brother, Karl Jorgenson. Elliott is my son."

"I'm pleased to meet you." The boy's handshake was firm.

"Dad," he said, turning to Garrett. "I went up to see Lib and her room was empty. They said Logan took her to New York. Is it true?"

"Yes, it is. Logan, as well as the doctor, thought it was for the best," Garrett replied.

"I didn't even get to say good-bye to her. It isn't fair."

"I know it's not. You can call her tomorrow at her grandma's place. I told her you'd get together this summer when you go out to see your mom."

"But what about school?"

"She took her work with her. She'll finish the year by mail."

"It's not right. She should be here with Anne."

"I agree, but you must remember this is Logan Prescott we're dealing with."

"Yah, Libby's dad. Well, she can have him. I hope I don't have to see him when I'm in New York this summer. I'd treat him respectfully, but it wouldn't be easy. Can I go up and see Anne? Did everything turn out okay when they took off the bandages? Can she see?"

"It all went well. She can see, but you can't go up to be with her just now. They have her sedated. I'll explain it all later. Why don't you grab something to eat?"

"I'm not very hungry. Maybe I'll go over to the mall. They guys wanted me to meet them there. If it's okay with you, I'll just meet you back at the apartment. I won't be late."

Garrett nodded.

"You have a fine young man there," Karl said, when Elliott left the room. "You must be very proud of him."

"Thank you, I am."

"What is he sixteen or seventeen?"

"He's fifteen. He has a very special relationship with your niece. Even with four years difference in their ages they've become best friends. Maybe it's because they're both summer kids and travel together so much."

"Summer kids?"

"Kids who spend summers with one parent and live with the other, kids who fly away on a regular basis. Elliott has been looking out for Libby on those flights ever since they first met."

"It seems you know my sister and her family better than I do. All I know is what I read in the papers. Her letters are very sterile. There's no excuse for our estrangement. We weren't close as kids, but with nine years difference in our ages it isn't abnormal. When she went to college, Papa had a hard time accepting her independence."

"I've never understood his reasoning. Anne tells the same story. I would have thought her success would be something to take pride in."

"Papa and Mama are very old-world. Girls don't go to college. They get married, they have large families, they honor their Papas, they obey their husbands, and most of all they are virgins when they get married. If their lives are hell, they endure it. If there is a divorce, it must be their fault. Anne may be successful, but she isn't like Mama and Kristen. She's wild and sinful if you listen to Papa and Johann. She's a poor lost soul if you listen to Mama and Kristin."

"What if I listen to you? What will you tell me about her?"

"Before this last weekend, I would have agreed with Papa and Johann. For the first time, I've stepped back from the family. I've looked at Anne in a different light. The newscasts, as well as you, have shown me the successful woman who is my sister. I want to get to know her."

Garrett smiled broadly. "I've prayed something like this would happen for the past five years. She needs her family. Since she's sleeping, I see no problem in taking you to her room. It's best if you get past the shock of seeing her before she knows you're here."

"What do you mean?"

"She has over two hundred stitches in her face. When she first saw them this morning, I know they shocked her. She handled it well, though."

AJ became aware of her surroundings. She felt as though she had been drugged. It certainly didn't surprise her. She'd been drugged ever since this nightmare began.

She tried to remember the last time she'd been awake. Were the bandages still in place? *No, they've been removed.* She felt an unaccustomed weight on her face. *The dark glasses. At least I have my sight.*

She didn't try to open her eyes. There was nothing she wanted to see. She only wanted to remember. Bits and snatches of the events of the morning came to her. Logan's announcement he was taking Libby to New York, the reading of Jo's will, the confrontation between Logan and Garrett, and then the bliss of sedated sleep.

"How is she doing?" she heard Garrett ask.

"It's almost time for her medication. She's been sleeping very peacefully."

The voice of the nurse sounded familiar, but it didn't belong to Rita. It must be late in the day and the night nurse had come on duty.

"If you need to get Anne's medication, I'll stay with her."

It was comforting to know Garrett cared. She wanted to talk to him, but she needed to sleep more. There would be time for talk, later, plenty of time for talk.

"You're certain she can see?" she heard a man say. At first his voice sounded unfamiliar and yet it seemed as though she knew his identity. She had to be imagining things. Karl wasn't here. He couldn't be. She vaguely remembered telling Garrett she didn't want Karl here. Garrett wouldn't have gone against her wishes.

"Yes, I'm certain," Garrett said.

"Whoever stitched up her face did a good job. She looks so small, so helpless. In the last pictures she sent, she looked so tired and drawn."

"That's what I tried to tell you earlier. I intend to see she gets more rest and slows down."

The conversation shocked her. Garrett and Karl were discussing her as if she wasn't even there. She wondered if she should let them know she was awake and aware of their presence, but decided against it. Tomorrow she would confront Garrett with his betrayal. Right now, she had no desire to see either of them.

Someone picked up her hand and lifted it to his lips. She forced herself not to react, not to show her displeasure.

"I wish you could hear me, Anne. Garrett says you don't want to see me, but I'll make you change your mind."

Never, she silently vowed. Unbidden tears sprung to her eyes and rolled uncontrollably down her cheeks.

"Anne, Anne honey, are you awake?" Garrett asked.

"Barely," she said, weakly. "Why did you bring him here? I thought I told you …"

"Don't blame Garrett, Anne. Coming here was my idea," Karl assured her.

"And your leaving is mine," she said.

"I'll be back tomorrow and every day after that until we clear the air. I'll swallow my pride, I'll beg for forgiveness, I'll do whatever it takes, but we will become family again."

"Garrett," she pleaded. "Tell him, tell him why. I don't have the strength to deal with it."

Before he could answer, the nurse returned with the sedative and asked them to leave.

"I tried to warn you," Garrett said, once they were back in the hall.

"She won't scare me away this easily. Like I said, I'll stay as long as it takes."

"Since that's how you feel, maybe you'd like to meet some of the other people who are willing to wait for as long as it takes. I'll make a few phone calls and pick you up at your hotel at seven."

* * *

"Just why did Garrett ask us to meet him here?" Marcia asked.

Around the intimate table of the restaurant's lounge, no one seemed to have the answer. Marcia, Mark and Norma, Ken, and Pam had all met at the lounge fifteen minutes earlier, but had no idea why.

"Are you sure she could see?" Mark asked.

237

"Positive," Ken replied. "The only thing I can think of is some kind of a setback after the blowup with Logan. I don't know what else it could be. I do know they're keeping her sedated."

"I can't believe that bastard," Marcia said. "How could he even think of taking Libby back to New York, when he knew AJ would need her here? I wish Garret had pulverized him rather than giving him just one punch."

Marcia's comment lightened the mood of the people around the table.

"That must have been a good joke," Garrett said from behind them.

Marcia turned and wondered if her eyes were playing tricks on her. "Karl?" she questioned. Automatically, she pushed back her chair and got to her feet. No matter what AJ said, she'd always liked Karl. He had been much less stuffy than Johann. He liked to tease her in a brotherly fashion. Of all of AJ's family, he was the one she missed the most.

Karl couldn't help the smile that crossed his lips as he recognized Marcia. Her immediate acceptance took the edge off Anne's rejection. As he hugged her, he remembered the girls as they had been during childhood. They had always been inseparable friends and it seemed adulthood had not changed their status. The memories triggered tears he felt too manly to shed earlier.

"This is Anne's brother, Karl Jorgenson," Garrett said, once Karl regained his composure. "Karl, this is Ken Aubrey, Anne's lawyer, and Pam Evans, her secretary. You know Mark and Marcia and this is Mark's wife, Norma."

Karl shook hands with everyone at the table then pulled up a chair to join them.

"Does this mean the rest of your family will be coming out to be with AJ?" Ken asked.

Karl shook his head sadly. "I'm sorry to say it, but no. This accident has opened my eyes, made me realize what I've been missing by not knowing her. I tried to make Papa, Johann and Kristen see it, but they still can't get past the hurt her career, marriage and divorce has caused."

"You can?" Mark inquired, his tone one of accusation.

"I want to."

"Have you tried to see her?" Pam questioned.

"Tried is the word. First I couldn't get her room number, then I had to get past Garrett. I went up just to see her, assuming they had her sedated, but she was awake. She wasn't happy about having me here, but I plan to change her mind."

"Where's Elliott?" Marcia asked.

Her question relieved Karl. He wanted the focus of the conversation to be off him and onto more neutral ground.

"I went to the mall to pick him up," Garrett explained, "but he didn't want to come. He decided he'd rather spend time with his friends at the arcade then eat at the pizza place. He said his friend, Josh, would see he got home. His dad was planning to pick the boys up at eight-thirty."

"Your table is ready, Mr. Lanners," the hostess said, breaking up their conversation.

Chapter Seventeen

"I think you're being unreasonable," Garrett said the next morning, as he sat by Anne's bed. "Karl is making the effort. It was his idea to come out here."

"His idea is about eleven years too late. I told you before I don't want to see him. If you're so taken with him, let him be your brother. Why don't you just give him some brotherly advice and tell him I want him to go back to Minnesota?"

"You don't really mean that. Sooner or later you're going to relent and allow him to see you. I've gotten to know him and I like him. He is sincere. Give him a chance."

"You aren't giving me a choice, are you?"

Garrett began to smile. "What do you think? You know there isn't much I deny you, but you're both missing something special by not knowing each other."

AJ closed her eyes. "All right, but later. I need to get used to the idea. Is Marcia here? I'd like to see her first."

"She wasn't here when I came up, but she said she'd be in by eight."

"What about the shops and the factory?"

"We closed down everything except the lodge and the shop there. We decided to reopen today. I have meetings set at the plant and the Crystal Creek shop this morning. Mark is meeting with the people at his factory as well as the Denver shop."

"Sounds like you don't need me at all," AJ said, pouting.

"Not until you're up to it, then watch out. You'll have more to do than you bargained for." He paused for a moment making her wonder if there was something else he wanted to talk about.

"There's something I've been meaning to talk to you about," he finally continued. "I think you should hire an assistant."

"An assistant?"

"Yes. You're going to have a lot more to do now. You'll be doing Jo's work, as well as your own. With another designer, you can increase the lines."

"There's no more room at the studio," she argued.

"We'll build a small studio at the plant."

"We can't afford to hire another designer."

"We can't afford not to. Jo and I were talking about it last week. She was planning to bring the subject up to you. The final word would be yours. We both know you need to slow down. I don't want you ending up like Jo and that is just what will happen if you keep up the pace you've set for yourself."

AJ thought for a moment. "You're right. You're always right. But I want to be able to pick the designer and personally oversee her work for the first year."

"Agreed," Garrett said, before he kissed her lovingly. "I knew you'd see it my way. I've got to run, but I'll send Marcia in to keep you company. I'll be back later and I promise Karl won't be in until you're ready."

AJ watched him leave. He was asking too much. She could accept an assistant and had been thinking about it herself ever since she accepted Garrett's proposal. Once they were married her twelve-hour days would have to end. After twelve years, she deserved to slow down and she did feel she could use some new ideas. She needed to protest if for no other reason than to show Garrett she was still in command of her senses.

As for Karl, could she accept him? If she did, would she betray the hurt she carried for so long? *Damn it. I do love Karl. I love them all. I was never good enough for them, never what they wanted.* She longed to cry, but remembered the sting of yesterday's tears and willed herself to remain dry eyed.

Karl sat in the small waiting area down the hall from AJ's room, with Marcia. They had been talking for a few minutes when Karl turned the conversation to AJ.

"Anne's a very successful, very powerful woman. What if Garrett is wrong? What if she won't see me at all?"

"If Garrett can't talk her into it, I'll give it a try. Don't worry, Karl, you'll get to talk to her. Deep down, I know she loves all of you. She's just had trouble showing it when none of you seemed to care."

"I couldn't agree more," Garrett said, as he joined them. "I think she's getting used to the idea of having Karl here."

Karl watched as Garrett turned to Marcia. "She wants to see you. I told her I'd send you in, if you were out here."

"Did you tell her about the new designer?" Marcia asked.

"Yes. She pretended to be mad about it, but I think she's been considering it herself. She gave in too easily."

"Well, it's a first step. I'll see you two later. I'm anxious to talk to her."

Karl waited for her to leave before turning to Garrett. "Did Anne agree to talk to me, or is that just something you said to appease Marcia?"

"She agreed, but asked me to have you wait until she got used to the idea. Before you do see her, I think you ought to get to know her."

"What do you mean, 'get to know her'? She's my sister. I've known her all her life."

"No, Karl, you know Anne. You don't know AJ and AJ is the woman you'll be meeting later. Very few people actually know Anne. I have appointments set up at the factory, the Crystal Creek Shop, and the lodge before the press conference at noon. I think it's best if you accompany me to see what I mean."

From the hospital, they drove the short distance out of town to the Fashions By AJ factory. The building was a new two-story unit with windows on both floors. To the front, a smaller one-story building was attached, also studded with large windows. The lettering between the windows read, Fashions By AJ.

Garrett parked is car in the already full lot in front of a plaque which read G. Lanners. The next two empty stalls read AJ and J. Bergandahl.

"This is where we start," Garrett said, turning off the ignition.

"Her designs are produced here? I never imagined such a large operation."

Together they entered the one story building. Karl was surprised to see Pam sitting at the reception desk, answering the phone. Behind her, 11x14 pictures of AJ and Jo greeted each visitor.

"Fashions By AJ," Pam said, sounding a bit weary. "They just walked in, Ken, just a minute." She handed the phone to Garrett and acknowledged Karl.

"I thought your office was up at Anne's studio," Karl said.

"These last few days, my office has been wherever I'm needed. Today it's here, tomorrow, who knows? I'm only helping out so Leslie can go to the meeting."

Garrett hung up the phone and Karl followed him down a corridor to a large lunchroom where men and women were crowded around the long tables. The room buzzed with conversation, but when they entered everyone became silent.

"It's good to see you all here this morning," Garrett began. "We wanted to tell you what's going on before it hits the press. AJ's eyesight is not impaired."

A sigh of relief sounded through the room and Karl realized his sister was not only respected as an employer but someone they considered a friend.

"You must be AJ's brother," a woman in a wheelchair said. "I heard you were in town. I'm Colette Rollins."

Karl took her hand, remembering the story about the Olympic skier who had been paralyzed in a tragic accident. The story Jo told them when they first met. "Karl Jorgenson," he replied. "Word certainly spreads quickly here."

"It does when it concerns AJ. I'm sure you know what Garrett is going to say. Would you like to see the plant?"

Karl nodded and pushed her chair from the crowded room.

"As you can probably tell, this plant has been expanded many times. When we first started all we had was the reception area. The growth has been phenomenal. The offices are on the other side of the reception area. The first floor houses the original line, Fashion Knits By AJ and Fluffy Fashions By AJ. The top floor has AJ'S Junior Fashions, AJ'S Teen Fashions, and the mail order phones. Behind us here is the shipping department. We run two eight-hour shifts, five days a week, year round, and most of our people stay on. In other words, our turnover is very low."

"And none of this existed before Anne came out here?"

"Right. This was Jo's dream and when it came true it was a godsend to this area."

"I wondered where you two went?" Garrett said. "Has Colette given you the grand tour?"

"Pretty much so. It's hard to believe Anne is responsible for all of this. Do all of the people in there work for Anne?"

"Correction," Colette said, "work with her. There's hardly a job here she hasn't done when it's been necessary. With the exception of working on the loading dock, she can step in anywhere."

"I'm sorry to break this up, but we have to get on to the shop," Garrett interrupted. "Several people want to see Anne, Colette. I'll leave it up to your discretion who they are. Just get me a list so I can approve them. It will be a few days, though."

Throughout the morning, they drove from the plant, to the shop, to AJ's studio. Karl remained in a state of shock. No matter how impressive the shop and the plant had been, he could not have prepared himself for Anne's studio. Here, her personality shone through. Her wall sported her diploma and several awards she'd received. Next to them, a U.S. map with colored pins marking franchise locations attested to her success.

Garrett said nothing as Karl walked around the office, touching each piece of furniture as though trying to touch AJ's soul. He paused at the drawing table and studied the half finished sketches, before moving on to her desk.

"So this is her world," he finally said, sitting down in the leather desk chair.

"Yes. As you said, this is her world. There's something else you should see."

As Garrett opened the desk drawer, Karl focused on the three-sided gold picture frame, containing a picture of Jo, one of Libby and one of Garrett and Elliott. They were Anne's family, not the people in Minnesota.

In front of the picture was a daily desk calendar open to Saturday's date. Printed across the date, he read Karl & Janet's 12th Anniversary. Maybe they were her family now, but a small piece of her remained in Minnesota. She did remember.

"I doubt anyone other than Jo and I know about this," Garrett said, handing him a photo album. "I walked in on her one day when she was feeling particularly alone. Jo was in Denver and Libby was in New York for spring break. She was looking at this and crying."

Karl opened the book, surprised to find family pictures dating back to his wedding. Every photo they had ever sent her was carefully taped to the pages of the album. She'd kept them all to comfort her, to remind her she did have a family. No wonder Garrett was so certain Anne would want to see him.

* * *

Marcia and AJ talked about everything but the subject, which was foremost in their minds.

"Look, AJ," Marcia finally said. "We need to talk about Karl."

"There's nothing to talk about," AJ replied, firmly.

"Yes, there is. Karl came out here because he's worried about you. We had a long talk last night at dinner. He wants to make amends."

"It's too late, Marcia, the damage is done. My family exists only on paper."

Before any protest could be made, the phone rang. Marcia answered saying only a few words before hanging up. Using the remote, she switched on the TV and sat next to AJ as a picture of the Lady Jo flashed on the screen.

"We come to you live from the Lady Jo Ranch. Garrett Lanners, spokesman for AJ Prescott, has a statement on the condition of Colorado's most famous fashion designer."

AJ listened as Garrett described her condition. His voice was calm, his smile reassuring.

"He made everything sound optimistic," she commented, when Marsha turned off the television.

"It is optimistic. You should have heard the press conference on Saturday when he didn't know if you would live or die."

"Every time I think of Jo, I wish I had died. How can I continue without her?"

"You don't mean that. You're tired. I'll let you get some rest and see you later."

AJ gave into her need for rest and fell into a troubled sleep, dreaming of Papa and Mama, Johann and Kristen, Karl, Garret, Logan and Libby. They were all pulling her in separate directions, all making impossible demands.

"I saw you on TV," AJ said, when Garrett entered her room, later in the afternoon.

"I'm glad it's over. Everyone is worried about you."

"I wish it would all go away."

"But it won't. Are you ready to see Karl?"

"No, but you aren't going to leave me alone until I say yes, are you?"

AJ couldn't miss the smile tugging at the corners of Garrett's mouth, the smile she so loved to see. "No, I'm not. Karl has spent the day getting to know you. I think he's better prepared than he was last night."

"Getting to know me? What do you mean by that? He's my brother. He's known me all my life."

"I can certainly tell the two of you are related. He asked me the same question. He knows Anne. I introduced him to AJ."

* * *

Karl waited while the operator placed the collect call to his home.

"Mommy, Mommy, it's someone for Daddy," Michael called, dropping the phone. "Some lady wants Daddy."

"Hello," he finally heard Janet say.

"I have a collect call from Karl, will you accept the charges?"

"Yes, yes, of course I will. Karl, how's everything going? Have you talked to Anne?"

"Only briefly. I had dinner with Marcia and her dad last night and today Garrett introduced me to AJ."

"I don't understand. If he introduced you to AJ, why do you say you haven't had a chance to talk to her in length?"

"I toured the Fashions By AJ plant, saw two of the Jo's dress shops, was given a guided tour of the Lady Jo, and spent time in her studio. Her touch is everywhere. The people here love her. She's more than the woman behind their jobs. She's a trusted friend. Anne's an extraordinary young woman. I should have known what I would find. She's special. Papa will never admit it, but Anne is the reason God brought us here from Norway."

"Listen to yourself, Karl," Janet said. "You're finding out what I've been trying to tell you for years. Do you think she'll see you?"

"Garrett says she'll agree to it, but I don't think it will be her idea. I don't care where the idea comes from, I just want to talk to her, to make things up to her. I'm sorry to cut this short, but I see Garrett coming. Be sure and watch tonight's news and I'll call you tomorrow."

"You can go up and see her now," Garrett said, once Karl hung up the phone.

"Thank you."

"Don't thank me yet. I'll give you fifteen minutes before I come to your rescue. You'll be on your own while I call Elliott."

"No need to worry about me. I can hold my own."

Karl left Garrett then went the few feet down the hall to AJ's room. He paused before entering the room. *Am I ready to see her? Can I accept it if she rejects me?*

"Anne," he said softly, as he entered the semi-darkened room. "Are you awake?"

Without answering, she turned her face toward him.

"I'm pleased you let me see you. I've been so worried."

"Look Karl, I agreed to see you to please Garrett, not you."

"It doesn't matter, because I'm going to change your mind. I've, we've, been wrong. I want you to ..."

"Want me to what, Karl? To forgive you? Forgive you for what? For playing the game?"

"Game? What game? What are you talking about?"

"Oh, Karl, you've been playing it for years and you don't even know it. You've all played it and now I've learned to play it, too. It's the game where you write sterile little notes saying absolutely nothing. They come for birthdays and Christmas and if we're real lucky they get here on time."

"Is that how it seems to you? What about Libby? What does she ..."

"You exist only on paper for her. You're Uncle Karl and Aunt Janet, who send her something for her birthday and Christmas, someone she has to write a thank you note to. If it wasn't for Mama and Papa, she wouldn't even know your last name. Do you know they've never even sent her a gift? Not even for her birthday or Christmas. All they do is send a card signed Grandma and Grandpa Jorgenson. Is that how they treat your children, Karl? Have they ever told them they love them?"

"I didn't know, honestly I didn't. I want to change things. I want to be part of your life."

He took her into his arms, but she turned away from him.

"I don't want you here. I don't want you to be part of my life."

Karl forced her to face him and took off her dark glasses. "What are you doing? I need those, the light hurts my eyes."

"You can have them back in a minute. You can have them back and I'll leave, but first I want you to look me in the eye and tell me you want me to leave. Tell me you don't want me to care about you."

AJ hesitated for a moment, while Karl held his breath in anticipation of her answer. "I--I don't ... I can't, I can't lie. I want you to care. I want someone to care. I've been so lonely, so alone."

Karl held her tightly, comforting her while she cried.

"Is it safe to come in?" Garrett asked a moment later when he entered the room.

"Perfectly safe," Karl said. "We have a long way to go, but we'll get there."

Chapter Eighteen

The first of July was fast approaching. It had been almost six weeks since the accident and Jo's death.

Over a month ago, the doctors had dismissed AJ from the hospital. Although her progress remained steady, Garrett worried about her. She refused to leave the house, conducting all of her business from the security of her studio. No amount of argument could persuade her to go to the plant, the shops or the lodge.

"I'll not have people seeing me in this damn walker. I hate the way I look. As soon as I can walk and have plastic surgery, I'll go out."

They argued about her obsession almost daily. Recently, Garrett consulted a psychiatrist.

"She needs counseling," Dr. Morgan agreed. "She has to come to grips with JoAnna's death. I've seen cases like this before. The only hope I can give you is once she gets into therapy, it will take time."

At first he said nothing, knowing she would never accept the idea willingly. He had merely taken over the more taxing tasks himself. Although he had not scattered Jo's ashes, he did see to the cremation before AJ was dismissed from the hospital.

He persuaded her to choose three of the designers who sent portfolios to interview. Jacque Kane, Sylvia Udey and Cathie

Fountain all showed the same promise AJ had twelve years earlier.

"You have to make a decision, Anne," Garrett said, as they again reviewed the interviews they had conducted over a week earlier.

"You choose, Garrett. I really don't care. They're all qualified."

"Qualified? Is that all you care about? I'd think you'd want someone you could relate to, someone you like."

"How do I know if I like them?" she shouted. "I don't even know them."

"Jo didn't know you, either."

At the mention of Jo's name, she burst into tears.

"This isn't working," Garrett declared. "You need to get some counseling. You have to come to grips with what has happened."

"And you need to get the hell out of my house. For that matter, get the hell out of my life. I got along quite nicely before I met you. I'll do the same again." AJ's voice was cold, her tone betraying her hidden anger.

"You don't mean that, Anne," Garrett said, as he tried to take her hand in his.

"Don't call me Anne," she shrieked, pulling her hand away. "Anne is dead. Do you hear me? She's dead. Only AJ exists."

Rather than upset her further, Garrett left the studio. He would call Dr. Morgan from the phone in the kitchen.

Anne sat alone at her desk. At that moment, she hated Garrett. She hated them all. With great effort, she got to her feet and made her way to the door. She slammed it shut and locked it against Garrett and the world.

When she turned back to her desk, the phone began to ring. She hadn't seen Pam at her desk and was certain she'd gone down to the lodge to have lunch.

"Fashions By AJ, AJ speaking," she answered, once she eased herself into her chair. The business tone that replaced her earlier outburst amazed her.

"Anne, Anne, is that you?"

Her heart skipped a beat as she recognized Johann's voice. "Yes, it's me. Is something wrong?"

"You have to come home immediately."

"That's impossible, Johann. Karl knows it's impossible."

"Anne, Papa passed away this morning. I haven't been able to reach Karl. You have to come. Mama wants you home for the funeral."

Johann's insistence annoyed her. She couldn't allow the people of New Oslo to see her using a walker, to be horrified by the scars on her once beautiful face.

"I can't come," she screamed. "Why can't anyone understand? Anne is dead and AJ can't make a trip of such magnitude. I just don't have the strength for it."

Without waiting for Johann's reply, she slammed down the receiver. "Papa," she sobbed. "Oh, Papa, did you ever know I loved you? Did you ever care? Were you ever proud of me?"

Sweeping her arms across the top of the desk, she sent pencils, paper clips and the three-sided picture frame clattering to the floor. The sound of breaking glass pushed her deeper into despair.

The walker stood next to her chair mocking her. With all her strength, she shoved it out of her way. Pulling herself to her feet by hanging onto the desk she took several hesitant steps toward where the picture frame lay, the glass littering the floor.

"No!" she screamed. "No!"

Pam had just returned from lunch when she heard the phone ringing. Before she could pick it up, the line stopped flashing and she assumed AJ had answered.

She paid little attention to the closed door of the studio. More than likely, AJ and Garrett were engaged in a private meeting.

Even through the closed door, AJ's cry of *Papa* sent chills up Pam's spine. She strained to hear more, but couldn't make out the words. The sound of breaking glass, things clattering to the floor and AJ's shout of *no*, brought her to her feet. Unable to open the locked door, she began to scream. "AJ, AJ, answer me AJ."

"What's going on?" Garrett asked when he appeared at Pam's side.

"I don't know. I heard glass breaking and then AJ screamed. When I tried to go in, I found the door locked."

"Stand back," Garrett said, hoping kicking open a locked door would be as easy as it looked in the movies. "I'm going to try to kick in the door. You find Rita."

To his amazement, it took only two kicks to break the lock and give him access to the studio.

AJ sat, amid the broken glass, her hands and legs bleeding from numerous cuts. In her left hand she clutched the picture of Jo. Rocking back and forth, she cried. "Jo's dead, Papa's dead, Anne is dead. Why, why, why is God doing this to me? Am I as sinful as Papa says? Should I die, too?"

Garrett snatched the jagged piece of glass from her right hand and gently lifted her into his arms. When he left the studio, Pam and Rita were just returning. AJ wrapped her arms tightly around his neck and buried her face in his chest while she sobbed.

He knew the blood on his shirt and face, as well as that on AJ's hands and legs shocked Rita. "Get her to her bedroom," she ordered. "I'll give her a sedative."

"Just grab your stuff. I'm taking her to the hospital," Garrett replied.

Turning to Pam, he continued. "No one is to know what went on here. Try to reach Karl and when you get him give him the number on the pad in the kitchen. He can reach me there."

Pam watched them leave, feeling at a loss. She wondered what had happened. What had pushed AJ over the edge? She had no time to question further, as the phone rang insistently.

"Fashions By AJ, how may I help you?"

"I want to speak to Anne. This is her brother, Johann."

"I'm sorry. AJ is away from her desk just now. May I take a message?"

"Don't give me that. I just talked to her. Now put her on the line."

"I'm sorry, Sir, but AJ is out of the office for the remainder of the afternoon."

Pam hated the lie, but she stuck to it. The shock of what she'd witnessed in AJ's studio, gave her no other options.

***

Karl was just finishing his speech. He and Janet had been in St. Louis at the medical conference for three days now and he was glad his prepared presentation was finally over. As he answered the last of the questions, he saw Janet frantically motioning to him from the back of the room. Collecting his papers, he wrapped up the session with his closing statement and hurried to her side.

"Is something wrong?" he asked, once he was close enough to see the tears in her eyes.

"When I got back from this morning's tour and luncheon, there was a message from Johann. I returned his call and he said your Papa died this morning. He said he called Anne and she hung up on him."

Karl didn't try to disguise his concern. During his last conversation with Anne, he sensed the depression in her voice. His call, later the same day, to Garrett confirmed his suspicions.

Garrett told him about the psychiatrist he talked to. It didn't take long for Karl to check the man's credentials.

From what he learned, Dr. Morgan's reputation was excellent, his approach unique. In his clinic, he combined physical healing with one of the spirit, resulting in surprising successes. Once back in their room, he placed a call to Johann.

"What happened when you talked with Anne?" Karl asked, when Johann finished giving him the details of what transpired that morning.

"I told her about Papa and told her she should come home."

"You know coming home is impossible for her," Karl said. "She hasn't left the house since she got out of the hospital. She can't even get around without her walker."

"You're being overprotective, Karl. I wasn't asking her to make a pleasure trip. She should have the decency to come to Papa's funeral. She told me Anne was dead and then she hung up on me. When I called back, her secretary gave me some line about her not being in the office. There was no sense in trying to argue with that woman. It was plain Anne didn't want to talk to me."

Karl hung up the phone. He didn't mind admitting his worry over Anne. As worried as he'd been these past six weeks, he was now more concerned than ever.

Pam's voice on the other end of the line sounded businesslike, but strained. He had anticipated a breakdown. It came as no surprise, but he'd prayed it could be avoided.

* * *

Garrett and Rita sat in the waiting room while Dr. Morgan examined AJ.

"I hope I did the right thing," he said, breaking the silence.

"Be assured, you did. She may not realize it now, but she will."

256

"Mr. Lanners," Dr. Morgan said, as he entered the waiting room.

"How is she?" Garrett asked, getting to his feet.

"The cuts were superficial. You were right. The depression is severe. We talked about it and she agreed to therapy. The fact she can't remember smashing the pictures and getting cut came as the deciding factor."

They talked about the treatment and the length of stay until they heard Garrett being paged. When he answered the phone, it did not surprise him to hear Karl's voice on the other end of the line.

"Anne can't remember much of what happened," Garrett explained. "From what I can gather, your brother called to tell her your father passed away. I'm sorry."

"Thank you," Karl replied. "Johann said he insisted that she come home for the funeral, then she became hysterical and hung up."

Garrett went on to explain the crazy events of the morning, as well as where they were. He needed a friend, someone he could confide in. He prayed Karl wouldn't betray his confidence.

"She didn't do any major damage to herself, did she?"

"She has some minor cuts on her hands and legs, but what convinced her she needed help was the fact she couldn't remember the incident."

"How long will she be at Morgan's facility?"

"About a month, give or take a few days, depending on her progress. We won't be telling people what actually happened. Other than Ken, Rita, Pam, Marge, you and me, we're telling people she's spending a month in the mountains to rest."

When he finished his conversation with Karl he returned to the ranch with Rita. Once he dropped Rita at the house, he drove into town.

His apartment seemed strangely quiet, as if it were in mourning for what happened to Anne earlier in the day. Elliott's picture on the wall opposite the door reminded him his son was in New York, spending his summer with Susan, in order to be closer to Libby. He was glad he didn't have to worry about leaving Elliott alone. As he told Dr. Morgan, he wanted to be close to Anne.

Dr. Morgan recommended a small hotel about a mile from the facility. Before leaving for the ranch, Garrett made a reservation.

Once packed, he called Marge. "I expect this to be held in strictest confidence," he said, once he finished telling her about Anne's hospitalization.

"And what do you want me to tell Libby?"

"I've given it a lot of thought. I think it's best if she thinks Anne has gone to the mountains to get some much needed rest. She'll understand the need. It's imperative the press doesn't get wind of this. I'm almost embarrassed to say it, especially to you, but Logan can't know either."

"Don't be embarrassed, Garrett. I know my son. I have wondered if Libby should consider going to school out here, at least for the first semester."

"Absolutely not!" Garrett exploded. "The worst fear Anne has is the possibility Libby won't come home. When the summer ends, Libby will return to the ranch. Under no circumstances will she remain in New York. Do I make myself clear?"

"I'm sorry. I didn't mean to hurt AJ with my idea. I only wanted to give her time to heal."

Garrett finished the conversation and hung up the phone. He wished he hadn't blown up at Marge. He'd have to watch himself or he'd end up in the same shape as Anne.

* * *

The altar of the church was filled with flowers and the organist softly played his father's favorite hymns. Beside Karl stood his mother. She looked very old and tired. In front of him were Lars and Kristin and in front of them Janet and Sharon. They were all waiting for Johann to nod for them to take their seats, so the heavy oak casket could be taken to the front of the church.

At last they were seated. The casket carrying his father's body wheeled past him and he couldn't help but think of Anne, alone in the hospital in Colorado.

Across the aisle stood the church council, who were the pallbearers. Throughout the church, women and men alike sobbed.

Karl sat dry eyed as Johann's sermon droned on and on. His emotions were in knots. He loved his father, but since he'd so recently stepped back from his family, so recently became reacquainted with Anne, he didn't know what his feelings were. Could they be called sadness or despair over the fact his father would never know Anne, never know Libby, would never be able to reconcile himself to the fact that Anne had become a very special person?

He again thought of Anne and worried. This had been the culmination of a breakdown for her and he couldn't even tell his family why she wasn't at the funeral.

Automatically, he helped his mother follow the casket out of the church and supported her at the cemetery.

Back at the parsonage, the women of the church had prepared a luncheon for those who attended the funeral. Karl accepted a plate of food he didn't want, while he stood next to his mother. Again and again he expressed gratitude to those who came to pay their respects.

Late in the afternoon, when most everyone left, a woman he recognized from church, but couldn't put a name to, came up to him. "Where is Anne?" she asked.

It amazed him the question had not been posed earlier and yet it annoyed him to hear it voiced.

"Anne couldn't come," Solveig answered, a hint of buried anger in her voice.

"But she should be here. Erik was her Papa," the woman continued.

Karl looked at her in disgust. "My sister is recovering from a tragic car accident. There is no way she could have made the trip to be here."

The woman said nothing. After embracing Solveig, she left.

"Are you telling us the real reason, Karl?" his mother asked, when she turned to him.

"Yes, Mama."

"Johann said she hung up on him."

"She was distraught," Karl said, defending Anne.

"She doesn't want to come home, Karl. Can't you see it? I thought you understood what she did."

"What she did, Mama? What did she do that hasn't been done before? She got carried away on a delightful fall afternoon in a secluded valley and had a child. When she married the man who fathered her child, she thought it would make you happy, but it didn't. You even refused to go out there for Libby's christening."

"Your Papa didn't approve. He said going would condone her actions."

"And what support did she get from any of us when he divorced her?" he pressed, his voice becoming louder as his aggravation became greater.

"But divorce is sinful, Karl. God says ..."

"For the first time in my life, I don't care what God says. Logan divorced Anne. She didn't leave him. If Papa cheated on you all your married life, would you have stood for it?"

"Your Papa wouldn't do such a thing."

"But Logan Prescott did. From the day they were married, he cheated her. He wasn't even in Crystal Creek when Libby was born. It took him two days to show up and learn he'd become a father."

"It doesn't make it right. Divorce is never right."

"You all refuse to see her for what she is. Do you understand how successful she is? I doubt it. I didn't until Garrett introduced me to AJ when I went to be with her after the accident."

"It was foolish of you to go out there."

"No it wasn't, Mama. I found my sister."

"Mama's right, Karl," Johann said, joining the discussion for the first time. "You were foolish. She's never going to come back here."

Karl knew anger radiated from his eyes. "I honestly don't blame her. What a bunch of hypocrites you all are. You stand up in church and talk about the grace and forgiveness of God and yet you can't forgive Anne."

"She never wanted to be part of us," Kristin said, siding with Johann.

"Well then, maybe I don't want to be part of us either. I've found my sister. I've met a beautiful, intelligent, wealthy, successful woman who has just now found someone who can make her life complete. She's suffered a tragic loss and she has an ex-husband who is threatening to take her daughter from her."

"Perhaps it's what she deserves," Kristin said, interrupting him. "Any woman who ..."

"Any woman who what, Kristin? Do you think she's sleeping around? I did too. I actually accused Garrett of being her lover. He said she wouldn't allow it to happen until they were married. That's the way Anne wants things. If you ask me, she's still worried about what Papa might think about her. They were planning the ceremony for just about now. A lover? Not hardly. She's lucky to have found a man who not only loves her but is a very dear friend."

Turning away from them, he made eye contact with his wife. "Get the kids ready, Janet, we're leaving."

Again he addressed his family. "I thought I was small minded, but I'm nothing compared to you."

"Do you think you should have said those things, especially today?" Janet asked, as he sped away from the curb.

"You heard them, they don't want to give her a chance. For all their self-righteousness, they can't find it in their hearts to forgive her."

"They've listened to your Papa and he was wrong," Janet commented.

"I can't see where your explanation makes things right. They're being cruel to her. It is cruelty, whether you believe it or not."

* * *

Garrett pulled into the parking lot of the hospital. Could it possibly be five days since he first brought Anne here, since he'd seen her? Dr. Morgan kept saying she wasn't ready to see him. He remembered the last words she'd spoken to him as being cold and cutting. He could still hear her telling him *to get the hell out of her life*. He prayed she'd come to feel differently. He knew he couldn't possibly begin to live without her.

He paused in front of Dr. Morgan's office, almost afraid to knock, afraid he would, again, be denied access to her room.

"Come in, Garrett," Dr. Morgan said. "I've been expecting you."

"Can I see her today?"

"Yes, I think seeing you would be good for her." Together they went to her room. When Dr. Morgan entered, Garrett hung back. Thoughts of rejection mingled with the memory of Karl entering another hospital room months ago. Would Anne be as reluctant to see him, as she had been to see Karl?

AJ propped herself up in bed. Her morning bath completed, she pondered her stay in this place. The last five days seemed very strange, very strange indeed. Although Dr. Morgan talked her into staying here, she knew Garrett was somehow behind it. How could she love someone who thought she was crazy?

She'd been so certain she knew him, but now she wondered if she ever knew him at all. Was he, as Logan said, another golddigger, out to profit from her misfortune?

She concentrated on her surroundings, not wanting to think about Garrett. As a patient here, she'd seen only Dr. Morgan and a handful of nurses. Dr. Morgan spoke to her each morning, but you could hardly call it counseling. The nurses brought meals she barely touched, gave her pills to calm her and make her sleep, and gave her back rubs.

She hadn't tried the door, hadn't gotten out of bed for more than attending to her bodily needs, and to take a daily bath.

"Good morning, Anne," Dr. Morgan greeted her as he entered the room.

"Good morning," she answered, her eyes lowered so she wouldn't have to look at him.

"Garrett's here."

AJ looked up. Did she want to see Garrett? The mere mention of his name made her mind stir with excitement. "How special for him."

"This is the first step, Anne. You have to see him sooner or later."

Afraid to show any feelings, afraid to trust the man who put her here, she sat quietly for a moment. "I'll take later, thank you," she finally said.

"You're going to see him now."

"All right, now," she replied. She certainly knew she was being given no choice in the matter. In fact, she found herself too weary to fight.

When Garrett entered the room, his appearance shocked her. He looked drawn. The dark circles under his eyes belied his lack of sleep. He said nothing, until he sat on the edge of the bed and held her hand. "I've been so worried about you."

"So worried you think I'm crazy. I'm not stupid. I know you talked me into checking myself into a mental institution."

"You can check yourself out again at any time," Garrett assured her. "No one thinks you're crazy. You just need help adjusting to everything that's happened."

"You've suffered a tragic loss," Dr. Morgan said. "Under the circumstances, anyone would need help."

"Come on, Honey, give me one of those beautiful AJ smiles." Garrett looked deep into her eyes and squeezed her hand ever so slightly. "I'm sorry it had to be this way, but I couldn't let you sit in the house and brood. I couldn't let what's happened eat at you and fester. I love you too much to loose you."

Garrett's words made the distrust dissolve. Suddenly, she wanted nothing more than to have him hold her in his arms and comfort her. "Papa's dead, isn't he?" she half whispered.

"Yes," Garrett answered sadly.

"I seem to remember talking with Johann. He wanted me to come home for the funeral. After that everything seems to get fuzzy."

"You destroyed your office and tried to kill yourself. In other words, you suffered a breakdown. I hate being so blunt, but Dr. Morgan says it's best we don't sugarcoat things. We must tell you the truth."

"Yes, I agree. I do need to hear the truth. Have you talked to Karl?"

"Every day. He's very concerned."

"What are you telling people? What are you telling Libby?"

"The official word is you needed to get away from the phones and get some rest. Libby, like almost everyone else in the world, believes you've gone to a cabin in the mountains with no phone."

AJ nodded, then turned to Dr. Morgan. "How long, Doctor? How long will I be here?"

"A minimum of a month. After that, you'll need therapy for a while as well as medication. Depression is a horrible thing. It's the deepest, darkest hole in the world. You'll find climbing out of it is far from easy."

"And after a month, then what?" AJ asked, needing a timetable, a schedule to follow.

"You'll go back to being AJ," Dr. Morgan replied.

"That's the first time you've called me AJ. Why is it everyone here calls me Anne?"

"Because it's the name you were checked in under. No matter how careful we could be, if AJ Prescott checked in, the press would know. Anne Jorgenson caused no such stir. Outside of Garrett and myself, no one knows you're AJ."

"Being aloof does have its advantages," she quipped.

"Until you're ready to face what's happened," Garrett said, "you don't need the press blowing everything out of proportion."

"Face it? Oh Garrett, I don't know if I'll ever be able to face it. How can I go on without Jo?"

"You're not without her. She'll always be with you. When you're well, we'll scatter her ashes, just as she asked."

An unbidden tear rolled down AJ's cheek. "In the valley, so she can watch over the ranch."

She took a moment to compose herself then continued. "Okay, whatever you say. When do we start?"

Dr. Morgan smiled. "Good. Up until today, you've been resting. Now you'll start working. I have a good therapist in mind for you."

"It won't be you?" she questioned.

"I see no patients and yet I see all the patients. I oversee everything. You'll find Kathleen Legion to be very qualified. You'll work with her only until she feels you're ready to meet with the group. Everyone is here for basically the same reason, depression. It's not a pretty word, but it describes the problem. They are people who have lost someone tragically, people who have been injured, as you have. We also have an excellent physical therapy team here. We'll not only ease your mind, help you cope, but we'll strengthen your body as well."

"It sounds like my life will be very ordered for the next few days. I certainly hope I'm up to it."

"You will be," Garrett assured her. "I'll be here every day."

"You've been with me since I first got here, haven't you?"

"I'm staying at a hotel close by."

"And things back home?"

Garret held her hand a bit tighter. "You're not to worry about them, but to put your mind at ease, things are running smoothly. Pam has everything under control and I check in daily by phone. I'm not so far away I couldn't be there if I'm needed."

"What about Libby?"

"She's worried about you, but she knows I wouldn't let anything happen to you. Right now, she's in Niagara Falls with Marge, Elliott, and Susan's mother."

"How wonderful." AJ realized her voice sounded strained, even to her ears. "She's not coming back, is she?"

"She'll be home by the end of August, so you'd best get your butt in gear, so you're ready for her."

"If you say so. I just find it hard to believe Logan will give up so easily. He wants her, I know he does."

"He can't have her. Ken will make certain none of this is made public. Like we told you in the hospital, there's not a court in the world that would judge you an unfit mother. As for you, young lady, you're going to do as you're told."

Little by little, AJ came to grips with her life. She made peace, of sorts, with her family. Even though she knew she would never see most of them again, she could forgive them and turn the other cheek.

At last she came home. It pleased her to be again able to communicate with the outside world. The first call she placed was to Libby.

"Oh, Mom," Libby squealed with delight, "did you enjoy your vacation?"

"It was lovely. The mountains were beautiful and with no phones, I got lots of rest. I missed talking to you, but it was worth it. I'm almost one hundred percent again."

"Do you still have the walker?"

"No, I left it behind. I'll have a cane for a couple of weeks then I'll be on my own. I've missed you so much. I can hardly wait to have you home."

"Elliott and I have reservations for two weeks from today. We'll be home soon."

AJ hung up the phone, secure in the knowledge Libby would soon be back on the ranch where she belonged.

Without hesitation, she dialed Karl's number and waited for him to answer. "Karl, it's Anne."

"Thank God. It's good to hear your voice again. Where are you calling from?"

"The studio, they have it all fixed up. No one would ever know I destroyed it. I'm sorry about Papa."

"Dying is part of life. It was his time to go home."

"How's Mama?"

"She's doing well. Johann and his family have accepted the pastorate there, so Mama is able to stay on at the house."

"And Kristin and Lars?"

"They're fine."

She noticed a strange tone to Karl's voice. "What's wrong?"

"Nothing."

"Don't start playing the game again. There is definitely something wrong. I can hear it in your voice."

"You're too observant. I haven't spoken with them since the funeral."

"Oh, Karl, don't shut them out. If you feel you must make a choice, choose those closest to you. Don't sever those relationships. Whatever words were spoken, make amends for them. I can't do that. It's been too long. I can't go home again, but you can. I refuse to be the cause of a rift between you and the family."

"You just don't understand. You don't know what they said."

"Words can't hurt me. I spent the last month finding that out. I'm sure you know where I went."

"Garrett kept me well informed. It was sheer hell not being able to come out there and be with you."

"I'm glad you didn't come. This was something I had to do for myself. I've been able to forgive them. I'll never see them again, but I've forgiven them. I've said it before and I'll say it again, if you being close to me jeopardizes your relationship with them, I'll understand if I don't hear from you again. Don't try to push me onto them. They don't want me. You came to me because you wanted to know me. They'll have to do the same."

"Morgan's place must have done you a world of good. At least you're not pushing me away by screaming at me."

The memory of their first meeting in the Crystal Creek hospital flooded her mind. "No, I'm not screaming. I'm just learning to live my life, to adjust."

"When will you and Garrett be married?"

"We're planning on the last Saturday in September. It will be nothing extravagant. Libby and Elliott will be standing up with us. We're working on writing some vows."

"I'd like to be there."

"If you come, I'd be very happy. If you can't, I'll understand. Before you make any decision, make peace with Mama, Johann and Kristin. If you can't, I don't want you here. I remember a verse I had to learn in Sunday school once. It went something like this: 'Don't try to remove the splinter from your brother's eye when there's a beam in your own.' I'm sure I'm misquoting. I have a tendency to make things sound the way I want them to, rather than how they're written. Either way, I think you know what I mean. Take the beam from your eye, Karl, make peace with the family."

* * *

With the wedding fast approaching, AJ worked on her physical therapy diligently. By the time Libby and Elliott returned home, she no longer needed her cane.

On September first, Jacque Kent arrived at the Lady Jo and began to work on the last of the spring line. AJ was pleased with her work and offered her full control of the junior and teen departments.

Midweek, just before the wedding, Karl and Janet arrived at the Crystal Creek airport. Garrett met their plane and took them to the ranch.

"Anne," Janet said, as she stepped into the studio.

AJ was on her feet and smiling as she crossed the room. "Oh, Janet, it's so good to finally see you again. I wish the children could have come as well."

"It was too difficult to take them out of school. My folks were delighted to baby-sit."

"Does the family know you're here?"

"No, they're talking to each other, but you aren't mentioned."

AJ nodded. *What did I expect, instant forgiveness, instant reconciliation?*

The Cowboy Chapel on the Lazy B was the perfect setting for the wedding. Erected by Paul Bergendahl's great grandfather over a hundred years earlier, it had originally been built as a place of quiet meditation for the ranch hands.

A few guests sat on the hand-hewn pews. Only those closest to Anne and Garrett were in attendance. At the front of the chapel, Garrett and Elliott waited for Anne and Libby to walk down the short aisle.

Libby wore a pale-peach dress and carried a bouquet of white cushion mums. As AJ watched her making her way toward the front of the church, she realized she seemed much older than her eleven years. AJ took a deep breath before she started down the aisle, escorted by Karl. Her dress was deep rust. Her flowers were gold and bronze mums. At the altar, Karl placed her hand in Garrett's and kissed her cheek.

When it came time for their vows, AJ and Libby placed their flowers on the altar and turned to face Garrett and Elliott.

In a clear voice, AJ began. "I, Anne, take you Garrett and you Elliott, to be my husband and my son. I will love you, cherish you and honor you for richer or poorer, for better or worse, in sickness and in health, as long as we all shall live."

Garrett's smile affirmed his love as he repeated the same vow to Anne and Libby.

To everyone's surprise, Libby spoke up next. "I Elizabeth, take you Garrett and you Elliott, to be my father and my brother. I promise to make you proud of me and to love you dearly, forever, as I do at this moment."

When Elliott repeated the vows and the rings were exchanged, the guests applauded enthusiastically.

Once they were back at the lodge, in the dining room, Garrett and AJ faced the press. One by one, they asked the questions needed to get their story. "Was any of your family here?"

"My brother, Karl and his wife Janet, came from Minnesota, and Garrett's sister Linda and her husband, Tom, are here from Colorado Springs."

"No one else," the reporter pressed.

"No one else," AJ replied sadly.

"What about a honeymoon, Garrett?"

"We've decided to wait," Garrett said, holding AJ's hand a bit more tightly. "It's been a trying year. There's always time for a honeymoon. We just plan to settle down and lead a quiet life."

Garrett's comment brought a chuckle from those assembled. "It's hard to believe there's anything quiet about your life, AJ," one reporter, who seemed to be at every interview AJ ever gave, said.

"Well, Janice, you know my life. It's not a quiet one. It seems this man I married doesn't approve of twelve-hour days. He wants me to slow down. I guess that's why we hired another designer. Jacque Kent joined us the first of September. You'll be seeing her designs in the spring line and then she'll be taking over the junior and teen departments. It's going to be an exciting year."

"Are you all recuperated?"

"Do you see a cane? I'm doing very well. I'll need a lot more physical therapy, but it gets easier ever day."

"Did your daughter really inherit both ranches?"

"Yes, they were Jo's legacy to her. She will be able to do anything she wants when she's of age. I can only pray she'll choose the life she's grown up with."

The questions continued until at last, Garrett called a halt to the session. "I don't want to tire my bride before she even has a chance to cut the wedding cake."

* * *

Karl and Janet were home only three days and the wedding was still overwhelming. The love Garrett held for his sister seemed almost too good to be true.

They were settling into their normal routine when Johann called. "I read you gave the bride away."

"You read right."

"Don't you think it was a bit much?"

"No. Look, I promised Anne I'd make peace with you and Mama and Kristin. It was the only way she'd let me come to the wedding. Anne is more than just my sister. She's become my friend. She doesn't want to hurt anyone. She's not asking for acceptance from you. She just doesn't want me to lose contact with the family."

"You don't need to talk to me about her."

"She doesn't want me to. How's Mama?"

"It's good she's been able to stay on at the parsonage. Remember how upset she was when we first came here and Aunt Ruth had to give up her home for us?"

"Yes, I thought about it during the funeral. What about you? Is the ministry going well?"

"I realize God meant for me to take over Papa's work here. This is where I belong."

"And Kristin and her family?"

"They're well. Did you take the children to Colorado?"

"Not this time. We plan to take them next summer and let them get to know Anne and her family."

The exchange continued and Karl considered it strained. He now knew what Anne had meant when she said she'd become tired of one-sided conversations. Johann asked curt, to the point questions, expecting his answers to be elaborate. Karl wondered what his brother wanted of him. Did he want him to say going out and getting reacquainted with Anne had been a mistake? He couldn't lie, not even to mend the rift between himself and Johann.

Libby

Chapter Nineteen

Brochures from colleges located all over the Midwest littered Libby's desk. AJ looked over Libby's shoulder at the colorful pages. They were from small colleges and large universities, Christian schools, and academic seats of learning. Each campus looked inviting, each curriculum seemed interesting.

"Any reason there's nothing from the University of Northern Colorado in that pile?" she asked. "Elliott likes it."

"You know why, Mom," Libby said, sounding annoyed. "It's the same reasons there's nothing from MIT. I want to be on my own, far enough away not to be under your thumb or Daddy's either, yet close enough to come home easily."

"Whatever you say. Just think about the University of Northern Colorado, to humor your old mother."

"Okay, Mom, I'll think about it, but don't get your hopes up. I've narrowed it down to three."

"Which ones?" AJ asked, pulling up a chair.

Libby handed her three brochures. The first one came from the University of Wisconsin, the second from Concordia, and the third from Gustavus Adolfus.

"Good choices," AJ said. "Any special reason you zeroed in on Gustavus Adolfus?"

"Other than the Christian background and the academic standards?" Libby teased.

AJ smiled. "Could it be your Uncle Karl? Is it possible you want to find the rest of the family?"

"Maybe," Libby confessed. "I'll have four years there. I'll get a good education, taking courses I really like. If sometime during that four years I get up the courage, maybe I'll look for them. If I don't, it won't matter."

As Easter vacation approached, Libby began to get acceptances from the three colleges of her choice. AJ knew none of them would be as enticing as Gustavus Adolfus. None of them had the pull of her uncle.

"I won't be here for Easter, Mom," she said, one afternoon while she was enjoying the view from the studio. "I called Uncle Karl. He said if I flew in on Saturday, he'd take me on a tour of Gustavus Adolfus on Easter Monday. I'll just fly from New York to Mankato, then come home from there."

"I won't try to change your mind," AJ said, giving her a hug. "Secretly, I'm pleased you want to be close to Karl. As for finding the family, that must be your decision. I can't make it for you."

Libby flew to New York, as usual, for spring break with Elliott. "This will probably be our last trip together, won't it, Elliott?"

"I'm afraid so, Lib. Once graduation is over, I'll be working for Eastman Kodak and next fall you'll be in Minnesota at school. We're all grown up. We certainly aren't kids anymore."

"I wish we were. I wish it would never end. I love you, Elliott." Libby leaned across the seat and kissed him tenderly.

"I love you too. I think I've always loved you, but it isn't proper. You're my sister."

Libby nodded, knowing he was right. They had spoken the vows to be brother and sister at their parents' wedding.

When the plane touched down, and they entered the terminal, they were met by Logan and Susan.

Libby knew her father had something on his mind. She also knew, or thought she knew what it was.

"Will you and Grandma be coming out for graduation?" Libby asked, knowing the question would lay the groundwork for what was on his mind.

"You know, we are. I've been wondering what your plans are? Since I know you're interested in going to college, can I push for MIT? I've arranged a tour of the campus for tomorrow."

"No, Daddy, not MIT."

"Then you're going to school in Colorado?"

"No. Uncle Karl lives in St. Peter, Minnesota and one time, many years ago, he mentioned a school there, Gustavus Adolfus. My counselor got me the information and it sounds like what I'm looking for."

"What kind of a school is it? I've never even heard of it. Are you sure you want to be stuck out there in the middle of nowhere?"

"It's a very prestigious college. It's Lutheran based. I'd be taking some religion courses."

"I don't like it, Honey. Are you sure this is what you really want? It sound so ... so stuffy."

"Yes, I really want to go there. I know I'll like it. They have courses in Scandinavian history and Scandinavian languages, along with excellent business courses."

"Is that what you want, a business education? You could get that anywhere."

"You don't understand, Daddy. I think I can get the best possible education at Gustavus Adolfus."

"I think you ought to go to MIT. Just think how close you'd be."

"That's right, Daddy, I'd be close to you, too close. I don't want to be close to you, just as I don't want to go to school in Boulder. You and Mother think I'm a piece of taffy. You pull me to New York. She pulls me to Colorado. I love you both dearly, but I need to find me."

"So, have you been accepted?"

"Daddy, I'm valedictorian of my class. I wouldn't have much of a problem being accepted anywhere."

"I suppose you're right. I'm not going to stop trying to get you to MIT, though."

"Try all you want. It won't do any good. There is nothing either you or Mom can say to change my mind. I'm very excited about going to Gustavus Adolfus."

Logan shook his head. "So, will your mother be going out to tour the campus with you?"

Libby averted her eyes, so her father wouldn't guess at her true feelings. "She's not very excited about my choice of colleges."

"I don't blame her, but don't parents usually go out and tour the campus with their kids?"

"I guess they do, but Mom's pretty busy these days, so Uncle Karl agreed to show me around."

"Good old Uncle Karl," Logan sneered. "What would your mother do without him? He's a convenient excuse to neglect you."

"Oh, Daddy, Mom doesn't neglect me and you know it. You've been telling me that every time I've come here, since I was five. I didn't believe it then and I certainly don't believe it now. She doesn't neglect me and I'm very happy."

* * *

As usual, Garrett and AJ lingered over their morning coffee in AJ's studio.

"Easter Sunday will seem quite lonely this year," AJ commented. "I know, with Libby going to Minnesota and Elliott deciding to stay in New York until Sunday, then flying straight to Boulder, it will just be the old folks at home. Would you like to get away for the weekend? We can go anywhere you'd like."

Before she could respond, the phone rang. "So it begins," she said. "Good morning, Fashions By AJ, AJ speaking."

"Well, good morning to you, too, Anne. It's Karl."

"Karl? What's up so early in the day?"

"I wanted to catch you before your day started. What are you doing this weekend?"

"Garrett and I were just talking about that, but we hadn't come to any decisions, yet. Why?"

"Janet and I want you to come out here and spend Easter with us. It would mean a lot to Libby if you toured Gustavus Adolfus with her on Monday."

"Are you planning a reunion, or would it be as you've said, just us?"

"I promise you, just us. We usually don't spend Easter with the family, as Janet and Vicki are so involved at church. No one else will be there. You know I wouldn't do that to you, as much as I'd like to. Garrett can fly that new toy of his right into Mankato."

AJ covered the receiver and discussed the proposition with Garrett. When they finished, Garrett took the phone. "We'll fly out on Friday. Just tell Janet I like my coffee black and hot."

Libby was surprised to be met by Karl and Garrett at the airport. "I didn't think you'd be here," she said, as she hugged Garrett tightly.

"Your uncle thought you might like company when you toured the college on Monday."

"Of course, I would. I just never thought Mom would come to Minnesota again, so I didn't push the issue."

"Don't try to outguess her. You know she'd do almost anything in the world for you."

Easter was a joyous celebration in Karl's church. Vicki worked with the youth in the kitchen, preparing a breakfast of baked omelets, hot cross buns, juice and coffee. To Libby's delight, her cousin asked her to join in the fun of serving the members of the congregation.

AJ and Garrett sat in the small church with Karl and Michael, while Janet sang in the choir.

"Why aren't you in the choir, Karl?" AJ asked. "As I remember, you have a great voice."

"I'd like to, but with my schedule, I can't make the rehearsals. I just like listening to Janet and the others."

"I know what you mean. Our church in town has a choir, but there just aren't enough hours in the day for me to be as active as I'd like to be. The only thing I really do there is offer to sing a solo every summer when they're in need of special music."

The next morning, Karl took them to Gustavus Adolfus. AJ gasped as the beautiful campus loomed in front of them. The brick buildings were impressive, the classrooms and physical education center were modern, and the dorms were inviting.

Although AJ had read over the brochure, she was not ready for the impression the campus made on her. She knew Libby had made a good choice.

June brought graduation and visits from Susan and her mother as well as from Logan and Marge. Libby remembered the tension of past meetings. As much as she wanted her parents together for her graduation, she knew with her father in New York and her mother in Colorado, life was easier. Unspoken hostilities boiled below the surface, and Libby was relieved when at last life returned to normal.

For the first time, Libby didn't go to New York for the summer. With school only three months away, she decided to spend her vacation working on the ranch. Although her mother suggested helping out at the Lady Jo, she opted for working on the Lazy B.

She knew the Lady Jo well, knew what it was like to cater to the guests. Instead of spending her summer as she had in the past, she wanted to work, really work, on the Lazy B.

Charlie Carter, the herdsman for the registered Angus herd seemed only too willing to accept Libby's helpful presence. He never became annoyed with her questions about the operation.

"You'll make a good owner, Miss Libby," he told her. "Just keep asking questions and remember all the answers. You'll never know when something you've heard will come in handy."

When she wasn't in the barns, she rode with the cowboys, checking the beef cattle or watching them break new saddle horses. She enjoyed every aspect of ranch life. Over the summer she'd done her share of leading the colts around the corral and mucking out the stalls. She'd even gotten to the point where she did some of the training. As much as she wanted to help in breaking the horses, she knew it would be too much to ask.

At times like these, the Lady Jo and her guests seemed far away. As August came to an end, she reluctantly prepared to leave for Minnesota. College and being on her own fascinated her, but leaving Colorado and the Lazy B would be hard. Unless she became dreadfully homesick, she would not return until Christmas, as it was her year to spend Thanksgiving in New York. She would miss her parents, the ranch and the hands. Was this what growing up meant?

Chapter Twenty

Libby loved school. Although there were times when she wished she had registered under the name of Libby Prescott rather than Beth Prescott, she knew it was best she not be known by her real name.

Libby Prescott was well known at home and she had never liked the notoriety. Even though most people here didn't even know her last name, she relished the privacy of being Beth rather than Libby. Perhaps she'd been over cautious. Here in the Midwest, no one had ever heard of her, but she preferred it this way. She didn't want purchased friendships. If they weren't genuine, she wanted no part of them. All her life people had been her friends because of her money and her mother's fame. For the first time, she'd found friends who liked her because she was Beth and for no other reason.

Across the hall she heard Sonja Olson's high-pitched giggle. Sonja was the type of girl Libby wanted as a friend. Her family lived on a farm close to Minneapolis, and instilled in Sonja a good Christian background. She represented the kind of woman Fashions By AJ catered to, the kind of woman who made her mother successful.

Libby laughed to herself as she picked up the mail she'd put on the desk when she first got back from class. It amused her to think of how much her mother dominated her thoughts, especially since she'd purposely moved halfway across the country to become independent.

Thanksgiving vacation was only three weeks away and as she shuffled through the letters, she looked for one from her father containing the tickets to New York. Finding an envelope from her father, she sat down on her bed to read it. The fact it seemed too light to contain tickets worried her. Carefully, she slid the letter opener under the flap and slit open the envelope.

Dear Libby,

I know it's my year for Thanksgiving, but something has come up. I've met this woman. I know what you're going to say, but it's not like before. This time it's real. This time I'm really and truly in love with Marie.

My newest book is being released in Europe. We're going to be married the weekend before Thanksgiving and spend our honeymoon on tour.

This will give you the opportunity to be with your mom. I know she misses you. I just hope you aren't too disappointed with the change in plans.

Be happy for me Honey.

Love,

Daddy

The next letter she opened came from her mother.

Dear Libby,

I miss you terribly and I'd give anything if we could have Thanksgiving together, but I know it's your dad's year and I won't fight him on it.

Garrett has come up with a wonderful idea. He's taking me on a cruise. Since I loved our cruise to Alaska two years ago, he's booked us on a Caribbean cruise. We'll be leaving from San Juan and cruising the lower Caribbean as well as South America.

I'll think of you in New York with your dad and grandma.

Call me on Sunday night.

Love,

Mom

Libby thought her heart would break when she finished reading the letters. For the first time in her life, no one wanted her.

I won't let it show, she silently promised herself. *I'll just buy tickets and go somewhere by myself.*

"Beth, Beth," she head Sonja call from outside the door. "Are you in there, Beth?"

She got up from the bed and quickly put the letters in her desk drawer. "I'm right here," she said, once she opened the door.

"What are you doing this weekend?" Sonja asked, as she hurried past Libby into the room.

"Studying, I guess. Why?"

"I just got off the phone with my mom and she said you could come home with me. I told her it just isn't right for you to stay here alone, just because your folks are so far away. You haven't been away from here, even for a weekend, since school started. So, what do you say? Do you want to come home with me?"

"I'd love to, but I don't want to impose on your mom."

"You wouldn't be imposing. My mom will love you, I promise."

Libby smiled. "Oh, all right, but I want to take her something. What does she like?"

"Get real, Beth, you don't have to take my mom anything."

Libby laughed at the difference between them. "It's something I want do. It's only polite to take a hostess gift. What's her decor like?"

"Decor? I don't know, it's just home."

"Does she like candles?"

Beth nodded.

"Good. I saw a beauty in a gift shop in town. I can pick it up before the weekend."

"Honestly, Beth, it isn't necessary," Sonja repeated.

"Yes, it is. I really appreciate her offer. My mom says it's only polite to take a gift when you're invited to spend time with friends, in order to show your appreciation."

"You'll love the farm," Sonja said, changing the subject.

"I'm looking forward to it. Does your dad milk cows?"

"Yes, but why?"

Libby regretted her question. Nothing about her suggested she might be interested in dairy farming. "Oh, I'm just interested. The place where I live runs a herd of registered Angus. Once in a while, the herdsman will let me come out and help, doing whatever I can. I enjoy it."

"Papa won't even let me in the barn when he's milking. He says the barn isn't a place for a young lady. I can't believe your mom would let you do such a thing."

"She says it's good for me to get to know all aspects of life by learning about people."

"What is it your mom does?" Sonja questioned.

"She works in a dress shop."

"She must really be something …"

"She is. I wish the two of you could meet. I know you'd like her."

Sonja went back to her room to call her folks, leaving Libby alone. Sitting down at her desk, she realized it didn't matter that no one wanted her for Thanksgiving. She was going to spend the weekend with a real family on a working farm. She'd been invited, not because she was Libby Prescott and someone wanted to impress their parents with her, but because she was Beth, and Sonja really liked her. It would be almost as good as going home. She could hardly wait for the weekend to come. Realizing she couldn't just leave without telling Uncle Karl, she placed a call to him.

"Hi, Uncle Karl, it's Libby."

"Hi, to you too. What's up?"

"One of the girls here has asked me to go home with her for the weekend."

"Where might home be?"

"I'm not sure. I do know it's up around Minneapolis somewhere. I know it's not far. It will be fun."

"It sounds like fun," he assured her. "What does your mom think about the idea?"

"I haven't called her. I always talk to her on Sunday evening. By that time I'll be back here. She won't mind, though."

"So, have you received your tickets for New York, yet?"

"I'm not going to New York. Daddy is getting married. He'll be in Europe on his honeymoon and doing the promo for his new book. Don't let Mom know, though. Garrett is taking her on a cruise since they'll be alone this year. I don't want to spoil it for her."

"So what are you going to do? Do you want to come here?"

"No. I'm going out on my own. I'm going to take a real vacation. I can afford it. Maybe I'll go to Florida."

"Don't make any hasty plans. I don't like the idea of you being alone. Plan on spending Thanksgiving weekend with your Aunt Janet and me."

"Look, I know you spend Thanksgiving with your sister and brother, as well as your mom."

Before she could finish, Karl interrupted. "They are your aunt and uncle and grandmother."

"I know, but I don't think I'm ready for them. They've made no move toward me, don't push me on them."

"They don't know you. Once they meet you, they'll love you. They aren't ogres. At least think about it."

Libby knew her uncle would like nothing better than to have her meet his family, her family. Maybe, one day, she would, but on her terms, not his. "I'll think about it," she promised. "Anyway, I just wanted to let you know about this weekend so you wouldn't worry when I wasn't in church."

"You have a good time. I'm glad you're meeting some nice people, making new friends. If you need anything, just give me a call."

"I will," she said, ending the conversation.

It was almost four in the afternoon, when Lars Olson arrived at the Gustavus Adolfus campus to pick up his daughter and her friend.

"Papa," Sonja said, "This is Beth."

Lars looked at the girl intently. She was beautiful, the type of girl you expected to see on a magazine cover. Everything about the girl was perfect, right down to her expensive designer original clothing. She certainly wasn't the type of girl who would feel comfortable on a farm and yet Sonja said she wanted to see the cows and the milking operation.

"Beth, this is my papa, Lars Olson."

286

"It's a pleasure," Beth replied, extending her hand. "Sonja tells me you have a large farm."

"We run about two hundred and fifty acres. It could be larger, but it's enough for my sons and me."

"And you milk cows. I'd like to see your operation."

He marveled at her. Either she was genuinely interested or she'd done her homework well.

"Now, why would a pretty girl like you want to get all dirty in a cow barn?"

"If I went home, I'd be in the barns. Charlie, he's the herdsman, let's me come out whenever I want."

"Do your folks live on a farm?" Lars questioned.

"Ranch," she corrected. "My dad's the accountant there. The job comes with a house on the property.

Beth's statement confused Lars. "Didn't Sonja tell me your folks are divorced?"

"Yes, but my mom's remarried. My stepdad and I are very close. My real dad's in New York. He works in the publishing business ..."

Lars thought over what Sonja had told him about Beth. He remembered her saying that Beth's mother lived in Colorado and her father in New York. It could be only a coincidence. On the other hand, could this young woman be Libby? He dismissed the idea. The chances of the girl being his niece were astronomical. "So, that's why you came to Gustavus Adolfus? Because it's halfway between?"

"You might say so. There are a lot of schools halfway in between. This one had a good reputation. I had my choice and Gustavus Adolfus offered the best education, as well as a Christian background. The ratio of students to teachers was a deciding factor as well."

"And she gets straight A's, Papa," Sonja added.

"Maybe you'd get straight A's if you studied more."

"Oh, Papa, all Beth ever does is study. She never has any fun. I couldn't be like her. Don't get me wrong Beth. I really like you. I just wish you got out more."

"I'm glad you could join us, Beth. We'll make sure you have fun this weekend."

Libby enjoyed the trip from Gustavus Adolfus to just outside of New Oslo. The only thing to mar her trip was the way Sonja's father kept looking at her. It was as if he knew her, or at least thought he knew her.

"I didn't think you'd ever get here," Sonja's mother said, as she embraced Sonja.

Libby fought the urge to turn and run. The woman was an older version of her mother. Even her voice sounded the same. "Mrs. Olson," she said, extending her hand. "It's a pleasure. Thank you for inviting me."

"You're very welcome, but please, call me Kristen."

The name came like a slap in the face. How many times had she read it on the cards she kept in her dresser drawer at home?

Happy Birthday, Libby, Love Uncle Lars and Aunt Kristen.

It had been seven years since she'd heard from them. How many times had she reread the old cards, the ones she'd saved? Every year on her birthday and Christmas, she pulled them out and pretended they'd just arrived. For years she'd pretended Uncle Lars and Aunt Kristin, Uncle Johann and Aunt Sharon, and Grandma and Grandpa Jorgenson really cared about her.

Her mother always said it had something to do with Grandpa Jorgenson dying and her not being able to attend the funeral, but she never really understood it. Maybe it had something to do with her. Maybe Uncle Karl was wrong. Maybe they all hated her for some unexplained reason.

She wanted to turn and run. More than anything else she wanted to make the excuse she'd gotten sick. If only she could take a bus back to school, but it was too late, she was already here, already facing her family.

"Beth," Kristen said, taking her hand. "Sonja has told us so much about you, do come in and sit down. Supper is ready. Erik will take your bags up to your room."

Libby sat down at the table. She had been famished earlier, but now the food lost its appeal. She wanted nothing to do with these people and yet she found herself liking them. Perhaps if she wasn't around her Aunt Kristen too much she wouldn't guess who she was. She'd have to choose her words very carefully.

"So, how do you like Gustavus Adolfus?" Kristen asked, as though trying to pull her into the conversation.

"I adore the school, the people, the classes. I especially like the one-on-one contact with the professors. It's fantastic! I don't think the University of Northern Colorado or MIT has the capability for such personal relationships. Those schools are just too big."

With dinner finished, Libby went upstairs to unpack. When she returned to help with the dishes, she held out a perfectly wrapped gift box. "I have something for you, Mrs. Olson."

Kristen took the package as though surprised by the gesture. "I wish you'd call me Kristen. You must know this isn't necessary."

"It's only a small token. I really appreciate you inviting me for the weekend."

"Why Beth, it's beautiful," Kristen exclaimed, once she opened the box. "I particularly like the verse. It says everything."

"What does it say?" Sonja asked

"It's John 3:16. *God so loved the world that he sent his only begotten son, that whosoever believeth in him should not perish, but have everlasting life.*"

"I bought one for my mom as well. I'll be taking it to her for Christmas."

"Not until Christmas? What about Thanksgiving?"

The thought of Thanksgiving brought a lump to Libby's throat. She certainly couldn't tell these people no one wanted her this year. "I'll be spending Thanksgiving with my dad in New York, but I'll be in Colorado for Christmas. It's not too far away."

Even with the small lie she'd told, she found her tears were very close. She didn't want to talk about her family and the holidays. Suddenly, she felt very alone. "I'm sorry, I'm very tired. Would you please excuse me?"

Without waiting for a reply, she hurried out of the room to the security of the upstairs bedroom where she'd unpacked earlier. Lying across the bed, she cried until there were no more tears left. She couldn't keep up this game of pretense with her aunt and uncle. She wanted to go home. How hard would it be to go into town and buy tickets to Crystal Creek? She wanted her mother to tell her everything would be all right.

The next morning, when Lars came down to milk, he was puzzled to see lights in the kitchen. He was certain he'd turned them off the night before. To his surprise, Beth was up, dressed in jeans, a chambray shirt, and boots, drinking a cup of coffee.

"I hope you don't mind me making coffee. Would you like a cup?"

He accepted the steaming brew from her. "I didn't expect to see you up so early. I thought all college kids slept in until ten."

"Not me. I'm anxious to see your milking operation. I'm not bad help, either. I can carry a pail of milk if I have to."

"What's this?" Erik questioned, coming into the kitchen. "Did I hear you right? Do you want to carry milk pails?"

Beth laughed. "That and more."

"When we're done maybe you'd like to take a walk up to the woods with me."

"Woods?"

"That's right, it was dark when you got here last night. There's a big woods behind the barn. It's about a mile up. It's a long walk. Are you sure you're up to it?"

"I do a lot of hiking back home. This is flat country, compared to the foothills and mountains. I'd love to go with you."

Libby relaxed. Lars and Erik posed no threat. If anyone was going to recognize her, it would be Kristin. Spending the day outdoors would be a welcome, relaxing change of pace.

By seven, they were back in the house for breakfast. The smell of bacon and eggs frying made Libby's mouth water.

"Mom and I are going to Minneapolis shopping," Sonja said between bites of food. "Would you like to go with us, Beth?"

"I don't think so. Erik offered to take me hiking, I mean walking, up to the woods. The trees are so beautiful. It seems like you've had a very late fall this year. Back home, the aspens would have already lost their leaves and there would be snow in the mountains."

"Do you ski?" Kristin asked.

"Yes, but not as well as my stepdad and stepbrother. I also ride horseback and go hiking."

"She's not bad with the cows, either," Lars said. "She knows what she's doing."

"I take that as a high compliment," Libby replied. "I like helping out at home, but if I get on your nerves, you'll have to tell me."

"Well," Sonja declared, "I'm going shopping. There's a party at school next weekend and I want a new dress. I wish we had some decent shops around here."

"What do you mean decent shops?" Libby questioned.

"Places that carry clothes like yours, Beth. I love everything you own. Even your grubbies are great. Where do you get them if you don't shop?"

"Oh, here and there. I pick up things at different shops. My mom makes a lot of my stuff, and I sew for myself as well." She looked intently at the food on her plate, praying no one would question the white lie she'd just told.

"You know how to sew, too?" Sonja inquired.

"I told you, Sonja, being able to sew would increase your wardrobe," Kristin said.

"It all seems academic," Libby commented. "Since I didn't bring a machine, I haven't done any sewing in a while. Homework seems to take precedence over needlework."

That evening at supper, Beth was quiet. It seemed as though the girl who was so bubbly with Lars, Sonja and Eric was unusually quiet around Kristen.

"So, how did you like your walk to the woods?" Kristen asked, trying to draw her into the conversation.

"It was beautiful. I miss the mountains, but this is a lovely part of the country as well. I guess I wouldn't mind living here, but my heart is back home."

Talking about Colorado seemed to be relaxing to Beth, and Kristen took the opportunity to get to know her better. "Does your mother know you're spending the weekend with us?"

Libby's eyes radiated a moment of indecision about her answer. "No, I usually call her on Sunday evening. She's hard to get hold of during the week. Her work keeps her very busy."

"Didn't you say she works in a dress shop?"

"Yes, but it's a busy time of the year out there. They're getting ready for the ski trade."

"Just where in Colorado is it you're from?" Kristen inquired.

She watched as Libby took a deep breath, as though she were afraid she would say the wrong thing. "We live just outside of Denver."

"On a ranch, right?"

"Yes. It's one of my stepfather's perks from his job. It gives me an opportunity to ride and ski, and well, a lot of other things."

"What kind of a ranch is it?"

"A cattle ranch.

When Kristen and Lars went to bed, Kristen voiced her fears. "Do you know who she is, Lars?"

"I'm beginning to think I do. She's Libby, isn't she?"

"I'm afraid so. What do you think she wants from us?"

"I don't think she wants anything. I don't think she knows who we are."

Kristen shook her head. "She knows who we are all right. She knows Karl. His picture is on the piano. She was so evasive when I asked her about where she lives, where the ranch is located. She knows that ranch inside and out. She should, from what Karl said she owns both the dude ranch and the cattle ranch."

Lars took her in his arms. "Well, if she does own the ranch, she doesn't need anything from us."

"I don't know. I really wish we hadn't insisted Sonja bring her here for the weekend."

"Why? She's a delightful girl."

"I didn't say she isn't, but what are we going to say to Mama and Johann? She's going to want to go to church with us tomorrow and we're going to the parsonage for dinner. How are they going to feel about meeting Anne's daughter?"

"Why don't you just keep your suspicions about who she is to yourself? Let them make their own judgments. You might be surprised. They might like her."

Kristen switched the light back on and faced Lars. "They'll like her. I like her. What I want to know is why is she trying to hide her identity? Why does she call herself Beth and not Libby?

"You know Libby Prescott is a very wealthy young woman. Maybe she just wants to be one of the kids. Maybe she thinks we don't know who she is. Have you considered such a possibility?"

* * *

Libby took special care in dressing for church. She prayed Lars and Kristen had not guessed her true identity. They couldn't have recognized her since they'd received no pictures from her mother since she'd been eleven.

Holding up the new suit her mother sent from the fall collection, she was glad she'd had the foresight to bring it along. The print of autumn colors suited her well and the rust-colored, silk blouse made a perfect accessory.

Today she would meet her grandmother and uncle. Once she did, she would have to decide if she wanted to be part of this family. She hoped they wouldn't realize who she was.

Taking one last look in the mirror, she found her appearance pleased her. She wore a minimum of make up and the neckline of the blouse accented her Black Hills gold cross perfectly. As she clasped the necklace, she remembered Elliott giving it to her for confirmation, then adding the matching earrings for her birthday.

"Do you attend church at home, Beth?" Kristin asked, as they drove the short distance to New Oslo.

"Yes, I go to the church in town. If the weather is bad or the whim strikes me, I attend the Cowboy Chapel on the ranch."

"Cowboy Chapel?" Erik questioned.

"It was built about a hundred years ago by the man who founded the ranch. He meant it as a place for meditation for the hands. He realized they couldn't always get to town to worship, so he built the chapel to serve their needs. If they didn't have an itinerant preacher, the owner would conduct the services. It was a unique concept. Now a pastor comes out once a month for communion. A wonderful old cowboy named Josh presides the rest of the time. His sermons can rival those of anyone I've ever heard. I guess it's because he talks from the heart about the things around us, the prairies, the hills and the mountains." Libby's mind drifted, until she could see Josh standing in the pulpit, preaching one of his wonderful sermons.

"You'll like Uncle Johann's sermon," Erik said, causing the mental picture to dissolve.

"I'm certain I will," Libby commented, hoping he was right.

As they entered the church, she cringed just a bit. This was the church of her mother's childhood. Things her mother described were as she pictured them. Little had changed.

Once she seated herself in the pew, she checked the hymns in the bulletin. She was pleased to find them to be ones she knew. Lifting her voice in praise, she smiled at how well it blended with those around her.

Johann Jorgenson took the pulpit and began his sermon. "Our topic for today is 'Let he who is without sin cast the first stone.'"

She listened to it half-heartedly. She had to admit, her uncle came across as a powerful speaker. As he talked about tolerance, she wondered if he had cast the first stone at her mother.

In the pew ahead of her sat an older woman, a woman about Kristin's age, and two teenagers. "That's my Grandma and Aunt Sharon. My cousins, Mary and Alan, are sitting next to them," Sonja whispered. "You'll love them. We're having lunch at their home."

Libby cringed. She wished this day would end. Wished she was back at school. Wished she'd never come.

When the last song ended and the benediction had been said, Johann dismissed the congregation. As Libby waited to greet the pastor, Kristen pushed her in front of them. "Johann, this is Sonja's friend from college, Beth."

Johann held her hand a bit longer than necessary. It seemed as though she noted a glimmer of recognition in his eyes. She decided her imagination suddenly started to work overtime. He couldn't possibly know her identity.

"I enjoyed your sermon, Pastor," she said, amazed at how sincere, how calm her voice sounded. "I especially liked your topic this morning."

"Why thank you, Beth. Have you known Sonja long?"

"Just since the beginning of the school year."

"Well, it will be a pleasure to have you at our home for lunch today."

"The pleasure will be mine," she replied.

When he released her hand, she took a deep breath before leaving the church.

Sonja soon joined her. "Didn't I tell you he's great?"

Libby nodded.

"What's wrong, Beth? Are you crying?"

"I'm just a little homesick. I didn't realize how much I missed my mom until I saw your whole family in church today. I'll be fine."

"Oh, is that all? Well, come on, Mom said Aunt Sharon could use some help with lunch."

"I really feel like I'm imposing. Maybe I'll just take a walk or something. I'd rather be alone for a while."

"Nonsense," Sonja persisted, pulling on Libby's arm, "come on, you have to eat lunch."

Reluctantly Libby followed Sonja to the parsonage, the house where her mother had grown up.

"So, where are you from?" Johann asked, as they ate their lunch.

"Colorado," she replied, trying not to make eye contact.

"Why did you choose Gustavus Adolfus, when it's so far away from home?"

She felt as though she had answered the same question a dozen times in the past two days. "A lot of reasons. Mainly I wanted to be far enough away from home to feel independent. The reputation of the school did play a big part in my decision. It's small enough to have a good ratio of students to teachers, and yet it offered everything I wanted."

"Besides," Sonja interrupted, "her folks are divorced. Her dad lives in New York and Gustavus Adolfus is halfway between."

Libby shot Sonja a glance she hoped said more than words. The last thing she wanted these people to hear was that her parents were divorced.

"You're a lovely girl," she heard her grandmother say. "Your parents can be very proud of you."

"Thank you," she said.

"I'll bet your parents weren't happy with your choice of schools," Johann said.

"I guess they weren't. Mom wanted me to go to the University of Northern Colorado. Daddy was pushing for MIT. I just told them I was old enough to make my own decisions. I'm certain it didn't make either of them happy."

"I still don't understand why you chose this school," Johann commented.

Again she repeated all the logical reasons, while in her mind she screamed *I chose it because it was close to Uncle Karl.*

The questions continued until Libby felt almost violated. She hardly touched her food and was relieved when, at last, the young people were excused.

"It's so nice out," Mary said. "Let's go outside."

Libby followed them, feeling even more like an outsider with her cousins. She listened as the boys talked about girls and the girls talked about boys. The idle chatter irritated her. "Where are you going, Beth?" Sonja asked when she saw her heading toward the house.

"I have to use the bathroom," she replied, as she went up the steps to the porch. "I'll be right back."

* * *

Lars watched as Beth left the room with the other young people. He'd studied her closely all through lunch and wished he could have stopped Johann's insistent questions.

"I take it you didn't know who she was when you invited her to spend the weekend with you," Johann commented.

"How could we?" Kristin asked. "It doesn't matter, though. She's a delightful girl."

"She's Libby, isn't she?" Solveig asked. "She's Anne's daughter."

"Yes, Mama, I'm afraid she is Libby."

"What do you have to be afraid of?" Lars snapped. "You said it yourself, she's a delightful girl."

"She may be a delightful girl, Lars, but what does she want from us?" Johann questioned.

"I don't think she wants anything. I don't think she even knows who we are. If she does know, she hasn't let on, and we've done the same. We can only pray we've done the right thing."

"But why here? Why now?" Johann asked.

"I don't want anything from you."

Lars looked up, surprised to see Libby enter the room. "Yes, I'm Libby, Anne's daughter. I don't have two heads or four arms or horns, for that matter. Until I got to the Olson's farm, I didn't know who you were. Olson is a very common name, and since I hadn't heard from any of you in seven years, it didn't ring any bells."

Lars could see that Libby was trembling. Tears were running down her cheeks as her voice faltered.

"I don't know what I ever did to any of you. How have I hurt you so badly when I've never even met you? Having a friend like Sonja meant everything to me. For the first time I'd made a friend from a real family who didn't care if I was Libby Prescott or just plain Beth. I like her, as I like all of you. I guess it's the reason I got so scared when I realized who you are. Maybe I wasn't supposed to like you. I don't know, but I promise you, you won't ever have to deal with me again. I'll find my own way back to school, thank you. Just have Sonja bring my things."

To Lars' surprise, Libby turned and ran out of the room. He immediately got to his feet to follow her. He no more than put his hand on the screen door, than he heard the squeal of tires and the thud of impact. Before even the startled teenagers could react, he was at Libby's side in the street.

* * *

Karl checked the television listings then looked at the clock. Being only one thirty he'd have to wait for the beginning of the Vikings-Forty-Niners game, as they were playing on the West Coast. Switching on the set, he settled for the Green Bay-Chicago game. He half listened to the game, while he read the Sunday paper. He knew he should be raking leaves, but it was football season. The leaves would be there next weekend when the Vikings were playing on Monday night.

"When is the game on, Dad?" Michael asked.

"Not until three. I've got on Green Bay at Chicago."

Before Michael could settle down to watch the game, the phone rang. "I'll get it, Dad. It's probably one of the guys.

"Jorgenson residence," Michael answered. "Sure Aunt Kristen, just a minute.

He covered the receiver. "Dad, it's Aunt Kristin and she's crying."

Karl took the phone from his son. "Kristen, Kristen, calm down. What's wrong?"

"Oh, Karl, there's been an accident," she stammered.

"Who? Mama? One of the kids?"

"No, Libby."

"Libby? It can't be. She's spending the weekend with a friend from school."

"She spent the weekend with us. Her friend is Sonja. She didn't know-we didn't know. It's been an awful weekend. There were some hurtful things said and ..."

"What are you saying, Kristen?"

"We're at Johann's and she ran out of the house and into the street. A car hit her and ..." Tears obscured the rest of her words.

"How badly is she hurt?"

"I--I don't know. The paramedics aren't here yet. She's just lying out there, so still. She's bleeding. Oh Karl, I don't know if she's dead or alive."

"Let me talk to someone who is making sense, Kristen," Karl demanded.

It took only a few seconds for Lars to come on the line. "I don't think she's too badly injured, Karl. The car was almost to a stop when it hit her. She's unconscious. There's a cut on her head from where she fell, and possibly some broken bones. We thought it best if you called Anne. We think she ought to be here."

Karl knew his voice sounded cold. "I won't ask any questions now. Just make sure someone is at the parsonage. I'm certain Anne and Garrett will be flying in. I'll need to know what time they'll get here so I can pick them up. I don't want anyone but me picking them up, though."

"I understand," Lars said.

"What is it, Dad?" Michael asked, when Karl hung up the phone.

"It's Libby. She's been in an accident. Get your mom and sister, we're going to New Oslo as soon as I call your Aunt Anne."

As he dialed the number, he prayed Garrett would be the one to answer. Instead, Anne's cheerful came across the line.

"Hello," she said.

"Hi, Anne," Karl replied.

"Karl? What a surprise. What's going on? I thought you'd be glued to the television set watching football."

"Is Garrett there with you?"

"Yes, he is. Do you want to speak to him?"

"I want to talk to both of you. Are you using the speaker phone?"

"No, but I can," she said, her voice beginning to waver.

"Put me on it." He waited until he was certain they could both hear him before continuing. "There's been an accident."

"Libby?"

He could almost see the tears spring to her eyes. "Yes. I don't think it's serious. I do think you should be here, though."

"What do you mean you don't *think*? Where is she?"

"It's a long story. She's in New Oslo."

"You promised me ..."

"She promised me, too. She didn't know exactly where she was spending the weekend. She only said she'd met a new friend at school and she'd been invited to spend the weekend with the girl's family. It turned out her new friend was Sonja."

"Oh, dear God," AJ said.

"I'll explain everything when you get here. I'll give you Johann's number at the parsonage. When you've filed a flight plan, leave a message for me there. There's a private airfield just outside of New Oslo. I don't think you should encounter any problems using it. Just call Johann's. Someone will be there to answer the phone. I don't know if it will be Sharon or one of the kids, but they'll get the message to me."

"Oh, Karl, not my baby!. If you want me to come out, it must be bad."

"Don't jump to conclusions, Anne. I don't know any more than I just told you. When Kristen called, it had just happened. The paramedics weren't even there yet. Lars said she ran into the path of a car. When he came into the house to talk to me, she was unconscious. The car had slowed down by the time it hit her. At the worst she could have some broken bones."

"We'll be there as soon as we can," Garrett assured him. "Flying time should be three to three and a half hours. With the plane right at the ranch we can leave almost immediately. As soon as I have arrival times, I'll call Johann's. Now give me the number and location of the air field."

AJ didn't listen as Garrett repeated the information after he'd written it on the pad by the phone. When she heard him thank Karl and hang up, she hugged him tightly. "Oh, Garrett, not again. I can't lose her."

"Don't jump to conclusions. You heard Karl, he doesn't know any more than what he told us. We'll just have to wait until we get there. Once we know more, we'll call Logan."

"Dear Lord, Logan, I'd almost forgotten about him. We can't wait to call him. If we do, he'll be angry. I'll call him from the studio while you file the flight plan."

Chapter Twenty-One

Johann knelt beside Libby. She lay so still he wondered how bad her injuries were. There had never been a doubt as to her identity. Libby looked just like Anne. At least the way Anne looked when she left for Colorado. If Libby's hair were blond rather than brunette, they could pass for twins.

The paramedics arrived amid a frenzy of activity. Libby's vitals were taken and they placed a cervical collar around her neck.

"Do you know who this girl is, Pastor?" one of the paramedics questioned.

"Her name is Elizabeth Prescott, but they call her Libby."

"Age?" the paramedic continued.

"Eighteen," Johann replied, surprised at how easily, how automatically the answers came.

"Does she have family here, Pastor?"

Johann hesitated only a moment. "I'm her uncle. She's my sister's daughter. She is visiting here from Colorado."

"Have her parents been contacted?."

"They will be," Johann said, knowing by now Kristen would have called Karl and Karl in turn called Anne. The confrontation with his youngest sister loomed only a matter of hours away. Was he ready for the inevitable meeting?

"We'll need consent."

For some reason the comment upset him. "She's of age, but since she's unconscious, I'll give consent."

"Can you tell us what happened?" an officer who had been measuring skid marks and talking to the driver of the car asked.

Before Johann could comment, Lars came out of the house. "I witnessed the accident. There had been an argument. Libby ran out of the house and into the street without looking. The driver did everything she could to avoid the accident. I doubt if Libby even saw the car."

"It wasn't my niece's fault," Johann protested. "If anyone is to blame it is us. Blame it on prejudice, stupidity, anything you want, but it wasn't her fault." All the time he was speaking to the officer, Johann kept his eyes and thoughts glued on Libby.

"There's no use going into anything now, Pastor," the officer said. "They're ready to take her to the hospital. Would you like to ride in the ambulance?"

"Go ahead, Johann," Lars advised. "Sharon is staying here with the kids. I'll follow you with Kristen and your mama."

Johann seated himself in the passenger's seat of the ambulance. Lights flashed and sirens screamed as they pulled away from the curb and headed for the hospital.

"Can you hear me?" he heard one of the paramedics say. He could only assume Libby was unconscious.

"Yes," her voice sounded strange, far away.

"Can you tell me your name?

"Libby, Libby Prescott."

"How old are you?"

"Eighteen."

"Do you know where you are?"

"Colorado, no, not Colorado, Minnesota."

The ambulance pulled up to the emergency entrance of the hospital. Almost before the vehicle stopped, Johann opened the door and ran to the back in time to see Libby lifted out on the gurney. He reached out and touched her hand. He wanted to comfort her, to take back the words spoken only minutes earlier, to turn back the clock to the moment he'd seen her in church. Her response was to recoil, as though his very touch hurt her.

"Libby," he said.

She looked up at him, her eyes reminding him of those of a wounded deer. Just seeing her looking at him in such a way saddened him. He could lay blame on no one but himself. He hadn't kept in touch with Anne. Why should Libby trust someone she didn't even know?

The trip from St. Peter to New Oslo seemed to go on indefinitely. The dashboard clock read 3:15 when Karl arrived at the parsonage. He listened as Sharon recounted the events of the day, the argument, and the accident.

"Have Anne and Garrett called?" he finally asked.

Sharon nodded. "They were able to get into the private air field you suggested. They'll be arriving at about five thirty. I didn't know they owned their own plane."

"How could you? You and Johann know nothing about them," he accused.

Sharon asked no further questions. There were no questions to ask.

"Karl," she finally said. "What is she like? Does she hate us?"

"She doesn't hate you, Sharon. I don't know how she does it, but she doesn't hate you. She's a remarkable woman. She'll be here soon, and you can make your own judgments."

He tried to remember if Kristen ever told him where Sonja was going to school. Had she mentioned Gustavus Adolfus? He doubted it. He hadn't known where the other kids went to school. Perhaps he hadn't cared.

It was almost four when he entered the waiting area where Kristen, Lars, Johann, and his mama sat.

"Oh, Karl," Kristen cried, when she saw him. Her eyes were red, her face tear stained.

"Have you heard anything?" he asked, after giving her a hug.

"Nothing," Johann said. "It's as though the doctors have forgotten we're here."

"It takes time to make a diagnosis. They're only being thorough."

They all looked at him as if expecting harsh words, perhaps even a lecture.

"Well, aren't you going to say it?" Johann inquired.

"Say what?

"Tell us how foolish we've been all these years to ignore them."

"Would it do any good? Would it change what happened today?"

Johann shook his head. "I just don't know what I'll say to Anne."

"You'll find the words. She's not hard to talk to. I promised her there would be no confrontations, at least not unless Libby asked for one. I even asked her to join us for Thanksgiving, but she said she wasn't ready for you yet. I can hardly believe we had the conversation only four days ago. She had no idea she'd meet you so soon. When did you know her identity?"

Kristen smiled. "The minute I saw her. She's Anne at her age. How could I not help but know her?"

"It was the same for me," Johann added.

"I tried to tell myself it wasn't her," Kristen continued. "I wanted to believe I'd been mistaken. All I needed to do was listen to her talk. When she speaks of the ranch where she lives, you can tell she's proud of everything there. It's hers, she owns it and yet she's content to be cleaning the barns with Lars. Her grades are excellent. She's a delightful person. I like her, I really like her."

Karl couldn't help but smile. Perhaps something good would come out of this after all. "There's nothing about Libby not to like. It's the same with Anne. You've just let Papa's prejudices get in the way."

"You should not talk so about your papa, Karl," Solveig admonished.

"Mama, Anne will be here in less than an hour. If it weren't for this accident, she wouldn't be coming back. Thank God it did happen. Maybe I can get all of you together. Maybe I can get you to see what a beautiful person Anne really is."

"I dread it," Solveig admitted. "You'll never know how much I dread it."

Karl knelt in front of his mother and took her hands. "Enjoy her, Mama. Enjoy Libby. They're both beautiful people."

Turning to Johann, he continued, "I have to leave for the airport soon. Before I go, I'll see if I can find someone to talk to."

A young doctor entered the room, interrupting him. "Is Miss Prescott's uncle here?"

Both Karl and Johann were on their feet. "I think it's you she'll want to see," Johann said to Karl.

"If you'll follow me, I'll take you to her room."

"How badly injured is she?" Johann asked.

"Her left wrist is broken as well as two of her ribs. She has some minor facial cuts and a concussion. The worst injury is a punctured lung. It happened when one of her ribs was fractured. It's nothing that won't heal, but we do want to keep her here for a few days for observation."

Johann felt his heart sink. A punctured lung sounded serious. How would he live with the knowledge this had been his fault?

He saw Karl turn to him. "If she wants to see her uncle, I think she'd better see both of us."

Although skeptical, Johann followed Karl to Libby's room. All of the harsh words they'd spoken earlier rang in his ears as Karl made his way to her bed. It nearly broke Johann's heart to hear her whisper Karl's name and grip his hand. Even worse were the tears rolling down her cheeks. Luckily, he stood behind Karl, out of her line of vision.

"I'm so sorry this happened," she sobbed.

"Maybe this is God's way of getting this family back together," Karl replied, then bent to kiss her cheek and wipe away her tears.

"The saddest thing is that I like them. I like all of them and they hate me."

Her words touched Johann's heart. "We don't hate you," he said, moving toward her bed. "We like you very much."

If his presence surprised her, she didn't show it. Perhaps the painkillers had dulled her emotions. "I heard you, Pastor. I heard you ask what I wanted from you and I want nothing. You have nothing to give me."

"Let us get to know you, Libby. Let us give you our love."

"Love?" she questioned. "Can you ever give me love when my mom, your sister, is a stranger to you? I don't need your kind of love."

"Give us a chance. Please, let us get to know you. Your mother will be here soon. We want to get to know her as well.

"Mom's coming here?"

"You bet she is," Karl assured her. "She needs to be near you. Since I've confirmed that you're all right, I'm going to pick her and Garrett up at the airport."

They stayed for only a few more minutes before Libby began to give in to the medication. As they made their way to the elevator, Johann did little to hide how shaken the encounter left him.

"How can she be only eighteen? Her perception is that of someone so much older."

"Their lives haven't been easy," Karl replied. "She'll need time to adjust to you. I remember a scene almost identical to this one when I first met Anne."

When Karl left the hospital, Lars went as well. No matter what was going on, Lars still had chores to do. He took Solveig with him. Karl realized how draining all of this had been on his mother. He told them he thought it best if she relaxed in familiar surroundings. He knew it would be easier for Anne to have to confront Johann and Kristen without their mother present.

The airfield was only a few miles from the hospital. When Karl inquired about Garrett's flight, the controller told him they were securing the plane and would be in the hangar in a few minutes.

What I should expect? Will Anne be hysterical? To his surprise, she appeared amazingly calm, almost to the point of scaring him.

"Karl," she said, as she allowed him to embrace her. "How is she?"

"She's going to be fine. I promise you, she'll be just fine." Anne nodded. She seemed content with his answer. As they went to his car, he marveled at her appearance. She certainly didn't look like AJ, the famous designer. She was dressed as he knew she did around the house. The split riding skirt, the plaid blouse and the expensive boots were like the ones he'd seen her wear when they visited her last summer. Her blond hair was pulled back from her face and secured with a ribbon of the same material as her blouse. Not even the strain of today's happenings could mar the fresh glow of her natural beauty.

"Lars took Mama home," Karl said, as they pulled out of the parking lot. "Kristen and Johann are still at the hospital."

"When we get there, I want to see them alone. Garrett and I have talked about it and decided it's the thing to do."

"Do you think it's wise?"

"Yes. I faced you alone. I want to do the same with them. I have to do this my way."

Karl replied, smiling at her words. It was easy for him to recall how he had met her on her terms. Now it would be the same for Johann and Kristin. "Whatever you say."

"Exactly what happened?" Garrett asked. "What caused the accident?"

Karl explained, as best he could, the events of the weekend. "The best thing to come out of this is she likes them and they like her. They've all agreed to get to know each other."

"They'll love her. What's not to love about Libby?" Anne asked.

"Really Anne, deep down, what's not to like about Johann and Kristen? Go easy on them."

"Touché. I promise you, I won't jump all over them."

Karl and Garrett watched as she got out of the car and went into the hospital. "I can't believe you're letting her see them alone," Karl said to Garrett.

"Why not? I let her see you alone. She has to face it. She's much stronger than she was seven years ago. She forgave them while she was at Morgan's place. She'll be just fine."

Kristen fidgeted. She wished Lars wouldn't have had to go home to do chores, wished he sat next to her. She knew it was best her mother went home. Mama hadn't had enough time to get to know Libby, hadn't felt the barrier she'd built up over the years begin to crumble.

When Johann returned from Libby's room, she'd seen the acceptance in his eyes. He would easily accept Libby.

Across the room from them sat a man. He'd entered the room about fifteen minutes earlier and merely picked up a magazine. He said nothing to them. She assumed he wanted no conversation with them. She wondered if he, too, waited for word from an accident. He sat, with his back deliberately to the door. Although she knew her actions impolite, she watched him intently.

When Anne entered the room alone, it took Kristen completely by surprise. The minute she came in, Kristen got to her feet. "Oh, Anne," she cried, as her sister held out her arms. "I'm so sorry. We never meant for anything like this to happen."

Anne held her sister at arms length, assessing her. "You couldn't have anticipated an accident. It wasn't your fault. Karl explained everything. I can't blame you any more than I can blame Libby."

To her surprise, Johann came to her side then held her close. She wanted nothing more than for the moment to continue, for them to accept her. She stepped back, realizing just how much Johann looked like Papa, but hoping he didn't think like Papa. No matter what, she wanted him to love her.

"You can be very proud of her," he said. "She's a delightful, perceptive young woman.

"Thank you," she managed to say, through her tears of joy.

"You'll be meeting Garrett soon," she said, once she composed herself. "He's doing some paperwork at the desk. Karl has gone to check on her."

"I wondered why you were alone," Johann commented.

"I had to face you by myself. It had to be my way."

"It always has to be *your way*, doesn't it AJ?" the man who had been sitting by the door said, as he suddenly stood by her side. He gripped her arm tightly and spun her around to face him.

"Logan!," she gasped, trying to remain calm. "I didn't expect to see you here."

"Did you think I'd be content to stay in New York when my daughter had been in an accident? They wouldn't tell me anything at the desk. I don't think they believed I was her father."

"There are times I have trouble believing it myself, Logan."

"I want some answers. How is she?"

"She's going to be just fine. I would have called and kept you informed. I planned to ask you to come out tomorrow."

"As you can see, I didn't intend to sit there waiting for you to drop me a few pieces of information, as though I didn't matter."

"Well, I guess it doesn't matter what I planned. You're here now, so take your hands off me."

"You're trying to shut me out of her life. It's your fault." Logan's face was so close to hers, she could smell the brandy on his breath.

"My fault! How is it my fault?"

"You let her come here."

"I didn't let her do anything. She's eighteen. She made her own decision."

"You should have pressed harder for the University of Northern Colorado."

"Like you pressed for MIT? I heard about it. She chose her own school. I didn't choose it for her."

"She chose it all right. Isn't it strange how conveniently it's located to your brother? She told me Uncle Karl would be close to her."

"Why is it you have such a problem with my family?"

"My, how your tone has changed over the years. Why can't you see them for what they are?"

"What are they? Are they like you? I certainly hope not. You tried, seven years ago, to make Garrett's and Libby's lives a living hell. You didn't succeed then and you won't succeed now. I won't let you destroy us."

Without warning, he released his grip on her arm and slapped her. The blow sent her reeling backwards, until she fell over a low table.

It was Johann who interceded. "Don't ever touch my sister again."

"She's my wife," Logan spat.

"She's your ex-wife," Karl said from the doorway. "You gave up your rights years ago."

"Libby is still my daughter ..."

"Yes, she's your daughter. She'll be fine. You can see her in the morning."

"Let him see her now, Karl," Anne said, choking back her tears. "Give him her room number. I'm too tired to fight about it."

Garrett could hear the commotion as he neared the waiting area. He hurried into the room, shocked to witness the confrontation between Karl and Logan. Anne lay on the floor, with a man and woman whom he assumed to be Johann and Kristen, at her side.

"What have you done now, Logan?" he demanded.

"It's none of your god-damned business, Lanners. We had a discussion. It got heated."

"I ought to ..."

Anne interrupted him. "Let it drop Garrett. Just get him out of here. Let him go to Libby."

"You can be grateful to my wife," Garrett said. "Have your time with Libby. We'll be up soon. I want you gone by the time we get there."

Logan said nothing as he left the room. Garrett watched him walk down the hall, then turned back to where Johann and Karl were helping Anne to her feet. He noticed the redness on her cheek from Logan's blow.

"What happened?"

"I tripped."

"Don't give me that. I don't buy it."

"He slapped her, for no reason," Kristen explained.

"I'll kill him. I ought to have the son-of-a-bitch arrested."

"No, Garrett. Think of Libby. His anger has been building for a long time. It came out."

Garrett watched as Anne leaned against Karl. She sucked in her breath as soon as her foot touched the floor. "Are you all right?" he asked, noting the pain in her eyes.

"Yes, I am."

"No you aren't. I can tell when you're lying to me. I want you checked over."

"It's nothing Garrett. I just turned my ankle."

She tried to put her weight on her foot for a second time but the pain he'd seen radiated in her eyes earlier caused her to stumble into his arms.

"That does it," Karl said. "We're taking you down to emergency to have some x-rays taken."

"I said I'm fine. All I did was twist my ankle. You'd think I broke my neck."

"I agree with Karl," Johann said. "We're going to take you down to check things out. It's better to know it's just a twist and nothing more serious."

Garrett watched as Anne rolled her eyes. "It seems as though I'm outnumbered. I'll do what you want if it will make you happy. I just want to see the looks on your faces when they tell you I'm in perfect shape."

Karl disappeared, only to return a few minutes later with a wheelchair. Garrett smiled as he watched her brothers help her into the chair, then push her toward the emergency room. This was what he'd prayed for since the first time he met her.

"I feel so silly," Anne sighed.

"Don't," Kristen commented. "Listen to them. They know what they're talking about."

While Anne went to x-ray, Karl made the proper introductions.

"It's good to meet you Garrett," Kristen said. "I've heard wonderful things about Libby's stepfather this weekend."

"I've been wondering about this weekend. Why did you ever invite her to your home?"

Garrett listened as Kristen explained the events of the past few days. When she finished, he almost felt sorry for Anne's family. They certainly hadn't been prepared to be confronted with the niece and granddaughter they didn't know.

"Mr. Lanners," a doctor who entered the room, interrupted. "Your wife is back from x-ray. It's a bad sprain. She'll have to be off her foot for a week. We'll have it wrapped and get her some crutches. Then you should take her home for some rest. I'm going to give her a prescription for some Tylenol 3 and the name of a doctor at the clinic for a follow-up exam."

"We'll make certain she rests, Doctor," Karl replied. "We'll take her up to see her daughter and then get her to take some of the medication."

A nurse wheeled Anne out of the examination room, her foot wrapped in an ace bandage and propped up to avoid further swelling.

"I hope you're all happy," she said, pretending to be annoyed by their concern.

"Not so much happy as relieved," Johann assured her. "Kristen and I will wait for you downstairs while you and Garrett go with Karl to see Libby."

"We won't be staying long," Karl commented. "Libby needs her rest and if Logan is still there ..."

Anne interrupted her brother. "There won't be another confrontation. He'll back down. He always does. He has a temper and it gets him in trouble."

"I'll say it does," Karl agreed. "So what do we do now? Logan certainly won't leave while Libby is still in the hospital."

"I'm planning to take Anne to a hotel where she can rest. Your kids have to get back to school," Garrett began.

"Janet can take the kids back. I'm going to stay here, too."

"Please stay with us Anne," Johann pleaded. "We have plenty of room."

"No, Johann. Garrett is right. I'll rest more comfortably in a hotel."

"Don't be silly, Anne," Kristen interrupted. "There's plenty of room at the farm. I'll feel better if I can keep an eye on you."

Garrett saw Anne look to him for reassurance. "I'm afraid I agree with your sister. The way I see it, there's no sense in arguing. You said it before, we've got you outnumbered."

"Whatever you say. I can see there would be no use in protesting."

"Since you're so agreeable," Johann added, "Sharon has supper ready for us. Lars should be back from doing chores by now."

Garrett knew the offer terrified Anne, even though she said nothing. He wondered if her mother would be as forgiving as Johann and Kristen had been. Would the differences between them melt away when they saw each other?

Seeing her father enter her room surprised Libby. The strange look on his face made her wonder what was going on. No matter what questions she asked, his answers were evasive.

"Is Mom here?" she finally asked.

Logan nodded. "I saw her and Garrett downstairs with your aunt and uncles. They said I should come up and see you first."

"What's going on, Daddy?"

"Nothing, Honey. I'm going now. I'll see you in the morning."

Logan left the room and Libby couldn't help but wonder what happened to make him so accommodating to her mother.

It didn't take long for her to get an answer. She was horrified to see Garrett push her mother into the room in a wheelchair. The expression on Uncle Karl's face said more than his words ever could. She wondered if they really expected her to believe her mother had tripped getting off the plane.

The painkillers were starting to take effect and she began to relax. The last thing she remembered was her mother telling her she'd be back in the morning.

Logan waited for them in the hall. They hadn't seen him when they first arrived, but he leaned against the wall when they came out of the room to leave.

"I--I'm sorry, AJ," he said, his voice low.

"You're always sorry, Logan. It doesn't matter this time. I'm not going to forgive you. I've been forgiving you for the past nineteen years. I'm tired of your excuses. I've heard them all. You're always sorry about an affair or making a scene over Libby. It doesn't work anymore. Just be glad I'm not pressing charges. I could charge you with assault, but I don't want Libby's name dragged through the mud. It has nothing to do with you. I'm doing this for Libby. It's bad enough that she's at fault for this accident. The press will have a heyday with it. I won't add the humiliation of having you arrested."

Without saying anything more, Anne nodded to Garrett, indicating she was ready to leave.

Johann waited for them at the elevator. "I thought I should warn you, when you get downstairs, there are several reporters waiting for you."

"Damn the press," Anne said, to no one in particular.

"I'll handle them," Garrett assured her.

"Could we be lucky enough to have Janice be one of them?" she questioned.

"I hope so, but it seems rather unlikely. I doubt if she could have gotten here this fast."

They got on the elevator and pushed the button for the lobby. Anne's heart beat faster, causing every beat to echo in her ears. She knew Kristen would be waiting for her, but so would the press. When the doors opened, they were greeted by a surge of reporters, including Janice.

"Good Lord Janice, how do you get places so fast?" Anne asked, as soon as she saw her.

"I was in Chicago. The wire services picked up on Libby's name," Janice said. "I just happened to be in the office of the Trib and caught it. I flew up as soon as I heard."

"Look Janice," Garrett began, "it's been a long day. We're all tired. For the record, Libby is going to be fine. She has a broken wrist, a couple of broken ribs, a punctured lung and a mild concussion. Why don't you give me the number where you're staying?. I'll arrange a press conference with you tomorrow. We'll know more then and you'll get the story you want."

"Fair enough, Garrett," Janice conceded. "What about you, AJ? What did you do to your foot?"

Without hesitation Anne became AJ, ready to answer the press, even if the answer needed to be the fabricated one she gave Libby earlier. "I twisted my ankle when I got off the plane. My overly protective husband and brothers insisted I have it checked out. They didn't give me much choice in the matter."

"Mr. Prescott," another reporter called out, "what are you doing here?"

"In case you've forgotten, Libby is my daughter, too." He said no more. The answer seemed to be enough for tonight.

Anne knew the reporters wanted more, but with Janice's acceptance of their terms, they would have to wait until tomorrow.

"You're on a first name basis with the press?" Johann asked, as they left the hospital.

"Janice and I go back a long way. I met her at my first fashion show and we've been friends ever since. She's covered everything from my wedding to my divorce and back again. She works for a paper out of Denver. She started out as a fashion reporter, but she's become so much more. We're good friends. She covers everything I do. It was just ironic she was in Chicago and picked up on the name. If it hadn't been Janice, it would have been someone less understanding, someone who wouldn't have accepted Garrett's request to wait until tomorrow. When AJ Lanners and Logan Prescott show up in the same town on the same day, it's news, especially when Libby is involved."

"I didn't realize."

"I'm certain there's a lot about me you don't realize, Johann. You don't know what it took to get me here. I vowed I'd wait for you to come to me. I'm here and I'm talking to you, but going to the parsonage and facing Mama scares me to death. I have some bad memories associated with that house."

Johann helped her to her feet and then into Karl's car, while Karl returned the wheelchair to the hospital. "We'll all be with you. You'll be just fine. We've been wrong. Now it's time to put things right. It won't be easy for any of us, but we'll work it out, together. We won't let you slip away from us again."

* * *

Solveig paced the living room of the parsonage. How would she react, once her children returned from the hospital? Anne had been so wrong, so very wrong to be pregnant before she married, to divorce her husband. Erik had said so. Had she been wrong to agree with him, wrong to have promised never to question his decision of over forty years ago?

Libby is such a beautiful child. No, Libby isn't a child. She's a young woman. I missed seeing the child, missed watching her grow into a beautiful woman. It's all been Anne's doing and she's done a wonderful job.

"Mama, please sit down," Sharon said. "They'll be here soon."

"Do you know how long it's been since I've seen my daughter?"

"It's been too long. I've never even met her."

Although Solveig heard Sharon's comment, she didn't react to it. "What if she hates me?"

"She doesn't hate you, Mama," Janet assured her, as she helped her to sit down. "She made up her mind, a long time ago. She wanted you to make the first step."

"She didn't even come to her own Papa's funeral. It wasn't right."

"This is something you should ask Anne about. I can't tell you why she didn't come."

"You know why, don't you?"

"I've always known, Mama. I just couldn't tell you. Karl promised Anne we'd keep her secret. I even understood why the big blowup happened on the day of the funeral. I also know why Karl walked out, and why he's always been Anne's champion. Maybe now you'll understand as well."

The closer they got to the parsonage, the more tension Garrett could hear in Anne's voice. From the back seat, he could see her stiffen every time Karl mentioned their mother.

Once in the driveway, he helped her get out of the car and stayed close beside her as she made her way to the front door.

"Anne, what happened to you?" Janet cried, as soon as they stepped into the foyer.

"It's nothing, really. Logan was waiting for me at the hospital. We had a fight and he created a scene. He hit me. I tripped over a low table and sprained my ankle. If I'd been home, I would have said nothing and limped around for a few days until it healed by itself, but between your husband, my husband and Johann, they insisted I have it looked at. I've been poked, probed, x-rayed, and proclaimed injured. I have to stay off it for about a week. It's a real pain, in more ways than one."

Garrett couldn't help but smile. He knew her so well, knew she would have done just what she said if she'd been home.

"You're just tired," Sharon said. "You'll be glad you had it looked at, once you're rested. How's Libby?"

Garrett ceased listening to the conversation between Anne and Sharon and concentrated on his wife. He loved her so much. He couldn't help being overly protective of her.

Just as he was about to suggest they go into the living room to sit down, he heard her ask, "Where's Mama?"

"I'm right here, Anne."

Garrett assessed the woman who stood in the doorway. She was tall and big boned, but her skin seemed to hang on her frame She'd begun to show her age. Her hair was the most beautiful color of white he'd ever seen, and her eyes were a clear blue behind her glasses.

"Oh, Mama," Ann cried, no longer able to control her tears. "It's so good to see you. You don't know how many times I've wanted, needed ..."

"My poor baby, my poor child."

Anne handed her crutches to Garrett then hugged her mother tightly.

"I think we should get you in to sit down," Garrett suggested, forcing them to break their embrace. "Let me help you."

When Lars and Erik returned from doing the chores, they all sat in the living room eating the supper Sharon and Janet prepared.

Garrett couldn't help but notice the expression on Anne's face. He knew it had been a long time since she'd had home cooking like this. At home they usually ate at the lodge because time in the kitchen came at a premium. He'd never minded, but seeing Anne's smile, he knew she'd missed it.

"I have only one question," Solveig finally asked, breaking the din of chatter and laughter of the meal. "I can overlook the fact you were pregnant when you got married and the fact you divorced your husband. When I saw Libby it seems very trivial.. She's a beautiful girl. When I see the love Garrett has for you, it warms my heart. What I can't understand is why you didn't come to your papa's funeral?"

"Oh, Mama, I don't know how to tell you. I've never told anyone." Anne's tears were coming so fast, Garrett knew she couldn't continue.

"What is said here, stays here," Garrett began, taking the burden of explanation from Anne.

Slowly, he began to relate the story of Anne's breakdown and the time she spent at Dr. Morgan's hospital.

It was Johann who first found his voice, who knelt beside Anne's chair. "A breakdown? Why did you feel you couldn't tell us about a breakdown, Anne?"

Garrett ached as she continued to cry softly. This was the first time they'd talked about the horrible events of the day her father died. It also constituted the first time she'd faced it since leaving the hospital. They purposely told no one what happened. Not even Libby knew where she went or why.

"I couldn't," she finally managed to say.

"Let me try to explain it to you," Garrett said, again taking the burden from Anne. "The company had been in turmoil since

Jo's death. Anne's holdings are widely varied. Maybe we should start there. At the time we had maybe thirty or thirty-five franchises scattered around the country. There are more now. Anne inherited all the franchises, which meant she needed to oversee them, and to visit them. Jo's will also left her the three shops she owned outright and Fashions By AJ. Then there were the ranches. The Lazy B and the Lady Jo, were left to Libby. They were all enterprises that meant a lot to the city of Crystal Creek. They meant jobs."

"I guess I don't understand," Lars commented. "What does all of this have to do with the breakdown?"

"I'm getting there. We read the will early so things could get back to normal. Even though we assured everyone things would continue to run smoothly, Anne was unknown in the business world. When the breakdown happened, we knew if anyone even guessed at what occurred, it could ruin her. At the time, we told literally no one about it."

"What about Libby?" Kristen asked. "Did she know?"

"I decided it was for the best if she didn't know. She'd gone to New York with Logan and his mother, so we told her Anne went to a cabin in the mountains to get away. We had to tell Logan's mother the truth, but like everyone else, we swore her to secrecy."

"How did you keep it a secret?" Johann questioned. "There had to be doctors, nurses. Did you swear them to secrecy as well?"

"We didn't have to. They only knew a young woman by the name of Anne Jorgenson had checked in. No know equated her with AJ. As Anne said, being aloof did have its benefits. There weren't a lot of pictures of AJ around at the time. Very few people really knew her. They were all suffering from depression. Many of them were recuperating from accidents. They'd lost people they loved and they needed physical therapy. They didn't have time to come to the conclusion Anne Jorgenson and AJ were one in the same. It became very easy to keep her identity a secret."

"I'm amazed," Johann commented. "How were you able to keep it a secret for seven years and not have Libby question you about it?"

"What was there to question?" Anne said, her composure returning. "She knew, like everyone else, that I spent some time in a mountain cabin. You see, this is the first time I've talked about it to anyone, outside of the few who knew, since it happened."

"I'm pleased it was us, dear," her mother said.

"I'm sorry I've caused you such pain," Anne replied. "What you have to remember is I'm not the Anne who left here nineteen years ago. I'm not even the AJ Karl found in Crystal Creek. My life has changed so drastically. My love, my designing, is almost nonexistent. I only do special orders such as designer originals. I have four designers who work for me and do what I tell them. I am no longer a little girl and if you are going to accept me, it will have to be on my terms."

Johann got up from his chair and seated himself on the couch next to Anne. "I don't know how we can ever make up for what happened. It's odd, for years the fact you were pregnant when you got married, then divorced your husband, seemed so damning. Then I met Libby and it no longer mattered when she'd been conceived. She's a beautiful person."

"Thank you," Anne said, allowing him to hold her hand.

"When I met Garrett, I wanted to forget about Logan. He'd shown his true colors at the hospital. How you stayed married to him for six years, why you didn't have him arrested tonight, I'll never know."

"I told him I didn't intend to press charges, because of Libby. As we told you, when AJ Lanners and Logan Prescott show up in the same town on the same day, it's news, especially when Libby is involved."

She took a deep breath before continuing. "I didn't file for the divorce because I knew Papa wouldn't accept it. Few people even knew the real Logan. He'd been with hundreds of women, he told terrible lies, and I supported him while he wrote his first novel. I gave him Libby as well as his start. When he no longer needed me, he tossed me aside like yesterday's newspaper. Accepting Garrett's proposal was the hardest thing I ever did. I didn't know if I could ever trust anyone enough to say I'd spend the rest of my life with him. Garrett's patience could only be compared to that of Job. He took his time and showed me how much I need him and how much he loves me."

Anne's voice had begun to slur, to sound as though she were drunk. It was a sign Garrett constantly watched for, something Dr. Morgan warned him might happen. He'd seen it only a few times in the past, when she pushed too hard for deadlines. "I think we'd better get you to bed," he suggested.

Anne looked up at him questioningly. "Is it evident?"

"Yes. You're overtired. I can hear it in your voice and see it in your eyes."

Anne made no reply. Garrett knew she'd accepted his suggestion without question.

Chapter Twenty-Two

Anne awoke to the sun streaming through the window. Even without her bearings, she realized the sun didn't stream through anyone's windows early in the morning in November. It had to be much later than she usually got up.

Yesterday's events flooded her mind. Had they left a note for Pam? Would she wonder where they went? *No,* she thought, *Garrett would have called and filled her in by now.*

A light rap at the door brought her back to the reality of the moment. "Anne," Kristen said, softly. "Are you awake?"

"Yes, Kristen, I'm awake."

Her sister entered the room and handed Anne a steaming mug of coffee, keeping the matching mug for herself. Carefully, she seated herself on the side of the bed.

"Where's Garrett?" Anne asked, after taking her first sip of coffee.

"He went with Lars to take Sonja, Janet and the kids back to St. Peter. He wanted to pick up a few things for Libby and explain what happened to the officials at the school. Karl thought it was best if Janet and the kids went home."

"Then Karl's still at the parsonage?"

Kristen nodded. "How are you feeling this morning?"

"Drained, very drained. Yesterday was extremely difficult for me."

"We've been such fools," Kristen said, taking Anne's hand in her own. "We all believed what Papa wanted us to believe and never looked for the truth. We never even realized what we'd done to you."

"You weren't terrible for not questioning Papa. I let him dominate my life for twelve years. It took months of counseling to see that I mattered, too. Have you talked to Mama this morning?"

"I think you're changing the subject."

"I think you're right. I need to talk about something positive. I usually don't dwell on Papa and his opinions."

"Since that's the case, I have talked to Mama. She's beaming. She's so pleased to have you home. I think she's coming to the realization Papa was wrong. You are very special. I hope she's not nineteen years too late. Can you possibly forgive us?"

"I forgave you seven years ago. I've prayed you would someday want to see me."

"I Guess none of this happened the way you planned. No matter how it happened, I'm glad you're here. How long do you plan to stay?"

"Until I'm certain Libby is well and the doctors say I can go back to work. I'm sure there will be some legalities. I want to talk to the woman who hit her. I have to be certain she knows it wasn't her fault."

"Are you saying you're not going to bail Libby out?"

"I don't think so. Libby will have to get out of this on her own. I've never had to do it before. There's never been any trouble. I can thank Garrett for that. He and his son, Elliott, have been a good influence on her. Thank goodness Janice is here. She'll make certain the press doesn't blow this out of proportion and crucify Libby."

"I have to admit, I was as shocked by the press as Johann. Do they pry into every aspect of your life?"

"As many aspects as I allow them access too. It's funny, last night when we talked about the breakdown, it frightened me, but once you knew I felt relieved. It seemed as though someone lifted a ton of weight from my shoulders. I think now is a good time to go public with it. Maybe I can help someone who is in the same predicament."

"Aren't you afraid of what could happen?"

"This can't hurt me now. If it can help someone else, it will be worth it and any humiliation it might cause."

"Let's not think about such things now. I want you to take a nice hot bath. Lars and Garrett will be back soon and then everyone else will be coming out."

"Why? I saw them last night, what more is there to say?"

"We've discussed it. We feel we need to sit down and talk, but not the way we did last night. If you remember, our reunion seemed very strained. There are a lot of things we think you should know and a few things we want you to tell us."

AJ wondered what more they needed to know from her. Didn't they already know more about her than most people?

Before she could ask the question, Kristen continued. "I saw the way Garrett packed your suitcase. Men certainly don't know how to pack. I've pressed everything, but it all looks so dressy. Would you be more comfortable wearing what you had on yesterday?"

"I'll never get those boots on again, but the outfit is comfortable."

"I washed everything up when I did the laundry this morning. All I have to do is run an iron over the skirt and press up the blouse. I didn't see any tennis shoes, though. Do you still wear a size seven?"

"As a matter of fact, I do."

"Good. I have a pair to fit you. You won't be putting your bound foot into anything. When you get out of the tub, give me a holler and I'll rebind it for you. Karl wants to check it when he gets here."

"Honestly, Kristen, everyone is making far too much of this. It's only a silly little sprain. If I'd been home …"

"I know. You would have hobbled around. Well you aren't going to hobble around here. Didn't anyone ever tell you a sprain can be worse than a break? They said this is a bad sprain. There's nothing silly about it. Let me pamper you for a while. I'm certain it's been at least seven years since anyone made you rest. You look exhausted."

"Well, thank you for the compliment."

"You know what I mean. I'll go and draw a nice hot bath for you. You'll find towels, soap, shampoo, and anything else you might need in easy reach. If you want anything else, you'll have to let me know."

AJ swung her leg out of bed. Carefully she unwrapped the bandage from her injured foot. There was a lot of swelling and the area sported an ugly bruise, reddish purple in color. This certainly wasn't something that would heal in a couple of days.

She glanced up and caught her reflection in the mirror. Kristen was right. She did look tired. The bruise on her cheek from Logan's blow, the small cut on her mouth, reminded her of the days when they'd been married. She would need to carefully apply her make-up to conceal it.

* * *

Karl went to the hospital. He wanted to see Libby before they went to the farm, just to reassure himself she was doing well. Anne would want to know, and he wanted to be able to give her a positive answer.

He'd seen the picture of Anne in the wheelchair, flanked by her family and Logan, in this morning's paper.

Colorado Heiress Injured In Traffic Accident
Fashion Designer, AJ, Rushes To Her Daughter's Bedside.

The headlines and accompanying story were burned into his memory. Luckily, the reporters respected Garrett's request and had printed his statement almost word for word.

He'd cringed a bit when he looked at the picture and saw the worried expressions on their faces. No matter how worried the family looked, Anne, Garrett and Logan were smiling. These were the happy faces he knew they often wore for the press.

He wasn't surprised to find Logan in Libby's room.

"Good morning, Logan," he said, straining to be polite.

"Good morning, Doctor. You are the doctor, aren't you? I didn't get a lot of introductions last night, but I assume you're Uncle Karl."

"Yes," Karl answered, "I am. How are you doing Libby?"

"I'm sore and tired of all these machines they've hooked up to me. I don't want to be here. I want to be with Mom."

"She'll be in this afternoon. Right now she needs you to rest and relax."

"I'm already tired of resting and relaxing. I have things to do at school."

"I'm sure you do, but you'll have do as you're told for the next few days. The doctors want to keep you here for observation."

"The woman who was driving the car won't be charged, will she?"

"No, but there will be charges against you. I called the police station this morning. They said you'd be interviewed later today and then be charged with sudden pedestrian movement into traffic. From what I can find out, the fine is about fifty dollars."

"I know it was my fault. I deserve whatever I get. I would like to meet her and apologize for what happened. I want to pay for whatever damages happened to her car."

"Don't worry about the fine," Logan said. "I'll go down to the police station and pay it for you."

"No, Daddy. This is something I have to take responsibility for myself. I don't want you or Mom bailing me out."

"Good for you," Karl said, proud of Libby for taking responsibility for her acts. He leaned down and kissed her forehead. "I have to go now. At least I can give your mother a good report when I get to the farm."

"The farm? Mom stayed at the farm last night?"

"We all had a long talk last night. We cleared the air, you might say. We have a lot more talking to do, but we'll mend our differences."

Libby nodded.

"I'd like to talk to you, Logan," Karl said, as he left the room and went out into the hall.

"I don't think I have anything to say to you, Doctor," Logan replied, after he shut Libby's door.

"Good, then you can listen to me. I didn't see it, but I know you hit my sister last night. I don't think it's the first time it happened."

"Just what did AJ tell you? What kind of stories has she been spreading?" Logan snapped.

"Anne told me nothing, but I'm convinced you've hit her before. From what my brother said, your anger was too easily provoked."

"She was my wife," Logan commented, not seeming to be shaken by Karl's accusations.

"Janet's my wife, but I've never hit her."

"Maybe you never had cause ..."

"Cause?" Karl echoed. "Anne has no cause to be hit. If you ever come near her again in anger, I won't care whose name goes through the mud. I will have you arrested."

"You and Garrett, you're both full of big talk and lots of threats. You sound more like brothers than brothers-in-law. I'm surprised you haven't hit me."

"I wouldn't give you the satisfaction."

"Garrett did. I haven't forgotten it, either."

Karl fumed. "As I recall, that happened seven years ago. The statute of limitations has run out."

"He had me by the balls then. If I went to the authorities, he and that lawyer of AJ's would have made sure I never saw Libby again. Things are different now. Libby's an adult. She doesn't need his permission for anything."

"You're right, she is of age. If you cause any trouble for her mother, she won't need anyone's permission to cut you out of her life. Be careful what you say and do."

Karl turned and headed for the elevator, hoping what he said would sink in and give Logan Prescott something to think about. He prayed he'd made it clear not to tamper with AJ Lanners or anyone connected with her. If Logan or anyone else did, they would have more than Garrett to answer to. He would be there, as well as Johann, to protect Anne.

Logan returned to Libby's room.

"What did Uncle Karl want?" she asked.

"He wanted to let me know where your mother is so I can reach her if necessary."

"That's not it, and you know it, Daddy. You hit her, didn't you?"

"What are you talking about? I wouldn't hit your mother," Logan replied, shaken by Libby's question.

"Don't lie to me, Daddy. I was only a little girl, but I wasn't as ignorant as you thought. I know what went on and so did Jo. I remember the fights, the bruises and the phony explanations Mom used to make. It was the same last night. I could see the mark on her face where you slapped her. She didn't sprain her ankle getting off the plane. You aren't fooling anyone. You haven't changed, not at all."

"You knew?"

"Yes, I knew. We lived in the same house. The walls weren't thick enough to block out your fights. As soon as you moved to New York, there were no more bruises. I was only five, but I remember. I asked Jo about it, just before you left. All she would do was shake her head and say we couldn't do anything about it."

"I never meant for you to know."

"That might be, but I did. Just like I knew last night would be another of those mysterious bruises nights when Mom had to make up an excuse for a bruised face and a sprained ankle. I'm giving you fair warning, Daddy. If you ever touch her again, you can forget you have a daughter. You and your new wife can start your own family. Maybe all of this will have taught you something."

Once Lars and Garrett returned, Kristen insisted they take the rest of the morning off.

Even though Anne knew the rest of the family would be coming out to the farm, it still surprised her when Karl arrived with Johann, Sharon, and their mother.

"I'll get you some coffee," Kristen offered.

"Sit still," Sharon said. "I know where your kitchen is. I think I can find the coffeepot."

"Good morning," Karl greeted Anne, as he leaned over to kiss her cheek. "How's the patient this morning?"

"Impatient," she replied. "I hate this inactivity. Kristen washed my clothes, ran my bath and insists on waiting on me hand and foot. After she did the laundry, I did have something comfortable to put on. Everything Garrett dragged out of the closet is so …"

"I did all right," Garrett interrupted. "I only picked out work clothes."

"I know. You did just fine." She turned back to Karl. "How's my baby? Have you seen her this morning?"

"I stopped at the hospital. She's doing well, but she's worried about you. I am too. We've got a lot of talking to do. I'm going to start by asking you to tell me something."

Anne wondered what more there was to tell. Of all the family, Karl knew her the best. What more information could she give him and why did he look so serious?

She received a reprieve when Johann and Sharon returned with a tray of coffee mugs and the pot for refills.

"What do you want me to tell you, Karl?" Anne asked, once her cup was again brimming. "There's nothing more to tell."

"I agree with Anne," Johann commented. "If anyone knows her, it's you. Did you learn something more at the hospital?"

"I most certainly did. I learned the truth and I'm willing to bet it's something even Garrett didn't know."

"What truth are you talking about?" Garrett questioned.

Anne's heart beat wildly. Her woman's intuition told her what Karl wanted to hear, what she'd kept hidden for so long.

"This wasn't the first time Logan hit you, was it?"

Anne lowered her eyes, ashamed to have to admit the truth. "N-no, but it was a long time ago."

"How often, Anne?" Karl pressed, making the memory even more vivid in her mind.

"Once a month, once a week, twice a week, I don't know. I lost track. I just prayed each time would be the last. It was always after he'd been out with some other woman at the lodge. It didn't matter if they'd been having drinks and dancing, or if he'd been teaching her to ski or to ride. I knew the minute he walked in the door he'd been with someone else. As soon as I'd say he needed to spend more time with Libby and me, it would start. The physical pain ended with the divorce, but the emotional pain will never end."

Garrett's eyes were filled with amazement and with tears. "Why didn't you tell me this before?"

"What good would it have done to tell you? The physical scars were gone. It would have made you angrier than you already were when you hit him in the Crystal Creek hospital."

"How did you know I hit him?"

"I knew, at least I thought I knew, so I asked Ken to be sure. I thought I heard you say something about it when that idiot doctor tried to sedate me. The only way I would have ever known for certain was to ask."

"He beat you. Why did you stay with him?" Johann asked, his voice echoing his disbelief.

"I had no other choice."

"No choice," Johann echoed. "Of course you had a choice."

"Did I? The only thing keeping you writing was my marriage. When he dumped me, your letters stopped."

"As did yours," Johann reminded her.

"Yes, as did mine. I knew what divorce meant. It didn't matter if I was right or wrong, beaten or cheated on, I'd shamed you. The most painful thing was when the birthday and Christmas cards stopped coming, even to Libby. If it hadn't been for Karl, I probably wouldn't have kept my sanity at all."

"I think it's time I tell you about your Papa," Solveig said, as she cried openly.

"Mama, what more is there for us to know?" Anne inquired.

"There is much you don't know, much no one knows but me. I was younger than you when your Papa first experienced the dream."

"The dream," Anne interrupted. "Wasn't that just a story you told us?"

"No. It really happened. At first I didn't believe him. I'd heard about it for weeks and was sick to death of it. Every morning, he'd say the same thing. 'I had the dream, Solveig. I had the dream.' Then one morning everything changed. He convinced himself God spoke to him. I ranted, I raved and I cried. I swore I could never leave Norway. I couldn't be so far away from my Mama and Papa. It horrified me when even they assured me it was God's will and I would have to accept it. I prayed and prayed for another sign. Then we received the call from America. Your Uncle Sven told us he had cancer. The church council wanted your papa to take his place. The news devastated me. I was certain he'd become sick because of my prayers."

"Oh, Mama, how could you believe such a thing?"

"It was easy. I led a very sheltered life, never knew anything but doing the will of God. I thought I'd tested God's patience too much. I promised your papa I would never again question his judgment. That is the reason I couldn't go against him, even though I wanted to come to Colorado not only for your wedding, but to see Libby christened. I allowed his opinions to become mine, and I missed more than I can ever hope to regain."

Anne couldn't help her tears. All the time she thought her Mama didn't care, she now realized she'd been mistaken. Her father had been as abusive as Logan, only the bruises he inflicted didn't show.

"Your papa always thought God saved us for a reason. For years he convinced me it had been for your twin brother, but he died at birth. Now I know the truth. It wasn't for Sven, but for you. God helped us to leave Norway so your talent could shine through, so Libby could be born and become the beautiful person she is. I have no right to ask, but can you ever find it in your heart to forgive us?"

"Oh, Mama, I forgave you years ago. I just couldn't take the first step to come home. Karl came and found me, but I harbored too much pride, too much hurt to come to you. I knew you'd have to want to find me as much as I wanted to find you."

The room became quiet, the women's soft crying the only sound. Anne noticed Garrett's smile and realized he'd prayed for this reunion for most of their married life. Karl, too, appeared to be pleased. As for Johann and Lars, she knew they were trying to sort out their feelings. No matter what they were feeling, she knew none of them could have ever guessed the turmoil Solveig had endured over the past forty years.

"I have dinner in the oven," Kristen finally said, breaking the silence. "Is anyone hungry?"

"You know me, I'm always hungry," Karl replied.

Solveig smiled. "You sound like my brother, Thomas. I remember how he was always hungry, too."

The comment seemed to ease the tension in the room. "How about you, Anne?" Garrett asked. "You need to eat. We have to meet with the press this afternoon. How much do you intend to tell them?"

"Only what's necessary. I do plan to give Janice an exclusive on my breakdown, though."

Once Johann and Garrett helped her to her feet, Johann asked, "what good will it do so long after it happened?"

"It might help someone going through the same thing. If it helps one person, I'll be happy."

The reporters were assembled in a small meeting room at the hotel. Anne noticed Janice as soon as they entered the room.

As usual, Garrett conducted the conference. He gave out only the facts before opening himself and Anne to questions.

When at last it was over, Anne motioned for Janice to stay.

"How's the ankle, AJ?" Janice inquired, her tone one of genuine sympathy.

"I'll live. If I remember correctly, it's what Garrett said in the release," Anne teased.

"I want to know, not as a reporter, but as your friend," Janice pressed.

"It's a bad sprain. Karl says I'll be on crutches for at least the rest of the week, if not longer. I can't imagine being inactive for so long."

"Maybe it will do you good. It will give you some rest. I've thought you needed to slow down for a long time. Everything happens for a reason, so make the most of your time off."

Anne rolled her eyes. It seemed as though everyone, even Janice, had suddenly become concerned about her. She disliked being the center of attention, especially when the attention remained beyond her control. She found herself more comfortable talking about Fashions By AJ than AJ the person.

"I'd like to have you meet my family, Janice. I'm certain you remember my brother, Karl Jorgenson."

"It's good to see you again, Dr. Jorgenson," Janice said, extending her hand.

"This is my brother, Johann, and his wife, Sharon. Johann is the pastor of the Lutheran church here. My sister Kristen Olson, and her husband, Lars, run a large dairy farm just outside of town. And this is my mother, Solveig Jorgenson."

"It's a pleasure to finally meet AJ's mystery family. Until I met Dr. Jorgenson, I wondered if she even had a family."

The words hurt. "We haven't been close," AJ admitted. "It took something like this to bring us back together."

Janice nodded.

"What I wanted to talk to you about," Anne continued, "is what happened seven years ago when I dropped out of sight for a while."

"You were at a mountain cabin, everyone knows the story. You're not telling me anything new."

"Yes, I am. I didn't go to the mountains. I spent the time in a private hospital, not far from the ranch."

"At Morgan's place?"

"Yes. You see, after Jo's death, I had trouble coping. When I received word my papa died, it all became too much."

"I see," Janice said, true compassion in her voice.

"I stayed there for five weeks. I want you to do an exclusive on it."

"Why tell me, AJ? Why now?"

"Because it needs to be told. I trust you to get it right, to tell it the way I want it told. Why now? I don't know. I just know I'm coming to grips with it myself. Maybe I can help someone by going public."

"When you get home, call me. We'll get together and work on this. I promise, nothing will be printed without your consent. So, where are you going now?"

"To the hospital. I have to tell Libby what I just told you."

"She doesn't know?"

"No, and I can't have her read it in the papers."

"I agree with you. You're a very giving person, AJ. There aren't many people in your position who would go public with something like this."

"It's easier to do now. The company didn't go under, no one lost any money, I didn't lose custody of Libby, and it's a way to reconcile with my family. Once I told them, I knew I had to tell you."

Janice seemed pleased to be AJ's confidant, although AJ knew she still had questions.

"Why wasn't Logan here this afternoon?" Janice asked.

"I don't know. Maybe he wants his own press conference. One not tainted by my point of view," AJ replied.

"Aren't you afraid he'll hurt you?"

Janice's choice of words seemed almost ironic. How could Logan hurt her any more than he had in the past? "No, there's too much at stake. He thought the divorce and Jo's death would destroy me, but I surprised him. By hurting me, he would only hurt himself. Libby is old enough to understand what he would be doing. He can't afford to lose her."

"It will be interesting to see what happens," Janice commented. "I haven't heard from him."

"You won't. You've always covered me, not him. Just keep your ears to the ground. I'll be anxious to hear what happens."

Chapter Twenty-Three

Garrett dropped AJ at the hospital. She knew he wanted to go the police station to hear for himself the charges against Libby. "Will you be all right?"

"I'm not up to running the marathon, but I can certainly make it to Libby's room. It's three now, I'll see you at what, four-thirty or five?"

"Probably. I'll see you later." He leaned across the seat to kiss her. "If you get tired before I get here, just call Johann. He'll come and get you."

When she entered the hospital, she looked nervously around the lobby. She almost expected to see reporters waiting for her and was relieved to find only people hurrying to see loved ones. No one took notice of her as she made her way to the elevator and pushed the button for Libby's floor.

When she arrived at Libby's room, she saw Logan coming out the door.

"She's asleep," he greeted her. "How are you feeling today?"

"Rested."

"And the ankle?"

"I have to have it rechecked, but Karl seems to think I'll be on these crutches for a while."

"I'm sorry, AJ."

"Don't, Logan. We went over that last night. It's over. It's done with. Let's talk about other things. How's Libby?"

"She's going to be just fine. They gave her something for pain about an hour ago. It made her sleep. She's concerned about you."

"Well, I'm here now. Why weren't you at the press conference?"

"What need was there?" Logan inquired, his tone one of sarcasm. "I'm sure your brothers and Garrett were there."

"The press wanted a statement from you as much as they wanted one from me."

"Would my side be any different from yours? Libby had an accident. As usual, I wanted to believe you were to blame."

AJ nodded, agreeing with everything Logan said.

"Libby will sleep for a while. Let me take you down to the cafeteria and get you a cup of coffee. I think you need to get off your foot."

The cafeteria was quiet. It relieved AJ to sit at a table by the window, while Logan went for coffee,

"I couldn't resist this," Logan said, as he put a piece of cherry cheesecake in front of her.

"You remembered," AJ said. She smiled at the memory of sending Logan out for cherry cheesecake on one of the rare nights when he stayed home, while she was pregnant with Libby.

"How could I forget? Thank goodness they had cherry cheesecake at the lodge."

He tasted his chocolate cake before saying anymore. "I found something out today," he finally began. "I didn't think Libby was old enough to understand what went on between us while we were married. I was wrong. She understood everything. The fights, the women, everything."

"Does it amaze you?"

"Yes, it does. She said you never told her."

"Until this morning, I never told anyone how you used to hit me. Admitting it shamed me too much."

"When did you tell Karl?"

"I didn't. He told me. What are you getting at?"

"Nothing, he seemed so certain I'd hit you before, I just wondered how he knew. I have a temper AJ. You know it better than anyone. I just want you to know I'm going to get some therapy before I get married."

"Married? I didn't know. I'm happy for you. What's she like?"

"It's funny, she's a lot like you, sweet, trusting, beautiful …"

"And wealthy?" AJ inquired.

"Not at all. She's a secretary in my publisher's office. She's about your age and a widow with two grown sons. We're planning to be married just before Thanksgiving."

"Thanksgiving? What about Libby?"

"Didn't she tell you? I'd written to let her know she could spend Thanksgiving with you. We're going to be honeymooning in Europe. I didn't think either of you would mind."

"Oh, Logan, I had just written her myself and told her Garrett decided to take me on a Thanksgiving cruise. She may have even gotten the letters the same day. My poor baby. Not only did she find the family she wasn't actually looking for and heard terrible things. She must have thought we didn't want her. No wonder she became so upset when she heard them talking. I doubt she told anyone about it."

"I think we have a daughter to see. Speaking of we, where is Garret?"

"He went to the police station and wanted to contact the driver of the car. I think he planned to make some calls to Colorado, as well."

"So, how are you getting back to the family farm?"

"If I'm ready to go before Garrett gets back, I'll call Johann. He said he'd come and get me."

"The names come so easily now. It's certainly not like when we first got married," Logan said, taking her hand. "I'm glad you found your family. I remember how much you missed and needed them."

* * *

The ringing of the phone awakened Libby. She wondered who could be calling. Uncle Karl had visited this morning. Her father had been there when she fell asleep. Could be someone calling about her mother? Could something be wrong? Was it possible she wasn't coming to see her?

Tentatively, she answered the phone, almost afraid to hear the voice on the other end.

"Lib," Elliott's concerned voice sounded in her ear.

"Elliott?" she questioned, relief evident in her voice. "I was worried. I didn't know who would be calling. I thought maybe something went wrong with Mom."

"Lib, there's nothing wrong with your mom. She's being well cared for. How are you? I heard about the accident on the radio and called Pam. She gave me the number for the Olson farm. I had to practically bribe your uncle, Lars, to get your number. Are you okay?"

"My pride seems to be more wounded than my body. It was a stupid thing to do. I'll tell you all about it someday, when you've got about a year. Broken bones will heal, but I don't know if my relationship with Mom's family will come out as well. I acted like an idiot," she said choking back her tears.

"Don't cry, Lib. I'm willing to bet they're all excited about getting to know you."

"Then you must be privy to information I don't know about. Oh, Elliott, I just want to go back to school and forget this weekend ever happened. It's all been so terrible. Nobody wanted me here and to make matters worse, now Daddy's come. He and Mom have been fighting. He hit her and ..."

"Calm down," Elliott coaxed. "Everything is going to be all right, I promise. Look, I'm on a break, so I have to make this short. I want to come out there right now."

"It would just confuse the issue. It's crazy here. Everyone is on edge. Daddy and Uncle Karl had a confrontation this morning. Even though I was pretty much out of it last night, I could see the strain on Garrett's face. I felt sick when I saw Mom. She has a bruise on her face and a sprained ankle. It just isn't a good situation. Why don't you wait until the weekend? You can't be missing work. You'll get yourself fired."

"If I told them the accident happened to my sister ..."

"No, as much as I want you here, please wait and see what happens. I'll call you at the end of the week."

"You won't forget?," Elliott cautioned.

"You know I won't. I'll call you Thursday night, at seven your time, at your apartment. Is there a lot of talk about the accident?"

"Not to me, but then who would equate Elliott Lanners with the wealthy Colorado heiress, Libby Prescott?"

"Anyone who knows us. You must have seen the same headline I did. I wanted to barf when I read it. Anyway, you have to get back to work. I'll talk to you on Thursday."

"If you need me before then, promise me you'll call."

"I promise. Good-bye, Elliott."

She hung up the phone and wiped away the last of her tears when she heard a knock at the door. "Come in," she said, not bothering to learn the identity of her visitor.

"Hi, Champ," Garrett said, as he entered the room carrying an arrangement of red roses.

"Oh, Garrett, they're beautiful. Isn't Mom with you?"

"I left her off here two hours ago. I thought she'd be with you."

"As you can see, she's not. I haven't seen her. I fell asleep while Daddy was here. Maybe they ran into each other and went down to the cafeteria."

The look on Garrett's face worried her. "It will be all right, Garrett, there won't be a repeat of last night."

"What do you know about last night?"

"More than you think. I know what went on. Daddy hit her. It happened a lot before the divorce. Daddy and I had a long talk. He won't touch her, not if he ever wants to see me again."

"It wasn't a pretty scene last night, Champ," Garrett said, the tone of his voice saying more than his words.

"It never was. I can't imagine last night was any different." Libby closed her eyes in an attempt to dispel the memories that had been flooding her mind ever since she saw her mother the night before.

"Let's talk about something else. I just had a call from Elliott. He assures me Mom's family is eager to meet me. Should I believe him?"

"Of course, you should. I reached him at work, just after he got through to the farm. We had a long talk. He was as worried about you meeting the family as he was about you being in the hospital. I assured him they are really good people. They just let prejudice get in the way. Your grandmother is especially excited about getting to know you. She says she's missed so much she doesn't know how she'll ever catch up. She's afraid you hate her."

"How can I hate someone I don't know?"

"That's exactly what I told her. She was feeling better about the whole thing after we had our meeting this morning."

"Thank you, Garrett. I do feel better now. Why don't you go down to the cafeteria and see if Mom and Daddy are there? When you do find them, tell Mom I want to see her."

"Anything you say, Champ," Garrett said, bending to kiss her cheek. "I won't be long."

Libby watched him leave. A sense of peace flooded her mind. If she'd doubted Elliott, she couldn't doubt Garrett. He'd told her the truth. Her family did want to get to know her, just as much as she wanted to get to know them.

It seemed to Garrett that he waited forever for the elevator to the lower level. Once he stood in the cubical, there were stops at every floor. Nurses and doctors as well as visitors joined him on the descent to the basement.

When he finally entered the cafeteria, he found Anne and Logan seated at a table by the windows. Anne sat with her back to him, her crutches propped against the table. She seemed to be engrossed in conversation with Logan.

"I wondered what happened to you?" Garrett said, putting his hands on her shoulders and kissing her cheek. "I went to see Libby. It surprised me when you weren't there."

"Then she's awake," Anne said. "When I went up, she'd just fallen asleep. I didn't want to disturb her."

"Is there anything going on I should know about?" Garrett asked, pulling out a chair and joining them. He shot an accusatory look at Logan.

"No, Garrett, we're only talking," Logan replied. "You can be assured I won't ever hurt AJ again."

"Can I? I doubt it."

Anne reached out and touched Garrett's hand. "Logan's right. We've been talking. We could never just talk when we were married."

Garrett's eyes were cold and his voice carried an edge Anne had never heard before. "Are you going to meet with the press?"

he asked. "They were surprised you weren't with us this morning."

"AJ told me. I'm sure I'll have to give a statement, but it will differ little from yours. I don't plan to say anything derogatory. I know I've caused you and AJ a lot of grief over the years. Is there any way we can be friends?"

"No. Not after what I learned today."

Logan nodded. "I understand. I just want to say good-bye to Libby."

Anne knew Garrett wanted to tell Logan he'd had his time with Libby and now it was their turn. She hoped the look she gave him would make him hold his tongue.

"You look tired," Garrett said. "Let me get you a wheelchair."

She didn't argue. Logan took the crutches while Garrett pushed the chair. Without glancing up, she could feel the confrontation that bubbled just below the surface, threatening to erupt without notice.

Libby was sitting up in bed, smiling as they entered. Unable to contain herself, Anne got to her feet and embraced her daughter.

"Well, young lady," she began, once she seated herself in the chair again. "Your father says you have nowhere to go for Thanksgiving. Why didn't you tell us?"

"I got both letters the same day. I couldn't tell you and spoil your cruise."

Anne shook her head, trying to understand Libby's words. "Just what were you planning to do?"

"I'd considered going to Florida."

"Florida? Alone?" Anne and Logan echoed, in unison.

"Sure, why not? I've never been on a vacation alone before and I'm certainly not afraid to fly by myself."

"Change your plans," Garrett said. "Come with us on the cruise."

"Not on your life. I love you all, you know I do, but I've received a better offer."

"A better offer?" Anne asked. "What are you talking about?"

"Uncle Karl and Aunt Janet want me to join them. I'm going to accept their invitation. Last night Pastor Jorgenson said they want to get to know me. I'm more than a little scared, but I do like them. I'm sorry if it hurts you, but I want to give them a chance. I want to know my grandma and the rest of my family."

Anne couldn't contain her tears. "We had a long talk. We've all been very stubborn. We've missed a lot these past years. I can't think of a better place for you to spend the holidays. They'll surprise you. I know they did me. They have a lot of love to give."

"I promised your mom and Garrett I'd just stay long enough to say good-bye," Logan said, bending to kiss Libby's cheek.

"Before you go, Logan," Garrett said. "I think Anne has something to tell Libby, something you should hear as well."

As Anne related the story of the breakdown, Libby cried and Logan shook his head sympathetically. "I wanted you both to know before I went public. It's not meant to hurt either of you. I hope maybe it will help someone else. It's been seven years and until last night I couldn't talk about it. Being here, I knew I needed to tell my family the real reason I couldn't come home for Papa's funeral."

"Oh, Mom, I wish I'd known. I wish I could have helped you," Libby said.

"What could you have done? You were a child. Granted, you were perceptive and loving, but you were a little girl. This was something Garrett and I had to work through together."

The next morning, Logan called his own press conference. To everyone's surprise, he insisted AJ and Garrett be present.

Questions about Libby were asked and answered before Logan came to the real reason for calling the meeting.

"I found out something about myself these past few days," he began. "It's something I didn't want to admit and to be quite frank, it shocked me. Recently, I've heard a lot about men who beat their wives, men who beat their kids. Every time I heard one of those stories, I'd think poor slob, no control. Yesterday, I realized I'm one of those men. It's been a long time since I've had a confrontation with AJ. On the night of Libby's accident, it all came to the surface. I found nothing ever changes between the two of us. She didn't sprain her ankle getting off the plane, she sprained it when I hit her and she fell."

Behind him, he heard AJ gasp. He couldn't let it shake him. He needed to say the words he'd prepared before he lost his nerve.

"I had planned to be married in a couple of weeks, but I called the woman I was going to marry. We've postponed the wedding until I can get some counseling. I want to be confident I won't cause her the same pain I've caused AJ.

"When AJ and I were married, it didn't take much for me to hit her. All she had to do was say the wrong thing at the wrong time, and my temper would explode. It wasn't until I saw what I'd done to my daughter that I realized what I'd done to AJ. I understand how wrong I've been. I didn't think Libby was old enough to know what went on. I always told myself I had cause. My wife nagged me. I'm sure a lot of men use those same excuses. I would promise myself it would never happen again, but it did.

"I've decided to go public with this because I want people to realize it doesn't only happen to someone who is drunk or down on his luck. I had everything going for me. I'd married a lovely woman and she'd given me a beautiful daughter, but I found it easier to lash out than to talk. I wanted to have my cake and eat it too. I wanted women, success, and money. I wanted AJ to support me and give me a chance to do what I wanted without working. I wanted her waiting for me when I decided to come home. I didn't want to hear her questions about why I wasn't beside her, why I wasn't spending more time with my daughter. It seemed easier to strike out than to rationally talk things out. It can happen to anyone. It happened to me. I'm telling you this because I'm finally getting some help. Maybe someone will see this or read about it and decide to get help too."

"I don't know what to say, Logan," Janice said. "Congratulations. It took a lot of guts to say what you just did, to go public with something like this."

Logan watched as Garrett put his arm around AJ's shoulders. Leaning against him for support she cried openly. Secretly, Logan wished he could be the one to be holding her, the one to comfort her.

The reporters turned their questions to AJ and Logan listened carefully to her answers.

"Why didn't you ever tell anyone you were a battered woman, AJ?"

"It shamed me too much. Logan and I will never be close friends, but I do wish him luck and happiness."

Logan couldn't understand the pain her words caused him. After all these years, he realized what he'd lost. He really and truly loved her, no matter how many times he'd tried to convince himself otherwise.

By Tuesday evening, the Gustavus Adolfus campus buzzed with questions and speculations over the news of Beth's identity. Sonja found herself the center of attention. Several girls from her dorm gathered to discuss the accident and its impact on Beth as well as themselves. No one had known or guessed at her true identity, wealth, or prominence prior to the previous weekend.

Now they were asking questions that seemed to have no answers.

Sonja was as baffled as the girls who sat around the table in the commons area of the dorm. She wished she knew Beth a little better, wished she'd known they were cousins before any of this happened. Perhaps if she had, she could have handled things better.

"Why didn't Beth tell us?" Luanne Adams asked.

"Well," Sonja replied, "her Mama says ..."

"Her Mama?" Luanne interrupted. "Don't you mean your aunt?"

"My aunt," Sonja corrected herself. "She says Beth always thought her friends were only her friends because of whom and what she was. She wanted to have friends here because we truly liked her."

"I can't imagine anyone not liking Beth," Susan Gjertson said. "Do you think she'll still want to be called Beth when she comes back?"

Sonja shrugged her shoulders. "I don't think it matters much, Beth or Libby, she's all the same person, although I think I can see some difference between the two of them."

"What do you mean?" Susan asked.

"We all saw Beth here, at school. She's so confident, so Beth, her hair, her clothes, her grades are all perfect."

Susan giggled. "Of course her clothes are perfect. If my mom was AJ, my clothes would be perfect, too."

"Can you imagine having someone famous, like AJ, for your mom?" Luanne questioned. "Have you read *Lost Innocence?*"

Sonja shook her head. She'd never read Logan Prescott's books. Until this weekend, she had never even heard of Logan Prescott, much less read his books. From what she heard, it wouldn't be accepted reading at New Oslo High School, much less in her strict Lutheran household.

"Your uncle writes something that steamy and you haven't read it?" Luanne pressed.

"He's not my uncle. Not really. They've been divorced for years now. Anyway none of it matters. The girl we know here is Beth, but at my place I saw Libby."

"What do you mean?" Gail Martin inquired.

"She seemed more comfortable in the barn helping my papa milk than she would have been shopping in Minneapolis with Mama and me. She even walked up to the woods with my brother, Erik."

"Didn't you have any idea who she was? Not even a hint?" someone else asked.

"No, but why should I? But Mama did as soon as she saw her. Papa said he suspected it, although he couldn't be certain. Uncle Johann said he knew the minute he saw her in church. As for me, I had no reason to suspect anything."

Sonja fell silent, remembering how Beth had wanted to skip Sunday dinner at the parsonage, how she had picked at her food and made noncommittal answers to the questions people asked her.

"Why didn't you know her?" Susan asked.

"It's a long story. Until this weekend, I hardly knew Aunt Anne and Libby existed. Grandpa Jorgenson was very old world. He certainly didn't approve of women with careers, and Aunt Anne wanted a career. She wasn't like Mama, happy to marry her high school sweetheart and raise a family. Then when she did get married, it was because she was pregnant and then they divorced six years later."

"My folks are divorced," Gail interrupted. "What's so wrong about it?"

"Grandpa believed divorce was unforgivable. I guess it was about the time Grandpa died that Aunt Anne's picture disappeared from the piano. I must have been eleven or twelve then. I remember the big blowup because Aunt Anne didn't come from Colorado for the funeral. Uncle Karl said it was because she'd been in a bad car accident several weeks earlier and remained too weak to travel. Somehow, everyone seemed to know there had to be another reason. Uncle Karl confirmed it by storming out of the house. It took a long time for any of them to be comfortable with him again. Things have never really been the same since."

"They sound like an odd bunch to me," Susan said. "Did you ever find out why she didn't come?"

Sonja nodded. "It all came out on Sunday night. She did have a good reason, but I can't go into it now. If my Aunt Anne wants anyone but the family to know, it will have to be her decision."

"So, now they're one big happy family?" Luanne asked.

"I wouldn't go that far. When I left you couldn't call them exactly happy. I'm sure they'll get there, though."

"Are you going home this weekend or are you going to stay for the party?" Gail questioned.

"I wouldn't miss this weekend at home for anything in the world."

* * *

Upon Libby's release from the hospital Wednesday morning, she found a barrage of reporters waiting for her.

"How do you feel about your father's confession?" one of them asked.

"Confession, or the realization he was wrong? I've know about it for a long time. It just took a tragedy for him to come to the same conclusion."

"What about the charges against you?"

"I've been charged with running into traffic. I'm the first to admit being at fault. No matter what the reason, I can't blame the driver of the car. There's a fine to pay and I plan to take care of it."

"When will you go back to school?"

"Not until Monday. Garrett has arranged to have my lectures taped and he graciously brought my books, so I can study while I'm recuperating."

"Where will you be staying?"

"I was staying with my Aunt Kristen and Uncle Lars, but they have their hands full with Mom and Garrett. I've accepted an invitation from Uncle Johann and Aunt Sharon. I'll be staying with them and my grandmother."

Although there were unanswered questions, Garrett called an end to the meeting. "We don't want to tire Libby. I'm certain you can understand," he said, wheeling her toward the door.

"I don't think I'll ever get used to the press showing up every time Anne or Libby turns around." Johann said, once they were in the car.

"It isn't always like this," Libby informed him. "Unless Mom is introducing a new line, we lead a pretty normal life. You'll see, now I'm out of the hospital and Daddy is back in New York, they'll find someone else to cover."

At the parsonage, Anne and Kristen waited with Solveig and Sharon.

"I'm getting nervous," Solveig commented. "We said some terrible things on Sunday. I wouldn't blame her if she hated us."

"She doesn't hate you, Mama," Anne assured her. "You'll see. Libby is a very special young woman."

"Do you think Garrett's son will be coming this weekend?" Kristen asked.

"I'm sure he will. He's very concerned about Libby. Garrett said he wanted to come out on Monday."

"I can't imagine any of my boys being so devoted to their sisters," Kristen said.

"Oh, I can," Anne replied. "Remember how Karl came out and found me. Brothers and sisters are closer than you might think."

"Did I hear my name?" Karl asked, as he entered the room followed by Johann, Libby and Garrett.

"Maybe," Anne teased. "Don't let it go to your head, though."

They spent the rest of the day together, putting Libby at ease before Anne and Garrett returned to the farm.

The fact that Karl would be staying at the parsonage made Libby more comfortable. Over the next three days, she became better acquainted with her family. She spent many hours describing her life in Colorado, as well as hearing of life in New Oslo and Kinsarvik.

When she called Elliott on Thursday evening, she sensed his uneasiness at staying with her family. Since Janet and the children would be arriving with Sonja on Friday night, she would be moving to the farm once Elliott arrived.

"I heard your press conference," Elliott argued. "Your aunt has her hands full with your mom and my dad and you're staying with your uncle and grandma in town. I doubt if they'd be happy having me barge in. Just find me a motel room."

"They won't hear of it. I'll be moving out to the farm once you get here. I'll be staying with Sonja and you'll be bunking with Erik."

"And just who is Erik?" Elliott asked, his tone accusing.

Libby wondered if she noted a hint of jealousy in his voice. "Erik's my cousin, Sonja's brother. I hope you're up to milking cows."

"I've never been as handy around the barn as you. It sounds like we're going to be a family. Speaking of families, how do you feel about yours?"

"It's a little touchy yet, but we'll get there. It took nineteen years to build the barriers. We can't expect to break them all down in a week."

"Dad says you're staying out there for Thanksgiving. Why not come home, have Thanksgiving at the lodge with me?"

"You're sweet, Elliott, but I know you're going skiing. I don't think I'm up to it just yet. I need this time with my family."

"Guess I can't argue with you. I love you, Lib."

"I love you, too. I'll see you Friday at the airport. Just when does your flight get in?"

"Eight. I'll see you then."

When Friday came, Garrett and Johann drove Libby to the airport, while Karl and Lars went to Saint Peter to pick up Sonja, Janet, and the kids.

Elliott met them in the waiting area and hugged Libby tightly. Then holding her at arm's length, he commented, "Well, Miss Prescott, you don't look any the worse for wear."

"I'm healing quite nicely, thank you," she replied, hugging him again. Turning to Johann, she continued. "Elliot Lanners, this is my uncle. Uncle Johann, this is my brother."

Johann and Elliott shook hands. "I'm glad you decided to come, Elliott. I think Libby needs you."

"I wanted to come earlier, but she wouldn't let me."

Garrett clasped his son's hand. "It's been a very confusing week. It's best you waited."

They collected Elliott's weekender from the luggage carousel, then went out to Johann's car.

"Where's Anne?" Elliot inquired, as they pulled out of the parking lot.

"She's playing Becky Homecky out at the farm," Libby answered.

"She's playing what? Isn't the term Suzy Homemaker?"

"It's only Suzy Homemaker when you do it every day. For Mom, it's a once in a lifetime opportunity."

Elliott laughed at her comment. "I guess she's not very domestic. Is she off the crutches?"

"They proclaimed her quite well yesterday. The doctor even told her she could start using a cane. Now she's anxious to get home."

"Have you heard from your dad?"

"He called twice. He started therapy yesterday. He and Marie won't be getting married until after the holidays."

Elliott shook his head. "I can't believe so much has happened, so much has been aired. People will have a lot to digest once Anne tells everyone about the breakdown."

"It had to be hard for both of them. They're both basically private people."

"So where do you go from here, Lib?"

"Back to school on Monday. Gustavus Adolfus is my choice. What about you? How is Brenda?"

"Come on, Lib, Brenda is Brenda. I can't see myself spending my life with her, but we've had a good time together. She wasn't happy about my coming here this weekend. I'd gotten tickets for a concert in Denver. When I gave them to her, she didn't have any trouble finding an escort."

"So, it's on to the next conquest. Have you met her yet?"

"You think you're smart, don't you? Yes, I've met her. Her name is Abby and she works in the secretarial pool at the office."

After a hectic weekend, Libby was glad to return to school, pleased to once again become Beth. As she stepped from her dorm to go to her first class, she found a group of reporters waiting for her. Instantly, she became Libby, the Colorado heiress, who could handle the press as easily as she could handle the chores at the ranch.

"How does it feel to be back at school, Libby?"

"It feels good."

"Do you think the new popularity of your father's books is because of your accident or because of his confession?"

"I'd like to think it's because of their merits."

"Are you planning to stay on at Gustavus Adolfus?"

"I am, if a few certain reporters will let me get to class. I think it's time you looked for something new to report. This story seems to be getting stale."

Chapter Twenty-Four

Sonja sat cross-legged on the bed facing her cousin. Could it already have been three years ago when she first met Beth? Could this already be the beginning of their senior year of college? One more year and they would go their separate ways. At least, they would not lose touch the way their parents did. They'd become too close to allow such a thing to happen.

"Does it seem like three years ago when we first met?" she questioned.

"Are you kidding?" Beth replied. "It feels like yesterday when you took me home for the weekend and I met the family. I remember it as being a scary proposition."

Sonja said nothing as she silently remembered the weekend she first realized Beth's true identity. She recalled the uncertainty of how she and Aunt Anne would change their lives.

Now, three years later, it was as though they had always been part of the family. Their visits were quiet reunions rather than emotion-charged events, as the first one had been.

Even Grandma Jorgenson became excited whenever they arrived. They now spent the week before Christmas and the week after school let out in New Oslo. Knowing these were busy times at the Lady Jo made their visits even more special.

It had been just before school started this past summer, when Sonja spent a week with Beth. Seeing the Lady Jo and the Lazy B for herself, she became better acquainted with Libby.

When she said something about it to Uncle Karl, he laughed. "I remember your Uncle Garrett introducing me to AJ before I went in to see Anne. Like mother like daughter, I guess."

She thought of the first time she realized the difference between Beth and Libby. Although she liked and sometimes even envied Beth, she admired Libby. Beth was intelligent, beautiful and perfectly dressed. She remained quiet, rarely dated, and led a relatively private life. On the other hand, Libby seemed equally at ease riding horses, working in the barns, or meeting the guests at the Lady Jo.

"It's hard to believe that in a few months, you will actually be running the ranches," Sonja commented.

"Don't forget, Garrett will be my guardian for three years. Jo's will provided that he oversee my interests until I'm twenty-five. I've thought a lot about it and I'm comfortable with the arrangement. Three years will give me time to adjust to being a working owner. I can only hope someday Prince Charming will come along and sweep me off my feet."

"Don't you realize Prince Charming has already come?"

"Whatever are you talking about?"

"Elliott."

"Elliott? He's my brother."

"He's more than your brother. I had suspicions the first time I saw the two of you together. The weekend trips from Windsor just aren't natural brotherly behavior. I think he loves you."

"Now you are being silly. He has more girls than he knows what to do with."

"But, has he settled down and asked one to marry him?"

"Don't be silly. He's too busy playing the field. The right one just hasn't shown up yet."

"Maybe the right one is you. I know you love him. I can see it in your eyes whenever you're together. You date, but I don't see your eyes sparkle for anyone else the way they do for Elliott."

"I hate to admit it, but I'd cut off my right arm to be his wife, but it's impossible. When our parents got married, we took vows. We promised to be brother and sister."

"Get real, Beth. He's not really your brother. There's no blood relation. It's so evident. Why don't you just admit it? Confront him and see how he feels."

"I'll let you in on a little secret. The last time Elliott and I went to New York together, just before I graduated from high school, I told him I loved him and he told me how foolish it was. He said we were brother and sister, nothing more. Nothing will ever change between us, no matter how much I want things to be different."

"If you ask me, I think he's very much in love with you. You have to be blind if you can't see it."

"Even if you are right, which you aren't, I wouldn't hurt Mom or Garrett for anything in the world."

"You mean like Grandma and Grandpa hurt her?" Sonja paused to try to read her cousin's expression. "Maybe you're going to have to look past those fears and think of your own happiness."

Libby laughed. "You have it all tied up in a pretty little package. You've just forgotten one thing. Elliott is very busy with all his girlfriends and hasn't made any move toward me. It's a waste of time to dwell on impossible things when we both have papers to write."

Although Libby went back to her studies, her mind remained on Elliott. She loved him, but she knew she could never profess her love. The thought of his ridicule was more than she could stand.

She wished she'd never said the words that vowed her love was wrong at her mother's wedding. If only she'd met Elliott when she was old enough to know what love meant, old enough to realize brother-sister love would never be enough for her.

* * *

Christmas was fast approaching and as always Libby sensed the excitement. Although she no longer went to New York for the holidays, her mother and Garrett would be flying into Mankato to spend the week before Christmas with the family.

It saddened her not to be going to New York, but there was no longer a need. A month after the incident in New Oslo three years ago, her beloved Grandmother Prescott died. Her last trip east had been for the funeral.

With no remaining ties to New York, her father and his new wife, Marie, had moved to London to be closer to her family.

Now Libby's visits with her father were two weeks in the summer to play tourist in the exciting city.

As she waited for her mother and Garrett to land, she found herself a bit disappointed over Elliott not accompanying them to Minnesota. He'd done so in the past, but this year too many projects at work required his attention and he couldn't get away. She knew that if she hadn't had the conversation with Sonja, his absence wouldn't have bothered her.

Once everyone was finally together, Libby took the opportunity to approach Erik and make the announcement about his future. Since her herdsman would be retiring the following year and Erik would be graduating from the farm short course in January, she hired him to fill the position. His acceptance meant flying to Crystal Creek shortly after graduation to spend as much time as possible with Charlie to learn the operation.

Anne, too, had an announcement to make. She waited until they all opened their gifts before giving voice to her plans.

"I've decided on a graduation gift for Libby and Sonja," she began. "I think it's time we all went back to Norway. We will take the girls with us and basically, we'll all find our roots."

Before she could continue, the room buzzed with conversation.

"I want to give this trip to the family," she continued. "I'm going to buy tickets for all of us, each couple and Mama, as well as the two girls."

"We couldn't let you do such a thing," Johann interrupted. "It's such a lot of money."

"What good is all our money if we can't do something special with it?" Garrett questioned. "Anne has looked into the possibilities and has tentatively booked ten seats to Oslo from Minneapolis for the Wednesday after graduation."

"Ten seats?" Kristin asked. "But there are eleven of us."

"Libby will want to stop in London for a few days, to see Logan. He is her father and he will want to see her for a little while at least."

Excitedly, the family agreed to Anne's proposition. Once they accepted her generous gift, they began formulating excited plans.

Although the proposition excited Libby, she secretly wished Elliott would be accompanying her. Silently, she admonished herself for such thoughts. Her life would go on, but without Elliott by her side. They would never be more than brother and sister.

Libby found Christmas to be a very difficult vacation. Having confessed her longings to Sonja, she found it hard to keep her eyes off Elliott. His hair, his eyes, even his voice seemed to draw her like a magnet. Why couldn't he see how completely devastated she became when he mentioned the girls he currently dated?

"What's wrong with you, Lib?" he asked, when he followed her to the kitchen.

"Whatever gave you the idea something was wrong?"

Elliott turned her to face him. "You're acting strange. Are you having boyfriend problems?"

"Boyfriend?" Libby repeated. "What boyfriend? The guys I date at school are just that, guys at school. There's no permanent relationship there."

"Maybe that's what you need, a permanent relationship," Elliott said, taking her in his arms.

Exasperated, she pulled away. As much as she wanted Elliott to hold her, reassure her, she didn't want his brotherly sympathy. "That's your answer to everything, isn't it? Well, I don't see you in a permanent relationship. As far as I'm concerned, you shouldn't give out advice you don't follow yourself." Pushing past him, she hurried out of the room.

"Libby," her mother said, but she didn't stop to reply.

"Elliott." Garret said. "Did you and Libby have a fight?"

"Don't ask me," she heard Elliott say. "I just asked her what was wrong and she bit my head off."

That's because you're what's wrong she wanted to scream as she slammed her bedroom door. The Black Hills gold bracelet she'd received from Elliott earlier in the week mocked her as it lay on the dresser.

She'd just picked it up, when a light rap at the door interrupted her thoughts.

"Libby, can I come in?" her mother asked.

"Sure Mom," she replied, putting the bracelet back in its box.

"Is something wrong between you and Elliott?"

Libby laughed nervously. "Nothing's wrong. Elliott seems to think I'm acting strange. Maybe I am. There is a lot of pressure at school and all he can say is that I need a man."

Anne drew Libby into her arms. "You have plenty of time for men. I know how it is when you're in school. Maintaining high grades can be a strain. Your brother is just worried about you."

"That's part of the problem. Elliott's not my brother, not really. He's someone I met at the airport a long time ago. Just because you married Garrett and we said some words at your wedding doesn't make us brother and sister. He thinks he can tell me what to do and how to act."

"It only seems that way. We all care about you. Why don't you take a nap, and then we'll go down to the lodge for dinner."

Libby nodded. It relieved her when Anne left the room. She lay down on the bed and reviewed the conversation in her head. Had she said too much? Would her mother guess her true feelings for Elliott?

Returning to school came as a relief. Engrossed in her studies, she seemed able to shut Elliott out of her thoughts for several hours at a time.

"You haven't been out for an evening in weeks, Beth," Sonja commented. "If you're this miserable here, what will it be like when you're back in Crystal Creek and Elliott is in Windsor?"

"I don't know. I've got to figure out a way to put him out of my mind. I guess when I'm busy with the ranches maybe I won't have time to think about him."

Libby hoped her plan sounded plausible. With luck it would pacify Sonja enough to leave her alone. One good thing to come out of this was the amount of study time she'd been getting by staying in and brooding.

Elliott's phone call came as a surprise. "Hi, Lib," he said, cheerfully. "I called to congratulate you on your midterms. I hear you aced them. Your 4.0 average is something to be proud of."

"Thanks. I keep trying. A few more weeks and I'll be home free."

"Should I be worried about you?" he continued.

His question bothered her. "Why would you ask such a silly question?"

"Because of the way you were acting at Christmas, the fact I haven't heard from you, and because even Sonja's concerned."

"Sonja? Did she call you? What did she tell you?"

"I called her last weekend. I took a chance she'd be home. She told me I shouldn't be worried. I didn't believe her. She doesn't make a convincing liar. I could tell she's as concerned as I am."

"Don't exaggerate, Elliott. She's concerned about her grades, not me. You'll see. When I get back from Norway, everything will be different. I'm sure it's just the pressure here at school that's causing my slight case of the blues."

"Are you coming home for Easter?"

"With all the preliminary work that needs to be done before this year's renovations at the Lady Jo, of course I'll be home. Your dad promised me a desk full of swatches and samples."

"Good. We'll take some time and have a long talk."

"Whatever you say. In the meantime, don't worry. Things are getting better around here. You'll see, come Easter, you'll wonder why you were ever worried."

"I hope so. I love you, Lib."

Libby felt a lump form in her throat at Elliott's words. They were the ones she wanted to hear, but his tone sounded more like a concerned brother than committed lover. "I love you too, Elliott," she said, ending the conversation before her tears began to fall.

When Sonja returned from the library, Libby was still crying. "Why didn't you tell me Elliott called you?" she accused.

"I didn't want to upset you. Believe me, I didn't tell him anything."

"I know. He told me. He also said you aren't a good liar. He says we're going to have a long talk over Easter. I hope I can handle it."

* * *

Easter vacation was, as Garrett promised, very busy. Libby hadn't been able to spend much time at the Lazy B, as the Lady Jo demanded her attention. She became so involved in the work on her desk she didn't hear the door open, nor the click of the lock.

She was engrossed in reading a report Garrett had left, when she felt someone's hands on her shoulders. Startled, she turned abruptly, to see Elliott standing behind her.

"What are you doing here?" she asked, his smile a bit disarming.

"I told you on the phone, we need to talk. Now we're going to do just that."

"Your memory is great, Brother dear, but your timing stinks. In case you haven't noticed, I have stacks of work. Whatever it is, it will have to wait."

Elliott pulled her to her feet, so they stood facing each other. "No, Lib, this can't wait. We need to talk about us."

"Us? What do you mean us?" Libby asked, wondering if she'd heard him correctly.

"Just what I said. Us! I've been trying to deny there could ever be an "us" for years. At Christmas, I realized I couldn't deny it any longer. I saw the expression on your face when I mentioned a boyfriend. I saw how much my suggestion hurt you. I wanted to take you in my arms and make the hurt disappear. No matter how hard I tried, I couldn't forget the look on your face. I thought, maybe, I was mistaken, but then I called both Sonja and you. I could hear the same hurt in your voice. That's when I remembered what you said on the plane. You said you loved me, but you were only seventeen. What did you know about love? I knew I loved you, but you had college ahead of you, and young men to meet and date. I couldn't spoil such a special time in your life with my feelings."

Libby put her finger to his lips. "Are you trying to say, 'I love you?'"

"No, I've said it before. I'm trying to say, marry me, Libby Prescott."

"But you said ..."

"I said we were brother and sister, but not by blood, only by vows. There is nothing to stop us, nothing to hold us back. It's not incest. It's love. I love you, Libby, just like I promised when we took those vows. I'll love you for as long as we live."

Before Libby could say anything, Elliott took her in his arms and kissed her tenderly.

"What about Mom and Garrett?" she managed to say, once they parted, not really caring about the answer.

"We won't tell them, at least not until the plans are complete."

"What plans?"

"Anne is taking you to Norway this summer. We'll get married there. Isn't your cousin, Gunnar, a minister there? He could perform the ceremony and Johann could assist if you'd like. You'll be going to London first. I'll go with you. We'll tell your dad and my mom then. Mom just called. She'll be doing a show there this summer. The timing is perfect."

"You've convinced me. How can I say no? I love ..."

Elliott didn't allow her to finish as he kissed away every question, every protest. She knew this was meant to be. No one else mattered but the two of them.

When Elliott broke the embrace, he asked, "Did you really say yes?"

Libby nodded, nestling her head against his shoulder. "Did you think I'd say no?"

"I prayed you wouldn't. If you had I don't know what I would have done with this." Elliott reached into his pocket and produced a purple, velvet box.

When Libby opened it, she let out a squeal of delight. The solitaire diamond in the Black Hills gold setting was exquisite. Wrapped around the ring was a delicate gold chain. "Oh, Elliott, it's perfect, right down to the chain. Until we're ready for our parents to know, I'll wear it on the chain."

"Let's call your cousin Gunnar and start the ball rolling."

"Now?" she questioned. "Do you have any idea what time it is there?"

"It's between nine and ten at night. It's not so late."

Libby threw her hands in the air. "I can see there's no use arguing with you when you have everything planned so perfectly."

As she waited for the transatlantic call to be put through, she was glad she would not have to rely on her imperfect Norwegian to be understood. Gunnar, her mother told her, had learned English when recuperating in the American hospital in Germany.

"This is Libby, Elizabeth Prescott," she said, when he answered.

"Libby? Anne's Libby? Is something wrong? Has something happened to your mother, your grandmother?"

"No, nothing is wrong. The plans are all set for this summer. I'm calling to ask a favor of you."

"A favor of me?" Gunnar questioned. "What can I possibly do for you?"

"I want to be married in Norway," she said, hardly believing the words she just spoke.

"Married? This is the first I've heard of it. Your mother has said nothing whatsoever."

His comment seemed to put her at ease. "She couldn't have told you, because she doesn't know. It's to be a secret until we arrive in Norway. There are some things we need to have you look into for us."

"Such as?"

"What arrangements we need to make, what documentation we need to bring. Before you agree, I must explain our situation to you." As best she could, she explained the circumstances surrounding her engagement and forthcoming marriage.

"We've been in love for years," she concluded. "We've tried to deny it, but it's become impossible."

"I see no problem with it," Gunnar assured her. "I'll check on everything. If I'm not mistaken, I may even have a surprise for you."

"What kind of a surprise?" Libby asked.

"Never mind. Just give me your phone number and I'll call you on Tuesday."

"No. I'll call you. I'm very hard to reach and I'd hate to have you waste your money. I'll call at say eight o'clock in the morning, my time, before I start classes."

Libby hung up the phone and turned toward Elliott. "He foresees no problems and he promised to look into the legalities. He also said he might have a surprise for me."

"Well, I don't want our surprise to be spoiled, so here is my long distance card. When you call Gunnar, be sure to use it. We wouldn't want Anne and Dad to get suspicious over your phone bill."

Libby began to giggle.

"What's so funny now?" Elliott asked.

"I was just thinking, you're going to have to start calling her Mom and I'm going to have to call Garrett, Dad. It will take some getting used to."

Elliott, too, began to laugh, then took her in his arms and kissed her lovingly. "Oh, Libby, I love you so much. Now that it's out and you know, I don't want you to go back to school."

"It's only a few more weeks. Not telling anyone will be hard. I promise not to tell the family, but I have to tell Sonja. I can't share a room with her without telling her what's going on."

"All right, tell Sonja, wear the ring at school, but not a word to your family." He held her a little tighter. "I wish I hadn't waited so long. You'll be going back tomorrow."

Libby silenced him with a kiss. "It's best this way. Otherwise, we could never keep it a secret. Just remember, in June we'll be in London together."

Once Elliott left, Libby put the ring onto the chain and slipped it around her neck, allowing it to drop out of sight beneath her blouse. *Ours is a strange courtship,* she thought.

Garrett and Anne flew Libby to Mankato, where Karl would meet them. Once Libby was back at school, Anne and Garrett would spend the night with Karl and Janet before flying on to Chicago. The Chicago shop planned a show and Anne felt obligated to attend.

As they drove from the airport toward the school, Garrett turned to speak with Libby. "Your mother and I have been talking about the future. I'm going to have my guardianship ceased. You're perfectly capable of running your ranches. You've shown us just how capable you are this spring. I'll continue as business manager as long as you want me, but I'm certain you'll want a younger staff."

"Are you positive?" Libby asked, more pleased than shocked.

"Your mom is forty-five, I'm almost fifty. We want some time to enjoy ourselves, but you know you can always count on us."

Libby wanted to hug Garrett, but the seat separated them. She wondered how she would tell him about Elliott quitting his job, about their dream of a partnership. "I know I can, but I'm sure I'll manage quite well. I'm certain Mom can find lots of interesting ways to keep you busy. While you're having the paperwork drawn up, I want you to put the house in your name."

"The house?" her mother repeated, surprise sounding in her voice. "But, it's part of the ranch, your home."

"No, Mom, it's your home. You and Jo are everywhere. I've had some plans drawn for my own house. When I'm ready, I'll have it built."

"When did you have plans drawn up?" Garrett questioned.

"One of my friends at school wants to be an architect. Since he needed to draw some plans for the course, I suggested he work on my house. It's exactly what I want."

"Will you live there all alone?" Anne inquired.

"Perhaps, but it's not built yet. Maybe, by the time it's done, I'll have been swept off my feet by some Prince Charming."

Libby's statement met with nods of approval. "Just be careful," her mother warned. "If you remember, my first Prince Charming turned back into a frog."

Is that what my father wa,? Libby asked herself. *Was he a frog or a snake? No matter what, he is my father and I do love him*

When at last she settled in at the dorm, she lifted the chain over her head and slipped the ring on her finger.

On an impulse, she sat at the desk and began to write her name on the note pad. *Mrs. Elliott Lanners, Libby Lanners,* she laughed at the last one. She certainly couldn't use the two names together. She could become Elizabeth Lanners or Libby Prescott Lanners, but not Libby Lanners. Before she could come to any concrete decisions, the phone rang. She answered, expecting the caller to be Sonja saying she would not be coming back until Monday.

"Hi, Honey," Elliott sounded as though he stood in the next room.

"I just left you," she responded.

"I miss you," he replied, with a laugh.

"You'll think you miss me when you get your phone bill. Calls to me, calls to Norway, it will resemble the national debt."

"Don't worry about it. If I can't be with you, see you, I want to talk to you. Did you have a good flight out? Do the folks suspect anything?"

"The flight was great and I don't think they have any idea about our plans. Your dad did tell me he's going to relinquish his guardianship as a graduation gift. He said if I needed help with anything, I could come to him. I told him I could manage, I just didn't tell him how. I did ask him to put the house in his name. I told him about having plans drawn for my own, our own house. I'm afraid they think I'm crazy. I'll be sending you the plans this week, to see if you approve."

"You know if it's something you want, I'll approve. As soon as I get them, I'll find a builder. We can get started the day Dad and Anne leave for St. Peter for graduation."

"It all seems like a dream," Libby said. "You managing the ranches, me running them, we'll make quite a team. I love you Elliott, but we have to hang up now."

"I don't want to say good-bye, Lib, but I know you're right. Call me Tuesday night, after you talk with Gunnar. Good night, I love you."

She hung up the phone, with Elliott's words I love you, ringing in her ears. With the diamond sparkling in the light of the desk lamp, she daydreamed about her future with Elliott.

"I'm back," Sonja said, as she burst into the room.

Libby hugged her cousin and anticipated Sonja's excitement about the events of Easter vacation.

"I think I have a job," Sonja blurted out.

"A job? Where? When did you have the interview?"

"I interviewed for a newspaper in Denver. Remember your Mama's friend, Janice?"

"How could I forget Janice? She's been part of my life for as long as I can remember."

"She held the interviews in Minneapolis over the holiday. I didn't say anything about you and Aunt Anne, though. I wanted the job on my own merits. Anyway, she asked about you when we finished the interview. She told me that I'd been called because of my resume and the sample articles I'd sent, and not because of my ties to you. I won't know anything for a few days, but it does sound promising. What about your vacation? What did you do? Did you meet anyone exciting?"

Libby smiled slyly. "I worked on the Lady Jo more than I wanted. I didn't get over to the Lazy B very much. It was more of a working vacation than anything else."

"Come on, Beth, there's something you aren't telling me, I know there is."

She glanced down at Libby's hand. "You're engaged. Who? You haven't been dating anyone."

"It's Elliott," Libby replied, looking lovingly at the ring.

"I should have known. I saw it coming. The Black Hills gold is a dead giveaway. When did he ask you? When will you be married? What did Aunt Anne and Uncle Garrett say?"

"Slow down, one question at a time. He asked me yesterday and I still can't believe it. We're planning to be married while we're all in Norway, but you can't tell anyone in the family."

"Why not?"

"Because Mom and Garrett don't know. It's going to be a surprise. You know I'm going to be spending a week with Daddy in London. What you don't know is Elliott's mother is there too, so we're going over together. From there we'll go on to Norway. Gunnar has agreed to marry us and we're hoping Uncle Johann will assist. Will you be my maid of honor?"

"You know I will."

"Good. I talked to Jacque and swore her to secrecy. She'll be sending us some sketches so we can pick out just the right dress for you."

"What about your dress?" Sonja asked.

"I haven't decided yet. If I want something special, I'll let Jacque know. I just haven't had time to think about it. Too much has happened in the past two days."

On Tuesday morning, Sonja listened as Libby placed the call to Norway. As she frantically jotted notes, she almost forgot the promised surprise.

"Before we hang up," Gunnar said, "I promised you a surprise. I was almost certain when we spoke on Saturday, but I had to make sure."

"Make sure of what?"

"Your grandmother's wedding dress. I thought I'd seen it at Aunt Gerta's, so I asked her. She said she found it when she cleaned the attic several years ago and wants to have it refurbished for you. She asked me to get your measurements."

If Sonja wondered why Libby started giving her measurements over the phone, she said nothing until Libby hung up.

"What was that all about?" she asked.

"Grandma's wedding dress, I'm going to wear Grandma's wedding dress when I get married. Aunt Gerta is going to have it made over for me."

Chapter Twenty-Five

"I can't understand why Elliott didn't come for graduation," Anne commented, as they ate lunch at Karl's prior to the ceremony.

"I told you before," Libby said. "He couldn't get the time off work. This is a busy time for him. We talked it all over and decided to have our time together when I get back from Norway."

"There's no excuse for it," Garrett stormed. "I don't care how busy he is, he should be here. You're his sister, for god's sake."

"Get off it, Garrett," Libby teased, bursting to tell them her secret. "Elliott has his own life. He doesn't need to be chasing out here for graduation when I'll be home in a month and we can spend some quality time together."

"I'll say it once more, then I'll let it drop," Garrett continued. "He should be here. If I'd known he wasn't coming, I'd have gone to Windsor and made him come with us. Believe me, when we get back home, I'm planning to have a serious talk with him about family obligations."

Family obligation. Libby smiled inwardly at the words. In two weeks, she and Elliott would be married and family obligations would, in reality, be true. The ring hanging around her neck and resting between her breasts attested to it.

On Tuesday afternoon, they all went to the Minneapolis airport to catch their flights. Libby would be the first to leave.

"I can't understand it, Libby," Kristen began. "Why fly to Chicago and then to London? Why don't you get a direct flight from here?"

"I like the flight from Chicago, and besides, I'm meeting some friends there." Once she said the words, she knew she couldn't take them back. She would be expected to make up a believable story for her family.

"You've never told me about these friends, dear," Anne said. "Who are they?"

"Just a couple of girls I met on my first trip to London. We've kept in touch. It will be good to see them again."

"It seems strange I've never heard you mention them before. What are their names?"

Libby felt pressed and had to think quickly. "Kathy Simmons and Jeannine Connors," she said, making up names for her nonexistent friends. She cringed at the lie. She'd never lied to her mother before and for a split second she wondered if she'd get caught. From the corner of her eye, she saw Sonja smile and hoped no one else noticed.

She boarded the plane amid calls of, "have a good trip," and "we'll see you in Norway." Once seated in first class, she lifted the chain over her neck and slipped the ring onto the third finger of her left hand. She'd taken it off for the last time. From this moment forward, she would not need to deny her love or her future with Elliott.

When her plane arrived in Chicago, Elliott waited for her. They embraced as young lovers, not brother and sister. Here it didn't matter who saw them, who guessed they were in love.

"I didn't think you'd ever get here," he said, holding her at arm's length.

"Neither did I. I had to do some quick thinking at the airport before I left. If anyone asks, your name is either Kathy or Jeannine."

"What are you babbling about?" Elliott asked, before he started laughing.

"Just before I left, Aunt Kristen asked why I wanted to fly out of Chicago and not Minneapolis . I had to think fast, so I made up the story about two wonderful girls I met on my first trip to London and how we always meet the Chicago airport."

"Why you little liar. I love it. This is going to be one exciting marriage. We have time before they call our flight, would you like something to eat?"

"I'd like a soda. Were you able to get our seats confirmed?"

Elliott ordered two sodas at one of the small bars dotting the airport and returned to the table where he left Libby. "Here you are, and yes, I did get the seats confirmed."

"It will be a perfect wedding trip, won't it, Elliott?" she asked, squeezing his hand before leaning across the table to kiss him lovingly.

At last they heard their flight called. Once seated, she couldn't help smiling. For as long as she'd know Elliott, she'd loved him. In a few days she would be able to tell the world just how much. It was like a dream come true.

"Mr. Lanners, Miss Prescott, would you like a drink?" the flight attendant asked, once they were airborne.

"We'd like champagne," Elliott said, turning to smile at Libby.

"You two look like you have something worth celebrating," the attendant said, as she poured the chilled wine into their glasses.

"We're going to be married in Norway," Libby replied.

"Norway? You must be on the wrong flight. We're going to London, not Oslo."

"We're on the right flight," Elliott assured her. "We have to stop in London and see some people before we get married."

* * *

The flight to Oslo left on time, its first class section filled with AJ Lanners and party.

"Flying first class," Solveig said, once they were airborne. "I can't believe it. I've never even been on an airplane before. It is so different from when we came to Minnesota, when we sailed from Bergen to New York."

"Yes, Mama, very different," Kristen agreed. "In eight or nine hours we'll be landing in Oslo, then take the train to Kinsarvik. In less than twenty-four hours, we'll be with Uncle Thomas and Aunt Gerta."

"What do you want to see in Norway, Mama?" Johann inquired.

"Everything. I want to see my family and friends in Kinsarvik. I want to see the little church and the parsonage. I want to cruise on the fjord. I want to ride the Finicular in Bergen and I want to see a glacier. I want to do everything I've been denied doing for so long."

"Would you like to see the cave, Mama?" Karl asked.

"The cave? How did you know about the cave, Karl?"

"When I went there, Gunnar took me to see it. He told me how he stayed in such caves during the war. Then he told me the story of your cave."

"The story of Mama's cave?" Kristen questioned. "What story? I've never heard any such story. Please tell us about it, Mama."

"Well," Solveig began, "when I was a little girl, only about five years old, my brother and sister would go off to play. I was very jealous. One day I said to my Mama, 'I want to go with them,' but Mama said, 'Solveig, you are just a little girl. You are too small to go with them.' I was very disappointed and cried

until I thought my heart would break. When she could stand it
no longer, she made them take me along.

"They took me to a beautiful cave along the fjord, behind a
waterfall. I remember being very frightened. The path was so
long and so steep, I thought I would fall into the fjord. When I
saw the waterfall, I wanted to go home, but Thomas took my
hand and led me into the cave. I was afraid until he lit the candle
and the cave came alive for me.

"It has stayed vivid in my memory all my life. The way the
lights sparkle on the walls, the stream gurgles in the back,
everything about it. The cave became my special friend. The day
before I married your papa, I went there to say good-bye to my
childhood. I went there to say good-bye to Norway before we
left for America. It is strange, I had promised myself I would
take you children there when you were old enough. I never got
to take you there since we came to America. Is it still the same,
Karl?"

Karl smiled at her and squeezed her hand. "It is the same,
Mama. Caves don't change, only people do."

Tears welled in Solveig's eyes. "I wish I was not so old. I
would like to see it again, but the path is far to steep for an old
woman. I will have to leave the cave exploration to you children.
You will have to see the cave for me. That is, if you are not too
old to climb the path," she teased, her eyes twinkling.

"I know I could climb it," Anne said. "But then, I'm much
younger than the rest of you."

"You're forty-five Anne," Karl reminded her. "You're not
that much younger than we are."

"Perhaps not, but I am in much better shape. I ski, hike and
swim."

"On the weekends," Garrett interjected, "and that's only
when I make you get out from behind your desk. Face it, Honey,
Karl's right, none of us are children anymore."

"The question is not about our physical stamina," Johann said. "The question is do you think Gunnar will be willing to take us to the cave?"

"Perhaps not Gunnar," Karl agreed. "His last letter mentioned a flare up of arthritis, but I'm certain his son, Gustav, will take us." They talked on, oblivious to the passing hours, the time for sleep. Solveig told them stories of growing up, then raising her own family in the parsonage in Kinsarvik.

As the plane neared Norway, one by one, they fell asleep, until only Anne and Solveig remained awake.

"I worry about Libby flying alone," Solveig whispered. "It is such a long trip for a young girl. What if she is unable to find the train to Kinsarvik once she reaches Oslo?"

"Oh, Mama, please don't worry. Libby has been flying alone since she was five years old. She'll be fine."

"But you told me she has usually traveled with Elliott. When she has traveled alone someone has always met her. This time she will be truly alone. That is why I worry."

"You'll see. She'll arrive with no problems at all."

As Solveig drifted off into a peaceful sleep, AJ thought about her words. She, too, began to worry about Libby traveling alone in a strange country.

* * *

Logan and Marie Prescott waited at Heathrow airport for Libby's flight to arrive. He remembered the first time he had met Libby here. She had voiced her concerns as to why he left New York, why he moved to London. She had also questioned him about his motives. He had explained how at first, it was to please Marie. She had family in Sussex, her youngest son was stationed in Germany with the Air Force, and her oldest son was working for a large company in France. London put her closer to her family.

His book had met with rave reviews in London and he found a wider readership here than in the States. He had even looked up his mother's friends. They welcomed him with open arms.

When his mother passed away within weeks of the scene in New Oslo, just two years after his father's death, he knew he needed to leave New York behind. With his ties to the city cut, he had no reason to stay. No matter where he lived, he would make certain he saw Libby. Although he knew her visits would be curtailed, it did surprise him when she announced she would be coming in the summer for only a week or two.

Now he waited eagerly for her to arrive. He regretted the fact she would be there less than a week, but the trip to Norway was her graduation present and the stop in London was made only to appease him.

To his surprise, across the crowded room, he recognized Susan Elliott. "Look over there, Marie. That's Susan Elliott," he said, pointing her out to his wife.

"Susan Elliott? The actress? Is she someone you dated?"

He'd forgotten Marie didn't know his connection with Susan. "No, she's Garrett's ex-wife, you know, AJ's husband."

Marie nodded, as though trying to fit together the pieces of her husband's life. "Isn't she glamorous? She looks just like she does on her soap opera."

"I wonder what she's doing in London?" Logan mused. "It seems strange she would be here."

Before Marie could comment, Susan's shrill voice assaulted their ears from across the room.

"Logan-Logan Prescott, what are you doing here?" she asked, making a production of giving him a hug and a kiss.

"I'm meeting Libby's plane. How about you?"

"I'm meeting Elliott's plane. It's just like old times, isn't it? The children are flying in together."

"Yes, only we didn't meet planes then. We had our mothers do it for us."

"Well, your schedule, my schedule, they've always been so busy." For the first time, Susan faced Marie. "Why, my dear, you must be Logan's new wife. I've heard so much about you. I am so glad to meet you. Logan deserves the best."

"Thank you, Miss Elliott, the pleasure is mine," Marie replied.

"Please, do call me Susan. As I remember, your name is Marie, isn't it?"

"Yes it is, Miss-I mean Susan."

Susan tired of the conversation with someone she considered to be below her station and returned her attention to Logan.

"Now, Logan, how much did it cost Garrett to get you to make that god-awful confession? He must have had something over you, or twisted your arm, to get you to do it."

"No, Susan, the confession was my idea, something I needed to do."

"Well, at least you beat AJ to the punch. I'm certain she would have cut you to ribbons when she told the world about her breakdown."

Logan sighed. Had he been as obnoxious as Susan before he started counseling? "AJ never planned to mention it."

"For someone who didn't intend to say anything, she certainly gave some story to the press."

"She had every right to tell her side of things, once I brought it out into the open."

"Well, she did tell *her* side of things, every gruesome detail of it. Anyway, I've always thought Garrett put you up to it. He can be so moral, if you know what I mean. You poor dear, I do feel badly about the way AJ and Garrett have treated you."

"There's no need in discussing it, Susan. It's all water over the dam. We don't see much of each other any more."

"Oh, that's right, Elizabeth graduated this year. You didn't go to the ceremony, did you? At least they let me attend Elliott's graduation, but then I didn't tell the world I'd been a spouse beater."

"I could have gone if I wanted. You must admit, it's a long trip for one day. AJ gave Libby a trip to Norway for graduation. We decided it would be best if she stopped here for a few days first."

"Isn't it ironic? Elliott called at the same time and said he wanted to come and see me. Can you imagine flying all this way, just to see me?"

"I didn't ask you, but just what are you doing in London?"

"Haven't you heard? I'm in a play. The New York papers were full of it. We open this weekend, so it's especially sweet of Elliott to come and see me in my debut. He asked for four tickets. I'm certain he's bringing a nice young lady with him or perhaps he has some friends he wanted to invite."

"Does Elliott have friends in London?" Marie questioned, joining the conversation for the first time.

"Well, not that I know of, but what does a mother know? I never see him. You know how it is Logan, especially since you rarely see Elizabeth."

Before Logan or Marie could answer, passengers from the Chicago flight began to coming from the customs area.

"Oh, look, there they are, hand in hand, just like when they were children," Susan said, once she spotted Elliott and Libby. "Elliott, Elliott, it's Mother," she called, waving excitedly.

Logan watched as Elliott returned her wave. As he did, Logan saw Libby drop Elliott's hand and hurry through the crowd to embrace her father. "Daddy, Marie, it's so good to see you."

"You, too, Honey. I just didn't expect to see you getting off the plane with Elliott Lanners."

"When Elliott said he was coming to London, we thought it would be fun to come together, like when we were kids."

"Oh Elliott," Susan said, her voice so loud, Logan didn't comment on his daughter's statement. "I plan to take you to lunch."

"I thought you would, Mother, but Libby and I would like to take you and Logan and Marie to lunch."

"All of us?" Susan questioned.

"I hope you know some nice place to go," Libby commented.

Susan took only a moment to ponder her answer. "I had planned to take Elliott to Covent Garden."

"Is it all right with you, Logan?" Elliott asked.

Logan couldn't help but approve of Susan's choice. The food critics called it an excellent restaurant, or so he'd heard.

"Do you have a car, Susan?" he asked, once agreeing to accompany them.

"Oh good heavens, no. I wouldn't even try to drive in this city. It's much easier to take a cab or use the tube."

Logan wrinkled his nose at Susan's mention of London's version of the subway. He used it only when necessary. He much preferred driving his own vehicle to being committed to someone else's schedule. "Well, I don't mind driving and I do have a car. We have plenty of room. We can all go together and save the fare."

"Well, then," Susan said, gesturing wildly, "we're off to Covent Garden."

They didn't lack for conversation on the ride to the restaurant. Once they were in the car, Susan managed to talk nonstop about her show. She sat in the back seat, between Elliott and Libby, clinging to Elliott as though she thought to do otherwise would make him disappear.

"Four tickets, Elliott," she quipped, "I thought perhaps you'd bring some nice young lady with you. Well, whatever. Hopefully, you'll meet someone while you're here. You'll just love the show. It's fabulous. The producer saw me in *He Loves Me, He Loves Me Not*. He says he was so taken with me he just had to have me for the lead. He begged me to take a hiatus from the show. It wasn't easy, but I finally arranged it. I still can't believe I'll be working in London all summer. I've been shopping at Harrods. Have you been to Harrods, Elizabeth?"

"Yes, Marie has taken me several times. It's, ah, uh, not ah very interesting."

"Oh, I do love shopping at Harrods," Susan continued, seeming oblivious to the others in the car. "Of course, I've been to Fortnum and Mason. You know, the Queen shops there. I couldn't live if I didn't rub shoulders with prominent people. Then there's that darling little man in his tux that bags my onions. I've never seen such a fabulously marvelous shop in my life! Do you shop there, Marie?"

"I don't make it a regular practice. The Queen and I aren't exactly the best of friends. I do go when I want to treat myself to something special. It's a bit like Harrods, it's nice for a treat, but I find I have more fun shopping in the small markets."

"Well, I haven't been to any of the local markets. I figure if it's not good enough for the Queen, it's not good enough for Susan Elliott." She punctuated her statement with hysterical laughter.

"You children are so quiet," she continued, turning her attention to Elliott. "You've hardly said a word. How was your flight?"

Libby wanted to admonish her for the statement, wanted to tell her she had not allowed them to say anything. Instead, Elliott calmly replied, "We had a good flight."

"I am just so pleased you came for my opening. It was such a surprise."

"We thought you might like it, Mother."

"We?" Susan shot a glance at Libby. "Why, Elizabeth, you didn't come for my opening, did you? You came to see your father."

"I did come to see Daddy, but one of Elliott's tickets is for me to see the play. We thought perhaps Daddy and Marie would enjoy it as well."

"That's very generous, Honey," Logan said. She saw him look at her in the rear view mirror. "What are you buttering me up for?"

"Nothing, Daddy," Libby said, flashing him one of her brilliant smiles.

"Well, if it's your graduation gift, I have it with me. I was going to give it to you over lunch, but now seems to be as good a time as any."

Marie reached into her handbag and pulled out a neatly wrapped box, then handed it across the seat to Libby.

Carefully, she opened the package. As she did, she felt her eyes widen in surprise and delight. Nestled in a bed of cotton, lay an antique pendant watch. She wrapped the chain around her fingers and lifted it from the box. The case carried an intricate etching of a sailboat on one side and the initial E on the other. As she pushed the button on the top, the case flipped open displaying the delicately painted face. Tiny pink rosebuds represented the numbers and the fine gold hands indicated the hours and minutes.

"Oh, Daddy!" she exclaimed, "It's exquisite. It's the most beautiful watch I've ever seen."

"I found it when I cleaned out your grandmother's house. I remember Mom getting it when her mother died. I couldn't have been more than eight or ten at the time, but I remember being very proud when she wore it. She told me her mother had received it for her eighteenth birthday. Since her name was Emma, even the initial on the case told me it had to belong to you. I thought it would be something special for your graduation. I had it cleaned and refurbished. It keeps pretty good time, too, if you remember to wind it."

"It's perfect Daddy. I know just what I'll wear it with." As much as she wanted to wink at Elliott, she refrained. With Susan sitting between them, she knew the gesture would be lost.

Once they arrived at the restaurant, all trivial conversation ceased. Elliott helped Susan and Libby to get out of the back seat of her father's Mercedes, while Logan held the door for Marie.

Susan made even a simple lunch into a theatrical production. As they entered the restaurant, she waved to people she knew and pointed out local celebrities to the disinterested members of her party.

It was Elliott who ignited the conversation when the waiter left after taking their order. "Libby and I have something we want to tell you."

Libby smiled as Elliott reached for her hand beneath the table and tried to read the puzzled expressions on her father and Susan's faces.

"We are planning to be married in Norway," Elliott continued. His grip on her hand tightened as puzzlement turned to shock, and shock to anger.

"Married!" Logan exploded, once he found his voice. "How can you think of such a thing?"

"We love each other Logan."

"But you're-you're brother and sister!"

"*Step*brother and sister, Daddy," Libby rationalized. "If you remember, my parents and Elliott's are not one and the same."

"But you've lived like you are. It's almost ..."

"Incest?" Libby questioned, the word sounding like an accusation. "That's the stuff you write about in your books, Daddy. This is love, pure and simple love. We've checked several legal authorities and there is no reason why we shouldn't follow our hearts."

"But why in Norway? Who is giving the bride away for god's sake?"

"Why not Norway?" Libby argued. "Being married in Grandpa Jorgenson's church is like a romantic dream. As for who is giving the bride away, Uncle Karl is doing the honors."

"I should have known. Good old Uncle Karl. It seems as though he's always there for you. Did he help you plan this fiasco? Did he find a minister willing to agree to this abomination?"

Libby swallowed heard. They expected people to be shocked. Even though they expected opposition, they never anticipated such open hostilities. "Uncle Karl didn't help with the plans. He doesn't even know. Elliott and I made them through Mom's cousin, Gunnar. He's the pastor at Grandfather's church. He will be marrying us. He's been very helpful."

"I don't believe it. I just don't believe it," Logan said, his voice dropping to almost a whisper, as he shook his head.

"You don't believe it?" Susan shrieked, her voice so loud several other diners turned to stare at them. "I can't believe you're throwing your life away like this, Elliott. You have a good position. You could have any woman in the world."

"I *had* a good position, Mother," Elliott replied.

"Had? What are you telling me?"

"I quit my job. Libby and I intend to be working owners of the Lady Jo and the Lazy B. Once we're married, we'll be full partners."

"How can you be full partners when your father is her legal guardian?" Logan questioned.

"Garrett relinquished his guardianship as my graduation present. When we get home, we're filing papers to make Elliott a full partner."

"What do you know about ranching, Elliott?" Susan demanded.

"Not as much as Libby, but I can learn. My love is the Lady Jo. We will make a very good team. We'll both work the two ranches, but the Lady Jo will be my responsibility, while Libby will take care of the Lazy B."

"And you came here for my-my permission?" Logan stammered.

"We don't need your permission, Daddy. I'll be twenty-two soon. I'm of age. I know what I'm doing. We only want your blessing, as well as yours, Susan."

"Has your mother given her blessing?"

"Anne and Dad don't know," Elliott replied, coming to her rescue.

"They don't know? How can they not know? They're a party to it. They're taking you to Norway." Logan's voice rose noticeably with each statement.

"We told you, Mother and Garrett don't know, and they won't until we get to Kinsarvik."

The food arrived and as they ate, the silence was deafening. Libby picked at her food, barely touching the entree that had sounded so good minutes before. Unable to continue eating, she excused herself to visit the ladies room.

She stood momentarily, looking into the mirror. The happy face that almost betrayed her secret had vanished. In its place,

392

she saw the look of worry, of stress. Hearing the bathroom door open, she turned to face Marie.

"What's this, tears?" Marie asked.

Libby's tears came faster as Marie took her comfortingly in her arms. "Oh, Marie, I wanted Daddy to understand, to be different. I thought he'd changed. Why can't he be happy for me?"

"You're not wrong, he has changed," Marie assured her. "He'll understand. Now dry your eyes and come back to the table."

Elliott had wanted to follow Libby, but Marie had gotten to her feet and excused herself before he could react. He'd hated seeing the hurt in Libby's eyes, which threatened to spill over in the form of tears at any moment.

"I suppose the two of you are living together," Susan accused.

Elliott stared at her, as though trying to comprehend her statement. "I can't believe I'm hearing you correctly, Mother. Libby has been in Saint Peter, Minnesota, and I've been in Windsor, Colorado. Living together under those conditions would be impossible."

"Don't be flippant. You know what your mother meant," Logan said. "In this day and age, everyone does it. Is she pregnant? If you've hurt her, I'll make you wish you'd never met her."

"I don't believe either of you. You're so worried about my morals, as well as Libby's, that it's sickening. When did you become as pure as the driven snow? Our personal lives are none of your business. But no, Libby isn't pregnant and we aren't sleeping together. Maybe everybody does it, but we don't. I take love and marriage very seriously, and so does Libby. I've dated a lot of women, but I haven't bed hopped, like you, Logan. I'd like to believe you've changed, for Marie's sake, but I doubt it.

As for you, Mother, you're no saint either. What is it the tabloids call your latest conquest, a toy boy? How old is he, twenty-two, twenty-three? Is he a good lover? Does he make you feel young?"

"Stop it Elliott," Susan shouted. "None of us are making any sense. You and Elizabeth are tired. Logan and I are in a state of shock. My flat is just a few blocks from here. You and I will go there and rest for a while. Elizabeth can go back with Logan and Marie. Tomorrow morning we will have had time to think things over and be rational."

Libby and Marie caught the last of Susan's words as they returned to the table. "Tomorrow morning?" Libby questioned. "What are you talking about?"

"We've been having a discussion, Honey," Elliott explained. "We've had a long flight. We're both tired. I'm going to Mom's flat. You go with your dad and Marie. We'll get a good night's rest. I'll call you in the morning."

"I don't understand," Libby pleaded. "What about dinner tonight?"

"Marie and I have already made plans and I'm certain Susan has done the same. We can all stand a cooling-off period."

Libby said no more. They were all on edge, to say anything now might lead to further arguments. She nodded as she sat back down next to Elliott, facing her father.

"Would anyone care for dessert?" the waiter asked.

Around the table, everyone declined. Libby knew they all wished the confrontation was over. Everyone remained silent, as the waiter tallied the bill. When he placed it on the table, Elliott reached for it, but it had been placed closer to Logan and he snatched it away first.

"This was to be our treat," Elliott protested.

"I'll take nothing from you," Logan spat. "Isn't it enough you're taking my daughter? Do you want my pride as well?"

Libby bit her lip and pushed back her chair. Brushing past her father she hurried out to the car.

"Lib," Elliott said, as he caught up to her, and placed his hands on her shoulders. "It will be all right. They'll come around."

"How can you be so sure? They were so angry, so judgemental."

"Look Lib, let's play it their way, just for tonight. We're both tired." He took her in his arms and kissed her tenderly.

The sound of Logan clearing his throat caused Elliott and Libby to break their embrace and face their parents.

To Libby's surprise, her father opened the trunk and took out Elliott's luggage. "What are you doing?"

"It's all right, Honey," Elliott assured her. "Mom's flat is close by. We can walk it easier than your dad can make it through traffic."

Libby shook her head. This had to be her father's doing. Walking certainly hadn't been Susan's idea. Susan Elliott wouldn't walk anywhere. Anything so commonplace would be beneath her. Libby realized, for the sake of her father and Elliott, she must comply with their wishes.

"I'll call you early tomorrow morning," Elliott said, just before kissing her on the cheek.

Libby got into the car and watched until they turned the corner and Elliott disappeared from view.

An invisible wall separated Libby from her father on the ride from Covent Gardens to Lillieshall Road. Only Marie tried to make conversation, to carry on as though the ugly scene in the restaurant had never happened. "We have a surprise for you," she said, leaning over the back of the seat. "My sons, Philip and Dan, will be joining us for dinner tonight, along with Philip's wife, Jane."

Libby inwardly dreaded a meeting with Marie's sons, especially after the blowup in the restaurant. "Your plans sound lovely," she replied. "I thought they were both on the continent."

"They are," Marie said, seemingly relieved to be on more neutral ground. "Phillip and his wife were in London on business last week and took some vacation time. They were with us until Sunday, when they went to Worthing to be with her parents. Dan flew in from Rheinmain last week and went down to Worthing with Philip and Jane. We have family in the area. They invited him to stay with them. They are both looking forward to meeting you. They'll be spending tonight with us, then will fly back tomorrow."

Libby pretended to be interested, but she couldn't help dwelling on the situation at hand.

At last they arrived at the row house on Lillieshall Road. Libby waited in the house, while Logan took her bags from the trunk and brought them into the hall.

"I know my way to the guest room, Daddy. I'll take my bags up and lie down for a nap."

Logan stood mute, as Libby went upstairs, not saying a word until he heard the door close. "Go ahead and say it, Marie. I deserve it."

"What do you want me to say?" Marie asked, putting her arms around his neck. "Libby's announcement was a shock for everyone. None of us were prepared for it. You were just more vocal about it. Elliott is Libby's choice. If you weren't so against him, you could see how much they love each other. You have to put aside your former opinions of the child and get to know the man."

Logan reached up and grasped Marie's arms, taking them from his neck. "Know him? Oh, I know him. He was a smart-ass kid eleven years ago and he hasn't changed one iota. You weren't there when he tore into Susan and me."

"What did he say?"

"Susan asked if they were living together and he came back with a tirade about me being a bed hopper and his mother's boyfriend being a toy boy."

Marie began to giggle, and then to laugh.

"Just what do you find so damned funny?" Logan demanded.

"My dear husband, if you could only step back from this situation, you could hear how foolish you sound. You told me about your bed hopping while you were married to AJ. I certainly didn't need to hear you say it. I've been reading about you for years. As for Susan, the tabloids have been having a heyday with her latest affair. He is only twenty-three, which makes him younger than her son. Neither of you has the right to ask about their relationship."

Logan looked at her, almost in disbelief. "You're right. I guess that's why I married you. You're always right and you can make me see where I'm wrong."

* * *

Libby couldn't believe the clock read after five when she awoke. Beneath her bedroom window the garden was alive with the sound of birds gathering for the afternoon feeding frenzy. In the distance, she could barely see Big Ben silhouetted in the long afternoon shadows. Had she been one floor up, she could have seen the famous landmark more clearly, but she remained content with only a glimpse.

Before she laid down, she'd taken a jersey print skirt and white top from her suitcase for this evening's dinner. Although it wasn't extremely warm, she decided against stockings and slipped her bare feet into white sandals. Lastly, she ran a brush through her hair and applied lipstick.

When she stepped into the hall, she could hear the buzz of conversation from the sitting room below. She'd heard a lot about Marie's sons. Until now, she'd never found the opportunity right to meet them. She wondered about the timing of the meeting.

"Come in, Honey," Logan said, when he saw her standing in the doorway. "Can I get you something to drink?"

"A glass of white wine would be nice."

Marie made the introductions. As the evening progressed, it became evident Logan hoped she would be taken by Dan. How foolish it seemed to have him pushed onto her at every opportunity.

"So, now that you're finished with college, what are your plans?" Philip asked, over dessert.

"Didn't Daddy and Marie tell you? I'm going to be married in a week and a half. After our honeymoon, we'll be working owners of the Lady Jo and the Lazy B ranches." With the conversation steered toward more neutral ground, Libby relaxed. She loved talking about the two properties she called home.

"Will your husband actively work on the Lazy B?" Dan asked.

"Sometimes, but the Lazy B is my love. I'd rather herd cows than guests. I will have to attend several functions at the Lady Jo each week, though."

"How interesting," Jane commented. "I would think you'd enjoy the guests, you seem to be so at ease with people."

The comment made Libby laugh. "I've been charming the guests since I was five. It's no longer a challenge. I'd rather be charming the cows and the cattle buyers." Libby's comment brought a laugh from everyone but Logan. He'd always strongly disapproved of her involvement with the Lazy B. It had been a point of contention between him and her mother over the years, as well the root of most of her parents arguments.

By eleven, everyone had retired for the night. Philip and Jane, as well as Dan, were leaving on early flights from

Heathrow. Libby silently approved of the arrangement, as she'd made plans to tour the city with Elliott.

The activities of the next morning were chaotic. To ease some of the tension, Libby volunteered to make breakfast. When everyone finally departed amid promises to keep in touch, she began to clean up the kitchen. She dried the last of the dishes, when someone knocked at the door. Hesitantly, she answered it, wondering what she would say to whoever awaited her.

"Elliott?" she questioned, surprised to see him standing there. "I thought you were going to call first."

"I intended to," he said, taking her in his arms. "I couldn't wait. I needed to get out of Mom's apartment. Where are they?"

"They, as in Daddy and Marie, took Dan and Philip to the airport."

"Dan and Philip?"

Libby let him into the kitchen then quickly explained about the surprise meeting with Marie's sons and Logan's plans for setting her up with Dan.

"That hypocrite. I'm wrong for you because I'm your stepbrother, but it's okay for you and Dan when the relationship is the same. I hope you set them straight."

"I did and I loved every minute of it. Now, who did Susan have you set up with?"

Elliott laughed. "Kimberly Bannerman, the actress who plays Mom's daughter on stage. She's all of twenty and literally worships the ground Mom walks on. I'm sure she thought I'd be eager to take her to bed, as well as back home with me."

Libby handed him the last of the breakfast coffee. "They aren't going to be our staunch allies, are they?"

"Did you expect them to be? I really don't care. We don't need them. So, what are our plans for today?"

"I planned to meet you at Victoria Station, tour Westminster Abby, then have lunch at Harrods and see the Tower of London."

"Victoria Station?" Elliott echoed. "You actually want me to ride the subway?"

"The tube," Libby corrected, remembering Elliott's dislike of the subway in New York. "Where is your sense of adventure? No one comes to London without experiencing the tube."

"My sense of adventure is on the slopes back home. As for experiencing the tube, I think I will survive quite well without it. A cab will suit me just fine."

They left before Logan and Marie returned from Heathrow. It was almost six when they came back. They were met at the door by Logan.

"Did you have a good day?" he asked.

"We certainly did," Libby replied. "I thought you and Marie would be out to dinner."

"We discussed it and decided we need to talk to you and Elliott about your plans."

"Are you certain you want me here?" Elliott inquired.

Libby watched, as her father contemplated his answer. "No, Elliott, I'm not certain I want you here. The announcement the two of you made yesterday took me quite by surprise."

"Then, maybe I should go."

"No. I need to come to grips with my feelings, for Libby's sake. I love her very much and even though you're her choice, you must know you're not mine. Yesterday was an unfortunate episode. We all said hateful things, out of shock. I'll not stand in the way of my daughter's happiness. I'll give my blessing. I'll even swallow my pride and make no further protests."

Chapter Twenty-Six

As morning arrived and the Northwest flight neared Oslo, the first class cabin began waking up. For Karl, this trip and the excitement it generated came as a reenactment of the flight he'd taken years earlier.

Across the aisle, Anne sat with their mother. Both were just beginning to stir. He was certain they'd been too excited to get much sleep.

"Good morning," he whispered as Anne stretched, then reached across their mother to put up the shade. Her action filled the cabin with sunlight.

"Morning?" she questioned, rubbing the sleep from her eyes. "Already? I think I just fell asleep."

"You did, Honey," Garrett said, from the seat behind her. "You and your mother talked most of the night away."

"I guess we did," Anne replied, as she accepted a hot, linen towel from the flight attendant.

Karl couldn't help but smile at Anne's childlike enthusiasm. Sitting up all night talking was something Papa had never tolerated. It, like the brotherly-sisterly banter that now came so easily, would not have been accepted behavior in their childhood home.

The announcement of the flight's impending arrival in Oslo prompted a flurry of activities, as trays were stored and seatbelts fastened.

"I must look like a wreck," Anne lamented, as she reached for her compact and lipstick.

"No worse than the rest of us," Karl assured her.

Anne looked around her. They were all a bit disheveled from sleep, but then so were the other passengers. No one had access to showers or time to completely wash up in the cramped restrooms. She wished she'd given it more thought and made arrangements for rooms in Oslo or close by. Planning to make it all the way to Kinsarvik on their first day, after such a long flight, now seemed like a mistake.

Once inside the terminal, the men collected the luggage while the women assembled their passports for the customs agents. All went smoothly. Soon they were making their way into the waiting area.

"Karl, Karl Jorgenson," someone called.

Everyone turned to see who recognized him.

"Gunnar, what are you doing here?" Karl said, as he first clasped Gunnar's hand then gave him a hug.

"I see everyone made it," Gunnar replied, avoiding the original question. "I've come to meet you. You remember my son, Gustaf? He'll help you with the luggage."

Solveig's eyes filled with happy tears, as she greeted her nephew. "You look so much like your papa."

Before Gunnar could reply, Gustaf took over. "Come, come, everyone. We have a surprise for you."

Garrett and Lars wheeled the luggage carts and followed the others toward the exit. Waiting for them, just outside the door, stood a large tour bus.

"This is for us?" Anne gasped.

"We thought it would be more relaxing than the train. It gave the rest of us a chance for a holiday as well. Gustaf's friend from school, Hans Knuijt, rented it to us and agreed to be our driver. His Papa owns the company. The bus is at our disposal for the entire week."

When the luggage was stored beneath the seating area, they were surprised to find more family inside. Everyone seemed to talk at once as they reacquainted themselves with Thomas, Gerta, Gunnar's wife, Marta, and Gustaf's wife, Erica.

"Such an expense," Solveig exclaimed. "We could have taken the train."

"Must you always be so practical, my dear sister?" Thomas asked, hugging her tightly. "After nearly fifty years of separation, I see no need for practicality."

Once on the road, picnic baskets of food were opened and plates of cheese, dark bread, hard-boiled eggs, and lefsa were passed along with crocks of herring.

"Here, Honey, try this," Garrett said, handing Anne a caramel colored piece of cheese.

"What is it?" Anne asked, wrinkling her nose at the heady smell of the cheese.

"Don't ask so many questions, Anne," Karl teased. "Just try it."

Anne bit into the cheese, tentatively at first. Although it was strong, it was not distasteful. She found she rather enjoyed its flavor.

"So, do you like it?" Johann asked

"I think so. I do believe it would be considered an acquired taste, though."

"It certainly is," Kristen said. "Goat cheese is not one of my acquired tastes."

"What kind of a Norwegian are you?" Gunnar questioned. "Everyone likes goat cheese."

"Well, this Norwegian doesn't," Kristen declared.

For the first hour, the Norwegian and American branches of the family ate and became better acquainted. As the miles passed beneath the wheels of the bus, one by one the Americans looked for empty seats and gave into much needed sleep.

Gunnar assessed his newfound family. These Americans amazed him. In all their careful plans, they never realized Norway was not the fast-paced country America seemed to be. Although the actual mileage from Oslo to Kinsarvik was not great, the roads were not the super highways of America. Mountains stood as obstacles, and travel was done at a more leisurely pace. The trip of eight hours by train would be considerably shorter by bus. Still, they would not arrive home until late afternoon.

The bus was now quiet. Gustaf sat in the front seat speaking in low tones with Hans, while Marta and Erica chatted away in the seat ahead of Gunnar. In the back of the bus, his father sat on the bench seat with his two aunts, engrossed in eager conversation, sharing the secrets and experiences of the past fifty years.

Across the aisle, sat Anne. She had always fascinated him. By the time news of her birth reached Kinsarvik, the occupation had begun and he'd run away to join the resistance. Fifteen years separated them chronologically, but he felt a millennium of difference. Just watching her, she seemed so self-assured, so remote.

He remembered when Karl visited twelve years ago and the subject of Anne had been broached. It seemed as though a curtain dropped and the door closed on the subject. It was almost two years later when Karl wrote a long letter about Anne. It explained so much. Even more came to light four years ago, when he received the videotape of Anne's press conference in New Oslo, along with the newspaper clippings from Denver.

Even in the planning of this trip, Anne still remained a mystery. His communications had been with Karl, Anne's secretary, and of course, with Libby. He'd spoken with Anne only once, maybe twice at the most.

"Do you mind if I join you, or are you ready for a nap?" he asked, as he slipped into the seat beside her.

In one motion, the remoteness disappeared, as she broke into a radiant smile. "I'm too excited to sleep," she confessed. "I'd welcome the company."

"So, what do you want me to call you, Anne or AJ?"

"I left AJ in Colorado. This trip is strictly pleasure, exclusively family. No one but family calls me Anne, so Anne it is. You'll never know how much I've appreciated your help with this trip. I know it seems like I left everything to you and Pam, but I was aware of all you were doing."

"It seems you're a very busy lady," Gunnar commented. "I hope you'll get some rest on this vacation. Karl worries about you."

Anne laughed. "I suppose he does, and with good cause, I'm afraid. Relaxation doesn't come easily for me. Fortunately, this trip will be different. There are too many concerned people around to allow me to do anything else."

They talked on for several hours, until at last Kinsarvik and the fjord spread before them.

"It's breathtaking," Anne exclaimed. "It looks just like a postcard!"

One by one the others saw what so excited Anne. Their remarks made Gunnar smile. He felt the same excitement every time he returned home.

"It's just as I remembered," Solveig declared.

Gunnar could hear the tears in her voice. He knew his father would have tears in his eyes as well. They had been separated for a lifetime and this reunion was exactly what they both needed.

The first few days were spent in Kinsarvik. On Saturday, they crossed the fjord and took the train to Bergen. They checked into the old hotel where they spent the last few days before sailing for America, before world and personal events tore their lives asunder.

They spent the afternoon shopping and exploring. After dinner, they made their way to the Finicular. Solveig seemed childlike in her excitement. It was exactly as she'd described it. The little car made its way up the mountainside and at last they were at the summit.

Even at ten in the evening, the sun shone brightly enough for pictures to be taken without the use of a flash.

Anne stood transfixed, staring at the panorama before her, lost in her own thoughts. She pictured Libby and the evasiveness in her daughter's voice prior to the flight. Was there something going on, something she should know?

* * *

Elliott awoke. Before opening his eyes, he tried to acclimate himself to his surroundings. The constant click-clack of the wheels on the tracks reminded him of the last few days in London. The longer they were on the train, the more space he put between themselves and the confrontation with his mother and Logan.

Libby shifted her position and he looked down at her as she slept in the crook of his arm. He wondered what time it was. The brightness of the morning sun this far north could be deceiving. Glancing at his watch, he noted the time as being five-thirty. In an hour and a half they would arrive in Kinsarvik.

"Good morning," Libby whispered, when she opened her eyes. "What time is it?"

"It's just past five-thirty. We've got a little time before we have to face our parents. Do you want to freshen up before we get some coffee?"

Libby nodded, and headed for the restroom. Elliott watched her make her way down the aisle then followed. If nothing else, he wanted to look his best when they confronted Anne and his father

* * *

Anne bustled with excitement. Libby's train would be arriving in less than an hour. Unable to sleep, she got up early, only to find Marta already waiting for her in the kitchen.

"I thought you might be up early, Anne," Marta said, handing her a cup of coffee. "You'll be meeting Libby's train soon. I'll wait breakfast until you get back."

"I'm afraid we've been a burden to you and Gunnar," Anne replied, after taking her first sip of the strong coffee.

"Nonsense. We are happy for the reunion and I enjoy your company."

"You're a better hostess than I am. I'd be hard put to give up my life for a month and cook for a dozen strangers."

"You and I are very different, Anne. I would be a stranger in your world, as well."

Marta turned her attention back to the breakfast pastry, leaving Anne to her own thoughts. She'd never worried about Libby traveling alone in the past. What was it about this trip that kept nagging at the back of her mind? Could it be something her mother said, or the tone in Libby's voice when they waited for their flights?

She heard Garrett and Karl talking, as they entered the room. "So, are you ready to go the station?" Karl asked, tousling Anne's hair.

"I guess so."

"Guess so?" Garrett inquired. "What's eating at you?"

"I don't know. I just feel as if something is amiss with Libby. I wish I'd talked to her when she called. I would feel better having heard her voice."

"You worry too much," Karl replied. "I spoke with Libby on Sunday and there is nothing to worry about. I did persuade her to take a later flight yesterday, and then come the rest of the way on the night train."

Anne knew Karl's suggestion made sense, but she couldn't shake the feeling of anxiety. It pleased her when Karl offered to accompany them to the station. With him along to keep Garrett company she could be alone with her thoughts.

The train came in on time and as it pulled into the station, Anne searched the windows for a glimpse of Libby. To her disappointment, she couldn't see her daughter through any of the windows. Focusing on the door, she couldn't hide her surprise when Elliott appeared as soon as the train came to a complete halt.

"Elliott!" Anne exclaimed, as he helped Libby down from the train. "What are you doing here?"

"I decided to deliver Libby to you personally," Elliott replied, holding her hand tightly.

"I thought you couldn't get the time off for Libby's graduation. How could you get away now?" Garrett asked, accusingly.

"Don't look so stern Garrett," Libby scolded. "It's all part of the surprise." She hugged first her mother, then Garrett and Karl.

"Surprise?" Anne asked, catching the glint of morning sunlight off Libby's ring. "A diamond, but--but who?"

"I guess I'm going to have to learn to call you Mom," Elliott said, as he kissed her cheek.

Anne could feel the color drain from her face. Was this what she'd sensed? "What are you telling us?"

"Elliott and I are going to be married here, on Sunday, after church."

"But you're..." Garrett began.

"We've been all over this, Dad. We're brother and sister, but not really. We've checked and double-checked. There is no reason why we can't love each other. There are no blood ties."

Anne and Garrett exchanged glances. "It sounds like you have your minds made up," Garrett surmised. "What I want to know is how you managed to plan a wedding in Norway?"

"We had a lot of help, Garrett," Libby explained. "Gunnar, Thomas, Gerta, even Sonja were in on it."

"They all know?" Anne asked. "Why didn't you tell us?"

"We anticipated opposition," Elliott said. He went on to tell them everything that went on in London. "We wanted everything planned before we got here so ..."

"So we couldn't stop you?" Garrett questioned, finishing his son's sentence.

"Something along those lines," Libby agreed. "We decided to have everything set before we told you. We want you to be happy for us."

"You know we're happy for you," Karl said, kissing her cheek. "I think your folks are in a state of shock. You can tell us about the plans over breakfast at Gunnar's place."

Once they revealed their plans to the family, the room buzzed with excited conversation. Everyone seemed to talk at once.

"With all your careful planning, you seem to have forgotten one small detail," Garrett finally observed.

"What's that?" Elliott asked.

"Sonja is going to be Libby's maid of honor and rightly so, but who are you flying in to be the best man?"

"No one, Dad. The best man for me is already here. Would you stand up with me?"

"Of course I will. But who will give the bride away?"

"We were hoping we could persuade Uncle Karl to do the honors," Libby replied.

Anne merely shook her head. Libby planned everything down to the finest detail. Her grandmother's wedding dress, her cousin as maid of honor, Garrett as best man, and her uncle to give her away. She wished her daughter had allowed her to help with the planning. She also wished she could have spared them the pain and humiliation they had experienced in London.

It was midweek when Gustaf suggested they go to the cave. They'd all been asking questions about it since they got there, but agreed to wait until Libby's arrival to actually explore it.

"We'll have to go in small groups," Gustaf explained, as they neared the waterfall. "The cave is like hundreds of others up and down the length of Scandinavia. It is not very large. Only five of us at the most can fit inside."

"Did your father really hide in these caves during the war?" Elliott asked.

"Yes, they afforded the resistance the proper amount of protection. Even in the winter, they could stay warm without fear of detection."

Gustaf continued, but Anne quit listening. Gunnar had relayed the story earlier in their visit, and she was now more than ready to see the cave for herself.

Picking up one of the fluorescent lanterns, she entered the cave alone. The light reflected off the walls, casting shadows and highlights onto the floor. She ran her hand over the smooth, cool stone and let her imagination run away with her. She could hear laughter and saw three children, now in their twilight years, sitting at the stone table on the stone chairs.

"Oh, Mama," she whispered. "I wish you could be here. I wish you could see this." Tears ran down her cheeks. She was startled, when she felt someone's hands on her shoulders.

"Could you hear the laughter?" Karl asked.

Anne nodded. "I could see them, too. It's as though their spirits are here, as though they never grew up. This is such a special place."

"Gunnar told me the laughter is an underground river that feeds one of the waterfalls farther up the fjord. As for the children, I saw them too. I think we saw them because we expected them to be here."

The others entered and the magical moment passed. The children were gone. Anne knew they weren't real, but felt their loss. She wondered why she had been the one to experience the magic of this place. Why not Kristen or Johann, who had stayed so close to Mama? Why would the one person who felt Norway to be so alien, who spent a lifetime denying her heritage, have the experience?

Chapter Twenty-Seven

Libby awoke, drenched in sweat. The dream seemed so real, so vivid. Beside her Sonja slept peacefully, assuring Libby the unsettling events of the dream had not, in reality, occurred.

After getting out of bed, she put on her sweatsuit, before going downstairs. She wondered why she experienced the dream on the morning of her wedding.

In the kitchen, she started a pot of coffee. While she waited for it to brew, she reviewed the dream.

She'd been dressing at the parsonage when she heard her father's voice. She was ready to walk down the aisle when Uncle Karl became her father. She stood beside Elliott when her father said they couldn't be married. She turned to Elliott for help, for reassurance, when he became Dan. She wondered what prompted such thoughts. Her father gave his word. He promised not to interfere.

As the bright Norwegian summer morning filled the backyard with sunbeams, she sat in the small garden sipping her third cup of coffee. To her surprise, she heard Sonja call her name. "I'm out here," she replied.

"What are you doing up so early?" Sonja asked, when she joined her.

"Thinking."

"Not second thoughts, I hope."

"No, just dark ones. I had a silly dream, a premonition of sorts. Maybe it goes with this house. Isn't this where Grandpa had the dream about leaving Norway and taking the family to America?"

"Yes, but what does that have to do with anything?"

"I don't know. I just thought of how it must have been terrifying to experience such a thing."

"So, what was your dream about?"

"Daddy came to the wedding, came to spoil things. I know it's foolish, but it seems to be gnawing at me."

"You're right, it is foolish. Now, I'm supposed to keep you occupied this morning so you don't see Elliott. Why don't we go for a walk? We aren't expected back here until ten."

"Why at ten?"

"Because the women are all meeting here for coffee."

"Coffee? But what about church?"

"Grandma says we'll go to church this afternoon and the Lord will understand."

Libby was glad the Lord would understand, because she certainly didn't.

Once they returned from their walk, the others had already gathered at the parsonage. To Libby's surprise, each woman had a small, personal gift for Libby, including hand-embroidered linens and beautiful lingerie.

She hadn't expected a shower, especially since the announcement of her wedding came only a few days prior to the actual event.

It came as no surprise to learn the men were entertaining Elliott as well. Even though they'd planned not to see each other on the morning of the wedding, the family decided to help them out by keeping them separated.

Once the noon meal was served and the dishes were removed, everyone but Libby, Sonja, Anne, Kristen and Erika left. In one of the upstairs bedrooms, the two dresses were displayed on newly resurrected dress forms.

Erika took on the task of dressing their hair, weaving ribbons and mountain flowers into the French braids she deftly created. Kristen assisted them with their makeup and Anne helped them with the dresses and accessories.

When at last they were ready, Kristen stood back to assess their appearance. "Let's see," she began, "something old, the watch; something new, your shoes: something borrowed, the dress; and something blue, oh dear, there's nothing blue."

"Yes there is," Sonja said, as she reached into Libby's cosmetic case and produced a blue garter.

"I'd forgotten that," Libby said. "I got it at the shower the girls at the dorm gave me." She took it from Sonja and slipped it onto her leg, allowing it to rest just below her knee.

Kristen again repeated the rhyme. "Something old, something new, something borrowed, something blue, and a lucky penny for your shoe."

"What would Papa say about such superstition?" Anne teased.

"I really don't care. I just want everything to be perfect," Kristen replied, as she rummaged through her purse for a penny and a roll of transparent tape.

"Is there anything you don't carry in that purse, Aunt Kristen?" Libby asked, while Kristen taped the penny just beneath the arch of Libby's shoe.

Before Kristen could answer, voices could be heard from downstairs. Heard, but not distinguished.

"I'll see who it is," Anne said, as she left the room.

Libby almost stopped her mother, almost said she knew who was downstairs, but she didn't. Her father was in London. Her fears were prompted by nothing more than a bad dream.

Karl sat in the kitchen of the parsonage waiting to escort Libby to the church. Upstairs, he could hear the excited chatter as Anne and Kristen helped Libby and Sonja dress for the wedding. Only moments earlier, Erika left to join the rest of the family at the church. It would be only a matter of minutes before he would give Libby to Elliott. He wondered why he hadn't guessed their relationship before they made their announcement. In retrospect, he could see it in the look in her eyes whenever his name was mentioned, heard it in her voice when she spoke of him.

Rather than dwell on things he couldn't change, he closed his eyes. Instantly, he became an eight-year-old boy, sitting in his Mama's kitchen, smelling her bread in the oven and listening to his friends calling him to play. What had become of those friends in the past forty-six years? Some had died in the war, some had moved to Oslo, Stavanger and Trodheim. Some, like himself, had moved to America. Only Ole remained in Kinsarvik to run his papa's store.

In the long forgotten, make-believe world, he could see Mama making pastry in the kitchen. He could hear and see Papa when he called them all into his study to tell them they were going to America. In the vision he could hear his father relating what God told him in '*The Dream*'. He also remembered hearing his father tell them Uncle Sven was dying. As he remembered it, he could see the hurt in his mama's eyes, but then his own excitement overshadowed her concerns as well as her feelings.

A rap at the door interrupted his thoughts. When he answered it, he was surprised to see Logan and two women standing there. He would have known Susan Elliott anywhere. She looked exactly like the character she portrayed on television, phony. The other woman, he was certain, must be Marie, Logan's new wife.

"I didn't expect to see you today, Logan," Karl greeted him.

"I wanted to be here. This is my wife, Marie and Elliott's mother, Susan."

Karl swallowed the words he really wanted to speak. "It's a pleasure," he said to the women. Turning back to Logan, he continued, "how did you know to come here?"

"Libby said she wanted to dress here. I took a chance. Considering those are wedding flowers on the table, I see I guessed right."

Logan's smile irritated Karl. It was like Susan Elliott— forced and phony. Before he had a chance to say anything, Logan continued. "I didn't come here to take your place, Karl. I only want to see my daughter get married."

"What if Libby doesn't want you here?" Karl asked, wondering if, just once, Logan was being sincere.

"Then, I've made a long trip for nothing haven't I?"

"Karl," Anne's voice interrupted their conversation. "Karl, is someone here?"

"Yes, Sis, someone's come to see you."

Logan watched as AJ entered the room. She looked even more beautiful than he remembered, even with the horrified look on her face.

"Logan? I didn't expect to see you. The children said ..."

"I know," he interrupted her. "We had our time in London. Susan and I talked things over. We decided we have a right to see our kids get married."

"*Right!* What right do you have to spoil this day?"

"I've heard a lot about you, AJ," Marie said, coming to his defense. "I've heard how forgiving you are. Please let him stay. I promise nothing will happen to spoil Libby's special day. He wants nothing more than to see Libby happily married."

"It's not my decision to make. You're here. There's very little I can do about it. I want this to be a perfect day."

"I agree with Marie. I promise there will be no scenes. I only want to see her get married."

"Karl is giving her away," AJ said, firmly.

"I don't intend to ruin any of her plans. I didn't come to give her away. She made it quite clear while she was in London that she's not mine to give away. I can't lay any claim ..."

"But you're here," AJ accused.

"Look AJ, I didn't come here to fight. I came to see Libby happily married."

Before AJ could say more, Libby called her name then entered the kitchen. Like AJ, the color drained from her face as she saw him standing in the kitchen.

"Daddy?" the word was more of a question than a term of endearment. "What-what are you doing here?"

Before he could say anything, Marie intervened. "We came to see you get married. Is it all right with you?"

"I hadn't planned, I don't know ..."

Logan ached at the expression in Libby's eyes. Although she'd been speaking to Marie, she'd never taken her eyes from him. Dropping AJ's hand, he reached out to his daughter. "I promise you there will be no confrontation. Once I know you and Elliott are happy, I'll be gone. We can't stay long. Susan has to be back to do a show tonight. We chartered a plane. The pilot is waiting for us a few miles out of town."

He watched, as Libby looked past him, to see Susan standing in the doorway. The deep sigh, which passed her lips, said volumes. "Of course, Daddy. You've come so far. How can I say no?"

Logan took her in his arms. He didn't want her to see the tears in his eyes, even though he couldn't hide them from his voice. "Thank you," he whispered, before kissing her lightly on the cheek.

Libby watched in shock, as Logan, Marie and Susan turned and left the house. "I didn't know," she said, choking on her tears.

Anne put her arm around her daughter's shoulders. "I know you didn't. He promised no problems. We'll just have to hold him to it."

"I don't believe the two of you," Karl said, his tone stern. "I can't understand why you allowed him to stay."

"What could we do, Karl, make them leave when they've come so far? He and Susan have a right to see their children get married."

Libby half listened to the conversation going on around her. "It's just like in my dream. He'll ruin everything," she cried, as she sought Karl's embrace for comfort.

"We won't let anything spoil your day, Honey," he promised. "Whatever you dreamed, it's just that, a dream. Now, fix your face and take a deep breath. There's a young man at the church waiting for you. We don't want to disappoint him."

Anne entered the church and took her place next to Solveig.

"Is something wrong?" her mother questioned. "It's already ten minutes later than we were supposed to start."

Anne smiled, in the hopes of reassuring her mother. "Just a minor setback. Logan's here, with Susan."

"Here? But I thought he wasn't coming."

"So did we. We're all trying to make the best of it."

Before she could say more, Marta began playing the processional. All heads turned as Sonja walked down the aisle, her dress the same shade of blue as her eyes. She was met by Garrett, who escorted her to her assigned place at the left side of the altar.

The music changed to the traditional wedding march and Anne stood along with the rest of the congregation.

Libby waited at the back of the church, her stomach filled with butterflies. Beside her, Karl squeezed her hand reassuringly.

At the end of the aisle, Elliott waited for her. Each step brought her closer to the man she loved, closer to the rest of her dream. Every time she looked up, it was Karl beside her, Elliott waiting for her. Inwardly, she relived the dream. Outwardly, she remained calm. When they finally reached the altar, Karl placed her hand in Elliott's.

"Dearly Beloved," Johann began, "we are gathered today, in the presence of God, to join this man and this woman in the bonds of holy matrimony. If any man has just cause as to why they should not be joined together, let him speak now or forever hold his peace."

Libby held her breath, but the church remained silent.

"Who gives this woman to this man?" Johann continued.

"Her mother and I do," Karl said, before he took his seat next to Janet.

Gunnar gave the wedding sermon while Johann read the vows.

As Libby repeated the words, she felt her life change. In a loud, confident voice, she said, "I, Elizabeth JoAnna, take you, Elliott Garrett to be my husband." The words sounded so natural, came so easily, as she promised to love him forever, no matter what happened in their lives.

At last she slipped the Black Hills Gold ring that matched hers onto the third finger of his left hand. As she did, she felt a bonding take place. They would be forever together, forever in love.

When Johann pronounced them man and wife, Elliott took her in his arms and kissed her tenderly. Feeling so safe, so secure in his arms, she clung to him just a moment longer than necessary. Only the snickers of their guests reminded her where she was and relaxed her.

They turned to face their guests as Johann proclaimed, "It gives me great pleasure to present to you Mr. and Mrs. Elliott Lanners." The spontaneous Americans surprised their more conservative Norwegian cousins by breaking into applause.

Libby smiled as she looked over the congregation. In this moment, she prayed the scene at the parsonage had only been part of the dream, part of her overactive imagination. Instead, reality sunk in when she saw her father, Marie, and Susan sitting in the back pew, smiling at her.

She knew Elliott felt her tense. After giving her a quizzical look, he followed her gaze to the source of her fear.

Libby turned to Sonja to take back her bouquet then she and Elliott began their first walk as husband and wife. At the last pew, Logan reached out to touch her. Pulling her hand out of his reach, she looked into Elliott's eyes. It was too painful to face her father. How could he have come here on her special day? He'd kept his promise not to spoil things so far, but would his new, mellow attitude continue?

Once outside, Sonja and Garrett greeted them. "Did you see him?" she asked, her voice hardly more than a whisper.

"Yes," Garrett replied. "I saw him. I certainly wasn't expecting him. I saw Susan, too. Just take a deep breath. I doubt they'll do anything to spoil your wedding day. More than likely, they only wanted to share it."

As the guests filed out of the church, Anne and Solveig joined the wedding party. Libby followed her mother's lead and greeted each of their guests with excited appreciation for their attendance. All the while, she worried about the last people in line.

"I only wanted to see you get married," Logan said, when he kissed her cheek.

"That goes for me, as well," Susan told Elliott. Her voice sounded so soft and loving, it surprised Libby. For the first time in years, Libby knew Susan was the mother Elliott remembered. She wasn't putting on an act or making a spectacle of herself.

"We didn't want to wreck your wedding, but you are our only children," Logan said, as he shook Elliott's hand. "We wanted to see you happily married."

"Thank you ..." Elliott replied, as though searching for the proper title.

"You don't have to call me Dad. Logan will do just fine."

"Will you be staying long?" Garrett inquired.

"No, we only came for the wedding. Susan has a show this evening. We chartered a plane to fly us here."

Anne moved to Libby's side then put her arm protectively around her daughter's shoulders. "I think it's time your father and Susan met our family."

"I agree, Mom," Elliott said before Libby had a chance to protest.

"I don't think you've officially met Marie, Mom," Libby added."

"No, I haven't, but I can see you are good for Logan. Libby speaks highly of you as well."

Libby watched as her mother embraced Marie then kissed her on the cheek before making the necessary introductions.

Aunt Kristen was hesitant, but to everyone's surprise, her grandmother acted more composed.

"It is good you are finally meeting your children's family," she began, when at last they were introduced. "It's a shame you never met us before."

"Better late than never," Logan observed. Turning to her mother, he continued, "thank you for letting us stay, AJ."

"Don't thank me, it was Libby's decision."

"I didn't want to hurt anyone. I just wanted to attend the wedding."

"I can understand," Solveig admitted. "I know you've hurt my daughter, and at times my granddaughter as well. As I see it, if Anne can forgive me, I can forgive you."

Logan said nothing. It made Libby smile. She'd never seen her father at a loss for words before. She knew he hadn't come here expecting forgiveness, and he certainly hadn't found it in her aunts and uncles.

"I have food at the parsonage," Marta announced. "You're welcome to join us."

"Thank you," Susan replied, taking Marta's hand in a genuinely sincere gesture. "I'm afraid we must leave. I have only three hours to get to the theater.

She turned to Libby and Elliott, then handed them an envelope. "I hope this is something you two will enjoy. It was a beautiful wedding. Be happy."

Marie, too, handed them an envelope, before they turned to leave.

"What's in the envelopes?" Garrett asked.

Libby opened the gifts. As she read the hand written notes, she began to smile.

> Dear Elliott and Libby,
> I have no idea what to get you. I hope you can find a special decorator for your new home. Let the master bedroom be my gift to you.
> Love,
> Mom

> Dear Libby and Elliott,

Susan's idea seems to have given us the perfect gift for you. When the decorator is finished the master bedroom, have him design the room of your choice, on us.

Love,
Dad and Marie

"It's hard to believe, but it seems the leopards have changed their spots," Elliott said, looking over the letters. "I never thought I'd say it, but I think we owe them an apology."

The day turned out to be beautiful. Gunnar and Gustaf helped Marta bring the food to the tables on the lawn. Tables groaned with an abundance of food. Fish, meat, bread, fruit and vegetables graced the tables along with a layered wedding cake.

The surprise of the uninvited guests seemed forgotten, as Libby and Elliott filled their plates and mingled with their guests.

"It seems as though this is a day of new beginnings," Solveig announced. "I think it is time for me to tell you of my plans. I have been talking with Gerta and Thomas. Now that I have, at last, returned home, I intend to stay here."

"Stay?" Kristen repeated. "You can't mean it. You have to come home. What would we tell people?"

Solveig shook her head. "You would tell them that I went home, home to Norway. I should have never left. I was never really happy in America. America was your Papa's dream, but Norway was always mine. I don't expect people to understand, but I plan to spend my last days where I am the most happy."

It was Libby who broke the silence brought on by Solveig's announcement. "I understand, Grandma. I'll miss you, but having you happy will reduce the miles. You're no different from the rest of us. Mom is happiest designing, I'm happiest running the Lazy B, and you're happiest here."

Solveig hugged her tightly, as the rest of the family reluctantly voiced the same opinion.

Chapter Twenty-Eight

Libby and Elliott borrowed Thomas' car and took the ferry across the fjord the morning after the wedding. Their first stop was Bergen. Like her grandmother, she fell in love with the quaint seaside city.

"I can see why Grandma loves it here. I've never seen anything to compare with it, not even the Rockies," Libby said, as they stood at the top of Mount Florin.

"It is breathtaking, but not nearly as beautiful as you," Elliott said, taking her into his arms and kissing her as he had so often in the past two days.

Libby was glad she'd saved herself for this. She was especially pleased she hadn't experimented with sex the way so many of her friends had. She knew now she'd always been waiting for Elliott, for the only true love she would ever know.

The wedding night was beyond her wildest expectations. She'd always known Elliott dated several women. She thought of him as experienced, but to her delight, he was as nervous as she. He'd been gentle and patient, his very touch sparking a fire within her that blazed every time his fingers brushed against her, even when he merely held her hand. Was this love? It certainly wasn't the love the girls in the dorm spoke of. It was the love she read about in books, the love her mother had for Garrett, the love her grandmother had for Norway.

From Bergen, they drove high into the mountains until they came to the secluded mountain lodge Gunnar had reserved in their name. The small hotel clung to the mountainside, mirrored in the crystal clear lake below. Their room was not elegant like the one they left in Bergen, but was beautiful in its simplicity. A massive dresser dominated one wall and a large featherbed covered with a summer tick and a down comforter rested against the other. There were no phones, no television, only hours for quiet exploration of the surrounding area as well as of each other. They ate simple meals with the other guests and felt more relaxed, more rested, than they could ever remember feeling.

"Mom and Garrett should find a place like this," Libby said, as she packed for the trip home.

"They should, but they won't. I've been thinking. You know that valley up behind the house, the one with the small lake?"

Libby broke into a smile. She'd always loved the area he described. She even called it her special valley. In her mind, she could see what Elliott meant. The valley was perfect for a lodge like this one. A place where the hustle and bustle of modern day life could be forgotten. A place where long walks and simple meals would be the drawing card.

* * *

Solveig sat at Gerta's kitchen table. Soon her children would return to America. Soon she would be alone with her decision to remain here in the place she loved. Could she let them go home without her? *Yes,* she thought, *yes, I can. I can give up my home in America and my children and grandchildren to be happy, if only for a short time. I know I'm being selfish, but I can do it. For the first time in forty-six years, I'm happy, truly happy, and at peace.*

"Supper is almost ready," Gerta said. "Thomas will be here soon. Help me set the table."

Solveig smiled at her sister. So little had changed between them. Once the children left, she would cease to be a guest in this house. The help Gerta asked for now would become the sharing of daily tasks.

"I still can't believe you are staying here," Thomas observed, once they sat down to supper. Solveig couldn't help but notice the concern in his eyes. "America has been your home for so long."

"Not my home," she replied. "America was Erik's home, Erik's dream. Had the decision been mine to make, I would have never left Kinsarvik. This is where I am happy. This is where I belong. I've talked it over with the children. They understand."

"Are you certain they understand? I am not as convinced as you."

"I did not say they accept it, but they understand. They boys and Anne are abiding by my decision, but Kristen, poor Kristen, she cannot accept my staying. It will not be easy for her to go home without her mama, but she will do it."

Solveig listened as her brother and sister talked, the conversation moving on to the everyday problems of life. Even though she listened, her mind remained on Libby. She wished she'd known her as a child. She loved all her grandchildren, but none in the way she loved Libby. Libby reminded her of Anne, independent, educated, wealthy and now in love with a good man. She realized how hard it had been for Libby to accept a family who had rejected her since before her birth. Thank God, she'd done it and grown from the experience.

Libby and Anne both reminded her of Gerta. Gerta had hungered for an education, had defied Papa, and had married for love. Secretly, she envied them.

As a young woman she thought herself in love with Erik. Papa told her she should love him. Now she could see it was not the burning love her children and her grandchildren carried for their spouses. He children had chosen their own partners in life. They had not had to endure the pain of arranged marriages. While her children enjoyed lives built on love, she and Erik had shared a quiet love. Love, because Papa said it should be love.

She could almost hear Papa when he presented the idea. "I think it would be best if you married the new pastor, Solveig. You've always lived in the parsonage. You're happy there. You'll make a good pastor's wife."

In one respect, her papa had been right, she had made a good pastor's wife. She'd been considerate of the sick and obedient to her husband. The only rebellion in her entire married life came over the move to America. She'd done as her papa said, and it took her on an adventure into a strange land. It also brought her heartbreak. How could she have denied her love to Anne because she had decided to follow her dream of education and a career? In following Erik's dream and abiding by her promise to never disagree with him again, she had alienated her youngest child. Even though Anne forgave her, she would never forgive herself.

"Don't you agree, Solveig?" Thomas asked, breaking into her thoughts.

"I'm sorry, I'm afraid my mind was elsewhere."

"I thought as much. I was saying how your Anne and Libby remind me of Gerta."

"Yes, in so many ways. Remember when you went away to college and met and married Alfred? It was never the same between you and Papa again. It's the same with Anne and Erik, although they never enjoyed a close relationship. She wasn't the son he was so certain God would send him. She'd been born a girl, a girl bent on getting an education. It wasn't easy when she went to Colorado and married Logan because she'd gotten pregnant. I don't know how many times Erik said he wished he could talk to Papa to learn how he handled you."

Gerta began to laugh. "Papa never handled me. He merely tolerated my decision to marry my professor, a man nearly twice my age."

"Please don't laugh Gerta. Did you ever forgive him?"

"Of course, I did. I forgave him right away and toward the end, when I came to visit before the Nazis invaded, we came to an agreement of sorts. I loved Papa dearly."

Solveig nodded. "It's the same with Anne, you know."

"I know. I prayed for her when she chose a different path. From your letters, I sensed Erik's feelings and I grieved for her. I knew her life would not be easy. How did you feel, Solveig?"

"The same, the very same. Anne says she has forgiven us. I believe her, I just wish she and Erik could have come to an understanding."

"She's a beautiful woman," Thomas said. "You can be proud of her as well as her daughter. They are cut from the same cloth."

"They certainly are. Anne has been so excited about this trip. Libby's announcement and wedding made it complete. I'm so glad you were able to find my wedding dress. It meant so much to her."

"Yes, she was excited," Gerta agreed. "She placed several calls to me to see if I needed anything. I must say, I am grateful I learned to speak English, as her Norwegian is far from perfect."

"Anne was never raised speaking Norwegian. Erik insisted she should speak only English. I am afraid it isolated her, made her into an outsider."

Thomas shook his head. "It's a shame, and add the fact that you and Erik missed so much of her. I still don't understand why now, when you're getting better acquainted, you've decided to stay in Norway."

"This is where my heart is. I have always loved Norway. I cannot think of calling anywhere else home. America is big, noisy and dirty. My children adapted to it, but I never did. I want to end my life, as it began, in the simplicity of this village."

They talked on as they ate dinner and made plans for the future. Gerta had invited Solveig to share her small house. It would be hard for her to say good-bye to her children and her life in America, but she knew she must follow her own dream.

When dinner ended, they took their coffee to the sitting room.

"I am so pleased my children married for love," Solveig said. "As much as Erik wanted to choose their spouses, he refrained."

"You resented Papa insisting you marry Erik, didn't you?" Thomas inquired.

"I never used to think so. I came to love him, but when I see how happy my children are with their chosen mates, I know I was cheated."

"Well, I never felt cheated," Gerta said. "I wonder who Papa would have married me off to, had I not met Alfred."

"Perhaps, Ole the goat herder," Thomas teased.

"Oh dear, can you imagine me married to Ole?. The smell of goats always made me sick."

"There was always Peter, the doctor," Solveig suggested, joining in the fun.

"Oh, not Peter. He has such a big nose and he used to pull my braids when we went to school. Just thinking of it makes me glad I married for love, not once, but twice. James and I also had a good life together."

It was nearly midnight when Thomas finally left. The dishes were stacked in the sink. They could wait until morning.

When the house became still, Solveig sat at the desk in her room, and put her thoughts on paper. This, she decided will be my gift to the grandchildren, my explanation of why I am staying in Norway.

* * *

Karl reflected on their time in Norway. It certainly strengthened the bonds between his brothers and sisters. He found it hard to believe the time would soon be ending.

As usual, they gathered at Gunnar's for breakfast to discuss the day's plans. Since Libby and Elliott were due to return sometime during the day, none of them wanted to wander too far. At last they decided to go over to Gerta's and see what their mother wanted to do with the day.

As they approached the small cottage, something seemed amiss. The windows were still closed and the kitchen door was not yet open. Karl knocked, tentatively. "Aunt Gerta?, Mama?," he called.

It took only a moment for Gerta to open the door. When she did, the expression on her face confirmed his fear that something was wrong.

"Did Thomas call you children?" she inquired, her voice flat and emotionless.

"No," Karl replied, as she led them into the kitchen.

"I thought he called you. Of course, he didn't have time. I only just hung up from speaking to him. I went to waken Solveig for breakfast and she was gone."

"Gone?" Johann echoed.

"It must have happened in the night, in her sleep, very peacefully."

"No!" Kristen cried, leaning against Johann for support. "Mama can't be dead!."

Karl didn't wait for further conversation. Johann could handle things with the girls and undoubtedly Thomas would call Gunnar and the others would arrive soon.

He took the steep stairs two at a time, locating the guest room at the far end of the landing.

His mother lay in bed, her face peaceful, as though she was sleeping. Automatically, he lifted her wrist, almost expecting to feel a pulse. Her skin was already cold to the touch and had begun to become ridged.

As a doctor, he'd seen death before, comforted the families, but nothing in his background prepared him for this moment. Eleven years earlier he'd lost his father, but by the time he returned to New Oslo, the funeral director had done his work. Now he faced this alone. He didn't want the girls to come upstairs. Even though he saw no signs of a painful death, she was not the mother they remembered.

He glanced around the room and saw a sheet of paper lying on the desk. He picked it up, recognizing his mother's delicate handwriting. Could this be the last communication she'd had with her children? It must be, as it carried yesterday's date.

To my dear children,

You'll never know what it means to me to know you are abiding by my decision to remain in Norway.

I write this letter now to send with you, for the grandchildren who cannot be here. I hope they will understand why their grandmother is not coming home with you.

Norway has been my home forever. It was the home of my youth, the home of my dreams. Having finally returned, I cannot bear to leave it to return to America.

I pray you will help your children to understand how sometimes following one's heart can hurt those they love the most.

When you return to America, I will follow my heart. I know this will hurt you, but for too long I have denied my own happiness.

For the first time in my life, I will think
of myself and follow my dream.

I love you all dearly and will miss seeing
you regularly.

Mama

He folded the letter and put it in his pocket. This wasn't the time for any of the others to read it.

When he returned downstairs, the rest of the family had crowded into the tiny kitchen. Kristen was crying bitterly, while Lars and Johann tried to comfort her.

"It was probably her heart," he said, knowing they wanted to hear something, anything that would ease the pain.

Anne looked up, as though she hadn't heard him. Her face, too, was wet with tears. "I think it was God's will. He knew how hard it would be for us to leave Mama here. He just wanted to make going home without her easier."

Everyone seemed to agree. Since nothing more could be done, Gunnar suggested they go back to the parsonage and make the necessary plans for the funeral.

* * *

Libby and Elliott stayed the night in a small lodge not far from Kinsarvik. They arrived there late in the evening and decided it best to return rested the next morning.

To their surprise, they found no one at the parsonage. They were just getting ready to go see if they could find someone when Anne entered the room.

"Libby," she said, embracing her daughter. "Your grandma is gone."

Libby stood in a state of shock, unable to begin to comprehend what her mother was saying.

It was Karl who took over when Anne choked on the words. "It was very peaceful. She died in her sleep last night."

Libby could say nothing, as she turned to find comfort in Elliott's arms.

Chapter Twenty-Nine

The funeral service was simple. Even as the words of scripture were read, Libby couldn't help but wonder why God had taken her grandmother. Only days before, Solveig seemed so full of life, so excited about the future.

Libby allowed Elliott to guide her away from the church to join the family in the small churchyard cemetery. She felt Elliott's arm around her shoulders, but her mind remained far away. Before her, the mountains rose to majestic heights and were mirrored in the crystal clear waters of the fjord.

Gunnar spoke words of comfort, but the only voice Libby could hear came from her grandmother. *Don't grieve for me. I am happy. I am content. Live your life by following your heart.*

She cringed as Elliott guided her toward the casket as it was lowered into the ground. Following the lead of her mother, she plucked a rose from the casket spray and dropped it into the grave.

Here her grandmother would rest in the family plot, next to her parents, close to where Thomas and Gerta would lie. Libby looked at them, amazed at how they had aged in the last few days. The death of their youngest sister had been a terrible blow, a grim reminder of their own mortality.

It was over. Solveig had been laid to rest and the family would continue without her. The remainder of the day would be spent with the Norwegian branch of the family. Tomorrow they would leave for Oslo and the next day they would board the plane for home. It had been a bittersweet month. Lives begun and a life ended. Family who were only names on paper and faces in photographs became close friends. Norway, which had been only a clouded memory or imagined dream became a reality.

On the flight back, Sonja, Libby and Elliott occupied the first three seats of the first class section of the Northwest 747. The rest of the family were scattered throughout the cabin. While the others were either engrossed in the movie or sleeping, the cousins conversed in hushed tones.

"Oh, Libby," Sonja began, "how can we go home without Grandma?"

"We knew she wasn't coming home at the wedding."

"I know. I guess I just hoped she would change her mind."

"We all knew she wouldn't change her mind. She loves Norway."

"Loved," Elliott corrected her.

"I think she's still there," Libby said. "Her spirit, I think her spirit will always be in Norway."

"Her spirit is in heaven," Sonja declared.

"What is heaven?" Libby pressed. "For Grandma, it was Norway, for me it's Colorado. I know God will reunite Grandma and Grandpa, but just maybe it will be in Norway. Maybe this time it will be Grandpa who follows Grandma's dream. She said America was his dream and Norway was hers. I think God took her before we left to ease the pain of leaving her behind. I'm certain her spirit is in Norway and it is happy. For me, when I think of Grandma, I'll think of Norway."

"Oh, Lib," Elliott said, squeezing her hand. "You graduated from a Christian college and you believe in ghosts."

"Not ghosts," she replied. "Just happy spirits."

The rest of the family met them in Minneapolis and drove them to New Oslo. With their
arrival so late in the afternoon, they decided to spend one last night together.

They talked about the trip, and at last, Karl read the letter he'd found on his mother's night table. With the reading of the letter, each of the grandchildren handled his grief in his own way.

The next morning, Karl and Janet prepared for the trip back to Saint Peter, while Garrett and Anne filed their flight plan from New Oslo to the Lady Jo.

"I hate the thought of everyone going home," Kristen said. "With graduation over, you won't have an excuse to come back to Minnesota."

Anne smiled, giving her sister a hug. "I think it's time this branch of the family came to Colorado. With Erik at the Lazy B and Sonja living in Denver, you'll have a good excuse for making the trip."

"Would you have made the same statement four years ago?" Johann questioned.

"Honestly? No, I wouldn't. So much has happened, both good and bad, I think God wanted us to get close again. We'll never drift apart now. We've been through too much together."

"It sounds like you're planning the next vacation before this one is over," Lars said. "We don't even know if the Lady Jo will have room for us. Just listening to the plans Libby and Elliott are making, it sounds like it will be sold out every week."

Elliott beamed at the confidence in the compliment. "There will always be room at the Lady Jo for the family."

The End

ABOUT THE AUTHOR

When her sophomore English teacher assigned a handful of students to write for an entire year, Sherry Derr-Willie fell in love. Since then, writing has been more than a hobby. With over twenty books to her credit, she has fourteen contracts for release dates in 2003-2005.

Married for almost forty years to her high school sweetheart, she describes her husband, Bob, as a saint, saying, "I doubt if a mortal man would put up with the eccentricities of a writer."

Along with her writing, she claims three children and eight grandchildren, ranging from infants to adults. Now that her children are grown, she and Bob enjoy their empty nest and the success of her writing career.

"If nothing else," Sherry often says, "I'm an overnight success after forty years."